SEPARATE BUT EQUAL

OTHER LA CAILLE NOUS TITLES

0-9647635-8-3	My Baby's Father G. Dan Buford
978-0-9718191-8-4	Songs of Life and Living Sam Adewumi
0-9718191-7-3	revolution|revolisyon|révolution: 1804 – 2004: An Artistic Commemoration of the Haitian Revolution Ella Turenne
0-9718191-6-5	The Eye of the Tornado Michelle J. Pinkard
0-9718191-5-7	Pick-Up Lines Michael T. Owens
0-9718191-3-0	Backfield in Motion Undra E. Biggs
0-9718191-2-2	The Canon of Loose Cannons Guichard Cadet
0-9647635-9-1	When He Calls Sharel E. Gordon-Love
0-9718191-1-4	Father's Footsteps Tony Cheatham
0-9718191-0-6	Bard From Par Taken Guichard Cadet
0-9647635-7-5	Water in a Broken Glass Odessa Rose
0-9647635-6-7	When You Look At Me Undra E. Biggs
0-9647635-5-9	Temples Vincent Williams
0-9647635-4-0	The Masks of Flipside Guichard Cadet
0-9647635-3-2	Party Ain't Over Yet! Tashia "Thema" McNeil
0-9647635-2-4	The A# Blu's William Laurence Jones
0-9647635-0-8	LoneWolf's Cry Guichard Cadet

SEPARATE BUT EQUAL

a politics of Black love novel
volume 2

G. DAN BUFORD

LA CAILLE NOUS

Cover Illustration & Design by Austin Greene

ISBN: 978-0-9718191-4-6
Library of Congress CIP Data on File.
LCCN: 2002024015

This book is available in print at most online retailers and bookstores.
La Caille Nous Publishing Company
https://lcnpub.blogspot.com
Send all correspondence to mailto:lcnpublishing@gmail.com

In memory of

Jason Singleton
William L. Jones
Richard Sanders

Acknowledgments

This is always the hardest part of the book to write because it is impossible to acknowledge every single person. As such, I always do it last because there are hundreds of you who have made the novel a possibility. My friends who taught me long ago that it is better to live to write, than to write to live; thus, this explains why it took nearly 15 years for the second "Buford novel" to publish. In all that I think and do, whenever people discuss friendship, I say: *Look at your friends. Now look at mine.* #old_spice

Many readers connected to the first Buford novel, *My Baby's Father*, and sent word of how that book captured the essence of their college life and/or fist love (or serious relationship), or simply their enjoyment of it. I would like to thank: Andrea Grant, Elliott Robinson, Kenney Robinson, Leon Caldwell, Nicole Jackson, Jarrod Johnson, Dion Baccus, Kim Sexton-Lewter, Donna Pryce, and the many others not named -- I say thank you.

I find it possible to connect with readers by staying true to a large portion of who we, as Black people, are culturally and historically. Since the writing of this current novel touched years in three different decades, I had a chance to do a lot of reading. Initially, the novel aimed to answer and join the canon of books published in the "relationship" genre of the late 1990's. I started doing this by relying in that day's tone while mixing it with the voice and fervor of two writers I hold in high esteem: John A. Williams (Click Song), and Sam Greenlee (The Spook Who Sat by the Door).

What started as a quest to represent the male view from two different ranges ended up, or became, an inclusion of a "strong female voice" I gained from reading the works of many women writers I have long admired: Toni Morrison, Alice Walker, Paule Marshall, Terry McMillan, Gloria Naylor, Edwidge Danticat and many, many others.

Though I am making a stylistic attempt to salute various women writers, this novel still comes from a male's lens. I make no claim to understand women and being capable of presenting their issues better than them. What I am doing is presenting a main character (Ernest LeGagneur) and his struggles with fidelity (monogamy) as it is locked with his involvement and quest to uncover the mystery of a secret society he has joined. Unbeknownst to him, he is caught in the middle of a war that predates the American Civil War – and people are being killed and/or being asked to kill themselves if/when they cross the line, an invisible one.

This is the part where I get to thank the people who struggled with me in writing this novel. I call them my Editorial Team, the ones who read this novel in raw form (shimmy shimmy ya) and prayed I didn't get angry with their feedback. Of course I tried not to; better yet, I did not. I start the appreciation with the first draft and Charmaine Bennett who read it and gave great insight. From there, I made many changes over several years until it got to the point (nearly 450 pages) where serious editorial cuts were needed and so I thank Meeta Pendharkar for being there. I then relied on several readers who brought so much to the novel that I earnestly say it would not be the book you are reading without their contribution: Earl G. Sharpe for always being "dat dude", the one who has had my back since ski hats and goggles; Cheryl B. Robinson who personifies the reader I picture myself replying to at readings; Odessa Rose, a writer I respect so much and who brought a smile to my face when she relayed how the book captured her imagination; fellow writer Gigi James for getting a few jokes others did not, and introducing me to her brand of humor; and Monica Cook, a friend with whom I reconnected after many years and though miles serve as distance, I know friendship will always be the room next door.

I would be remiss if I did not acknowledge Austin Greene, the prototype for the brother the 11 o'clock local news should interview, and Regina Brooks of Serendipity Literary Agency, a publishing professional who gave me a peek of the industry from a different angle.

Dedicated to JAM, Sponge and Control,
and all women who give us our voices.

Part One

VOICES FROM THE MARGIN

HOPE'S HOUSE WARMING

New York, circa 1993

"I don't need a man. A man needs me." Nothing, not even an abrupt end to a six-year relationship was going to find me caving and changing my stance.

Hope simply agreed with a "I hear that" then hung up the telephone. Her main satisfaction seemed to be that I would definitely come to her party. She gave no indication she recalled those words as the ones we heard Bliss speak the last time we saw her alive. Hope had also become part of this revisionist history of who Bliss was – not that I really knew her.

I only met that Bliss chick twice, back-to-back weekends at that. Her aura screamed of a duplicitous chick playing all sides of a closed circle. She played it well by mainly saying good things about people then quickly placed herself on a higher plane. Chick was as fake as they came. She irked me, for various reasons, but mostly for trying to play the role of an experienced, worldly woman when the word on the grapevine stated otherwise.

October 1991, the year of abrupt endings is how I now refer to it. It was the eighteenth, only a week after attending an event I tried my hardest to back out of. I saw Bliss for the second time, after having heard her name a few times over the years. Campus lore had suddenly morphed her into a mythic figure, the young woman credited with breathing life into the MAX boys. MAX boys were dangerous because they operated sans structure, where any man could crown himself king and be that, as long as he stayed within the barely visible territorial lines he drew for himself.

Dusk falling over Manhattan always felt like the evacuation scene of a movie where giant killer ants chased humans out of their domicile. I drove into Chelsea via the LIE and Midtown Tunnel because Hope said we should arrive together. She only had to ask once for me to tag along and attend Attitude's first major gallery showing. Gym and treadmill could wait. I left Queens at 3:30 p.m. but after fighting through rush hour traffic, by the time I reached her office, the city looked grayer than normal, almost comic bookish, like a web had been spun. A soft hug with a gentle spine rub as we reached across the gear shift.

Hope had not told me this was a society event! High society at that!

I should have known this, put the pieces together even before she gave me a glimpse of the invitation card that came to her job. There had to have been a reason why Attitude had not personally invited me. Two clicks of my brain to the left side would have told me that a MAX boy would not exhibit unless it was done to the maximum. That was how they lived life, even the negative sides.

Hope only found out about the event because her job received an invitation. She volunteered for the exhibit and they agreed because of the years she had known him. We were the same age but she chose to stay and do grad school at our alma mater, while I decided to push career and pursue my masters on a part-time basis.

Though the exhibit had been at the gallery for nearly a month, tonight's event was *invitation only*, sent out to major publications, competing galleries and art critics. Très chic meshed with overly-crowded; polished floors, bright teeth, low-cut expensive dresses and club ties. My first thought was that Attitude had sold out.

Hope, ever his defender, explained the basic story of how he lost a bet to Bliss, and had to agree on no longer being an "underground" artist. Bliss did not think he could pull it off, but every gallery she contacted wanted him, so she went with the Bienvenue Gallery. Known for only showing works by established artists who catered to the wealthiest of folks but not necessarily in need of patronage, pieces at Bienvenue rarely sold for under five-thousand dollars. Failure here was worse than doing so on the street level, simply because the published reviews would be harsh. And the artist's ceiling would have been set. Most artists dared not approach, crutching artistic integrity, claiming their art was pure all the while breaking bread and dawn with strung out junkies.

She guided me through his work, contrasting it with his first collection, calling it a major departure from his other works and previous collection. *Voices from the Margin* exhibited a dark sobriety, a bare canvas sliced and splashed in measured tones and compartments. The clarity lied in its boldness, wherein the brushstrokes baited the viewer to prejudge. The benefit of having chosen Bienvenue Gallery was that these patrons and critics had seen the worst and the best. *Voices from the Margin* claimed to be neither. The thirty-nine pieces that formed the collection built a wall around the past, the truth and showed an artist willing to *take the money and run.*

The attendees gushed over the pieces, and I absorbed the exchanges. And, there was Bliss, with the audacity to wear a sheer white dress with no bra nor panties, taking credit for having made him.

She proceeded to tell us how she had Attitude on a string and that he'd do anything for her. Of course her face cracked when he walked in, not disheveled but clearly not dressed for the occasion: T-shirt with a slogan, with some next chick, white girl wearing a matching t-shirt with an inversion of the same slogan – *Be Me; and Who's Me.* Bliss looked as if she'd had her period run down her leg when Attitude introduced the girl as his future wife. He held court with a champagne flute raised by a slightly bent elbow; interlocked fingers – caramel brown and canary yellow. His speech was short, gracious yet bellowed a distinct self-assured note, clearly meant for Bliss.

When they walked away to meet and greet, I simply told her, "Don't ever be fooled, 'cause there's never a time to play a skank." With the media there, all kind of bulbs flashed in the air; prominent people being quoted. True, I'm sure when Attitude gave that little spiel thanking Bliss for helping him craft the collection over red wine and good times – it made her feel special. But I made sure I took a picture of her, since no one else cared. I wanted to be sure if she ever tried to play dumb, I would show her what the flash captured, what people with real clear vision could see: erect nipples and bush- nun bush, at that, because I asked around when I met her last week; that Bliss chick had no reputation to speak of, yet confiding in me she was a sexual freak, who goes hard.

Bliss did not utter another word to us or anyone else, until the end of the night. She had retreated to the only empty wall in the space and observed the party, much like I had done after Hope gave me the tour when we first walked in. I knew to pick a place and keep my mingling to a minimum. After doing my best, these past two years, to slowly wean myself out of Society parties, I found no reason to get deeper as Attitude himself maneuvered a way to walk away. Then, as if a jolt of energy coursed through her, Bliss approached me as I waited for Hope to say her goodbyes. She got real close to me and shouted, "Barbara, I don't need a man. A man needs me." and then repeated the two short sentences two more times; these times adding my last, "Barbara Wilson…". She then walked back to the other side of the room, staring at me as if to say, 'your move'.

Bliss's last words had not registered or meant anything special to me, even after I saw how it turned Hope's right shoulder and spun her to where we stood and then immobilized her like a little kid playing freeze tag. She barely excused herself when she came out of her stupor. She rushed outside. I followed quickly but mindful I had spiked heels and a knee high skirt. She could run that fast because she wore charcoal gray slacks and flats. She responded to my call with rushed words that matched her pace. "I have to make a phone call."

I got to her as she dropped the coin. The phone booth on the corner did not have a door, only a back panel with perpendicular sides. She adjusted her body with a slight movement, indicating she needed privacy. I moved a few steps away but close enough to hear her only words when the person at the other end picked up. "The King is under attack!" Her voice flared, "no." She repeated her words, hinting that the person on the other line asked for clarification. The call took about thirty seconds from her depositing the quarter to hanging up the phone.

Manhattan, edge of Soho, now under the complete darkness, it felt smaller, the kind of place with short streets lined with garbage cans; alleyways where directors filmed movie rape scenes. Hope's eyes betrayed her words, "It's nothing. I'm glad you came. I liked how you came at Bliss. It gave me a different point of view." I smiled and we walked toward the parking garage to retrieve my car but my worries bubbled. When we got inside the car, I asked again. Hope's demeanor, a forced innocence as she played into her new haircut, a bob with a short bang split down the middle. She said something I thought no one had picked up on. "You have to decide whether you are in this Society or out of it."

"I just need to know if Ken is in any trouble."

She laughed and said, "This was a MAX event. It has nothing to do with the brothers." Traffic moved, with us catching a red light at every other intersection. Relieved that my first worry had been cleared, I made the worst mistake I could at the moment. I let my guards down. Hope's words came direct yet she maintained the supportive tone. "Why do you act like this was something given to you? You earned this. You have a right to tell anyone you meet who you are and how you came to be here. You have nothing to be ashamed of."

"I never said I was ashamed but it doesn't mean I have to claim something I am not, like Bliss is doing."

She laughed. "Is that what you think Bliss was doing?" When I didn't answer, she continued, "I thought you understood that she was standing there forcing them to look at her, letting them know she would support a man, no matter the situation."

I pulled in front of her building, a few feet behind the "No Standing Anytime" sign. "Would you do that?"

"I have. We have. Not under the bright lights like she just did but we have." Then her tone changed. A sadness ran across her face; it seemed to hold back the high pitch sounds because the bass came out of Hope's mouth. "You know what, you and I, we'll forever be friends and it is what I want. But, you don't have to be a part of this for us to be close. I hope that's not what you think."

"Sometimes I don't know what to think…"

She cut me off. "It's simple. It has always been and will always be this simple: you know enough to keep your mouth shut. You do know that, right?"

A small fear, beads of sweat fizzed on my brow, behind my ears and down my spine. I nodded unable to say the words because my mouth locked. Hope hugged me and promised to call for lunch.

She did. We did lunch, shopping, concerts and over the next two years we truly became girlfriends, best friends.

Two years of just enjoying life and the plush style that came with having a great income backed by two degrees on the wall. All I had to do was keep my mouth shut when it came to talking about the Society. That had become easy and then my world caved in one week.

My man of six years left me, and four days later, Bliss died.

October 1993

Forty degrees during the second week of October was not my idea of a nice night for a party, especially since it served no true purpose – not a birthday nor a holiday. Hope even warned guests not to bring gifts. My life had splintered less than three months ago, yet I felt so relieved. I had managed to hold my ground while everyone seemed to be running away, finding alternate routes to reshape their lives, even Hope.

I never pictured Hope as someone who would need to move to New Jersey, gentrified Jersey at that. Her move from Murray Hill, Manhattan now put two tunnels between us. She went from high rise to a community with a security gate, manicured lawns and assigned parking for detached condos in red brick-faced colonial style buildings. In some ways this could be seen as moving closer to how she grew up in the suburbs but Hope was city-slick and tough as any girl I ever met.

Until her phone call a few hours earlier, I had an iron-clad yet trifling excuse to bail out, knowing this party to be an attempt to mend rifts. People would smile but none would discuss why several tight friends went from seeing or talking weekly to needing a party just so they could say hello again.

We no longer had Bliss yet everyone pretended she continued to be or had been a big part of their lives.

I arrived early to help Hope with last minute details, and be there enough time in case I wanted to leave early without her feeling slighted. Plus, I needed to clear the air with her. Bliss's death brought back the uncertainty I felt two years ago when Hope made that phone call. I came early to ask her point blank whether something had been in the works to forever silence Bliss, the way Hope had silenced me. Hope's words served caution while taking away a core part of my personal history, rendering me only able to talk about the marginal stuff, for fear I would end up a suicide.

I was not early enough as nearly a dozen people beat me there. Unlike me, they brought gifts. Blenders, wine glasses and stuff I knew Hope possessed. They knew this, yet they seemed excited, at peace that Hope no longer lived in the past, like she had been reborn. This became my cue to observe, listen and forget quickly.

Her new apartment, an alcove studio, half the size of her previous place in Manhattan explained why she donated most of her furniture to charity. Miniature lithograph prints lined the exposed brick wall from the window at the opposite end, past the kitchen, up to across the bathroom's door. Instead of her straight-laced nature, Hope aligned the prints with top edge of one frame next to the center of the other, and no two frames on the same plane. Her aesthetics had expanded. Back in the days, she would have featured only the likes of Bearden and Gordon Parks. She now included Dali and Rodin; mounted glass shelves with very few books and a couple of statues she purchased over the years. Skylights throughout the apartment enhanced the artistic feel.

The layout managed to detract from the smallness, leaving me fascinated that she fit a futon, sofa, bed and could still entertain dozens of people. Many more showed than I expected. Of the seventy or so who came and went, thirty arrived within the first two hours. More than half left early, saying they came only to pay their respects...letting the word and thought hang like an unfinished sentence, as if Hope and Bliss were family.

Nearing eleven o'clock, even in a crowded tight space I felt alone. Just a pitch above boring, the party had served its purpose of retying alliances. I pondered the best way to excuse myself and call it a night, until Ernest and Devon walked into the party.

HARDWOOD FLOORS

Ernest stood up the steps on the landing near the exit, opened the door as I turned for a last glance. Nothing about this place, a condo on the sub-level of a three-floor colonial, registered as a purchase Hope would make. With a visitor's lot not too far from the secured gate where one signed in, it conveyed more than affluence and seclusion. Less than a five-minute drive, the Lincoln Tunnel separated and connected. The skyline faced us with windows lighted or dark in no specific pattern.

The short walk to the car found us silent, as if processing unconnected thoughts. Ernest had to be thinking two steps ahead or something. Wanting to sleep with him served many functions with lust being near the bottom of the list. If anything, loneliness but not in a needy way, yet I found myself on my way to Brooklyn at one in the morning with a MAX boy. I reasoned with myself – yes, he walked in with Devon, but Attitude only dealt with people of impeccable character. Still I kept thinking they were MAX boys, and their fraternity's notoriety included the ruthless, deceitful manner in which they dealt with women.

I needed more convincing. If, for all that I had done and accomplished in my life, I couldn't have a one-night stand with a MAX boy, then maybe I was still an eighteen-year-old freshman.

"Brooklyn, eh?" I exaggerated the words, letting him know my displeasure. "I haven't been to Brooklyn in months. Didn't you anticipate Devon leaving with Miranda?"

"Is that who he left with?" Ernest matched wits. His answer avoided telling his friend's business, while not having me think he condones Devon's behavior. "Where do you live?"

"Kew Gardens."

"Oh, oh! You Queens girls are very high maintenance."

I switched to a less-occupied lane then paid the toll for the Lincoln Tunnel. "Yeah and you Brooklyn guys are all crooks." He laughed. "Where do you live? In Flatbush?"

"Not all Haitians live in Flatbush, you know…but I lived there until recently. I just moved to Carroll Gardens to take over my brother's lease."

"I didn't know you were from Haiti. How long have you been here?"

"Going on 14 years."

A slight tension still existed between us, confirming the small talk we made screened our true intentions. I never had a one-night stand, but I could feel Ernest shared what I felt. I needed something to oil my engine, move me pass the point where I thought that relationships ruled, and sex required an emotional attachment. I kept thinking to be quiet and let him lead, yet I asked, "What have you been doing since college?"

"It's only been two years, but I've mostly been feeling my way around the advertising industry, hoping to land a job at a top-notch agency. What about you?"

"I'm the Executive Director of a school for children who have not done well in traditional schools." Ernest nodded, more than approval. "Do you currently work in an ad agency?"

"I was but I quit." I thought, quitter, loser…this guy's unemployed? As if he could read my thoughts of wanting to turn on the radio and make this ride quicker and less involved, he added, "Things got tough…after my friend, Bliss, killed herself, I couldn't focus. I needed to regroup. Did you know Bliss well?"

"No, met her and we spoke a couple of times. Why didn't you just ask for a leave of absence?" A shallow thing to ask, but quite logical; plus I wanted him to move from this topic. Ernest gave me this look. Had the light on the West Side Highway not changed to red, his silence could have meant he had not thought of the possibility. The look meant a dear friend had died and any past involvements had to be severed, and for me to ask that question confirmed my reputation - a cold-hearted chick. Even when I cared deeply, I did so in a cold, demanding way – that was my reputation.

Ernest reached for the radio. We both felt the same thing, so why not, why not turn on the radio. The clear starless sky gave a dark, empty feeling to the night. The sudden quietness between two relative strangers should have been uncomfortable, but it seemed to be what we needed. We drove across the Brooklyn Bridge. The sounds of WBGO, the NPR jazz station soothed a yearning in my heart, to be touched. October has always been my favorite month, although my birthday is in June. The cool, gentle, nightly breeze, sometimes peppered with moments of rain, the month anchoring the fall season symbolized my renaissance, my rise from the ashes of my summer of discontentment. Perhaps, having been in an academic setting since five years old, I viewed autumn as the first season.

"Make a left on Atlantic and a right on Nevins."

I decided to give him a quick test to see where his heart lies and when it lied. I switched from radio to cassette. I had been playing the song over and over during the ride to Hope's, to steel me for the first time I saw my ex. Ken was a brother; I knew he would be there. It would be my first time seeing him since he left me a note, that note:

I have to leave. I'm not sure I will be back. You do what you have to do to survive. Always know that I love you and always will.

The song's first notes drew no reaction from Ernest. He stared straight ahead and I really could not... *You can never tell what's in a man's mind*

Ken played the role of the perfect man to the limit and though I claimed this as my favorite song, he embodied the lyrics, singing over the cassette whenever I played the song, replacing the next and many other lines with autobiographical sketches like, *And if he's* <u>Stay Black'n Die</u>, *there's no use of even tryin'*

SBD were the call letters of his fraternity and over the years the fraternity came to be known as *Stay Black'n Die* because of their fierce loyalty and willingness to die for the cause. Before then, they were simply known as 'the brothers'. As years went by and many other organizations formed and the term "brothers" got used for nearly every Black man, SBD veered away from being 'the brothers' even though those in the know knew what a person meant when they said 'the brothers'. The brothers were the glue and the fabric, the married, the fathers, the preachers, the doctors and the lawyers, the scholars; they were the men you saw holding hands at museums with the women who looked straight ahead- down, or with their nose in the air. The brothers had been betrayed, captured and sold; then they escaped, decided to stay, fought, marched to overcome. And, I had a brother; a fine brother… *Then he surprised me, leavin' me a note sayin' he's gone for good…*

The streets were empty and I was in a car with a MAX boy. His quietness confused me. Had he interrupted the song to give more directions then I would know. A red light. *You can have your Broadway,*

Then he chimed in…*give me* <u>Flatbush Avenue</u>…

Angels from the skies stroll 7th and for that thanks are due

I almost asked 'what' until I realized what he'd done; he replaced Ken's Harlem with his Brooklyn street. An invitation to come in, sing lead in an impromptu duet. Not only did Ernest know the words, he held tempo as I sang. He joined in at the end to let me know that he was willing…*To put some music to my troubles and call them the Harlem blues…*

He directed me to a parking spot. Feeling my hesitation, he asked, "You're not staying for breakfast?"

"Breakfast at one in the morning?" I wanted to know his exact offer, but he only nodded. To know, I would have to enter.

The two-block walk gave me a chance to survey the neighborhood, consisting of three-story limestone homes, with street-level entrances, and another entrance up on the first floor. The landings were about twelve feet above the street. Parking seemed tight since most cars had very little space between them, and the hydrant across the street from his apartment had a car risking a ticket by being less than ten feet away. Up the block, a school. Across the street, a corner laundry. The streets had no noticeable potholes. Ernest lived in the garden floor and basement level of the fourth house from the corner. "This is an interesting duplex," was all I could say because he hadn't done much to the place.

"I still don't feel at home here. It's gonna take some time to adjust."

The top floor had no furniture except for a coffee table surrounded by one sofa and throw-pillows. A small living room with a small bathroom situated directly behind the sofa. Next to the bathroom, an enclosed kitchen area. The main bedroom served as his den. A few canvases, reams of paper and large unframed canvases layered the floor near the computer desk. "Do you paint?"

"No, I just dabble. The computer is my main weapon. I do graphic design and I'm beginning to expand into writing copy." Ernest walked in from the kitchen and into the living room. We faced each other, adjusting to the environment, trying to reestablish a comfort level. For some reason, he held the locket again. He had done so at the party. I snatched it away and shocked, he asked, "What's wrong?"

"My father gave me that." I lied.

"Well call me George Michael then…I'll be your father figure." He winked then laughed to show that he served up the corny line on purpose, to make light of the moment.

I turned to leave, but he put his arm around my waist and pulled me to him. I talked forward into the open space in front of me. "Get off me! Get your hands off me!!"

Instead of letting go, he asked, "Why can't you relax and stop trying to control the situation?"

I turned to face him and spoke in a slow, measured tone. "My father gave me this chain and locket. White gold, he said when he gave it to me. That was the first and last time I saw him. He died two days later. He committed suicide."

I lied to Ernest again, totally going against my 'honesty is the best policy' nature. I could not tell him the truth, that when opened, the locket revealed a black and white photo of my brother, who could pass for my father when he was in his late twenties. The secret and my confusion was that my brother died at 20, so how could he have taken this photo.

Ernest took hold of my hands, pulling me closer. Our bodies leaned softly against each other. Our faces slowly closed the distance between us, we kissed, our fingers caressed. He kissed without squeezing body parts. Next, he did another thing that impressed me when it was my first time with a guy. He took off his top. Sure, I liked to be undressed and savored, but I preferred a man who took off his clothes first. Especially when the room was lit, even if by only the light from the next room, allowing me to see only his shape, the bulky shoulders, the well-defined chest, the shapely arms, the could-be a little flatter stomach, the stiffy with the pee-hole aiming at the ceiling, the strong thighs and calves, and the stiffy.

Ernest smiled as if asking for my approval. I approached and used the tip of my tongue on his chest then our mouths met. I wondered if he would carry me to the bed, instead he pulled me to the cold, hardwood floor.

ICE CREAM IN BED

For two days I filed my time with Ernest as a one-night stand, yet I kept wondering if I could keep it as just that. In the office, I called to check my home messages throughout the day. Every file I read or any other minor accomplishment, I rewarded myself by checking my messages. That Tuesday night, after rushing home to see if he had called and simply had not left a message, I lost my nerve. I rationalized it saying to myself with so many people knowing we left Hope's party together, a rumor could start. Before I dialed his number, I replayed Saturday night to make sure I had enough exits should he not be interested in seeing me again.

I first met Ernest at the end of my sophomore year in college, during his visit as a high school senior, star athlete scouting the local colleges. He stopped on our campus because Attitude, a mutual friend, attended my school. Introduced in a group setting, had he not chosen a nearby college, I doubt anything but his build would have stayed with me. My silent reaction as we exchanged greetings, *My, that's a big boy*. The thought resurfaced when he walked into Hope's housewarming party.

I saw him at a few parties over the years, but we never got a chance to hold a real conversation, just small talk in a group. Hope brought him over.

"You two remember each other, right? Barbara, Ernest."

"Yes, I remember Ernest," I said and gave him a hug, the kind you give a casual acquaintance, when you do not want to send any sexual signals. As I gave him the second pat on the back, he released his hold on me. I thought he would reciprocate my cue not to exchange any sexual energy, but instead

Ernest held both my hands, on the edge of my fingertips and said, "Lovely as ever."

That slight stare into my eyes froze me. Ernest broke eye contact, very slowly, smiled, then walked away as if the compliment was just small talk.

Standing in the middle of a room with a smile on my face had only one implication. Before I got a chance to throw a disclaimer, Hope chimed in, "Just like a MAX boy." She giggled, and then walked away. Then it struck me. She had said MAX boy.

I did not know Ernest joined them until the night of the charter ceremony.

"No MAX boys," I commanded myself then stole a glance at Ernest. MAX boys were the opposite of 'the brothers', especially on the major point that counted – women and long-term commitments. Everything else you could find blurred lines where individuality played a major factor. With MAX boys trying to squeeze as much life into the short span they estimated for themselves, they operated more as mercenaries, mere soldiers of fortune. Oft-times, women became the casualties. With this in mind, I made a slight turn to look at Ernest from a different angle, the obtuse lens of a MAX boy when it came to matters of the heart.

He had a trimmed dark beard encasing a round, dark-brown face; large eyes, with very short lashes, and perfectly, trimmed eyebrows.

He caught up with Devon.

They had this little icebreaking routine going. As they greeted a woman with a hug, they would say "Be a good girl, and give a grown man your seat." The double-entendre drew laughs from everyone, even the brothers who were chief rivals with Ernest's fraternity. Within minutes, their laughter and conversation transformed a dull party into a mini-jam. They recognized everyone in the room, enough to be on a handshake-hug or hug-kiss basis.

Thirty-two people in the room. Fifteen of us sorority sisters. Fourteen SBD brothers. And three MAX boys.

Another simple turn of my body and it clicked as to who, besides Hope, might have invited Ernest to this very private party. Attitude was one of the first friends I made in my first year at TGI. Though a MAX boy, he somehow slid into our side of fraternity and sorority life without any conflict as to his allegiance if ever a quarrel erupted. The two of them brought Devon over. "You remember Devon, right?"

Devon stepped forward but I hesitated to hug him. "Hey Barbara, where've you been?"

I offered a smile. "We all can't get around like you Devon, but I've been close enough." The word on the grapevine - Devon was a womanizer. He confirmed this minutes earlier by the hug and kiss he gave another one of my sorors. When he entered the party, they wandered down the hall, away from everyone else, to a dimmer portion of the apartment. Though only a soft peck on the lips, Devon had a wedding band and Miranda did not.

Devon grinned, knowing my last sentence meant I had no time for his duplicity. He slid away into another group's conversation.

The party had picked up. Most people danced so I decided to sit and make small talk with Ernest. I did not actually say anything, just sat directly across from him, with my legs slightly open. No, nothing that blatant. I wore a stylish lime green blouse, a black blazer, and calf-long skirt with a small split on the left side. He rubbed the brow of his nose, and Attitude whispered something in his ear. They both laughed then Attitude walked away. "What? What y'all laughing about?"

"Nothing, just at your MAXine pose."

"My what?" I knew he meant it as a female version of MAX boy.

"I've always been impressed how you SUM women lay down game."

"Boy, you must be out of your mind." My eyes drifted from his mouth to his torso – muscular beyond buff, shrouded in a designer black muscle-top. I looked hard, enough to detect the outline of the nipples on his firm chest. I pictured a smooth surface with not a sliver of hair and oiled with Egyptian musk. I could sense his read of me and how it intimidated him – that I had my game on, and only wanted him for one night.

The next move was his.

He walked away to the kitchen and filled his glass with the red wine he brought as his housewarming gift. I thought he would motion me over with a slight turn of his head, and perhaps ask me if I wanted a glass, so we could finish the conversation, the game.

A minute later, it came to me. He must want privacy.

I would forever remember the next moments; they defined our union. "What you thinking?"

Ernest turned quickly, startled. He had not been baiting me to come into the kitchen. Really, I thought, what was with the evasive maneuvers? "Would you like something to drink?"

"No thank you. I don't drink."

"Let me guess – alcoholism in your immediate family?"

"Very good," I pivoted around him, rested my elbows on the counter, enabling my back to curve and looked into his eyes. My patronizing tone to his last statement confounded him enough, into a reflex, a blink. I waited for his next words, to see whether he would apologize or make light that he had guessed correctly. He did neither, and that made my interest in him, a bit hostile, wondering what it would be like to match wits with him just to turn him down. My soft spot for his physique kept swaying my decision. "Seriously, what are you thinking?"

"Nothing. Just chilling, sipping some wine."

I leaned closer to him. "I'm amazed a MAX boy can be at a party with so many attractive women and not be on the hunt."

"Oh that's what it is! You're still on some college rivalry bull? Is that why you tried to call out Devon?" He bent over, placing his elbows on the kitchen counter. "And, how do you know I'm not on the hunt?" Just as I started to explain that I did not care about reputations, especially stuff dating back to college days, he broke my train of thought. He lifted the locket hanging from my necklace. A gentle motion but it happened instantaneously. I felt like I had sunk deep into a swimming pool; fighting to make my way back up to grab the edge. The sight of my heart-shaped locket resting in his palm angered me. Instead of snapping for the over-personal way he decided to come at me, I controlled myself by slowly lifting the locket out of his hand. "If I'm not allowed to touch your heart, then why leave it dangling out in the open?"

Not only did those words freeze me because that locket meant so much to me, not because it cost a few thousand dollars. The photo inside had given me a quiet confidence that my biological brother, long thought dead, could be alive. No, I thought, Ernest, you cannot hold my heart but you could comfort me for a night. I looked in his eyes to make certain he understood this.

At night's end when I went to the closet for my jacket and overheard Attitude saying his goodbyes, I ignored the coincide that Ernest got up to ask him for a ride. I then noticed Devon and Miranda had left. I made a mental note to talk to the sister. Attitude said, "I am actually heading to D.C. for a few days."

Ernest chuckled and said, "Don't worry about it! I'll hook up with someone else."

My proximity and timing gave Attitude what he thought was a great idea. "Hey Barbara, be a good girl, and give a grown man a ride!" He pointed to Ernest. Those who heard his words busted out laughing. "Get your minds out of the gutter! I'm just trying to see who's going to Brooklyn tonight."

Attitude hugged a few people then gave Ernest their frat grip. "Hope, give me a call during the week so we can meet for lunch."

Ernest used a faint whisper, "No pressure, but can you give me a lift into Brooklyn?"

"Yes, a ride. Sure. Why not?" He stepped out of the apartment with Attitude as I spent the next minutes saying my goodbyes.

>=<

Ernest picked up on the fourth ring and with his lone word 'hello'. This shed no light on whether he was expecting mine or anyone's call. It did say he did not need the answering machine to screen for him, as if dodging someone. I got right to the point but not with a pathetic 'why didn't you call'. I knew why. We agreed it would be a one-time tryst. Our lovemaking had been robotic and awkwardly hard, even after he rolled us around so that his back, not mind, rested against the cold hardwood floor. The movements improved, and then became more fluid when we made our way to the mattress and box spring laying directly on the floor inside the bedroom. He had no headboard so he used the wall to balance himself while I gripped his back and the side of the bed. We climaxed in deviated intervals, short bursts, paused breaths beneath sweated brows.

He did not recognize my voice when I asked, "Hello, may I please speak with Ernest" as I inadvertently switched to my office voice, diction and all. "Hello Ernest. This is Barbara. Barbara from Saturday night."

"Saturday night? I've never been there. Are you sure you have the right phone number?"

"Point made." I chuckled. "It didn't sound like you remembered me."

"Of course I do, we met years ago…"

I interrupted him, "Very funny. It's just that when we left and exchanged numbers the next morning, I sensed that your offer, like mine, to be more of a formality." He remained quiet and I could not tell whether I insulted by implying, that our interlude served no more than a late-night snack to the fridge, or the cupboard for just two cookies to hold one over until breakfast.

I wanted him to say that he was a MAX Boy. Why did I feel the need to call him? Where could it really head? That might have stopped me as I could not put the breaks on my mouth. "Ernest, it's just that the fear of people discussing my sexual history leveled me. One utterance would start a rumor. You seemed discrete enough, very sincere and earnest in your manners. So, I just thought that…"

"That's scary!"

"What is?"

"You putting thoughts together." He didn't give me a chance to object. "I like when you shoot straight as you did on the ride home. Whether it's in words or symbols, get at me. I'm solid and will never try to gas you up."

>=<

Two weeks later I still found myself haggling with my conscience, wanting to put an abrupt end to this dead-end relationship.

"I know. I don't feel obligated. It's just that these past two weeks have been real nice. More than I thought of, when I first drove you home."

He cut me off as if he sensed I wanted to set boundaries and expectations. It was one thing if we were doing the sex thing once a week, but we spent the night together eight times in two weeks. I had many concerns about being with Ernest. Small issues like whenever I called him, trying to get an invitation back to his place, he always ended coming to my place, using some contrived line like "I don't mind wearing my away jersey."

I figured he had someone special, besides me, in his life. I put myself in the special category because of how he treated me. Ever since the Tuesday after our first interlude, when I phoned because he failed to make the call to say he had a great time and we should go out some time, Ernest found new ways to pamper me. Simple things; showing up with home-cooked meals in Tupperware; or picnics at dusk – the beach, parked car with a scenic view...

Yes, the brother cooks up a storm, at least five times a week he told me over the telephone. That Tuesday night, I called his bluff even though I really did not care whether he was lying or not.

I just wanted to be with him again.

He showed up at my place an hour later with a supermarket shopping bag. Three containers. Pasta. Meat sauce. Baked chicken and a pint of Haagen Daz butter pecan ice cream. This gesture worked better than flowers and gave him an unlimited supply of brownie points.

My mind quickly changed his file, placing him under *he would have to do a whole lot to mess this up.*

We stayed up late, a little after two, even though my alarm clock buzzed weekdays at six in the morning. Usually by eleven, I am in deep sleep, but I wanted to talk, ask the important questions we skipped on Saturday. We spent most of the time in the living room, curled up on opposite ends of my sofa. He flipped through the television channels, as if searching for something real. "You're not gonna find what you're looking for in there."

We began to play these little games of pointed yet rhetorical questions. "How do you know I haven't found what I'm looking for?" He stole a quick glance at me. I took in his whole physique and slowly pulled the spoon out of my mouth, the ice cream coating my lower lip. My eyes fixed on him, noting that I so loved the creme V-neck wool sweater. The sweater, loose and flowing, looked like a sea of tranquility underneath his large neck. A tight vein ran from his jaw-line well into his shoulder. His brow, not creased yet he looked to be focusing, the look of someone contemplating life and all of its absurdities. We still had not talked about our past relationships. I guessed because the way we started, the past really did not matter.

Or did it? The ensuing days, I thought of asking friends who were not SUM women what they knew. Two months ago, particularly before Bliss's death, I wouldn't have had to do it this way. I could call any of the sorors, especially Hope and get the four-one-one. She never showed any concern about my relationship with Ken but oddly tried to get us back together by using her housewarming party as the smokescreen.

I had to find about Ernest through other sources. I never mentioned his name, only hinting my curiosity about the MAX boys. From there I got all the important story lines.

The proximity of two women he slept with concerned me. He lived with one soror and a rumor about another, not a concurrent storyline; still, it felt somewhat tacky. Diane and Lauren pledged together, but had a fallout, due to sheer competition, including over the men in their lives.

The word on Ernest confirmed my suspicion - he got his share. With extra words, those who really knew him spoke of a gentle soul who needed no dirt to bury the bones, mainly because he functioned as an empowering force, in that, after he left a woman, she literally became that - a woman.

Perhaps I needed him over a decade ago, when a young girl needed to believe in something else besides the evil that men do - in that they left, for no reason.

The more days passed, the question on my mind became my driving force. Each night we stayed up eating ice cream, with our backs against my bed's headboard, the stereo grooving something mellow and our silhouettes neatly tucked into one another: when will he leave?

MOTHER'S TONGUE

November 1993

Ernest left even on mornings I did not have to go to work. On workdays, as I showered he brushed then peeked through the curtain to smile his goodbye. The rare times we left the apartment at the same time, I drove him to the subway station. One day he surprised me and said he planned to walk home – to Brooklyn, from Kew Gardens. I would not say I spied on him but since my appointment was near, at the courthouse, I circled back before heading to the office.

The Interboro Parkway curved often so I did not spot him until my car got less than a quarter mile behind him. He walked at a brisk pace with his backpack over the right shoulder. On this part of the parkway, he had to walk off the shoulder. I hesitated, not sure whether to honk and wave, or pretend to not have seen him. Most cars probably took him for a vagrant but I knew him to be steel hard, layers of it, covering the vulnerability he laid bare on that first night we sat side by side, when he explained how Bliss had impacted him. The straight gait with the slight right shoulder tilt maintained the rhythm of his b-boy bop. The fact that he could or would even attempt to walk the ten miles from our two apartments made me aware of a discipline I overlooked. I switched to the outer lane and slowed to use the car behind and the one I just cut off as a shield. That night when I called, since he did not mention seeing me, I did not bring it up. Instead I waited for a morning when the things he kept hidden could open up another's world.

"I am picking up my little brother today. Do you want to come?"

"Why? What's up?"

"He made the high school junior varsity team so I thought you could impart some wisdom on him."

"OK. Kool!"

Just like that? I thought to myself. In the six weeks we never went anywhere. He refused to meet any of my friends from work, or those not part of our connected past. In fact, neither of us spoke of that past, any past. We basically telephoned, met up, laughed and spent the night together.

"I will come back to pick you up around one."

"Are you sure?"

"About what? Leaving you alone here? You're the one who always rushes out in the morning using every excuse from needing ingredients for a real breakfast, art to do, or exercise and basketball."

"OK, you got it. I'm still amazed you never saw me play in your last two years of school."

"Different schools."

"Yes, but Barrington played at TGI once a year. I assumed since Hope came to games, you did too."

I simply smiled and rolled my eyes that way, toward the exit. Ernest's first fishing expedition as to my interests while at TGI came at a bad time, though I doubted there would be a good time to explain to him why I stayed off the scene.

I fully expected Ernest to go through drawers, medicine cabinet and photo albums. The apartment had my life as it had been since I graduated from TGI six years ago. The place stored memories, mementos, photos and junk that turned a 1200-square foot, polished hardwood space with bare white walls in an upscale building into a home. A large one bedroom, it did not have a hallway and visitors basically walked into the living room the moment they crossed the threshold. The living room said a man lived here but not alone. There was a woman who asked that he put the curved pink stripe on the western wall. The crepe curtain layered over sheer white single panels in front of translucent designer blinds, at first glance seemed to contrast the plush brown leather sofa, and the two-cushion leather seat. Then, the antique pieces stood snobbishly to the outside – two standing lamps, a writing desk, frames holding original prints. This room still said together forever. Elsewhere the apartment never moved from amoeba status.

When I got back, I did not get to use my well-rehearsed opening sentence. Ernest had showered, boiled two eggs and drank some orange juice. He had no interest in my recent past but he asked many questions about my childhood. I told him he would learn enough in an hour.

I did not mean for him to learn this much.

>=<

I planned my visit to not see my mother. I got my life to the point where I only saw her once a season – Christmas; March, her birthday; June, mine; and September, my little brother's. I picked up Darren for our bi-monthly hangout because he reached that age where he needed a strong role model. Last March, as I drove up, I overheard my mother scolding him about having teachers calling her at work. His grades began to pattern the children recommended to my school for at-risk youths. Closer to home, it reminded me of how my older brother veered off the path of good student to juvenile delinquent, then teenage felon. My mother doubted I could handle the situation with Darren. It did not matter that I had a bachelors in psychology and a masters in sociology.

We scheduled alternate Fridays to coincide with my payday. My mother wanted Saturday mornings so she could join us when possible, but I preferred to take half-day Fridays knowing her work schedule could not accommodate such a practice.

Of all Fridays in over a year, she picked that one as her third sick day. In over thirty years with the same hospital, my mother had only taken two sick days. Her car was not in the driveway or out front but the moment I put the key in the locks, I felt her presence. Darren never turned both locks, if any.

The neighborhood managed to stay safe though the town failed to live up to the middle-class dream the early transplants had envisioned.

My parents moved to Wyandanch from The Bronx in 1963 when she turned twenty-one. They were two years into their marriage. My father, twelve years her senior, worked delivery for a supermarket chain and made decent money. My mother had completed high school and landed a job as a Nurse's Aide. Two years later, my older brother, Lincoln was born. Add two more years then you have me.

By then, *no man in the house, only a mortgage on one salary* – that's how my mother described her life. She worked sixty-hour weeks, counting on neighbors and friends to look after us. With barely enough to survive she clearly had not imagined this life.

Darren's father seemed like a Godsend. I knew this, even at twelve years old. The quick way he bonded with my older brother showed he had been a rough and tumble guy during his younger days. With us females, he curbed his aggression, letting me dictate how close we would get. My quick-to-the-point conversations, learned from how my mother dealt with her past boyfriends allowed us to deal on an equal level, much unlike the father-son bonding he shared with Lincoln. He moved us from the town's center to the edge, switching us to a better school district.

For whatever reason, my mother would not let go of the past. She carried the loss she took on selling the old house back to the bank the way a fifth-grader carried her school books to her chest, her initials and that of her first crush encircled by a heart with piercing arrows. Nearing thirty-seven, she balked at the idea of a second marriage and refused to file for divorce in absentia, even two years later, when she gave birth to Darren.

I still held the hope that I was misreading my mother's playbook, reasoning her sneers, frown lines and sarcasm were a cover; and that she played a more subservient sexier role when behind closed doors with Darren's father.

My mother's life and relations with men taught me strength and pride were required to get a man, but a whisper and a nod is what kept him. She had no time for my angst about boys during my teen years. A month after I turned eighteen, a two months short of my leaving for college; Darren was not yet three years old, when his father left for good. No one could have foretold his selling the partnership in one of the busiest auto repair shops in town. We rarely spoke but whenever he approached me, he usually bore that guilty, scared look under his left eye. The hesitant putter of his second word sounded the same as when he spoke with my mother. I sat at the kitchen table, eating a bowl of cereal, rushing to get to my summer job. My mother had not yet returned from her late night shift. He simply said, "Look out for the baby and be good." The obscure way he put it registered only because I looked up and saw him holding an old blue suitcase.

It took a whole lot of strength not to cuss him out but I figured my mother had already done so enough times.

Days later, when my mother realized baby father number two never planned to return home, she called in her second sick day. Sick, because he did not even have the nerve to tell her.

She often spoke of selling the house to let go of the bad memories, but never followed through with the task, lamenting how much she loved the neighborhood and its proximity to her job. Sandwiched between two major boulevards, the house stood second to the corner on the back-end of a street that only ran a quarter of a mile; with six houses on each side of the block. I loved it for its simple elegance: detached, white with yellow trimmings, stucco, driveway on the right side. Three steps led to the porch with a green bench to the right of a plexi-glass door.

The front door opened to the living room. Furniture from a store offering Ethan Allen knockoffs at decent prices but with cut-throat financing rates, making the customer wish she had bought the genuine article. Beige with brown Rorschach inkblot-like patterns; matching loveseat and armchair, organized in a U-shape around a marble coffee table with a crystal vase holding plastic flowers. To the left, near the windows facing the street, a dining room set that rarely got any use. The years had toned the room's yellow paint, fading it toward eggshell. The plush, forest green carpet had kept well.

I turned left toward the kitchen.

The slight tilt of her head revealed her first surprise: a man with me – a man who was not Ken, the man I told her I would marry. I introduced Ernest, and she took his right hand as he leaned down to kiss her on the left cheek.

A conversation with my mother flowed quickly. The words tumbled out akin to a person who had drunk a truth serum. She caught Ernest by directing her questions at me, even though she knew my normal time for picking up Darren. "What are you doing here so early? How come you're not at work?"

After I answered, she simply glanced in Ernest's direction. The pause of an open mouth, quickly closed and twisted right, revealed her second surprise: his admitting to being unemployed.

She cut me a sharp look, making sure Ernest had not seen it. The coldness of her eyes forced me to recall the major piece of wisdom she shared when I left home for my first post-collegiate apartment - *Beware of broke men with big dicks*. I shifted the conversation to Darren, who proceeded to brag about making the high school's junior varsity basketball team and that he's going to be *the man*. From my work with kids in his age group, I knew making JV as a sophomore was not that big a deal. Plus, Darren was well under six feet tall so checking his hoops dreams would not be too hard. His spirit and confidence so high, he challenged Ernest to a game.

The backyard had the same rim Darren's father posted using two two-foot iron extension beams over the garage, to make the basket regulation height. He and Lincoln spent many hours out there.

"Where's your car?"

"Inside the garage."

"How come you're not at work?"

"Just felt sick today. Couldn't figure it out, but now I know why." She stared through the upper portion of the back door, a glass sectioned into four panes. Standing side by side, my cursory glances allowed a quick study of my mother's physique. Though nearing fifty-two years old and carrying the bone structure she passed to me, she avoided obesity and even sloppiness. Most places we would easily be identified as mother-daughter, for we possessed the same round face, high cheek bones and firm, voluptuous body. With that said the stark differences of her shoulder length weave, full make-up regalia with extended lashes, shadow and mascara would cast doubt, especially when we enunciated our words.

She did most of the talking, a rarity when we got together. My mother had shown little liking for Ken but somehow she tolerated him, figuring I would indeed marry him, have a child or two, then divorce. Having never discussed my breakup with him, she took this first chance to give her take. I tried to convince her this generation approaching thirty with no kids and single was the norm. "Really?" She asked the question as if she would pull out a binder filled with documents stating the opposite.

"Yes, for some."

"Well, this one's definitely not the type you need in your life at this age."

"I don't need a man. A man needs me." After I said it, my mother laughed, not loudly, just a soft chuckle. To muffle the sound and suppress her words, she pressed her lips, teeth biting down guarding her tongue from moving forward. Her reaction summed up our failure to having ever bonded. We had never seen eye to eye. From as far back as I could remember, my mother wanted me to see her as this phenomenal woman. All I ever saw, frowns of disapproval, over the slightest miscue; heard harsh words, belittling my older brother and me. Everyone I have asked confirmed my father also felt her wrath, which explains why he left two months before my birth.

I thought of sparking our usual small talk, wherein I would comment she had not aged since we moved to this house about fifteen years ago. Coloring could explain her hair. A healthier diet, her slimming down a bit, but her face sported no worry lines, not even those of a woman who had been abandoned by the fathers of her three children, and lost her eldest son to prison gang violence.

She started fixing dinner, cutting vegetables into a pot and putting meat in the oven. While the three pots stirred, we sat side by side, in silence for nearly an hour. The kitchen table framed by two chairs, and the room curved on the side where all the appliances stood. She glanced outside more than she did at me. "He seems nice, seeing as how he's been out there for hours playing." Ernest and Darren battled the way two brothers would, knocking each other hard against the garage door or to the ground. My mother and I were impressed with the facile manner Ernest bonded with what most considered a moody, anti-social teenager. He heckled Darren to keep working on his outside shot. They trash-talked over every play the other made.

Her hesitancy to outright like Ernest had more to do with me than him. By now, she obviously caught on that I did the opposite of what she had done in life, or would do in a situation. It took her years to realize I did this on purpose. Nowadays she no longer voiced an opinion, just waited for me to make absurd claims so she could laugh.

>=<

Ernest came back into the house, and Darren did not seem to mind that our planned activity of going to the mall to buy him sneakers and athletic gear had been derailed. My mother offered dinner but I declined. Two hours with her was enough. She did not take no for an answer, so I decided to use the extra time to talk with Darren about his schoolwork.

While we did this, my mother gave Ernest towels to shower, and he went to the car to get his backpack with the clothes he had worn yesterday.

We ate in the dining room, using the good china. She served baked chicken, mixed vegetables, butter beans and white rice. Normally I had to coax Ernest into dialogue, even small talk. That night, he talked the most ever since I remade his acquaintance. My mother's tone and laughter reminded of the few happy days when she would come home with a bottle, a lottery ticket and a funny story about a co-worker. She would offer me a drink and not get too upset when I declined. My research from people I asked, those who knew her family and my father's, revealed why family and their old friends never visited us. My parents moved to Long Island to distance themselves from their parents, uncles and aunts who drank too heavily and smoked whatever object they could light.

My mother told Ernest stories but none of my childhood, as if she really did not know or remember me. How could she? When not working, she locked herself in her room with the television as her confidant. Her stories were of people bleeding and dying, of old age and loneliness, medical advancements and people's ability to survive and overcome. Ernest talked more of being a teenager, nothing too specific but he created a link to Darren, projecting the good future he saw for my little brother. He talked of being a tough kid, tough but with a head on his shoulders. My mother beamed, as if the credit for Darren was all hers. I kept quiet, smiling, thinking of how smooth words must have been how and why she fell for our fathers.

We stayed for another hour after dinner, making the four-hour visit the longest time I spent with my mother in nearly thirteen years. Darren walked ahead with Ernest, out of earshot. My mother again cautioned about wasting time dating a man like Ernest, but it was clear her words had more to do with her past relationships. She somehow got it twisted, thinking I brought Ernest home to meet her, when in actuality I brought him to meet Darren, giving the boy another shot at having a big brother, even if only for a day.

We hugged our normal embrace, complete with a hard kiss to her left cheek. Ernest waved since she did not come off the porch to the car. I rubbed Darren's neck, reminding him we needed to talk some more about school and to expect my call tomorrow.

MISSIONARY POSITION

Friday night traffic on the Southern State Parkway heading toward Queens normally meant congestion, lots of stop and go. I forced my eyes to stay on the road to avoid looking at Ernest but my mind drifted then locked on him and my mother. My mother considered it a premonition that she called in sick for only the third time in thirty years the day I brought Ernest home. She saw her sick days as my father, Darren's father, and Ernest. I could have told her how I came to be with Ernest, and why the thought of my marrying or getting knocked up by him existed only in her mind.

She could have come out and flatly admitted she did not want my life to turn out like hers. Instead she told me life with Ernest would be a dead end, a one-night stand, one that lasts years - what she had done for the better part of her life. I would have told her Ernest was just a fling, but she got him to open up more than I ever could.

For nearly two months, I did most of the talking. I took the lead while Ernest evaded or joked with cynical answers. In my mother's presence, he jumped right in. She pulled him in with the right questions, asked them in a very direct manner and he answering them without hesitation. She made me see the error of my circumvent way of asking him about his plans.

He had no plan, because he estimated a shorter life, based on bad decisions and quick results.

As I drove the highway under the autumn sky, a fairly warm night with temperatures in the early fifties, he actually noted, "Your mom's real cool. How come you never mention her? She's funny and straightforward. I like that." While he rambled, I thought of ways to change the course of our union, show my mother that a woman can see a man - for herself - as he is, never constricting him to the stories already told or written about what a man must become.

We had walked around the edges of each other's lives, not asking or telling too much. When I inquired about his life, Ernest remained steady with vague answers. When we spoke of family, we shared some commonalities; of our mothers we both said, "*She's alright.*" We loved our siblings. Unlike my family, he came from a much more stable unit. He knew and lived with his father. Ernest was the fifth of seven children; youngest boy, before the twin girls, the only two born in America.

I insisted we go to his place tonight, made it sound like I wanted to drop him off, so I could go home alone. When we got inside, I asked him to share his story for he had learned mine. He did not have any albums. For pictures, he had various boxes or film envelopes, assorted files that I rifled through in search of whether he had always been this earnest. I strolled through the pictures of his childhood while he nursed a beer. He wore a tank top and faced his computer, doodling an abstract piece. He spoke of the piece as I marveled at his resemblance to his mother.

Ernest gave the lowdown of a happy family who once struggled under a military dictatorship, barely eating three piece-meals per day, together. Meals provided by a father who did whatever job it took to carry the load, and by a mother who sold oddities at the local market. She bathed and dressed the five children each day for school and church on Sundays. His little limbs exposed, under pressed cotton short sleeves and khaki short pants, except for Sundays when the pants would be longer. Then a family stumbled into the mirage of New York City during the late seventies and early eighties, when inflation mixed with harsh winters to forge ties between depressed communities of immigrants - Haitians, Jamaicans, Panamanians, Puerto Ricans - with Yankee boys. Both brothers dead, he said. They got caught up in that life and faced pretty much the same elements as my older brother.

Later on, his pictures, those without the wrinkled edges and yellowing paper spoke of his progression, of college, its graduation, while maintaining the b-boy stance; then to the corporate world, a buppie by day and b-boy by night.

This was Ernest, a collage: The focus of his eyes on the computer's glare; the sports trophies on the shelves, basketball, track and football, during his high school years. Then as if overnight, art became his life, an abstraction to not deal with the emotional bonding and physical contact of sports. No more need for belonging to a team, a family, not even that of his fraternity, which he joined, following childhood friends from the neighborhood.

This apartment seemed to be the fault line, the change.

I noticed that, except for the sports trophies, nothing on the shelves or walls existed in the pictures. He boxed up the past, most items in storage, with the remainder downstairs.

When I first asked to see the old pictures, he gave me this quizzical look, wondering why the sudden need to connect to his past, especially since the person I now know no longer lived there and probably never really did.

The smile, a grin, he cracked shattered his newfound mask that he copped after Bliss's suicide. He no longer smiled the old smile. It existed in the past. His new smile, born out of a new laugh looked more like the result of a cough, the remnants of a late summer cold. I needed the old smile, to move from the edges, the margin of his existence.

Since art served as an extension of the artist, I moved from the photos to the design on the computer to piece together Ernest the collage. The work was incomprehensible but its depth quite obvious, yet it connected to nothing, nothing that could tell who he used to be. Its ambiguity resembled the etchings of a deceased artist, someone unwilling to account for his vision. One whose recognition would come decades after his death, perhaps start a movement. For now, in these times, for this type of art, he would suffer in obscurity. Ernest wanted an artist's immortality, a death wish to die young and have people forever wonder what could have been.

Next, I ruffled through boxes containing his commissioned works and those he had produced as a nine-to-fiver or for college coursework. These proved much more accessible. With his permission, I picked a dozen or so pieces, and coupled with the last updated version of his resume, I began to lay the foundation.

Two days later, after updating the language and style of the resume, I made twenty copies of the design pieces, got them bound and then wrote the cover letter. With twenty unsealed envelopes in hand, I asked for his signature on the cover letter.

He laughed a short sweet burst, and then gave me a hug then a soft kiss after he saw the great job I had done. Of the twenty companies, a dozen called for an interview. He accepted three and got a job offer from each.

THE FEAR OF SMALL, CLOSED PLACES

December 1993

New York City, big city dreams, beams of light on little people yearning to be big and no light on the people who are big, moving amongst the masses incognito. Ernest remembered the subway exit closest to the building's entrance. He definitely wanted to be at least ten minutes early. Walking underground, people moved more cautiously; it seemed like they feared being bumped onto the subway tracks.

The upside escalator had space for two, with an imaginary line in the middle, making the right side for those who had time to stand in place, and the left side for walkers and light joggers.

Ernest did not mind Manhattan. He never loved it like some who grew up in the outer-boroughs, harboring dreams of one day being able to afford *a deluxe apartment in the sky, moving up like The Jeffersons.* To him, Manhattan's beauty only shone at night particularly on an empty street where the architecture towered to give light on the artistry, especially in the Fall when vibrant fashion colors enlivened the gray and beige architecture. To Ernest, Manhattan epitomized the drone of corporate world, filled with building lobbies where Blacks, some with prior criminal records, stood as security guarding against the *buppie* wannabes. The something they guarded against was not money, but the freedom to think that silk ties and expensive suits and meeting with decision-makers freed strivers from the small closed places designated to hold Black people back. Elevators brought back memories, serving quick reminder of class. Elevators brought back his trepidation of being in small closed places. Grade school days when he ventured into many buildings to visit friends, some elevators got stuck between floors. Pissy smells. Playing corners. A few had cameras. Office buildings had hidden cameras for those who fear being in small closed places with Black men. Elevators also have people who stood directly in front of a striver even though there were other places to stand.

Only five people and the guy stood directly in front of Ernest. Sure, he saw Ernest, but he ported this faux snobbery, subliminally asserting Ernest should be happy to be here, to have people fear him and allow their fear to crush him piece by piece. As each floor emptied a passenger and finally only the two of them remained in the elevator, the guy did not move. The back of his head reaching up to Ernest's chin.

Hidden cameras and Black security guards in the lobby ready to pummel. Would they beat Ernest to show their loyalty and his ignorance? Would they simply restrain then throw him to the curb while suppressing wide smiles of approval? Simply put, Ernest thought, *this guy's my worst nightmare.* In small closed places, the fear contrasted the state of being afraid. It veered into the realization of someone smaller, living out some code of superiority, ignoring basic human evolution - *survival of the fittest.*

He knew the most the guy could do was claim Ernest instigated the fight. Though not giving the satisfaction of saying 'excuse me', Ernest felt ashamed of having to walk around him, even though only the two of them occupied the elevator. Ernest considered looking back at him, instead he made a mental note to use the camera as an ally, which it could be unless Ernest did something stupid. Ernest looked into the camera as if asking, *do you see this nonsense?*

The receptionist's successive blinks confirmed she did not think he would get the job when he left last week. She picked up the phone, "Ernest LeGagneur is here to see you." She hung it out, curved it like a question mark.

His manager appeared after four minutes, just as he decided to take a seat. He expected a wait of less than a minute, overlooking his manager's boss made the hire while the manager vacationed. She not advancing toward him confirmed the displeasure. She quickly let on with a brief education that he was the third person in four years to hold this position; she interviewed twenty people, half of whom, including a few internal candidates, she considered more qualifed, after her boss showed her Ernest's resume.

Ernest listened and blocked her out at the same time.

His job description acknowledged what her boss stated during the interview – *Account Manager, Lead Designer* to handle the company's second largest account. "This is your office. I will be back in a few minutes to introduce you to some of the people with whom you will interface." Situated on the twenty-fourth floor of a thirty-five floor slate-colored building that occupied half a north-south block, his ten-by-eight office felt more like a cage with an open door and a tinted fiberglass wall overlooking a crowded, bustling city he wished he could walk freely on a weekday, as opposed to sitting there, feeling like a rat trapped, like a token, a mere statistic the company needed to say it had Blacks at the junior executive level. That was how his manager made him feel.

Ernest had seen and even executed some cold power plays but his manager, Sharon Tunic, clocked him in five minutes and fifty-one seconds, if one counted the minutes she made him wait in the floor's lobby. The next hour passed slowly. He spent the time reading over the files in the desk drawer. The previous office-holders kept meticulous files but had done little to grow the accounts. Their creative logs showed too many revisions, with many ideas scratched instead of nurtured. By the time Sharon returned to walk him around the floor for the introductions, he got a better sense of her hands-on managerial style. The department's structure lent itself to numbers-people doing creative work. A true creative could combat her by taking a passive-aggressive approach, as opposed to the confrontational style of the Type-A personalities who impulsively applied for this position, to tap into their creative side.

She introduced the coworkers with names and faces blending into the same questioning look, *"Sharon Tunic hired a Black man?"* and with Sharon making a point to attach, "He was hired during my vacation."

He made no true attempt to memorize names, only the ethnicity and gender of those who occupied the smaller offices in the middle, the people one office off the corner, and the ones in the corner offices. The interior designer set the floor to lay bare the homogeny of the non-managerial staff. The cubicles ran back-to-back the length of the rectangular floor space. On his side of the floor, facing Lexington Avenue, he saw the first Black face, a woman, short, nice curves, flat chest, lots of make-up. He smiled, only to hear her exaggerated proper enunciation, "It is good to meet you." He read into it, as someone opting not to befriend him. Perhaps she was upset she did not get the position. She sent intense signals, letting him know- *No, you are not getting any pussy, or even a smile.*

Sharon led him around to the left, short side of the floor. A couple of white coworkers had that same questioningly look then finally a genuine smile, from a senorita with curvaceous hips, firm breasts, a pretty face and bronze skin. "Hi. I'm Lourdes. You came in last week, right?"

"Yes." He did not recall seeing her but the interview started at ten and ended close to noon. Quite a few people boarded the elevator with him as he left that day.

"Congratulations. If you need anything let me know."

"Thank you. I will." Not sure how he had slipped into the too-proper enunciation the sister had thrown at him, he smiled and Lourdes did the same to let him know that she was down with him. Further down the floor, the office before the corner had plaques on the wall. His fraternity's insignia mounted on oak. Ernest thought of acknowledging him with the recognition signal. Though quite subtle a move, Ernest read the brother as someone who could be over-joyous and respond by giving him a hug then the fraternal grip. Ernest had come to know the fraternity as a division, of those who flaunted their membership, and ones who simply shook hands and slipped the grip.

The brother felt Ernest's grip and nodded because he understood, for the time being, Ernest wanted to be an *Incog-Negro*.

Sharon stood by that office a little longer. Her small talk, a dead give-away that she wanted to read whether, as Black men, they would be allies or combatants. Ernest said few words, making it clear he was not here to make friends or enemies. The tour took longer than anticipated. "It's almost time for me to go to orientation."

"We don't work with too many people on this side of the floor, only two." They rushed down the long side facing west, the back of other office buildings.

Lena sat in the office closest to the exit leading to the elevator bank. Life had few coincidences. Everything happened for a reason. Name your cliché because bleached blonde, dry humping that passed for subway sex, her wide eyes made Sharon ask, "You two know each other?"

Earlier this morning, Ernest and Lena bumped into and then rubbed against each other during a crowded, frenetic ride into Manhattan. As with most random New York events, afterward they kept moving in opposite directions because the city (held) eight million people.

"No." They both denied any possible acquaintanceship in a very casual manner. Lena caught on to Ernest's poker face and came from behind her desk to extend a hand. "I am Lena McIntosh."

Ernest waited for Sharon. "This is Ernest LeGa...I still can't get the last name right."

"LeGagneur." Ernest squeezed Lena's right hand and caught the slick bat of her eyelashes, the subtle lift of a coffee mug with the left hand to flash the rock on the platinum, diamond-crusted engagement ring and wedding band. Her small talk with Sharon revealed a boldness he sensed when she leant into him this morning on the subway. The union had been an accident but she challenged him to apologize. He kept waiting for Sharon to slip in that his hire was not her idea, but she did no such thing in front of Lena, to whom she seemed to yearn for approval. As they walked away, he took a last glimpse into her eyes, wide and a glimmer. Yes, Lena could be trouble, he thought.

Sharon led Ernest through the elevator bank then re-entered to their side of the floor, skipping all the other offices, except the corner one and the cubicle next to it – Sharon's boss and his assistant. The assistant barely smiled as she said, "The corner boys are still in the Monday meeting."

>=<

Orientation lasted two hours and made him miss his old job. This company dwarfed the previous one. There, he would never have the chance to create designs that conveyed his abject disdain for the box an artist had to jump into, just to get the chance to be considered *out of the box*. He did not see himself as the type of artist who wanted to take a dump on the world, only to expect its inhabitants to tell him they loved it. He yearned to couple a brand with a logo and a slogan of less than five words. To see that pairing last a decade or more, and even after replaced, have people always associate the brand and logo with his old slogan.

A pile of materials sat on his desk but none dealt with the account attached to his job title. He then noticed the flowers with the card placed gauchely on one of the chairs facing his desk. The card read, *"So proud of you, honey - Barbara."*

She would not last a week - Ernest's assessment after their second sexual encounter. He only busted two weak nuts the first time, and one the second time. Barbara's body was wicked, a strong athletic build with fifteen-mile per hour curves, with the parts to satisfy, but her focus on form, technique and tempo, and unwillingness to just let go and be wild, led to him not enjoying himself. Simply put, the sex was terrible, and she talked way too fucking much. Yet, she possessed the credentials and disposition to make a man rich or successful in his chosen endeavor.

"Ernest, what are you going to do?" He asked himself when he noticed the caller's identification number, a 718 area code followed by a Queens exchange. His instinct ordered him to dodge her call. He decided to pickup the phone, hoping to tell her that he appreciated the wonderful gesture of sending flowers to the job on the first day, but how it could make his life. He thought better and simply asked, "How'd you get my number?"

"What? Are you serious?" He did not interrupt. "I called the main switchboard and they patched me through. Why? What's wrong?"

"Nothing's wrong. Just that the flowers and phone call caught me off-guard." By lunchtime of his first day, he already hated his job. It fortified his belief that job satisfaction began with one's co-workers. "Yes, it was a very nice gesture..." His boss, Sharon, popped her head into his office. She wanted nothing specific, only to give him hint that her phone line, his line and the department's assistant shared the same hub and lit up on each other's phone set when in use. She waited, leading him to tell Barbara, "I have to go. Yes. O.K. Bye."

Ernest did not like the way that played, feeling he got punked, knowing he would soon have to draw the line in the sand. His small talk veered into the workload she assigned. "It was not why I was hired."

"I'm not sure you're ready for that account. I think it's best to bring you up slowly."

Instead of saying fine, he attempted to draw the line in the sand. "I have two years representing commercial accounts, and if given the chance..." Sharon walked out halfway into his sentence.

YOU MAKE ME LAUGH

The clock struck seven and the television turned on by itself, another reminder of Ken. He allowed himself four and half hours each night and preset the television to turn on and off on its own. He did this the week after he moved into the apartment. We bought a bigger television because he kept his in his studio apartment in Harlem. That apartment served as the last fortress, a reminder of his non-commitment even though he spent the majority of his time in this apartment. I never had one in the living room and kept my television in the bedroom as I liked to read in bed or talk on the phone.

Except for their height, six-two for Ken, and six-four for Ernest, those two were polar opposites. So one hour more than it should have taken him to get here, I began to wonder about Ernest's first day at work. I doubted he had to work late his first day and he never ran late. The mere thought of being ten minutes late and he would call. Yes, that considerate; yet didn't seem to expect others to be that way towards him. It took up to the days leading to his first day at this new job for Ernest to accept my being there for him.

Last night he actually said, "I hope you're not one of those *I'd do anything for a Black Man* type of chicks."

"What would be wrong with that?" I put the pencil between my teeth, its horizontal hold drawing attention to my lips and eyes, as I seductively looked up at him.

"That is the worst type of woman -- so caught up on doing the specialty things yet a man still has to get another woman to handle the basics."

The whole notion of *doing anything*, knowing that was never me, but still curious to hear his thoughts. "What do you consider the basics?"

He just rolled his eyes and went to the sofa, drifting into the television, to yet another sporting event. I hated that posture, with the remote in his hand and the game on as my cue to leave him alone. My cue to leave him alone had become my way of testing the waters and finding out how he viewed relationships, in general, and me, in particular. Slowly, Ernest had gone from one-night stand, lover, to a man I admired. The way he bonded with my brother and mother, to the point they've both called to ask about him. One time they called during a visit and he chatted with both for an hour combined. His genuine laughter during the conversation aroused a part of me, then to see with just a push by me, how he could land a job making sixty-five thousand in just one interview. "So, what are the basics? Aren't you going to tell?"

He shook his head. "That's not really the issue. I really didn't want to leave for work from here."

"Come on now. You spend so much time here. What's the hurt in giving me the satisfaction of seeing you leave for work on your first day?"

I pushed the wrong button. I wanted to talk but not with a cantankerous tone. "The basics are about multi-tasking, doing about three things at the same time. Like you see how I'm watching the game. At the same time, I'd like to be eating some homemade chicken wings, and having sex, preferably getting a blow job."

He never bothered to look away from the television, attesting he didn't care how much, if at all, those words offended me. "Where does all the stuff I did to help you get this new job fall? You're about to make twenty thousand more per year than your last job and that's what's important to you?"

"It's cool. It's one of those specialty things."

"A job is a specialty thing?"

"No, Headhunter! That's not something I look for in a woman. It is not way up there on the scale when choosing a woman."

I needed to divert my anger so I left him alone to flick through various channels and catch highlights of the day's NFL games. The bedroom felt far once I turned on the music. I sat on the bed, reading through progress reports and notes on my students' files, jotting down calls I needed to make. Parents. Probation officers. Court-appointed lawyers. Most of these kids had turbulent homes; compounded with their insistence that life had shortcuts, my school served as their last chance before years of incarceration.

Whenever I got angry and dived into my work, I pushed myself to remember when I left home believing college would be a sanctuary until I landed my first recording contract. I had a message and rap would afford me a platform to speak of the ills and traps set up to consume youths like my older brother Lincoln. He pleaded guilty because he had done the deed but at just 14 years old, he got sentenced like an adult.

Rap had just begun to climb up the pop charts. Run DMC kicked the door open when they dropped their self-titled album after redefining the rap game with the seminal hit, *Sucker MC's*. L.L. Cool J's first single *"I Need A Beat"* signaled a turning tide in rap, but also in my choices. Music, like sports, always served as a legal way to escape the troubled streets. People searched hard to discover and nurture those talents, much more than hitting the books. I did enough of both but was average at best. I had a decent voice and loved poetry. Some guys around the way formed a DJ'ing crew and a couple of us girls tagged along with them to local parties, grabbed the microphone a few times, harmonized, rapped and started thinking of the possibilities. A friend's mother who burned out on men and drugs even before crack cracked open vulnerable communities, she took interest in my future. She spoke of college and how we women needed to take charge of the communities. My guidance counselor did the rest by finding a small, private liberal arts college that provided enough financial aid money. That's how I ended up at TGI.

I quickly fell in love with campus life and the various worlds it offered, especially in subjects showing how I could help my older brother and youths bound to fall through the same cracks.

By the time I finished organizing my work papers, Ernest had fallen asleep on the sofa. I knew he needed a good night's sleep for this new course in life, so I woke him to get him inside. We barely spoke in the morning. As he left, I gave him a hug then looked out the window, feeling a sense of accomplishment, oddly enough, the way a mother felt when she allowed her child to walk alone to school for the first time.

Mid-day, I felt bad for probably getting his first day off to a bad start. So I sent the flowers, even though I couldn't pinpoint the source of his ambivalence about the resume, the interview, job and flowers.

>=<

The downstairs bell rang and I shook off thoughts about lateness and the crude remarks he made last night. I approached the apartment's door but did not open it. I heard the elevator reach the floor. Three good strides and as he reached the door, before sounding the bell, I flung it open. "Hey hon! What's up? How was your day?"

"Crazy fucking white people. What else is new?" I glanced his frayed look with tie knot slid down from the open white collar of a stiff blue shirt with thin stripes. The suit looked a bit too staid for a designer but he convinced me that this look worked because of the firm's culture. After a soft kiss to my lips, he rushed to the bathroom, along the way, dropping his bag on the sofa. He planned on slowly dressing down a bit, but first he did so to his manager. "My boss is a bitch."

No, he didn't say that! "She's a WHAT?"

He poked his head out of the bathroom while washing his hands. "No I am not using it as a synonym. She is whack. She demoted me on my very first day."

"She what?"

He removed his tie like it was a noose and then sat on the sofa. "You know I was hired to be the Account Manager as the Lead Designer for the Walker-MedCo account, right? I come from orientation and there is this pile of entry level bull on my desk. Talking about she doesn't know if I'm ready for such a big account."

I made light of the situation because I didn't want him to start plotting a reason to quit. Something strange about the way he lived when he wasn't working worried me. He did his own art, cooked and came over here at night. It made me think he was looking to do the struggling artist, home-husband thing. For some women that's fine. I have quite a few girlfriends who supported their boyfriends or husbands while they were getting their advanced degrees. And many have broken up with those same guys with nothing to show for it. Don't get me wrong, I'm not into that *my husband gotta make more than me* crap, but the brother gotta have a real job.

Ernest continued to ramble and complain about his day, with a positive sentence thrown in here and there, then out of nowhere he asked, "What you got to eat?"

"Nothing. I was waiting for you to come so we can go and grab something."

His right hand went to his face, his way of showing displeasure, yet trying to keep his cool. "You made this big production about how I had to come over. I thought you were going to surprise me and cook a meal or something."

His voice didn't hint at anger, so I matched his composed tactic. "I've cooked for you before."

"Once!" Though he shouted, I still sensed no sign of frustration.

"I wanted you to come over so I could hear all about your day."

"I could have gone home and called you."

I whined, "Forget you then!"

He laughed. Sometimes he loved my whining. Other times he really hated it. "Do you at least have a beer in the fridge for me?"

"Picture that! If you want to poison yourself, go ahead. I ain't gonna help."

"But you cooked for me once."

"Forget you then!" No whine, but he still laughed. "You're gonna miss me when I'm gone."

He continued to laugh and I tossed a sofa cushion at him. He caught it then tackled me to the sofa, tickling me until I begged him to stop. "Come on," he said, folding his tie into his suit pocket. "I have food from yesterday afternoon. I made it while watching the games before coming here."

"I don't feel like going to Brooklyn tonight."

"You're always saying I don't invite you over enough. Come on then!"

"Let's just order something and eat here."

He sat near me and put his arm on the back of the sofa, behind my neck. His first step in trying to convince me to do something. "Either way we have to go to Brooklyn. I don't have work clothes here."

"What's this *we* you keep talking about?"

He chuckled, going with the lightness of my voice. "Oh, you're going out like that?"

I giggled. "Let's eat here and I'll send you home in a cab after we're done."

"Done what?" He squinted and pursed his lips.

"You mean you're not gonna give me some?"

He motioned me closer with his left index finger. "I'm not following you. Are you saying that I have to sleep with you for my dinner and cab ride home?" I nodded. "Well, Ms. Wilson, I'm sorry but I'm just not that kind of guy."

"Well you can break the rules for me."

"I've broken enough for you."

"Which ones?" By now, our faces were real close and we whispered.

"Don't date women who don't cook at least four nights a week!"

"What else?"

"Treat them with respect but don't take African-American females seriously!"

"What?" I knew I had to pick my battles but in one sentence, he disrespected the entire sisterhood, but also said that he was taking me seriously. I've wanted to have this *where do you see this heading* conversation for the longest. One night I even started it, right after the best sex we ever had. His answer: *going to the kitchen, 'cause I'm hungry like a motherfucker.* I could not let him cross this line. "What's this about sisters?"

"Love y'all to death, but y'all are queens. Major culture clash for brothers who realize they ain't jack, let alone a king." See Ernest got this spell over me! I could be dumb enough and say it's his looks, his cooking, and the other ways he pampered me. The truth, his philosophy bedeviled me, a real defeatist attitude I truly needed to understand because of my job. I am responsible for countless little Black boys who already embody precisely what he has come to accept as his reality. He changed back to the original topic. "What's up, you coming to Brooklyn?"

"Let's order some food first. I am starving."

"Why didn't you cook something then?"

"I haven't had a chance to go food shopping." He let out an earsplitting laugh complete with feigning holding his stomach to compose himself, knowing full well I rarely go to the supermarket. "You're gonna miss me when I'm gone."

He's quick with the counter-punch. "You're already gone!"

I tossed a sofa cushion at him. "What do you want Chinese or Pizza?"

"I'm not eating that stuff tonight. I had a sub for lunch. That's enough takeout for one day. Plus, it's a waste of good money."

"It's my treat."

"What does it matter who pays? We're together. And afterward, I gotta take a cab to Brooklyn. More money wasted."

Together? His linking us seemed inadvertent but made me wonder if he really saw us that way. Driving to Brooklyn right now would get us off-track. I stalled. "I'll drive you to Brooklyn if you give me some."

He stood up. "A deal, if you give Big Boy a kiss."

"I told you I am not into that."

"I thought you were just saying that because we were new to each other." Ernest sat on the coffee table. The quizzical look, knowing of any issue, this was the set in stone losing battle. One time I was extremely horny and he wasn't in the mood, so I used my tongue for a few minutes to arouse him. Brotherman got all excited and thought I was gonna swallow for him or something. So disappointed when I stopped to start riding him, that he told me if I didn't plan on finishing the job, I shouldn't have started.

We've been at a standstill ever since. That night he gave me an ultimatum. He would not do me until I did him. Fine with me since the oral tradition was not one of his better subjects. "What's it going to be?"

"What?" Not sure of the question because my mind had drifted.

"Are you going to take me to Brooklyn so we can eat?"

"I'll take you to Brooklyn, but let's eat here first."

"Don't bother!" Ernest walked out of the apartment. So immature, especially how he caught me off-guard, flipping the switch with no warning. All this time I thought we were kidding around, as to who could be the most stubborn. But two could play whatever he called this new game. I did some quick calculations. It took him at least an hour to get home using the subway. During that time, I would order Chinese or Pizza from a place near his apartment. Pick up the order. Be there in forty minutes, sitting in my car in front of his apartment.

>=<

"Hey Big Boy!" A slight second for my voice to register. He paused at the gate, the look on his face let slip he didn't know whether to smile or ignore me. The slow turn in his original direction revealed this side of my personality intrigued him the most, why he even bothered. I teased, "Do you want some Moo Goo Gai Pan?"

As he turned the lock, I stood two steps behind him, though being here indicated I might be one step ahead of him. Ernest did not own a car but he knew how long it took to get here from my place. The Interboro Parkway curves like the builders aimed to give the road the feel of a back country road, with an arch within each one hundred feet. Cement divider blocking four narrow lanes, two on each side. On a dark night with frost on the pavement, speeding cars slowing to hit a bend have been known to careen, only to bounce back into the adjacent lane. Tonight the few cars heading into Brooklyn appeared in no rush. Not even I who had to traverse Atlantic Avenue for five miles, catching practically every other light until Nevins Street. Not once did I go over 45 miles per hour. My coolness was not what Ernest noticed. He discerned the commitment I made to be in his life had nothing to do with sex or his becoming my man. Us being together long-term would be quite welcomed but first I needed him to get back to normalcy, his old life before this apartment, before losing Bliss.

The apartment emitted a mixture of potpourri and polished wood, betraying the easy-going nature Ernest passed as his innate self. By Sunday evening while watching the NFL games, he had cooked, cleaned and readied his wardrobe for the next work day. I knew this because after I called he arrived at my place within two hours. The kitchen floor shone the reflective gleam of a recent mopping. The stove, no stains of spilled sauce. I reached in the cupboard for plates and then carried the two table trays to the living room. He came from the bedroom wearing a T-shirt and shorts, a quiet sneer on his face as he looked at the food on my plate. He passed through the living room without uttering a word.

After he fixed himself a plate from the food he made yesterday - pasta salad and cold jumbo shrimps - he came into the living room and placed the plate on the other table tray. "I know why you came here tonight. After we finish, I'd like you to go home and sleep in your own bed."

Relieved we would recommit to our playful banter, I chimed in, "I'm not that kind of girl. I need the cuddling and to be talked to sleep."

He spoke in an unfussy tranquil timbre. "I can't accommodate your needs in much the same way you can't mine."

"Mine are simpler. They lead to a more enlightened and healthy life."

Ernest glanced to his right and into my eyes. "Did you come here to be enlightened or for some dick?"

I continued chewing and food went down the wrong tube, bringing out a series of coughs, followed by our laughter. "Why did you leave tonight without waiting until we came to a consensus?"

"We did. That's why we're sitting here."

"And, if I hadn't come here tonight would you have called me in the morning?"

Ernest swallowed. "I'm not that kind of guy. I get the phone calls."

"Is that why you deal with me? Because I don't always have to be right?"

"On the contrary, you have an exaggerated need to be right. That's why you came over here tonight, hoping I would get into a fight with you. But I know how to play you."

How misguided, I thought. "If you know how to play me, then how come you can't get any head?"

"That's not what I keep you around for." He paused to look away, for emphasis, then back at me. "I keep you around because you're funny."

I played along by doing the Joe Pesci character from the *Goodfellas* movie. *"I'm funny how, I mean funny like I'm a clown, I amuse you? I make you laugh, I'm here to fuckin' amuse you? What do you mean funny, funny how? How am I funny?"*

Ernest interrupted me, "Gimme a kiss."

"You or Big Boy?"

A gentle tug on my left elbow, pulling me to him, into a passionate kiss.

YESTERDAY

Yesterday,
Love was such an easy game to play,
Now I need a place to hide away,
Oh, I believe in yesterday.

--The Beatles

When times got rough which they have been ever since he became a teenager, Ernest's mind helped him cope by pulling out a song to lead him, comfort him, join him as he traveled the world alone. Mr. Speiser taught him the guitar his sophomore year in high school. He learned the basics, notes and chords; to play a few songs including *Yesterday*, his cross-cultural favorite. Corporate work life kept forcing him to pull out another favorite, Billy Joel's *New York State of Mind*. He wanted to get away from that state of mind, so he longed for something, someone who could remind him of what home felt like after flesh and bone had been buried and smiles and giggles began to fade in the deepest recesses of one's mind.

His new routine of buying breakfast in the company's cafeteria had its glitches. He thought of breaking the practice but he put it in place to ingratiate himself into the company's culture. The corporation made sure to keep prices low, vary menus and configure the seating area so tables sat no less than three people. But the man on the grill, dressed in orderly white, topped with funny hat, did not seem to know the difference between scrambled, sunny side up, or over-hard. At least when Ernest ordered, he did not know. On this, the third time that week, and at least the tenth time in the month since Ernest started working at the company, the cook screwed up his order, not by a slight variation, but mayo instead of butter on toast accompanying eggs. So, Ernest decided to confront the situation. It was not so much nerve he had to work up. He just wanted to avoid getting into a pissing contest and have someone misinterpret the dispute as some sort of class struggle. He grew up comfortably but not well-off, and knew the hassles lower-wage workers balanced while having their dreams veer drastically off-course, thereby surviving as best as they could. Ernest weighed the fear of being viewed as uppity. The cook's brash, underhanded glimpse served as the final straw. Ernest asked, "Blackman, you got a problem with me?"

His timidity suggested Ernest caught him off-guard, "No." Then, as Ernest headed to the cashier, the cook started with the drama, at first talking under his breath, elevating to louder minor jabs, to climaxing where he brought the laughter of his coworkers. The patrons, all of them whites, remained muffled. Ernest knew they would do so only until he got out of earshot or they returned to their workstations. The gossip would spread, that he got shook by the cook, a *real* tough Black. The thought of being seen as a broken slash safe Black, one to be befriended slash walked all over; this plight played in Ernest's mind. After paying, instead of walking out, he turned. Standing a good fifteen feet away and with a glass counter separating them up to Ernest's chest, he looked at the cook. Without raising his voice, Ernest asked him, "Bo, are you a tough guy?" His eyes transmitted he had no idea Ernest knew his name, producing a silence, from him and all the others.

Ernest nodded slowly, appreciating how his mordant pitch had frozen time. Patrons and cafeteria line workers avoided his eyes as he left the room.

>=<

The exchange ruined his plan to sit at the first open chair with a table of less than four people. He knew whomever he sat with would want to know the ins and outs of the clash. He still held no more than small talk with whomever he sat with during breakfast or lunch, but the random sit-ins had afforded him enough opportunity to know not only the workers from his company but those from the other companies with offices in the building.

At his desk and before even unwrapping his food, Lena appeared at the threshold with a half-smile and dark suit. Hair pinned up to show off diamond studs and a slender neck, she got right to the point, stating she walked in as he questioned Bo. He didn't get to answer as Lena's presence drew a crowd – Asian assistant, then two white Account Executives, followed by Lourdes. When Sharon popped up, like a repellent, everyone fabricated a reason to go away. Left standing there, she made awkward small talk with Ernest. Only the second time they spoke on matters not related to work, it confirmed they simply had nothing in common. Sharon, two kids and in a dull marriage, at least judging by the pictures in her office. A home in suburban New Jersey, with a shallow above-ground pool suited for children under age six. Her husband, a dweeb, probably a hockey fan, only to distance himself from the major sports with their minority fan following. He probably watched Xgames, NASCAR and skateboarding. A beer gut on a five-nine medium frame, a small town, below average boy who probably earned more than twice Ernest's salary.

Ernest could feel her words breaking the ice that encased her and he wanted no part of Sharon's warmth. He and Sharon could only relate on the extreme points that fooled people into thinking opposites attract and could stick together for long. Unlike Lena, she was not attractive. Not even average, and he had no attraction to her – he, who friends mocked for having a low barometer when it came to being attracted to a woman.

Sharon evoked that flawed breeding look. Her extremely flat ass like she had been pick-pocketed. No curves to her hips. Hair combed but looked a mess with that sloppy, shoulder-length curl rag. Her nose, the only redeeming feature, if one preferred the button-sized look, but the lack of angles on her face bracketed the true sign that she scored no more than a five on a good day. Yet, to Ernest, she routinely sported this look on her blotchy face; that she expected him to find her attractive.

He feared getting to know Sharon. His warning light simply said YIELD. Not STOP or MERGE! YIELD! She would want something, directions, not just sex. She would ask questions in the form of statements, leading him to pity her. He would begin to play therapist, forty-five minute sessions of sex, talk and understanding that might cause tears to stain his shoulders. Afterward, no matter how much he lathered when he showered, her stain would remain, contaminating him with feelings that might cause him to talk about himself. Then she would feel that they had connected. And, as if she foresaw no harm in such a union, she offered, "Next week, would you like to assist me on the InterFaith Alliance campaign?"

Definitely a smart, cunning woman, to phrase it as if he had an option. To offer him the opportunity to work on the new, top level account, one larger than the one the company hired him to head. Though a non-profit, pro-bono account, the displays for InterFaith Alliance would be all over the country's top cities and national highway billboards. Even if she allotted him only one of the six designs, that visibility could take his career to the next level.

So, he agreed.

>=<

Friday evening. Five-forty-five. Sharon sat behind her desk and computer. He made a right out of his office, instead of passing by hers, preempting any chance of her asking him to undertake a minor task. Though not sure whether those last minute tasks were power-plays or her just being a workaholic, the long way around validated Sharon overworked. No one was at their desk, not even Derrick.

Drained from days of brainstorming for the new account, Ernest wanted to just go home and take a nap. He had called Attitude to cancel the plans, then Derrick. Both persisted.

Meeting somewhat under the guise of introducing Derrick, he would convey to Attitude he wanted to end this mission. Even though Ernest believed in its importance, the mission had taken too many turns and a bit longer than he expected. Ernest yearned for his old life, knowing no way could someone have killed Bliss; chick was too thorough to be brainwashed into plunging a knife into her gut. The mission's answer lied not on a who, but a why?

The hangout session climaxed too quickly and he failed to get a moment alone with Attitude to debrief him.

He went to the pay phone nearest to Attitude's building. Normally his pager would tell him who tried to reach him but this morning he rushed out and forgot to take it with him. The six messages were from two females, Barbara and Paulette. Though he phoned back the few times she called since Bliss's funeral, he had not seen Paulette.

Ernest stepped away, out onto the avenue. Yellow cabs crisscrossed, to pull up and pick up passengers. He tugged his coat closed, holding the two flaps together, opting not to button since the subway's entrance was less than twenty feet away. Bleeker Street. Soho, Manhattan's art district. Lofts housing designers, photographers and painters, both commercial and underground. The retail stores sold hip, chic to totally avant-garde wares. Broadway overflowed with a swarm of worker bees who, at the end of the workday, transformed into party animals, most hoping to relive their campus days. Except this life bested the zenith of their collegiate days.

He resisted admitting nine-to-five beats cramming for exams on topics he will never use again. Each weekly paycheck brought almost nine hundred dollars after tax; a lifestyle way better than rummaging drawers to chip in four ways on a keg, liquor and weed. In the darkness of winter, Ernest fought the negativity craving to overtake him.

Going by Paulette's would not be an admittance she still fit in his life. He just thought it would be good to reach out, and to eat. One of her prime attributes, she always had a hot meal for a brother. They met a few months before Bliss's death. The atrium near his old job had a blend of takeout restaurants comprising a food court where people often ate with strangers. Paulette sat at the lone table with empty chairs. A fellow Haitian, she came to the States at twenty-one, only two years ago; whereas he got here twelve years ago, shortly before his twelfth birthday. They made love on the first date because that was his M.O., in that he tried to undress a woman the first chance he got. If she said no, then all future moves belonged to her, because he needed to know who or what had changed. He categorized it as love, for afterward, though she claimed to be more inexperienced than how she performed, Paulette's entire being coursed upwards in his body, past his heart and into his mind. The vibration brought a song, one he loved to play and croon but it never really registered even though he had moments, moments where even after feeling it from the shaft to the navel then to the heart, logic prevailed. This feeling had no logic as she lied there next to him, hours later, on the faux Persian rug. He looked at her, the way the crescent moon curved around her left temple and her nipple pointed in a ready fashion, as if begging for him to suckle, full himself from the infinite warmth she could provide. Neither uttered a word but in his mind, he knew the words. He reached for the remote control; forwarding, seeking the song on the mixed tape with the slow jams. The cassette never came into play because after their dinner and movie date, they came upstairs and she asked him to tell her what she could do for him and what he could possibly want from a woman like her.

The song expressed to her his feelings, for she looked scared. She turned and balled up under his shoulder, and her eyes stared ahead.

Please let me make a true confession
I have never been in love before

Ernest could easily admit the greatness of 1980's, particularly when it came to the music but that decade never let him get strong footing. He always had a crisis and so far, the 1990's continued the pattern. Deep down, like Bernard Wright had sung in "Who Do You Love", he knew who he loved but that really was *Yesterday*.

>=<

Having to transfer from the N, R line to the Number 3 train left him a bit disjointed. His thoughts of an hour ago, while deciding which high he wanted to ride, had him spaced out enough that the speed of the cocaine made the phone call; the mellowness of the ganja slowed him to think of her and what role could he possibly play in her life at this stage; and the volatility of the alcohol, though only a few beers made him want food and sex. When Paulette opened the door, her eyes quickly told she recognized the disconnect between them. She danced around the direct issues so he used his high as the reason. "Ernest, you know that's not what I mean."

He gave her left hand a squeeze, taking in the slow evolution of her style. She adapted, rapidly assimilated into the fashion, dialect and inflections. She never shied in what she wanted from him or any man: to get married and have kids. Paulette carried the air and mask of simplicity in beauty and demeanor, and came to personify the girl next door, not just in the homemaker mode but in the length of hair, as it hung just a bit over the shoulder, always done up with cute bangs she sometimes parted and pinned to the side. Her medium build held slender hips that would easily widen after a child or two. The slow, deliberate steps to move them only enough make men of distinction to wonder about her sexual proclivity.

Normally, Ernest could not resist that act, for these women spoke his language, but tonight, he felt the fear Bliss made him forget until she died. "You have to spell it out for me."

He followed her to the oven. Her reaction or lack thereof to his wrapping his arms around her waist meant she wanted to talk about serious stuff, but would only do so after he ate and only if he wished to discuss them. She sat and remained silent while he ate. Her elbow rested on the table with chin on her left palm. She only responded to the compliments he gave about her cooking and what she had done to the place. The first time he came to her new dwelling he almost caved to the point where he nearly invited her to live with him. The neighborhood did not appeal to him, edge of Crown Heights, heading into Bed-Stuy in one direction, and East New York in the other. A rooming house converted out of a large single-family unit, the only one who resisted developers who turned the entire block into four-story walk ups, four apartments per floor. The house with its perpetually dark hallways, each floor with three bedrooms, a kitchen, bathroom and a common area, except hers. Though she had to come down one floor for the kitchen and bathroom, the attic room gave her more privacy.

The angular shape meant he had to duck when walking in certain parts of the room.

The food, du riz collé avec poi et legume, filled him to the point where sleep crawled from around the corner. On the bed, together, she whispered, "It's nothing serious and I don't want you to be mad, but I am dating someone."

"Why would I be mad?"

She pulled his left shoulder to roll him onto his back, to make eye contact. "I would be mad if you were dating someone."

"That's funny because you know...forget it."

"No Ernest, don't forget it. I know it's been nearly four months since I last saw you so I don't expect that you haven't been having sex. Just don't tell me that it is something serious."

"Let me guess. You need to know how serious mine is so you can..."

"I already told you that it's not serious. We've gone out a few times, had sex for the first time last weekend."

Ernest spread his arms, palms flat up. "What does that have to do with me?"

Paulette squeezed his palms between hers. "Everything! I need to know if we're going to get married. If you are planning to stay the night. If you're..."

"Look, if you want me to leave, then I will leave." Ernest got up from the bed.

She rose after him. "I called you to see you. So you can stay. I don't want anyone but you but I can't be alone. Do you understand that?"

"Yes I do." Ernest hugged her to his chest and whispered, "I love you, and I want the best for you, even if it's not me."

"I love you too. You are the best for me." They lied back down and fell asleep in each other's arms.

WHERE HAS RACE GONE

The next morning as they walked up Eastern Parkway toward Utica Avenue, she wanted to hold hands. They used to do that even though Ernest never got comfortable where he would be the one to initiate it. A slight bump of her shoulder against his indicated she wanted his hand; next she would slip her arm through the slight open space between his arm and side. This time, he did not open up. Paulette cut him a dirty look. When he got to the bank, she waited outside. He did not tell her the stop was for her or she may not have come. When he got back outside and handed her the envelope, she did not even count the money before putting it into her shoulder bag. She had an expression on her face, one that contained words she only knew in Kreyol. She knew he would understand them even though he was no longer fluent. Instead she simply said, "You're so full of yourself."

"You don't understand my life."

"And you think you understand mine?"

"I'm not trying to." She laughed as if she had gotten the confirmation she long sought, that he thought he was better than her. "You know I'm in this until I'm dead, right?"

"Who says you're alive?" That she asked in Kreyol with all the spit she could build up without having any of it spill on his shirt, pants and shoes. *Ki moun ki di ou vivan?*

He grabbed her arm with such force she should have reacted to his hold but she stood there and sternly looked into his eyes. "You got it." As he let go of her, he repeated, "You got it."

She turned to walk away only to spin back and slam her body into him. Paulette held him and kissed him. A few pedestrians stopped, some clapped and others said, "Get a room!" But no one ignored their embrace.

She shouted at Ernest, "I love you. I love you motherfucker." Then she walked away.

>=<

Ernest spent the rest of the weekend and Monday dodging phone calls from Barbara. On Friday, The buzz from the drugs was too strong and good to be in Barbara's company. He took steps to slowly limit Barbara's access to him. No matter how stimulating the conversation, how humorous her personality, Barbara just did not fit him.

She kept filtering into his mind and he knew to be heavily on hers but after four months, he realized that they were using each other to not face the ghosts of their past. During Hope's housewarming party, her ex-boyfriend entered the apartment and after greeting everyone except Ernest and Devon, he came over to grab her away from him. He didn't even say a 'what's up' to Ernest because he knew the deal: Ernest had always wanted to sleep with Barbara.

But, at no point, did Ernest think she wanted him that way. Now she wanted him to keep moving further down the road and he could not. He respected her too much, so much so that he could not dump her; they had to come to a place where they both respected and cherished what transpired between them and why.

He dodged her during the holiday season because Christmas and New Year's good alibis were easy to fabricate. The plans with his family lasted many less hours than he claimed. He stretched one hour before and three after. For Christmas, they exchanged gifts but not tradition. He went to church with his family for both eves, while she simply went to give gifts and grab a meal. For New Year's, her planned four-day cruise to the Bahamas with two friends and their children morphed her from being fine with their mostly behind closed doors relationship, to her inviting him to events, private ones – a friend's dinner party, a function sponsored by her school's board member, and an actress friend's Off-Broadway play. He passed on all the gatherings, escalating the tension in their relationship- pretty much his desire.

Even a hangout with co-workers, on a Tuesday night, served to push her further back. Except for the people in his weekly meetings it got to the point where he spoke to no one except Derrick who kept pressing him to hang out these past few weeks. His last job he socialized with co-workers but made sure to keep everything platonic. That company had fewer employees and a more familial feel. This current job proved to be a totally different animal, very cutthroat, with little room for advancement and everyone fighting for the same boost up the ladder. The hostility lent itself to great sexual energy, for the men were fit and brash, and the women hot-tempered and cunning. The smiling ones, like Derrick served as a good litmus test, like dipping your toes in the pool.

Derrick told him the regular Tuesday night hangout at *The Last Stand* was the most laid back. He soon realized Derrick was a bit too entrenched in work politics and maneuvering to make moves on Lena.

As Derrick nursed the bottom of his fifth beer, Lena's eyes fixed on Ernest and he picked up on her simple message. Ernest did not like the steps he would need to close the deal so he slipped his hand into his pocket and sounded his pager. Three people shouted, "Booty call!"

Ernest laughed and as he walked away, he finalized that he had to limit frat's access to his personal life. He held no doubt in his mind that that fool Derrick discussed the hangout session over at Attitude's and other aspects of his personal life with co-workers.

By the time Ernest returned, the others loitered outside, with some ready to head to the same subway line. Derrick ran an end-around, trying to see if this one white guy and Lena wanted to shoot by his place. Lena declined. "What about you Ernest?"

Ernest winked at frat. "You know how Tuesdays are!"

The white guy surprised him, "Oh yeah! It's useless hookers night." Derrick gave him a high-five.

Caught off-guard by the fact Derrick blatantly, indiscriminately gave away codes, no matter how small, Ernest simply said, "Yeah, you know how we do."

They walked away, crossing the street to go west.

The wide avenue granted the wind enough access where even on a night in which it traveled about five miles per hour and in the same northeastern direction they stood, the chill factor rushed people off the streets. Taxis made up the majority of cars moving down Third Avenue. Their leisurely pace gave them the opportunity to entice people, who were not heading too far but whom the plummeting temperatures chased.

The first cab whisked by and Lena made no motion to hail it. Then another. "I would hail you a taxi but you know how it is for us Black men." She only smirked. "Do me a favor and get in a cab so when my date shows up, she doesn't see you."

"Why? You're having drinks with coworkers is a problem?"

"Now, don't pretend that you don't want something."

Lena laughed. "Ernest, I don't want to sleep with you if that's what you mean."

"Seriously, you don't want to give me some?"

Her laugh was louder this time. "Seriously!"

He held back his laughter, thinking she's cooler than he ever imagined. "Not even head?"

She turned her back then turned back around. "Do you want to go somewhere, for a drink or something?"

"No. I am waiting for someone, and I wish you would just get in a cab and go."

"Fine. Are you sure you wouldn't rather call her back and cancel?"

"No, she was in a meeting not too far away and we're heading back to Brooklyn together."

Ernest expected her to counter but the look on Lena's face signaled something different, a mixture of shock, more than that of seeing a woman hug him from behind. The shock shattered the parallel universes she and this woman had existed in for many years. It was as if someone has smacked her then quickly hugged her, the betrayal, love and confusion of an abusive relationship, of having walked away, to flee because the natural response to stay, at least for too long would mean that you were an accomplice; but the look revealed more than that; pigtails, knock knees, pretty pink dresses and a face made sticky from devouring candy – the past; adorned in all its glory, the mystery explained in bits and pieces.

Ernest could not stop looking at the bewildered expression on Lena's face. The two, three seconds felt like forever, slow motion of barely noticeable wince. He no longer saw Lena, the white woman, coworker, would be seducer. He saw a mirage, an abstraction, not much unlike the designs he created, not the ones to pay his bills, but the ones he uses to free his mind; a square, graph with points to be plotted, but only the bold creator went off the given path, and wrote outside the margins.

"Barbie? Barbara Wilson!!"

"Oh my god! Lena Strand. It's been, what, six years?. They hugged, like lost friends who just fell out of touch, not through quarrel but mere life and circumstance. "How have you been?" Barbara asked, "How do you know Ernest?"

He left them to feel each other out, like champion boxers with no animosity toward each other, only the need for the glory and prize money. "We work at the same company."

"Small world! We should do dinner."

He saw this as the time to step in! To not do so would mean that you wanted them to get chummy again and worse of all, you'd be using the renewed friendship as the conduit benefiting your thoughts of a tryst.

"OK. So I'll catch you some other time." Ernest placed a soft kiss on Barbara's lips.

"No. I meant all of us. Tonight. Right now…"

Ernest moved away a step. "No, it seems you two have catching up to do." He measured his words as to not totally take himself out of the picture, only to push Lena out because he had to get their story first before they could mend whatever rift caused them not to see each other for six years.

"Barbie, just give me your number. We can do dinner some other time." Ernest reflexively took a step back. They hugged and said goodbye, not only exchanged business cards, but they wrote their home numbers on the back of their respective card.

Lena and Barbara hailed cabs. As they waved goodbye, her head through the cab's back window, Lena asked, "How's Hope?"

Barbara answered, "She's fine."

KEEPING SECRETS / BARBARA SPEAKS

Our cab pulled up only seconds after Lena's pulled away. It might have been for the best because we were on the verge of instigating an all-out fight, not a physical one, but a verbal lashing. Ernest pushed that final button; at least that's what I thought. First to insult me by pulling these disappearing acts, using work or hanging out with friends as his excuse. After days of being avoided, I forced myself into his schedule to simply say good-bye. Then I showed up and he was nearly drunk and trying to set up an interlude. I spotted him as soon as I came up from the subway. The off-center tilt of his right shoulder with left hand in his pants pocket; his camel tweed coat blowing with the wind so the woman could see the layers of his outfit; I knew the game well. Then as I grabbed him to basically say, 'gotcha', my eyes met hers.

The cab needed instructions because the driver could not get confused and try to veer local or go uptown to catch the FDR Drive then BBT and not the bridge. My joy of seeing Lena after all these years dominated the early part of my conversation. I call it mine because Ernest considered my talkative nature, rambling. Normally he tuned me out when the banter did not relate to something that would benefit him. Yet that night, he seemed ready to digest every morsel, as if waiting for that one piece of information he could use to close the deal with Lena.

I veered off-course and asked, "How come you didn't tell me that you worked with Lena?"

"How was I to know you roomed with her or even knew her?"

"If you would open up and talk about your job, your life, your past then it would come up in the normal flow of conversation. It's like I don't even know you."

"The problem is that you are not listening. When I tell you what I need, you ignore it then…"

I interrupted, "Like what?"

"If you don't know by now, you will never know."

"That's exactly what I mean. Instead of giving me a concrete answer, you give these vague…"

"Answer me this, what do you want from me?"

"I need you to not to disappear when things aren't going well, to answer my calls and messages…"

"Is this what this is about? You wanting to keep tabs on me?"

"I'm not trying to keep tabs. I just need to know that after days of not seeing you…that you're not bar hopping with some white girl from your office."

"Hold up! Is this what all this is about? You're scared of a little white girl?"

That question smacked me way back, to grade school, 1979 precisely.

That year I discovered the nerve my mother liked to stand on, the one Ernest continually sought out. We moved during the school year so I had to finish sixth grade in a new school. My mother is one of these Black folks who always described white people as 'little', no matter their physical size or prominence.

When Darren's father came into the picture and we moved, my new grade school was pretty integrated. I made friends quickly because I simply walked up to people and said hello. My clique consisted of a few Black smart, pretty girls and not necessarily the toughest bunch in school. Years ago, all of them had gone through the picked-on phase. I never got picked on because in my old school, all of the kids knew my family because we lived in the neighborhood since before my birth.

At first, I saw no signs of trouble. Things went smoothly for weeks until one day, while I ate lunch at a table with four friends. Schooled and warned about the crew of so-called tough kids, I learned how to avoid them and had done a good job. But, for some reason, Millie, the lone white girl from the group of tough kids, found reason to come over to our table. She poked me, using her index finger to jab my left cheek, *poke, poke, poke.* I quickly turned and saw her hover over me. She was more a box of a person, no discernible shape as her limbs were meaty and her arms stayed close to her body.

That night when my mother got home, I told her what happened. Had my brother, Lincoln gotten home first, straight from school like he was supposed to, I would have asked him. He might have given better advice since he always ran with the tough kids. He already had a crew of tough friends at his new school, the local high school.

My mother made no effort to soothe my tears with a hug or something, for having my milk taken and the change I saved by not buying a big lunch. She just shouted, with no preface to her answer, "You let a little white girl take your lunch money?"

I tried to tell my mother, although also twelve years old, Millie was as big as a grown woman, with newly-formed breasts, slightly overweight, broad shoulders, no waist, rolls of fat on her gut, thighs that rubbed when she walked and a pudgy pink face. My mother took her purse off her shoulder then unpacked the groceries. Normally, it would be my job to unpack the groceries, the beginning stages of my training to be domesticated. After putting away the groceries, my mother would guide me on how to prepare the meals we ate. That night after we cooked and sat to eat, she said, "Make a fist. Now, the key is to punch her on the edge of her nose and the mouth, specifically the top row of teeth."

My words came out in a nasal whining pitch, which my mother really hated. "Her face is too big, her mouth and nose are too far apart and my fist is too small."

"Stop whining! Listen!! Tomorrow, buy your lunch as usual, open the chocolate milk and bring it to her table. As you hand it to her and she reaches for it, throw it in her eyes then hit her like I showed you, as hard as you can."

"Then she'll crush me!"

"She's already crushed you. She took your lunch money in front of the entire class, right? You cried to me, right? Then what more do you want?"

That night my brother got home close to 11 p.m. I could hear my mother screaming at him, the same stuff about how he's going to be just like his father, in jail by sixteen, then a parolee working menial jobs, but he was not going to be so lucky to find a woman to look past all of that and help him get on his feet, instead he'll become a junkie, strung out on some corner, and on, and on. My brother often told me, dating back to when I was six, that I had to learn to tune my mother out, that she lived in the past, an era that never actually happened as she retells it.

I made sure my mother fell asleep before I snuck next door to my brother's room. He sat on the bed with his back to the headboard, eating the food I helped prepare. "Lincoln, what do you do when someone at school picks on you?"

He motioned for me to come to my normal spot. I sat next to his knees, facing the TV, somewhat ashamed and afraid to look at him, for fear of breaking out into tears. "No one's ever picked on me."

I then told him my mother's advice and he said kids who he and his friends picked on never responded that way, and he doubted that response would work. "Then, what should I do?"

"Do what Ma says! Maybe she was picked on or somebody stopped her by doing what she told you."

"How do you make sure that no one picks on you?"

"Whenever I am out of my environment, I go look for trouble. By doing that, everyone thinks of me as trouble, and leaves me the fuck alone. You see my friends; we're not really the toughest kids in school, only the most troubled."

"OK, I will try that next time. For now, I will try Ma's way."

"By the way, what's that girl, Millie's last name? She probably has a brother that goes to my school or something. I will get him."

The next day at school, I did as my mother said, *milk then punch*. If it weren't for the school security guard, Millie would have probably killed me. She sat on me, choking me and must have punched me in the face five or six times before the guard showed up to pull her off me. The kids were frantic, yelling *fight, fight, fight*. The girls who I hung out with were nowhere to be found. The next day they said that they couldn't make their way through because Millie's friends had formed a circle around us. Some other kids told me that they looked scared and never tried to break through. Though I periodically hung out with them here and there up to high school, I never allowed myself to become closer with any of them. I think the only reason they even spoke to and hung out with me was because of my mother's actions the day of the fight.

My mother never had to come to school for me, and I knew she hated having to do so for Lincoln, but he usually was at fault. Since I wasn't technically at fault because I was doing what she told me, I knew she couldn't, wouldn't be mad at me, except maybe because I had gotten beat up.

We waited in the office for nearly three hours – me, the principal, Millie, her father and mother. The principal ordered us not to say anything until my mother arrived. Her parents seemed on edge, as if embarrassed of having to once again face the principal and yet another child's parent. They peeked at their watches to help time move along so they could then go on with their real lives.

When my mother walked into the office, she did not even look at me. The calmness in her must have duped Millie's father into thinking she neared to shake his hand. At the last moment, she closed her fist and punched him on the left cheek; and in the same motion, she used her left hand to grab the stapler off the principal's desk and slammed it to his face; then she switched the stapler to her right hand and threw it to Millie's mother's forehead. Millie looked scared but my mother never made her way toward Millie. She turned her vicious, psychotic stare to me, not halting at the sight of my bruised and blood-stained face. I charged at Millie and started pounding her. She did not fight back.

The principal grabbed me and as security rushed to restrain and take my mother away, she screamed, "Don't make me have to come back down here! And, don't fuck with my daughter!!"

Ernest laughed at the story. He laughed all the way to Brooklyn. He would stop me to ask a question so I could further detail a part, so he could laugh some more. Tears filled his eyes, followed by his last words, "I like your moms; she's kool."

While he laughed, I found it odd that he paralleled himself with my mother; therefore my friend Lena to Millie.

KEEPING SECRETS / LENA SPEAKS

Barbara had changed so much. I could tell by her face. When I first met her, not only did her beauty stand out but you could tell by her eyes that she really did not know how to react to adversity. At only eighteen, she stood ready for a fight but not ready to start one. Tonight, she looked fierce, emboldened by battles lost and some hard earned victories. Near each corner of her full lips, a sneer inched up toward her high cheek bones, as if daring someone to say the wrong thing. But, then she saw me, it all dropped and her lips parted, to radiate a smile that cleared any misconception I ever held about searching for her after we lost touch.

The hug she gave me placed me back to who I used to be, so many memories, mostly good ones, though at the time some felt bad. College memories challenged us to define growth and the nature of letting bygones be just that. Especially when one got to the real world, as we often called the nine-to-five, and run into men you allowed to take your blouse off on the first night you met them or acted out absurd fantasies such as blow job in the men's bathroom at one of the town's bars. Those men were now corporate decision-makers and cronies with your new coworkers; with many of their wives being the prissy, no put-outs who envied you in the college days, or the girlfriend who visited or received their visits during weekends. They also knew your scandalous history. My wild days did not necessarily bequeath me with a standing so indecent that I cannot walk hand in hand into the office holiday party with my husband, a prominent architect. Nor do those reckless nights and judgments vanish where I could be gleeful that my newest coworker's girlfriend is Barbie, my roommate during my wildest days.

September 1985 made it official, upperclassmen status, my third year at TGI and planning on doing my normal routine to not have a roommate. At the end of my sophomore year, when I filled out the next year's dorm application form, I placed all sorts of restrictions: non-smoker, early riser, no fragrance, then at the end of the dorm registration, NO ROOMMATE PREFERRED.

I had gotten very comfortable with the routine of college life, with the studies and town life. I knew Monday was domestic night; Tuesday, vodka night; Wednesday, dollar beer and two-dollar rail drinks; and Thursday, import night, my favorite night, especially in the winter when two of my closest buddies would brave the cold and snow of upstate NY, freezing while my lemon of a car warmed; the engine sputtering, smoke bursting out of the exhaust as we drove the two miles to town. The game remained the same, all of us vied for the attention of the same guy, no matter how dorky or handsome. One of us would pick the guy, flirt, throw out innuendos, giggle, but give him the choice of which of us he wanted. Then we girls would bet how many weeks the relationship would last. We didn't play that game every Thursday. Sometimes we did the bar thing just to get wasted. On those nights we would walk the two miles to town, and revel at the fun of being sloshy while walking back home at four in the morning, across campus, shouting nonsense as we walked past the first of two quads with dorms.

Those were the days but then my two running partners, my mentors graduated. I met them my freshman year in a general requirement class. They didn't care much for Poe Hall and its crudeness, calling it a cheap knockoff of *Animal House*. Our friendship bloomed because of the common exchange, each side had something of use to the other: the freshman with the car; the juniors with wisdom. They needed a place to hangout since they were roommates and lived far off-campus; I needed to bypass the predictable pattern newbies lived. With their counsel, I learned how to get rid of roommates by the second week of October, when students could start changing from their assigned rooms. Word got around the dorm and the various campus circles that I was a bitch to room with, so no one applied to live with me even with the long waiting list to live in Poe Hall. The start of the next semesters when a transfer student or freshman got assigned by the administration, all I had to do was keep my part of the bargain, live the history and be that bitch, and my roommate would move out by the semester deadline of the room change period – the tenth of November. For the remainder of the semester, the whole room would be mine, at no extra cost.

In Barbie, I saw a difference, a bit of myself, young freshman who didn't have TGI as her first option, a girl from Long Island; she from Wyandanch and I from Babylon. She was the only girl; I was the only child.

Her mother drove her up and as her younger bother helped her unpack and put up posters, Barbie and I took a quick liking to each other. The first night after her family left, instead of going to town for domestic night, I told Barbara what to expect from TGI and, specifically, Poe Hall. Halfway through the rundown, she asked about MLK Hall, where most Black students lived or socialized. I had no concrete details but gave her general pointers.

That first Friday afternoon, I geared up to play big sister or at least mentor. I handed Barbie the fake ID I promised to get for her. "Are you ready to go to happy hour?"

"Happy hour? What's that?"

She was green as hell, like someone just plucked her from the field. Not only did she not know, she did not care even after I filled her in on the schedule for the town's best bar. "Happy hour from three to eight. Rail drink specials and beer pitchers at half their normal price." She wanted me to pass up the year's first happy hour because the Black students were throwing a two-to-two, a twelve-hour party at the student union. She tried to convince me to go, and I actually considered it, until I remembered that no campus-based activity could serve or sell alcohol.

That afternoon, we parted ways in more than just our partying preferences.

Though we continued to share details of our lives and truly enjoy being roommates, her walking in at 9 p.m., catching me sitting on the floor, with my head between the legs of a nearly comatose drunk guy, surely caused a greater divide between us.

"Close the door!" I shouted, and Barbie stepped into the room then closed the door. "No. I meant for you to leave then close the door."

"I'm not leaving. This is my room too." In all my semesters of scaring off roommates, I never heard that answer. "You need to stop that nasty shit!"

I ignored her and wondered had she turned her face to the wall, her side of the room with the posters of RUN-DMC, LL COOL J, and MC LYTE, and clippings of articles from Jet, and Ebony.

The guy came and Barbie shouted, "Did you just swallow that?" When I didn't answer, she added, "You are a nasty white girl. I thought people were just telling lies about you."

I turned my head to her and took in the full disgust of her stare, which confirmed she had been looking at me the whole time. Though I did not intend for her to catch me in this position, I searched her face for the cracks, those indicating the contempt that roommates felt for me. Sneaking in a guy for sex or walking in drunk with my friends on a nightly basis while my roommate slept were surefire ways to get rid of roommates. My eyes must have asked the question, Did you just bring race into this? She made set to leave the room, her palm twisting the door knob. I ordered her to "Sit down!" I shouted louder the second time to make my point, and then I asked the guy to leave. He wore that 'after I come I like to nap look' in his eyes. I nudged him again. When he got up, he shook his dick at Barbie and said, "Not bad for a white boy, eh?"

She rolled her eyes and sucked her teeth and then walked to her side of the room. He pulled his pants from around his knees and blew me a kiss goodbye.

Poe Hall was a corridor style dormitory, where room doors opened into hallways, public space. For Poe Hall that meant people straggling the hallways or lounging in front of their rooms after happy hour. They sat on the carpeted floor, either stoned out of their minds or nearly dead drunk. Most considered my hall mates the dregs of the campus. I made my way past them and into the nearest bathroom to wash my face and rinse my mouth. I needed to be alert for either a heart-to-heart or bitter fight. Either way, I wanted to be ready.

When I came back into the room, my absence achieved what I had hoped. She had her eyes fixed on the wall over my bed, at the lone poster of Billy Idol, surrounded by various ad clippings, some contained only words but many had images of products. The clippings trailed to my closet where a door-length poster of Madonna celebrated her as the latest heir to the nation's Marilyn Monroe's blonde fixation and ambition.

As I sat on my bed, she said, "Lena, sorry for calling you a nasty white girl."

"Nasty is OK." I laughed to lighten the mood. "White girl, not cool! I have a hard enough time accepting a roommate. I don't need race stuff mixing into it."

Barbie laughed with me. "I didn't know you had a boyfriend."

"Boyfriend? That wasn't my boyfriend, just some guy I had a class with this past semester." Her eyes, the way she rolled them, first to the top, then left then back center; told me we needed to have a serious talk. We discussed sex a bit and nothing about her personal freedom indicated parents who kept her locked up, with a curfew or anything.

When Barbara saw me on campus, she would come over and chat with my friends and me. I did the same when I saw her. At first, our friends found it surprising we were still roommates and neither seemed to be trying to push the other out. Popular wisdom stated that women were overly-competitive but on the sly. Men showed their competitive nature, and that allowed them to get along as mere acquaintances as well as best friends. Barbie and I harbored no such petty grievances. We both looked good, had different fashion styles yet the sense to know what worked, and partied hard, albeit on different scenes.

Barbie partied and like most freshmen, she overdid it. She came to the room to sleep. Other than that she came to get me to go somewhere, while I stayed in except for my bar hopping. Studying proved second on her agenda. By the second month, she got involved in a slew of organizations, and became the singular reason for the large number of Black visitors who patrolled Poe Hall. Other Black Poe Hall residents socialized away from the dorm, or hung out with white students and took on white persona or had that facade before coming to the college.

Judging from the friends she hung out with, I swore she would move out of Poe Hall and into MLK, once the room change period began. I also thought I knew who would be her first campus fling. She said no, because she didn't see Manny that way; plus Hope liked him. She didn't seem to appreciate my honesty when I told her to go for it because she was prettier than Hope. She brushed me off, as if to show me that my comment came from my petty jealousy because she and Hope were slowly becoming best friends. She might have mistaken the fact that I had no true best friend, especially on campus, as a need for her to serve that role. Or that I hoped to fill that role for her. To me, having just one best friend spelled trouble.

From the way things progressed, with numerous and various guests knocking on the door, asking for Barbie and leaving messages for her, I saw Barbie as someone who also shied away from that one best friend model. Her female friends were always rude and brief to me. The males tended to give me the up and down then a smile; some seemed to come by only when they knew Barbie wouldn't be in the room. I would be civil because they were her friends but no more than that.

Manny never came by alone. He only knocked when accompanied by Hope. The first time I saw him in the room, I was returning from the laundry in the basement and not looking my best. Surprise guests, add that to the list of reasons why I hated having a roommate. The three of them sat on side of the Barbie's bed with their backs to the wall, leafing through her album. Hope said hi and Barbie introduced Manny. I immediately recognized him as the lone Black guy of the thirty people in my summer pre-admission orientation. Back then, two years ago, he wore his hair close to the scalp. He had filled out a bit but still looked on the light side with the same sneer under his left eye.

Though I had seen him on campus, particularly in some of my large lecture classes, we never spoke, much less look each other's way. As he looked up, I said hi and gave him a smile. I mistook his nod and smile as a prelude to a casual banter, of how we were in the same orientation, of how it's ironic that in over two years we have never spoken, and so on. Instead he insulted me. "Yeah, I know you. You're the unconscious blonde."

"The what?"

Hope and Barbie laughed. Manny continued, "We've called you that since freshman year, ever since you passed our demonstration line by Barclay's Bank. We were urging them to divest out of South Africa."

His statement knocked the legs from under me, so I went to sit on my bed to face my accuser. "Who's we?"

"The RSA. The Radical Students Association. It's a coalition of various student orgs who stage rallies for global change."

"Yeah, I've seen your flyers, and just thought you all to be social misfits."

Hope and Barbie laughed. Their laughter didn't faze him. "Baby, I'm president of the school's top frat. VP of the RSA. Dean's list? Should I continue?"

"Yes. You look good blowing your own horn."

"Word on campus is that's your specialty." He placed the emphasis on specialty.

Hope ooo'ed. Barbie playfully gave him a light slap on the back of the head. "Watch what you say to my roommate. Apologize!!"

Without hesitation, Manny said, "Sorry about that, Lightskin. You know how mean the dozens can get."

While I folded and put away my clothes, they continued their conversation. Twenty minutes passed and he made to leave, giving each of them a hug. As he left the room, both said, "Bye, Attitude!"

Though I was included in the y'all of his "Check y'all later," I wanted him to acknowledge me again to see if we had made a connection. "Attitude? Now that nickname fits well."

"Not a nickname. Frat name. So, that's Big Brother Attitude to you, Lightskin." He left.

No connection.

Like Manny, Hope only saw me as a white girl. As much time as Hope spent in the room, or when she came by when Barbie wasn't there and I told her she could come in, she would not. She evaded me as if I had a communicable disease.

As the room change deadline approached, I felt that Barbie would move out. She never mentioned wanting to move but Hope asked her, right in front of me, to move to MLK to be her roommate. When Barbie replied that Hope already had a roommate, Hope answered, "That girl's an *Oreo* and would be moving to Poe as soon as an empty spot opened. That spot being yours."

I bit my tongue because both, especially Hope, struck me as people who have had wide white cultural influences. But Hope had perfected the balance one needed to render someone invisible, in that from day one and onward, she could stare in my face and share no emotion. She dismissed me with her quick sentences, showed confusion in her eyes whenever I interjected a joke into their conversations, and often walked by me on campus without even a glance.

>=<

Our routine of living together yet socializing differently went on without a glitch because Barbara and I used a signal so she would know when I had a guest. Some nights she would go stay at a friend's. Other nights, she would come in. I got good at sex under the blanket, while making as little noise as possible. What could have been a point of tension made for some good humor and conversation. Barbie made it known she thought I should be less promiscuous. That one school year, I think I had some type of sex with twenty-some-odd men. I made it known she had to loosen up. Neither of us budged. We only laughed, went on shopping sprees, and used my meal card to treat her to the upperclassmen cafeteria.

Things were fine until one import night. I felt sick so I went back to the dorm early. There was no signal on the door. In fact, Barbara never had the need to put the signal on the door.

Had the red bulb not been burning, along with her incense and the music not been romantic, I would have thought the whole thing an accident. Hope sat upright, topless on Barbara's bed; eyes closed, head tilted back.; swaying to the song's rhythm. I would have thought that Barbara on her knees, her mouth caressing Hope's left breast to be a moment of weakness, something spontaneous.

The sight paralyzed me to the point where my mouth remained ajar and so was the room's door. Hope's panicky yet forceful tone and words released me, enabling me to move.

Hope sprung to her feet, shouting, "Close the door!"

As I entered the room then closed the door, Hope said, "I meant for you to leave."

"I'm not leaving. This is my room too!"

Barbara calmed her. She dressed and left after Barbara told her, "I will see you at the cafeteria for breakfast."

The red bulb forced us to see each other in shadows, like negatives in a dark room. I sat on my bed and she sat on hers. I could sense her looking at me, but I could not look at her so I buried my face into my palms. We sat in silence for about five minutes. When I finally looked up, Barbie asked, "Aren't you going to say anything?"

In my confused state, all I could muster, "I didn't know you were a lesbian."

She chuckled. "I am not a lesbian."

"What do you call what I just saw?"

"A moment of weakness and extreme horniness." She laughed and her tone made me realize a new maturity – it snuck up on me and signaled my talk about sex might have penetrated the iron curtain blocking her velvet expressions. "The whole campus dynamic is so screwed up, at least for Black students. There are like a dozen Black women for each Black male. Some of these guys milk it for all they can. They make little effort to hide the fact that they have multiple sex partners. Attitude, who're you so fond of, has like nine women he just rotates as he pleases."

"I do not have a thing for Attitude."

"It's so obvious. If he were white…"

"Why is everything black or white with you?"

"Because this is America." She paused for emphasis then asked, "How come none of the men you bring here are Black?"

"None are Asian or Hispanic. So, what's your point?"

"My point is simple. I am not a lesbian. Hope and I were hanging out and she got all emotional, talking about how close she feels to me…"

It was my turn to laugh. "You fell for that? You might not be a lesbian but she sure is. It's funny how I never picked up on it though the signs were there, especially her wanting you to move to become her roommate."

"Don't worry about that! I'm not moving to MLK. I like living here in Poe Hall. Some of these people got major issues, but they don't scare me."

We talked the rest of the night, with her reassuring me what I saw to be a one-time thing. As we turned in for the night, I asked, "Does Attitude ever ask about me or state an interest?"

"No."

"Why? Doesn't he like white girls?"

She laughed. "It's not that. Half of his rotation is white. He just has his hands full."

"Seriously?"

"Why do you think he treats me and Hope like his little sisters?"

"Has he ever tried a threesome with y'all?'

"Hell no! You know I'm not like that. Plus, Hope likes him. More like is in love with him."

"I thought she was gay."

"She's not gay! I am not gay. We just got horny, lonely and in need of attention, and we don't trust the men on this campus."

At that we turned out our night lamps and said good night.

ISSUES ONLY A LIGHT SKIN BROTHER CAN HANDLE

Two days after Barbara reconnected with Lena, Ernest knew he had a mess on his hands. Though many people could chime in and give advice, he knew of only one person who could handle this the way he really should. For all his shady acts, Devon never got lost in someone else's story. Ernest woke up feeling this way; he had all these women in concert, telling him the story of his life; trying to put all the pieces together, improvising, passing the baton to the next one when a particular part got too hard.

Devon came by his apartment on Thursday night. First, he agreed with Ernest that Attitude lied about not knowing much about Lena. Then, Devon threw a wrinkle into the equation, that Barbara was a lesbian or at least bisexual. Ernest was not fazed by that.

Next, Devon told him he should drop everything including the dumb job that had him working these crazy hours, but not because the boss lady, Sharon was coming onto him sexually. Devon embodied the philosophy Ernest's favorite uncle imparted on him the week before he left Haiti. He said, "Things are going to be completely different, especially the early years. So be prepared to drop everything about who you are now if that's what it takes to survive. The only thing you should never forget is to never turn down food and pussy. Since you can't give back either, and only evil people would poison food. So, why would you be that close to them?"

Then, Devon brought up Paulette and all the reasons Ernest should call her and marry her. "I can't. It was easy for you to marry Lucille because you know you're in this forever. I am not. I am eventually going to have to run and I can't risk her life by doing so. The most she can get out of me is a kid; that's it."

"Is that why you're still with Barbara?"

"Going to Hope's party, Attitude said it was a mission so I called you. I get there and that scene was the hardest read ever. I thought I was misreading the playbook until you left with Miranda, and then Attitude asked Barbara to drive me home. It didn't help that Barbara kept interrupting me all night, basically throwing me the ass, which is so unlike her. Then her man comes in and she blows him off after a dance."

Devon hesitated. He held the cognac glass in his left hand, stopping midstream on way to his mouth. His furrowed brow indicating a suspicious thought had entered his mind. "You think she knows something about Bliss's death?"

"No, but she is scared of something, and I think Lena might be the clincher."

"The white girl?" Devon finally gave into his confusion. He used his left palm to get up from his seat. Ernest observed the extra pounds Devon had put on, and not just his mid-section but the fit of the business shirt clung to his arms and his slacks hugged a little too tight, from the waist to the knees. Married life had either gotten too good or new stress factors had entered in his life. "No one knows nothing about her except that she slept with a lot of men."

"What's up with Miranda?"

"I shot straight and asked her. She said nothing was in the works, and that Bliss's death was a suicide. I tried to see if Barbara knew anything but Miranda barely talks to Barbara." Devon pulled from the blunt then downed the rest of his drink. "What's the next move?"

"I can't make one. Lena is avoiding me. Barbara hasn't called."

"To think, for a brief period of history, I used to envy you." Devon stood and grabbed his jacket. "Ern, you're my man and I know you think things always go against you but you got this Barbara chick…she's got issues only a light-skin brother can handle, so why don't you give me her number and let me take over from here?"

"How're you gonna goof when I tell you some real stuff?" Devon was the only person, MAX boy included who knew the ins and out of their relationship – everything. He wanted to tell Attitude but when he called asking about Lena, Atttitude said something strange, something that confirmed he had indeed misread the playbook. Attitude asked him 'Why is Barbara meeting up with you? When did y'all become so tight?'

Ernest clammed up by asking again about Lena and again he received an evasive maneuver. So he called Devon, who only people with real tough skin could handle. Ernest caught the last part of Devon's rant, "Because you're going out like Frank! You pass up on these real chill chicks like Paulette who have minor faults then progress to these women who, instead of being out there looking for a savior, they are looking to justify their fucked-ways, even going as far as blaming their mothers."

Frank? Frank DeLoose. While Ernest played that name and his story in his head, he brushed Devon off with a "Fuck you and…!"

"That's fine! I expect that. Just like you got my back in all manners and times, I got yours. If I'm the only one honest enough to tell you the real then I'll take the punishment." Devon reached his hand out for the frat grip. Ernest took it.

>=<

Devon woke him out of his stupor and made him realize he misread the playbook. This forced him to count the women in his life. As a MAX boy, he had to accept the responsibilities. He even had to count the women he was not sleeping with. He thought for sure Hope would call after Bliss's death but she continued to avoid him, to let him do as he pleased. The night Attitude invited him to her housewarming, he brought her a handgun for her to keep. He handed her his jacket and said, "Hold this for me." Her eyes showed she knew what that extra weight was, heavy metal, in the inside pocket. She did not even call about that. Did she know about his relationship with Barbara? If so, still no phone call. Hope was too sharp to not know there would be a response to Bliss's death. For this, he gave her one of his guns for protection.

Barbara obviously misread the playbook. She did not need his protection since she had Ken in her life, so he thought. Not one phone call from him whenever Ernest visited and laid up with her, but he knew a confrontation would soon come. Barbara did not need his protection in her life because she had nothing to do with Bliss's murder – she did not come to the funeral.

In the beginning, she played like it was just sex and good times. Nowhere in the rule book does it say a casual fling had to be disrespectful. In fact, he felt the opposite; treat the casual ones special and the word they passed around helped him not have to hunt too hard.

But then Barbara started getting into his business, acting like she, who had pronounced it on night one, had forgotten he was a MAX boy. She who shut him down when he told her how Bliss's death had impacted him. For a SUM woman, she had given him too many chances. That surprised him, pleased him and confused him to the point, he could not make the next move.

After another night of uneven sleep, he unlocked his office door then sat down to log into his computer, the de facto time clock. He checked his voicemail, to be greeted by Barbara. She made a new suggestion, that he should quit his job and come work for her. Her charter school had an unfilled slot for an Art teacher.

OK, not a terrible idea, he thought. But to be Barbara's employee would definitely not work if they were in a physical relationship. He found it odd she wanted him to come teach at her school, once she realized her mission of getting him a corporate job brought more strain into their lives. She skipped a move, the one where she, like Bliss did for Attitude, tried to make him famous. Ernest chuckled, knowing she did not think he could make money and a name for himself via his personal art.

As if on cue, Sharon appeared at his office door, with a design in hand as if trying to mark the office and this time slot as hers. Walking this deep into the office meant the matter was important. Normally she stood erect. This new posture had her bent forward in front of his desk, facing him, not looking at him. Her gaze, downward and focused on one of the designs / slogans; her blouse, with the top two buttons unfastened, revealed her cleavage, her breasts dangling in the cup because the bra strap was loose. He followed her finger as she pointed at areas in need of improvement; with her it was always needed improvement, to the point where he blocked her out because he came to realize her advertising designs and technique focused too much on delivering the message, even if it meant sacrificing the art. The plaques and awards on her office walls showed she achieved sales goals. The firm loved that her accounts made money, but to Ernest, those accounts would have made money regardless, because the placement budget sold those products. Even if she refused to fess up to it, those in charge wanted a balance and hired him, for the art.

Sharon didn't understand this, so six lead designers in three years, the word had gotten around the industry that only a hack could work for her. Ernest knew this going in so during the interview he told the director, of the job offers from two competitors, two top-tier agencies, one for its slogans and copy division, the other for its design division. Ernest learned they hired Sharon Tunic for her managerial skills. But this year, when they finally won another top account, the client company specified they needed to hire a designer, and not someone who just knew how to dilly-dally around with software. As the big firm explained and he knew all along, big firms with known brands needed the sizzle because everyone knew they got steak. But she balked and worked on the Walker-MedCo account and used a freelancer to supplement her work.

The InterFaith Alliance campaign wanted to let everyone know that they really did have a steak, and not just ground meat. But Sharon kept trying to remove the sizzle from the print campaign; her blue line pencil, its eraser removing the subtle abstract nature of his odd etchings; its lead point adding punctuation where she saw diction as opposed to the overlapping, flowing judgments, like the mind's freestyle, the bylines sectioned into two parts of equal distinction. Then, she did the unthinkable, unpredictable act of walking to his side of the desk; as if unaware that her left breast had touched, it leaning against his shoulder. Her gaze; still on the drawing, hinting that this was just business.

The phone's ring jarred her to the fact that Ernest did have a life, possibly a candidate or more yearning to be what her husband was to her. To hear him giggle then to agree to dinner plans for 8 p.m., without asking her what time the two of them will be done with work tonight, she backed then slipped away, as he hung up the phone. Feeling the rejection, the look in her eyes asking for a rain check, a life raft, Ernest simply looked away.

The more days went by it seemed as if Barbara and Sharon were in competition for the same prize, to change his mind. The problem was that neither knew his thoughts. They had read the books, seen the movies, listened to the songs, and so on. From those access points and pertinent items such as place of birth, age and the past, they built a profile. His voice, the persona of his vitals, heart, mind, body, soul; they seemed unable to decipher. They seemed to be using a filter to break down the essence of his words and being. But through the filter, all that passed through became raw, albeit profane to them; the nature of manhood simplified in hopes of imitating then rejecting it, then correcting it, but really trying to reinvent it.

RATIONALIZING FENCES

Ever since that cab ride home when I ran into Lena and didn't give you as much detail as you wanted about our life as roommates, I've actually felt us growing apart. Before then it was just you using work or hanging out with friends as his excuse. Thursday – I paged you over and over until you finally answered. Friday – you claimed to be hanging with friends. Saturday – I phoned three times and you never picked up or called back. Sunday, I didn't call and neither did he. You called that Monday during work, as if knowing I would be busy. We spoke briefly and you blamed it on the new project, and said it wasn't a very good night. By Tuesday, I needed you to come out and say whether or not it was over. You cannot get away with simply blowing me off, after all I had done for you.

I knew from day one that a real relationship was not possible. But it's like you want to burn this bridge we built. I don't see a need to do so. We were both rebounding. It's like I told my ex as our relationship was winding down. I paraphrased one of Jesse's speeches, the one about us having houses on the same block. What Jesse failed to mention was that, some of us, we have fences around our homes.

I can respect that. True, I had no business popping up in front of your house uninvited. Perhaps, I had that right, then lost it. HOW?

Perhaps I failed with you because I tried to mold you instead of accepting you as is. Truthfully, ruefully, I don't know what you are, who you are, what you want to be, who you want to be. At the same time, you have too many demands! So, If you can't take me as I am then you should leave.

Yet, it hurts me deeply to think that you and I cannot be friends, that you dodge my calls. Simply put, it's not all that. I am not your enemy. I am your friend, your sister. There will always be a place for you in my heart. I will always love you.

Yours,
Barbara

He read the letter, for the eighth time. This last time he recalled the night. Blistering cold, with a strong wind cracking against the cardboard boxes leaning against the dumpsters of the neighborhood stores that lined Flatbush Avenue where Nevins Street starts. Traffic was not heavy and he only saw one other pedestrian before he reached his block. The forecast called for heavy snow. He stopped at the liquor store for a fifth of Beefeather's gin. He stepped out and glanced at the clock atop the Williamsburgh Bank Building. Though he wore a watch, he always checked that clock, a force of habit from when he first came downtown with his parents, a week after arriving in the U.S.

He got to his block and saw the 1989 light gray Nissan Sentra parked across the street and then it dawned on him that he forgot to go by her place for dinner. He debated whether Barbara had come for a confrontation. His block was not good for such scenes since it housed young married couples, with most having inherited the property from their families. Most lived on the upstairs portion, and rented the lower levels to people in their mid-twenties. He wondered how his brother passed the screening process and got to buy such a building.

Her body looked charged as if on edge, waiting to leap out of the car. He expected her to come charging out of her car and to make a scene. But she calmly looked at him, making eye contact to be certain he saw her. She then started the car, pulled away from the curb and drove through the green light.

Earlier that day, at 4 p.m., he checked his home messages - four from Paulette. He last saw her a month ago, and since her blow up in the street, she never called. Still Paulette never called back to back. So he called her quickly; she had a dream last night. It scared her. In it, Ernest died. Since they both believed in dreams, they stayed on the phone a bit. Not only did time escape him, so did thoughts of dinner with Barbara.

>=<

Barbara's letter came that Tuesday, with a time stamp of Monday. He saw it as the weirdest of letters, uncertain how to classify it- *love, dear john, untitled*. To not accept this offer of friendship meant he wanted to be enemies or wishes they could remain intimate. No, Ernest preferred things the way she suggested in the letter.

He called Barbara that Wednesday morning. She placed him on hold while she cleared the other caller. When she returned, she didn't speak about the letter. She too wanted to bury the past, no matter how recent. "I'm glad you called because if you hadn't, I wouldn't have known whether to call and invite you to my party."

"You're having a party? What for?"

"In celebration of me!"

"Me? Who's me?"

"Very funny! It's this Saturday night. No gifts!"

"Seriously! Are you having a party?"

"Yes, I'm having a party to celebrate being me. Attitude is doing the music, like old times, only difference is that he's not spinning, he's bringing his CD collection."

"Oh, that crazy mother…" Ernest stopped mid-word, mid-sentence. He wanted to add, *it figured because you're both on some next shit,* but he chose not to, just to keep the peace.

>=<

That last conversation with Barbara plagued him for two days. As he ate breakfast at his desk, Lena, who had been avoiding him since learning he and Barbara were intimates, popped up and said, "I guess I'll see you tomorrow."

"What?"

"I just got off the phone with Barbie. The party!"

Ernest got his confirmation that Barbara was indeed on some next shit, so he might as well be too. "I am not sure if I'm going. I don't really deal with Barbara on that level anymore."

Lena stepped into the office. She had remained behind the threshold, as if not crossing that barrier signified respecting Barbara's space, but now she came right to the edge his desk.

So on casual Friday, with a crème crocheted calf-long sweater, unbuttoned over a black lycra body suit hugging breasts and home plate, she stood there saying "Is that why I have yet to again bump into you on the subway?"

To confirm he understood her question, he answered with a question. She looked too good, not average. Firm jaw line, evidently lined with teeth that had been tightened by braces. Pearly white teeth, light brush of make-up, and sky blue eyes. "Did Barbara tell you we were done?"

"Yes. She told me you two had a fallen out but nothing so serious that you can't be friends."

"Did she tell you she was stalking my place?"

Lena took a seat. "No. I've been avoiding you these past few weeks because it caught me off-guard that you and Barbie were an item. At first, I figured she would call me to put a gag order on me but she didn't call until today. Yes, she invited me to her party, but I see it for what it is. She wanted information about you."

"Gag order about what? And, what did you tell her?"

"I am not getting in between whatever's going on with you two. But, I did lie for you and say that I haven't heard anything about you in the workplace."

"You don't have to lie for me." He paused to give a half-smile, a flirtatious one. "Plus, there isn't anything to hear. I am a free man."

"Well, don't hit on me to get back at Barbara." Lena got up to leave.

"I actually stopped because of her. It's been hard because I know you want to give me some."

She turned around to counter his joke, and without completing the full turn, just enough to glance at him. "Not really, I don't just do anything for a Black man."

At that she turned to leave, without waiting for his question of what she meant by that. It gave him enough to know the extent of their conversation. So he called Barbara to say he was bringing Devon with him to the party.

WHO INVITED THAT WHITE GIRL?

When Barbie invited me to her party, I accepted quickly but had my doubts about going. Neither telephoned after we ran into each other. The fact she waited until her party to reach out meant she too needed an explanation as to why my story with her ended rather abruptly. She should know the simple answer, that I never got over what happened the last time she invited me to a party. True time healed certain wounds but I knew the moment we sat face to face, I would need an explanation.

Going to the party was the entry point.

When we arrived, we missed a left turn and thought a right turn would allow us to square the block. Instead it led to a small hill and eventually a few one way streets that seemingly formed a maze. We circled the block once then found a parking on Metropolitan Avenue. We retraced our path and found her block. The neighborhood was dark with hills curving around bends.

My husband, Larry fought to contain his excitement about meeting some of my college friends. I held a hint of fear, not knowing what type of welcome to expect. I again explained to him that these were not my college friends. If anything I only considered Barbara a friend; with Hope and Manny/ Attitude/Davenport or whatever his new moniker might be, as mere acquaintances. I actually did not expect to see him at the party, but the moment I walked in, I spotted him near the entertainment system, playing his usual role of deejay.

A subdued affair and total contrast to the party Barbara and Manny invited me to my senior year at TGI. This party featured a mixed cast of players: Black, White, Latino, Asians and mixed-race people. Before I even had a chance to go over and say hello to them, a couple of Barbara's sorority sisters and brothers stopped me for idle chit chat.

Surprising to say the least!

In college, their fraternity and sorority did not socialize with whites. True some whites went to their parties and other events as if drawn by guilt, but not one of those people. College for me was all about bar-hopping and sex, no time for idealism-filled guilt. My husband never asked and I never presented him an oral history of those days.

After introducing Larry to Barbie and the pleasantries, I held his hand and walked over to Attitude. He hugged me in a very familial way and I returned the hug. That hug brought me way back. As the thoughts ran through my mind, beginning to replay the night that changed my life, I heard Larry say, "The Manny Davenport? I heard you were dead."

"No, that's what the PR piece is saying this year. You're Lawrence McIntosh. I heard through the grapevine that Lena married you. She did well for herself."

"Thank you. Were you two close in college?"

"No, we swam in different rivers, but she roomed with my good friend Barbara. When Barbara told me they ran into each other, and with the party coming up, I definitely asked Barbara to invite her."

The nerve of that jerk! He just admitted something he should have admitted on the spot, when asked why I came to the SUM surfacing party. I felt a rush of tears, angry ones coming on, but I was not going to cry, at least not in front of them. If they wanted to become friends, they were not going to do it over my body. I simply turned to walk away and then it hit me. There were two men staring dead at me. One was Ernest and he looked puzzled. The other I met once, in passing, years ago. Monk too looked puzzled.

I could not tell whether it was my link with Manny or Larry that concerned them.

Their eyes took me back to the place, memories I continually fought to block.

October 1986, particularly the week leading to the SUM surfacing party, had been cold and rainy. For October in upstate New York, that was not a big deal, normal Fall weather. For me it mattered. Never one to acknowledge the cold, especially when temperatures barely slipped under 50 degrees at night, the light rain, the chill in the air affected my body. I had the shivers and consumed lots of tea and soup. Months ago, during the summer my two best friends died in a car crash. The guilt plagued me through nightmares, flashbacks of good times had. I cancelled plans with them because Barbara wanted to catch a movie and I had not seen her in weeks. They did not drive and relied on others to drive them. I let them hold my car and they asked another friend to drive. That driver could not hold her liquor as well as I could.

All three died. I felt guilty.

Though Barbara did not like them based on the one time they met during the previous winter holiday, she felt guilty. Convincing her she had no reason to feel this way allowed me to put some of my own guilt aside and return to school even though I planned to either transfer schools or stay out of school for a year. Barbie's friendship was my rock.

Since the previous year, her freshman year, she talked of joining a sorority. It never made me a difference. I respected that we led different lives. Same as the previous year, her friends came by the room. Most of the girls, especially Hope, remained hostile. The guys showed respect, flirted on the sly and stopped by to test the waters when Barbara was not expected to be around.

That day came back to me clearly. I hid from an overcast, windy day that kept me under the covers, forcing me to miss my two morning classes. Barbara came into the room and handed me an envelope containing a typeset invitation. I had seen flyers for the party around the campus but this invitation was personal, special. "There is a party. You are invited."

She had invited me to other parties but I never went, so I wondered why she thought I would go to an off-campus party. "I will think about it."

"Also, I will not be around much this semester. Only to pick up clothes and stuff."

"Why?"

"Don't you know anything?" She snapped. "I've been pledging for the past couple of weeks and we are surfacing at this party. Once the line surfaces, I can only interact with my line sisters and members of the sorority and brother fraternity."

I didn't say anything because I like to feign ignorance on these matters. It's funny how just because someone didn't chime in on topics that may or may not be of concern, people assumed the person did not know. True, when it came to what the Black fraternities and sororities did, I knew nothing. But when Barbara started expressing an interest, I did pay more attention than previous semesters. I saw few differences from the white ones, especially the ones with members living in this dorm. So, I figured with the surfacing party in three days, the pledging would be, at most, a semester-long process. Afterward we would go back to normal. That worked for me! I didn't factor in how others felt.

Barbara hardly came by the days leading to the party. In fact, few people were around. Poe Hall remained its usual loud self, with people drinking, getting high and being rowdy because they could. I asked around and no one knew or cared about the surfacing party. As if a different world, if you eavesdropped around campus, every Black person knew of the party.

And, I was invited! Invited?

Saturday, a simple of choice of what not to wear? How do I go, style-wise? Do I go like a knockout blonde bombshell with something tight, real form-fitting with the make-up adorning my face like war paint, as if I came to take the man of my choice? I hardly dressed like that. In fact my mom made me understand at an early age the power of fashion. For my junior prom, I wanted to look simple and cute. She sucked her teeth at me and told me that as her daughter, when the occasion called for it, look your best.

Junior prom! I lost my virginity that night. I also lost my innocence, for I realized the power a slim figure with C-cups had over men and how other women started seeing you as a threat. So for the SUM surfacing party, I decided to only look decent. I did not want to take any one's man because I did not need more women's animosity. My roommate invited me to support her with my presence.

In a town as large as Trafalgar, being way off-campus was hard to do. Everything one need was about half a mile and no more than a mile from the main gate: bowling alley, dry cleaners, supermarket, bars. To be this far off-campus was to make a profound statement. Quickly to the left off the main road, the neighboring town which led to the highway out of Trafalgar. The taxi driver actually turned around to look at me when I told him my destination.

As he made the right turn, he asked, "What are you going to that house for?"

"There's a party." I didn't offer any more to see what his next words would be, but he didn't say anything else.

TGI formally known as Trafalgar Garrison Institute is a former military school in western New York. Its position on the lower bank of the mountain range made it hard to attack and was used as a place to retreat during the Revolutionary War. The twenty-five acres of land consisted of five stone buildings capable of housing five hundred people. Before the Civil War the federal government sold the land to a retiring Army General who used it to house, school, and train orphans, male and females, in the art of war. General Trafalgar raised funds from wealthy patrons to buy more land and build more buildings. The institute and its care rested in their hands and subsequently the children of these trustees. After World War One, with many of these families garnering wealth from other sources and few staying in military life, they decided to change the focus of the curriculum to the liberal arts.

During the same period, another institution grew to prominence in the same valley. Semline Seminary went from a monastery serving all faiths and secularists, a place that brought young visiting scholars to fellowship to teach the prevailing wisdom to an all-male science and engineering college. The scholars would then return to their communities and spread the Semline philosophy. Its exclusivity angered those who funded and managed TGI, so their rivalry extended from around 1877 up to today, with 1946 being the turning point. At the end of World War Two, Semline admitted its first class of female students. The college did this to combat the state government's plan to build a state college with a primary purpose of furthering the educational goals of women. With scant numbers of women in either of the two existing private schools, the new state college, Barrington Graphics Institute became a major obstacle to the other schools ever developing a reputation as a place students came unless they were fully funded or legacies of those who had attended either school when they were the only game in the region.

TGI maintained its relevancy because there were certain student-life organizations unwilling to offer a charter to the two neighboring schools. Semline dominated all sports except basketball and enrolled the most eligible bachelors. No one really visited Semline unless invited because even though there were no gates that visitors had to check in and give their identity, the campus was open and gray. Even in its new additions, the campus remained true to its oval landscape so that the main circles were for communal prayers and lectures.

TGI was the opposite. One road led to the front gate. To access that road the driver had to come from the eastern side, Semline; or the western front, Barrington. When the roads converged, cars drove another mile to pass through the small town with shops catering to student needs and off-campus housing for upperclassmen.

A towering spiked gate with an intercom allowed the visitor to reach the main gate's security officers. One officer would then call the student the visitor identified. The student would then come to the main gate where he or she would provide student identification and sign a form to state the nature of the visit. The visitor would then countersign the form.

This type of rigidity discouraged visitors especially since those rules remained in place for parties. At a TGI party, most revelers attended the school. It built a sense of community and trust. These sign-in rules did not apply to students leaving or reentering campus. A simple mention of the number on your campus ID into the intercom and then showing one's campus ID. A small campus with two quads in a rectangular maze. The buildings were brown stones, all with similar design on the outside but vastly different inside. Administrative buildings on the far left side and northern section faced the open quad, the one where a statue of General Trafalgar stood. On the right side of the western quad, the newest structures, towers whose height conflicted with the existing architecture. The faculty and classroom buildings faced a grassy field where students congregated on warm days and even cold ones, after meals and between classes. Instead of making the walk past the gym, cafeteria and the student association building, students stayed on the grassy field.

The taxi arrived and I got out. From the sudden stop and gaze of the people milling outside the house, I could tell I should not have been there. A Victorian style house with silver and gold trimmings on a beige house, it looked something out of the South before the Civil War. Up the steps, still more people gave me these funny looks. If I had driven, I may have decided to simply return home. I walked through the open door and the music grew louder but there was no mistaken the words being uttered behind my back as I crossed the threshold. The couple looked young, most likely freshmen, said it as if it was the most normal thing to say. They uttered everyone else's thoughts, "Who invited that white girl?"

Out of habit, whenever I walked into a place with music playing, I located the source. He wore headphones; his head down, moving to the beat; his eyes on the turntables. The crowded dance floor made it difficult to cross the twenty feet to get to him. The living room and dining room combination had been cleared to create the dance floor. For every other couple I passed, I heard the same whispers, *"Who invited that white girl?"* When I would turn my head, no one would look away, but no one would say anything else. I felt a mixture of hurt and fear. I wondered why Barbara would invite me to a party with these types of people?

"Hey Mr. DJ!" I did my best to put on a brave face as I approached the DJ's platform. Attitude looked up and gave me a warm smile, and it helped me hold back the urge to confront someone. Whenever he came by the room with Barbie, I always felt or wanted to feel a connection to him. Attitude let the record play so we could talk. He motioned me over to the side so he could observe the crowd. "I haven't seen you by this semester. You and Barbie not friends anymore?"

"We'll always be friends. She's my sister."

"By the way what's up with your fraternity brothers and sisters making snide comments to an invited guest?"

"These are not my frat brothers. I am just DJ'ing for the night."

"I thought you were in a frat?"

"Yeah, there are nearly a dozen Black frats and sororities on this campus. This house is SBD: Stay Black'n Die! Summa Beta Delta."

"What's your frat? I've never seen you wear letters so I didn't know the difference."

"I hardly wear letters. In fact it's rare for any of us to wear letters. Once in a while we wear subtle reminders of our colors: navy blue and silver too. We're Fly MAX Beta - Proud I'm Black!"

"How come they don't have one of their own DJ'ing?"

"I formed a DJ team with Ken, their chapter president, our first semester here before either of us pledged a frat. So, I'm splitting time with him so he can take care of fraternity business tonight."

As the song ended instead of mixing in the new record he prepped, he abruptly picked up the needle to mute the stereo and I heard the words, "Who invited that white girl?" Then he mixed in the new record.

I lost my cool. "You think that shit is funny?" Too many people looked at me.

"Only as funny as you making Barbara think living in Poe Hall is okay for a Black girl." He caught me off-guard because I could not tell he was serious, particularly the claim that I was making fun of Barbie. "Also, what's with the nickname Barbie? Her name is Barbara."

"If she didn't like it, she should have said something."

"No, I don't like it!"

"Fuck You! Who do you think you are?"

Just when we were about to really get into it, this guy came over. I recognized him from campus but didn't know him. "Ken, what's up, baby?"

"Yo, Attitude! We're cool! But the brothers are heated at you! Why did you invite her?"

Though he said her, I knew what he meant!

"Barbara invited her!"

"No she didn't, man! Trust me she didn't!" He paused and looked at me and turned back to Attitude. "She better had not."

At that, Attitude frowned and ordered me, "Be a good girl and go get me a Heineken!" He pointed in the direction he wanted me to go. When I didn't move, he shouted, "Now!"

I walked to the left side of the room, through an archway that separated the dining room. I reached into the garbage can filled with ice and water and pulled out a beer. I waited a few minutes, studying their body language, trying to read their conversation. About twenty people milled about in the kitchen, fixing themselves drinks, tapping the keg and eating. I could feel their stares as if trying to unnerve me but I just stared straight ahead at Attitude. When Ken walked away, I returned by Attitude's side.

I could only guess on what they discussed. Either Attitude put him in his place for what sounded like a threat to Barbara, or he confessed to having invited me. "Is everything OK? I guess I shouldn't have come."

"Thanks for the beer!" Two loud knocking sounds and the party came to a halt. I mean no noise whatsoever. Even the music stopped. The pledge line came in. I counted nine women standing in increasing size order next to each other. It was difficult to pinpoint Barbie because all of them had their hair shaved near to the scalp. Then I noticed her. They did a general greeting to the big sisters and brothers. After the greeting, I saw Ken approach Barbie and whisper something in her hear. To take the focus away, he motioned at Attitude to restart the music.

People regained their party spirit while the pledges stood against the wall adjacent the entrance. Even though he never stopped playing records to look at me, his words soothed my angst. "She's OK. The hair cutting is to take away all vanity and to restore the hair's natural texture."

"Did you invite me or did she?"

"What does it matter? She's my sister. And you claim she's your friend. Will you be there even when she's not there for you?"

"What do you mean?"

"I'm there for her even when or if she deserts me. That's what I'm asking you."

As I turned to look at him, I felt a tap on my shoulder. I turned to see Barbara, Hope and Ken standing in front of me. Barbara's voice but the words sounded cold, formal, unlike her sing song melodic flutter. "I am sorry but you have to leave. No outsiders are allowed for the remainder of the surfacing ceremony."

Her words and tone left me speechless, frozen in place.

Attitude's words shook me out of the trance. "Ken, handle the turntables for me while I walk Lena out."

Hearing my name temporarily separated me from the whole experience of being considered an outsider. As we passed through the crowd no one snickered or made any comments, until we reached the front door and I heard the pledges whisper to one another, nine times, in a ripple effect, "Who invited that white girl? Who invited that white girl? Who invited that white girl? Who..."

Hurt feelings could not begin to describe how I felt, but I suppressed tears, suppressed them way down in my belly. The time for that had passed. I wanted to smack someone, and that person was standing right next to me. We cleared the porch side by side and made our way down the steps, far enough so no one could hear our conversation. "Why did you invite me here tonight?"

"Are you back at this again? What does it matter who invited you? Tonight was to give you a glimpse as to what you are facing."

"I'm not facing anything."

"I understand politics is personal, and all that. You built a bridge and Barbara crossed it. Now she's building this bridge, can you cross it?"

"If I joined the klan and invited you to a ceremony, would you come?"

"I may not be part of their frat, but that's not what they're about. They take a strong separatist stand because of the choices whites made them take in the past."

We remained quiet. My eyes wandered off to the darkness of the street, the sky. He obviously was not going to add anymore so I shifted the topic and dropped my voice to a sexy reverberation. "All this time, I thought we had a connection."

"Everything is sex with you! Let me guess, if I took you home and we had sex everything would be forgotten."

"It depends on how good the sex is." I paused so he could chime in. "Where do you live?"

"Paine and Hancock."

"On the northern side of town?"

"You see how your prejudices work? I can't live on the north side of town because of what, money?"

"What does that have to do with you and me? We all prejudge each other. I am not the only one who has a reputation. I did some asking and heard you get around."

"Well, you could be the next notch."

I laughed to give myself enough time to think of the best retort for his flirtation. "OK, you can't take me home. Can you at least drive me home?"

"Nah, I want to see the song and dance presentation. Plus, I have to finish DJ'ing."

"To get a cab, I have to walk down the hill and that's like a half a mile. And then there's no telling if one is anywhere nearby." As he turned to return to the party. All I could do was scream, "Attitude, you're an asshole. You're a real fucking asshole."

He just laughed.

I had not even walked two short blocks when an old maroon Buick pulled up a couple of steps ahead of me. Thinking that Attitude had been pulling my leg, I jogged up to the passenger door, expecting to see him. As I reached for the handle, I noticed two Black guys with shaved heads in the car. I froze until the passenger asked, "Do you believe in the kindness of strangers?"

Very familiar words for me, so I said, "Yes."

The passenger stepped out and folded the seat forward, so I could slide into the back of the car. We remained quiet the entire ride. They did not even speak to each other. All sort of emotions ran through me during the ride back to Poe Hall. Most of all I felt like crying because I realized I lost my sister, Barbara, that night. The feeling of loss over death can at times be surpassed by that of seeing someone you trusted go in a direction which you can never travel.

They dropped me off a few feet before the campus' main gate, as if they did not want to be seen. As I left the car, they both said, "You know enough to keep your mouth shut. You do know that, right?"

I nodded.

Barbara did not come to the room for four days. She showed up on a Wednesday. When I told her I planned to move during the room change period, she simply said, "I can't focus on that right now."

>=<

These past few years I often thought of the friendship that could have been, so when I first saw Barbara again, I wanted to fill in these missing spaces. No matter how much I blocked out that night, it became my daily existence until I met Larry. The oddity of watching my husband talking to Attitude, my standing alone in a festive atmosphere, and Ernest sitting alone and in a very pensive mode should have told me that something was amiss.

My mind shifted away from my past and to the going-ons at this party.

Barbara and Ernest recently broke up, yet Ken played host as if he lived in the apartment. For every step she took, he held court, greeting guests and helping to serve drinks.

Forty minutes passed then the full force of the danger lurking in the place hit me though I could not determine the source. I caught my husband's eye to motion him away from Attitude. Instead he called me over, "Lena, I've given Davenport my card and wrote your office number on the back. He has a painting I've long coveted. We will work out the price. He will call you so you can pick it up at his loft. By the way, have you met Major?"

Major held out his hand and I shook it. My thoughts veered and I held back from exclaiming *wow*! I felt like a little girl again. The best way to describe this man was to call him a distraction, the same claim men made about a woman wearing a low-cut blouse. Staying to chat and stare into his hazel eyes could would make me lose my focus of wanting to kill a few minutes and leave. So I politely pulled Larry away with a simple, "Let's go mingle with some other guests."

Attitude simply nodded to me and I smiled. As I pulled Larry away to make small talk with other guests, I paid attention to everything going on around me. Everything seemed normal enough until Attitude played a rap song I had never heard before. At first I could not make out the words, then as I caught the rhythm, I detected the chorus, *"Polly wants a cracker..."*

The cause: Hope.

He played the song over and over. At least three times. People whispered, "That's Public Enemy, right? *Fear of a Black Planet*, right? He shouldn't be playing that here."

Hope made her way around the room. I sensed something different about her. A bubbly bounce to her voice to replace the dourness that surrounded her back in college. I had seen her giggle, but never smile or show joy. Her body looked virtually the same from years ago. She wore a tan knee-high skirt with burgundy etchings, camisole and a navy leisure jacket, a very expensive necklace, and she had her haircut in the day's preferred short asymmetrical style. Then I caught the change, the rift, in between her smile and as she introduced the guy with her.

I glanced over at Attitude. He was looking directly at Monk, who stared in Ernest's direction. Ernest gazed nothing in particular. The music played on. As Hope made her way to my side of the room, I expected her to veer off and act like she hadn't seen me. Instead she nudged Monk and asked, "What's up, stranger? How've you been?"

"I'm good." The curt response, as if stating for her not to bother introducing him to her date.

Then she took a couple of steps toward me, directly in front of me then she extended a hug and kiss on the cheek. We made small talk as we introduced our significant others. "Barbara told me she ran into you. I'm surprised not to have seen you all of these years."

"I turned into a regular homebody after college. I see things have changed with you also." The words got no reaction. She simply squeezed my hand and asked for us to talk later, perhaps do lunch. She continued working the room but she avoided Attitude. Yet he needled her by replaying that song. A few people asked him to play something else, but he ignored them, including Barbara.

It all came to a halt when Hope shouted from across the room, "Why don't you play *Lethal Injection*, track Five next?"

People reacted with laughs, *ooohs and ahs!*

Attitude stopped the music and slowly walked over to her. "You want to talk race with me?"

"No, I don't want to talk anything with you!"

By now their raised voices forced some fraternity brothers to step in.

Attitude shouted, "Get your fucking hands off me!"

Ken stepped between the brothers and Attitude. "Yo A! Chill man! It's not all that."

"Why you in this? Anybody ask for your input?"

"Yo! You better take it down a thousand." The rest of the brothers closed in around the argument. Those who didn't, stood on the periphery, in fighting poses. The three men with Attitude – Ernest, Monk and Major – did not budge. I could not determine whether it was a way of showing no fear, or their plan not to get involved. Larry took a step as if to go stop the altercation, but I grabbed his left wrist.

"Check it, Ken! I know we're cool but you're crossing the line. This ain't your argument. It's not your house. So, stop trying to act like you're the king of the castle..."

Ken stopped and looked at Barbara. It was as if the whole argument with Hope had been a charade. Ken clenched his fists as if preparing to swing. His brothers stepped to close the circle. Attitude's crew still did not move.

Barbara grabbed Attitude by the arm, and pulled him out of the circle and he said, "You're right. I'm out."

She pleaded with him. "Don't leave! What's the problem? Why are you being this way?"

He hugged and whispered to the side of her ear, "I love you sis. We'll talk." He turned back around. "Yo Monk! I'm bouncing. You're with me?"

"Nah, I'll catch up."

Attitude nodded to Ernest. Ernest nodded back. Afterward he reached out his hand to Ken, who did not shake it. He gave Hope a soft kiss on the cheek. "It's all love, sis. OK?" He headed to the closet near the entrance. He and Major exited the apartment.

The remaining guests shifted uneasily, with most finding a reason to leave. Ernest and Monk still had not budged from their positions. Ken tried talking to Barbara but she avoided him. Hope had an uneasiness about her as if feeling out of place. She whispered something in her date's ear to which he smiled.

When she left, only Barbara hugged her. The others simply waived.

I surveyed the room, realizing I could stay and socialize. Instead I asked Larry if he was ready to leave.

"Whenever you're ready."

I gave Barbara a hug and kiss, with a promise to call and do lunch or something.

MISREADING THE PLAYBOOK

The truce she called forced Ernest to come to the party. He knew it would not be good, at least not the type of party he liked, but for a good period it had a very festive mood until he walked in. He spied the party and the arriving guests from the floor landing upstairs. He almost did not knock and enter since MAX boys never rolled alone. When Barbara said he could not bring Devon, he balked. Then she said he could bring anybody else, but Devon, the brother he rolled with; the one who not only sparked a light on any dull party, but also a magnet for trouble which must have been her concern. Ernest knew Attitude would be there and he would have reinforcement if anything popped off.

Why would Barbara throw a Society party? The first day he met her, he learned she wanted out of the Society. Back then he did not have a formal name for this thing that entrapped him. Whereas she wanted to bow out gracefully, Ernest had revenge on his mind. He replayed all the angles since Lena got an invitation but he could not exact a conclusion. He would not know the answer unless he walked in. He had to enter before Lena arrived, so he could contrast the party before and after her arrival. What could her arrival mean, especially with so many of Barbara's co-workers there? Ernest kept a low profile when it came to these parties. He had too much mistrust for all the sides.

When Ernest visited Barbara's apartment, at first he used to look for signs that Ken still factored in her life. She made it clear, very early on, that their relationship was done. *For good*, she said. Their initial night together Ernest figured Barbara did it to get back at Ken for cheating with Ernest's woman, her soror, Diane. Then he realized she did not know about that tryst so Ernest never mentioned it.

But Ken arrived with the second group of partygoers, accompanied by several SBD brothers. After not hearing a peep from or about him, he not only showed up but played host as if the past few months never happened.

Then as the party progressed he sensed something very different. Attitude started instigating something and it made no clear sense as to why he objected to Hope dating a white guy. *Skits and Calisthenics*, he quickly figured because Attitude couldn't care less about such a thing. *Skits and Calisthenics*, the mainstay of MAX boy training, a way of diverting attention by creating an implausible scene.

Yet, Ernest could not figure the real target until Attitude said Ken was no longer king of the castle. He linked it to what transpired earlier, when Lena's husband knew something false about them, that Attitude was dead. Both pronunciations silenced everyone; Ernest resolved to learn the essence of their conflict at a later time.

To his right, he could feel Monk's presence. Obviously Monk felt trouble ahead. Ernest knew his exit had to be smooth which would be hard because the crowd had thinned and now each person's exit became very noticeable. Enough SBD brothers had left, but he sensed they waited around the corner, in the shadows. Ken lingered along with his two tightest lieutenants. He and Ernest had never been friends, nor were they enemies. But swimming in another man's pool, no matter how gentle the strokes always seemed as if one had gone in with muddied boots. Ken dated Barbara for nearly a decade, ever since she finished the SUM pledge process. Being that he was a senior at that time, a fourth generation SBD legacy and she a sophomore, a first generation SUM - their union spoke volumes as to how thorough she must have been.

Though thorough, Ernest knew from the onset that Barbara would be an in-and-out mission. Attitude forced his hand yet never gave him the reason he wanted Ernest in Barbara's life. Since Attitude treated her like a sister, he figured she needed protection. Barbara turned out to be a complete surprise, nothing like he expected. For a woman to have dated the same man for so long, she proved incorrigible in remedying the ways a woman pushed a man out of her life. Many days he sat up and thought that she could be home, but those days were outnumbered by the ones where he really cared less whether he ever saw her again.

With less than a dozen people still in the apartment and with one of them being Ken, Ernest decided to leave. Though he got up, Monk held his position. If anything, Monk knew the nature of the beef. Ernest noted how Monk eyed his movements while keeping a sideward glance at Ken. "Barb, thanks for a great party. I gotta make my way back to Brooklyn."

"You're not staying over?" They chatted near the apartment's front door, out of anyone's earshot. "I need to talk about something, about us."

"We've been through that and it's not in the cards. Look Ken's here and he's making every effort to say that whatever happened between us will not affect what could be between the two of you."

"That's what I want to talk to you about." With her back turned, she did not see Ken approaching. In most situations, Ernest would have taken major offense to an ex or any guy interrupting his conversation with a female, especially one he's intimate with, but he and Barbara had their run, way past the finish line. "I've been going through this relationship..."

"What relationship?" She turned at his voice. "What's the real deal between you?"

Ernest rubbed his mustache because Ken pushed the envelope past the imaginary line Ernest had drawn in the sand. This time he didn't glance at Monk. He counted how many people left. He once saw Monk fight and knew Ken's two lieutenants would be no match. One on one, Ken would be a challenge for him because of his Golden Gloves boxing background; Ernest felt up to the challenge. Barbara, he was not sure which side she would take. The other five other people in the room, he didn't really know any of them. But if they jumped, he would have to pull out his gun. If he pulled it out, he would use it. So he took the short! "Yo, Monk! Let's Be!"

He tried to goad Monk into saying, *Max, Be*. Instead Monk replied, to let him know tonight would be the last night of this conflict. "Nah, I'm gonna lounge for a moment!"

"Ain't nobody lounging." Barbara walked over to Monk and grabbed his elbow. "Monk, baby, you know I love you like a brother, but you have to go home. In fact, the party is done. Everybody please leave."

Those words pleased Ernest. As they made their way out, he would hear what Monk volunteered but ask no questions. He thought of extending his hand to Ken to let him know that he was and is up to any challenge, but Barbara stole the moment. "You too, Ken! OUT!"

"What?"

"What, what? You don't get it do you? I know! I know!" Her proximity and tone shut him down to the point he simply grabbed his coat from the stand and left without uttering a word.

As Ernest turned to leave, she grabbed his arm and said, "I need to talk to you."

What she knew she obviously wanted to share with Ernest but in his mind, no matter what, he would not stay the night. He only stayed to learn the knowledge that bowed Ken's head in defeat, and caused Monk to nod and leave him behind, in enemy territory. Ernest stepped back into the center of the apartment, over to the table serving as the bar. Of course for a party she tolerated booze, but whenever he needed her to stock the fridge with a few beers she objected. Had she changed? Or was it for show? Gin on the rocks, twist of lime. After locking the front door, she disappeared to the bedroom. He was not going in there. He went to the sofa and surveyed the room, at the major cleanup ahead of her, complete with putting the furniture back in its proper arrangement.

She came back into the room as he had never seen her. Her nudity was too late and too much underneath the bright lights. He knew her naked body under dimmed lights or candles, as she held the pretense that they needed romance to have sex. She stood directly in front of him, but far enough that he could not reach her while seated on the sofa.

OK, Ernest thought, you are beautiful; we already established that. A medium yet thick build; hair cut close to the scalp, enabling one to see the range of beauty from hairline, arched eyebrows, flat nose, full oval lips, angular jaw line, succulent neck, curved shoulders, large breasts, flat stomach, slim waist, wide hips, protruding and wide behind, well-toned calves, slender ankles and to smooth feet.

Deep down she got to him for she never showed this level of vulnerability. Her hands held behind her back. The slow rise of her breath, from lungs to chest, a slow heave. If she cried, he probably would too. But, she held it in, as if suddenly realizing it was not that he did not care. Ernest did not know. "You know how you said I should mind my own business about Devon and Miranda?"

"Not that again!"

"It's more. While working the grapevine, I also found out that your ex, Diane, my soror had slept with Ken. Did you know that?"

"Yes."

"Why didn't you say something?"

"I did. At the Semline Charter Ceremony. I walked in your direction..."

She interrupted, "That party was over two years ago, and you didn't say anything."

"I walked in your direction while you were holding your man's hand. Didn't you sense something was wrong?"

"You MAX boys have all these symbols that normal folks don't recognize. Why didn't you say something, say actual words?"

"That's not our way. Also, Attitude walked over to where we were standing, basically saying he would handle it."

The first tears fell. She wiped them with the back of her right hand. "Well, he never said anything to me. Well fast-forward to a few months ago. I never understood or knew why Ken broke up with me. Now I see – it was his guilt or fear that someone would say something."

"So, kool, it worked out in the end."

"No! No one told me! Not even Hope! But in the end, that's why she fixed us up!"

"Hope fixed us up?" Ernest let his brain click a couple of times to fathom an equation where Hope would willing set him up with Barbara. Since he could not think of one, he tried to end the conversation. "OK, so? We had a good time. We'll always share a bond."

"Listen to you! Ready to move on, off to the next mission. You're such a played out pretty boy."

Ernest stood up, gave her the timeout signal and came closer to her. "I understand you're hurt about Ken and Diane, but I don't need your abuse."

"You still don't get it, do you?"

"Get what?"

"Bliss! Ken left me because of Bliss." As if she had undressed for the wrong man, Ernest's confusion made her laugh and cover herself by shielding her pelvis with her palms and turn her arms so that they covered her breasts. The humility she came to show dissipated. "The break-up to hook up!"

"What?" Ernest got it but couldn't believe it.

"Yes, your dear Bliss! Hope told me she was fake, but this takes the cake. Everything from Diane up to Ken!" Barbara kept piecing it together. "We exchanged numbers at the Semline Charter Ceremony. Correction! She offered me her number so we could hang out as friends, then slept with my man."

"What? You're saying it was not Ken's guilt but Bliss's love that took your man away?"

"Love? What she was putting out there was not love. That was pure garbage…"

"You need to get a reality check. What you are putting out here is slum. Bliss had gold, from her heart to her toes. And, your man knew what he wanted."

"If he knew what he wanted, why is he begging to come back?"

Ernest shrugged his shoulders, "Beats me!"

"I will tell you why. It's because I don't need a man, a man needs me."

The equation clicked. Ernest now understood why Hope would hook him up with Barbara. The urgency in his voice struck her as Ernest grabbed Barbara's shoulders, "What? What do you mean by that?"

"I'm just repeating how your girl Bliss sees relationships."

"When did you hear her say that?"

"Bliss. She yelled it at me, a week after the Semline Chartering ceremony, at the gallery ceremony for Attitude's art collection, the night before he left town and went AWOL for two years."

"What happened after that?"

"Hope ran outside and made a phone call and said, 'The King is under attack'."

"Who did Hope call?"

"I don't know." She moved away from his grasp. "So, you're saying he bailed on me because he's a coward?"

"No, someone was trying to kill him."

"No, she made that call two years before he left, before we broke up."

"Well, that's how long the plot must have been in effect, how long it took to get to him. But first they had to get Attitude out the way. But why would Bliss step aside?"

At that, Barbara took a hard swallow and did not utter another word. She now understood her role.

"The real question is if you thought the King was under attack, why did you step aside? Why did you not do something?"

Ernest ran toward the door and slammed it as he exited her apartment. He did not bother press for the elevator. A feeling of paranoia rushed over him.

He was indeed in enemy territory. He felt their presence as if they were everywhere but he couldn't see anyone.

>=<

"NO!" He screams as he flies down the stairs, not caring whether he wakes her sleeping neighbors. "Shut up!" He screams but the words are not audible. It's as if he is screaming into his subconscious at the various people trying to play from the sidelines. "SHUT UP!"

The street is quiet but Ernest thinks that the darkness has a voice. To be sure that the darkness knows to stay away, he pulls out his gun and fires two shots in the air. In the darkness, perhaps an echo, two shots ring out. To Ernest the response comes as a relief; someone has his back. Part of him wants the police to come for him because...

These voices from the margin of his life. This is too much to deal with...

Part Two

SEPARATE BUT EQUAL

DAMN, BLISS! HOW COULD YOU?

When Attitude came back to town, on the night Bliss committed suicide, and started talking about how someone killed her, I didn't want to hear it. Too many reasons existed why he shouldn't breathe such a thought. The foremost one lied on the fact that life was not a linear exercise. We learned things in year twenty we should have experienced in year three. We also faced things in year three that we didn't get to apply until year twenty.

I wish I knew that back then - in October 1991.

>=<

Bliss was a newly formed puddle of rainwater. No matter how much rain had fallen, she existed as an unfilled until we declared war.

As MAX boys, though we declare war, we have the option to make love and leave gun play and death out of it. For pragmatists like Girard, when anyone asked why Bliss had to die; why she killed herself – he always answered even to me, *"Ernest, she got caught in the crossfire between us and society."*

Who knew what Bliss represented? She always stood apart even when standing solidly in a large group. She looked fairly much the same my last day seeing her as she did when Girard first pointed her out. Bliss maintained the same five-five, medium build, never gaining the freshmen fifteen; never doing a drastic cut to her near shoulder length hair. She rarely smiled without following it up with many words or a loud giggle. I could never say she laughed, as a laugh could oft-times be impure, hold a hidden message or strike a severe blow; Bliss giggled.

How could I have known her plans? How could any of us, especially since we do not know anything, not even our own role in the greater scheme of life. Even then, our strings are being pulled.

The first pull took place October 1991. I sat in a rental – 1991 Lincoln Towncar, white with leather interior – bopping my head to hardcore beats. Girard, kid I knew since the end of the sixth grade, a good ten years held the wheel, doing about sixty, switching lanes on the FDR Drive. G remained that kind of dude, that no matter his clothes or occasion, he looked as if he wore a polo shirt with a pair of denims. A b-boy forever, he worshiped material and upheld a code based on love while giving the impression that he admired recklessness. He maneuvered the road while his head and shoulders expressed the music's essence. The ride reminded me of a bumper car ride at the amusement park, better yet Go-Cart, since G never got into an accident.

A peaceful afternoon with temperatures approaching sixty degrees. The car windows cracked enough so our sound blasted and announced our advancement. The chill in the air emboldened our kool posture. We packed jackets because upstate New York would be in the high thirties later that night. No rain in the forecast for either locale and the sky lay flat, translucent blue with few streaks of white clouds. We headed to Semline, a school that neighbored our alma mater, for the charter ceremony for our fraternity. Though our frat had been in the region for seventy years, Semline never held a charter because no one from there ever pledged. So this past year, the other two neighboring schools agreed to pledge under Semline's rules to help obtain a charter on the campus. That became Bliss's entry point into my life.

Before then I knew her on the hi-and-bye tip, as she once dated Semline's star basketball player, a dude I played against since freshman year in high school. He and I weren't friends at that time, nor were we ever enemies, only on-court rivals. At Semline and the region in general, Bliss had name recognition, mainly as everyone's little sister, a good girl with brains, body and bliss.

Bliss lived up to her name much the way I matched mine: Ernest, earnest. She brought joy whenever she popped up on a scene. She took over and dominated even without trying. Her bubbly personality and calculating mind brought her doubters, not enemies. Her cold stare when challenged made her one of us.

MAX boys as we are simultaneously, affectionately and derogatorily called; we loved Bliss, even I who really did not know her, at the time of the Semline Charter ceremony.

Devon organized the weekend with a little coordinating help from other brothers. The only MAX boy still taking classes at any of the three schools, and the only Semline pledge to be initiated. The rest of us attended either TGI or Barrington. Though we became fast friends our freshmen year, while attending different schools, our pledge period put Devon on top of my list when it came to a rolling partner.

Out of respect, even alumni of rival fraternities and sororities made time in their schedule to attend the ceremony.

Since neither of us took the day off from work, chances were G and I would be the last Fly MAX Beta brothers to arrive. Phone calls from the campus and two surrounding schools poured into New York city since yesterday afternoon.

The ceremony was a big deal for all of us, so G had the video camera and I had the flash photography. "Oh, yo! G, son, don't kill me but I forgot my camera."

"So it's forgotten!"

"Nah, you know I need to take my own pictures. My artistic eye calls for that." G shot me a quick glance as if to say *Negro, please!* I knew he would make the Ueee back to Brooklyn 'cause I never did mindless stuff. Forgetful or irresponsible could never describe me though I came nowhere near as organized, some say as anal, as G.

We got off the highway and circled back down, not too far from the United Nations, to re-enter the FDR.

With most folks he would have been sour at having to combat traffic down the highway. The rush hour traffic on the Friday before Columbus day staggered all the way down to the Brooklyn Bridge. Traffic had been thick heading north on the FDR. Now we had to cross the bridge back to Brooklyn and drive deep into East Flatbush. The dashboard clock showed 6:58 p.m. By the time we got to Semline's campus, it would easily be after 11 p.m.

Four months ago, after graduation, I thought of moving into a less crowded block but something about this block appealed to me. It being sandwiched between two major thoroughfares, Flatbush and Nostrand clinched it. I grew up about a mile southeast. This new neighborhood also fascinated my lady of nearly a year. The block, with its four floor walk-ups, reminded her of when she lived near the Polo Grounds. The familiarity helped her decision to make a major step in life and move in with me. We met a little over four years, right before freshman year, during my visit to the three neighboring schools, same day I first saw Bliss.

Diane and I kicked it a little over the years; you know sticky fingers, ice cream and an occasional tryst but we never coupled. Our college, Barrington Graphics & Art Institute suited the quick hit and undercover liaisons, not open courtships and monogamy. Students before us cultivated an environment and culture too political and cut-throat. One week, one month, rarely would a couple last a semester. So for us, neophytes of our respective organizations, to deal symbolized a major step.

As a SUM woman, Diane had restrictions she could not tell me. I had orders I planned to follow: A MAX boy never openly dated a SUM woman unless it's for keeps.

No one frowned on friendships or clandestine affairs but unions like ours unnerved people and heightened Diane's fears to the point where she changed her mind over a dozen times when it came to attending the Semline Charter ceremony.

Everything about living together was lovely. We cooked together. The simplest stuff brought me joy, especially seeing her wearing my boxers with just a tank top and socks, as we cuddled on the sofa, watching TV, reading or chatting.

But the love ended on Friday, October 11, 1991. The apartment's wall to wall carpet, and the fact I always entered quietly muffled my steps.

There stood the maintenance man, naked, standing behind Diane.

There bent Diane, with butt in the air.

Sweat dripped from his forehead, nose then chin to the small of her back. The look of ecstasy on both their faces. The sudden pause in mid-stroke. The words fighting to escape her larynx. My simply walking to the closet and reaching for my camera. At that moment, in the periphery, I could see him step toward his clothes. Jeans, blue denim shirt and briefs, he had tossed on the lounge chair she bought at a yard sale. She called it her comfort chair. She sat there to read, watching me while I did hand-drawings with my back to the headboard. Or, as I sat on the computer to her right.

Perhaps he thought of reaching for a gun, assuming my mind traveled there. He obviously knew details of me. If he didn't he would not be in my bedroom playing my role. Diane obviously did not know me as well as she thought because she called out to me after I said, "Don't mind me! I am just reaching for my camera."

As I made my way to the door, her bare feet swimming through the plush carpet followed my casual steps. "Ernest, it's not what you think!"

"Oh, OK! I was beginning to think you loved me." I closed the door, ran down the steps and made my way out of the building. Friends know friends, and brothers want to take your place when they sense trouble. As a friend Girard knew immediately that a part of me had died but I knew better than to tell him right there on the spot. Basically, I anticipated his words; he of the rational, handle everything as it comes mindset.

"Yo, you're going tell me what's wrong or what?" He asked again after we crossed the Brooklyn Bridge. We passed that first park overlooking the East River. When I told him, he swerved out of the left lane, crossed two lanes and pulled over to the right side of the road, a few feet past the overpass. G looked at me like I had lost my mind. I was real angry but played kool. I already formulated a plan based on the conclusion I drew from Diane's reaction to mine. My problem meant my solution would be implemented not G's. "We gotta make a Ueee and kill both of them. Do you know what happens if you let that kind of disrespect slide?"

"Yeah, but I also know what killing two people means."

"If you had smoked them right there on the spot, you could have pleaded temporary insanity. There's a defense for it: crime of passion."

I made to calm him, by getting him to focus on self-preservation. "Son, she's not worth the hassle."

His eyes widened and eyebrows arched up. "It's not her. It's you. When word gets out on this, you, us…collectively will become the laughing stock."

"Oh, word is bound to get out, but if we declare war, dude in my bedroom with my woman will be like a medal of honor. You feel me?" G understood my logic but I could tell he would never choose this method, so I had to drive the point home. "Yo, what's the pecking order? Devon is the rock, the monarchy. I am the president. You are the military. I declare war! Are you in?"

"Of course I'm in. Just let me know when it's time to kill the joker in your bed."

"That joker is not a wild card; he's nothing more than a clown, a mere pawn. Someone's pulling his strings." I took my stare off Girard and looked directly ahead at the people, staring into our car, wondering why we parked on the side of the highway. "I need you to pull into the service station before the Tappan Zee Bridge on I-87. Make a phone call. Diane is SUM so this was an attack. If she's on the prowl, then chances are one or more of them Stay Black'n Die dudes were creeping behind my back. Therefore…"

G finished my sentence, "…they're behind this scene" then gave me the frat grip. "Did you forget your camera on purpose?"

"No, I am not that smart. But I do remember packing it. I think she took it out my bag. She wanted me to catch her and dude together." I should not have told him the last part because his eyes screamed for murder. "G, make love not war!"

Girard's driving lacked the carelessness he previously displayed. The toughness he comported lied not on size even though he trained hard, running a dozen miles a week to stay fit. His confidence originated from a quick mind backed by quick hands, and the ability to take a punch but only when needed. He believed if you hit first and your hardest, only those of your ilk could retaliate; and if such people existed then you should have long befriended them.

Someone hit me hard, but I categorized it as a sucker punch and nowhere near hard enough to keep me from my destination.

G pulled into service station and I stayed in the car. I never asked who he called. It would be the same if he asked me to make a call. In this situation the protocol followed along these lines. "I got word that Ernest's woman is fooling around behind his back. Send word ahead of us! We are heading to Semline. We'll be there in three hours. It's War!"

We crossed the Tappan Zee Bridge a bit after 8 p.m. then continued north heading toward I-90.

To prepare for what lay ahead, I used thoughts of Diane, to think of why she would do such a thing. We took a chance on each other because she treasured her family's legacy and wanted to carry it forward. She held no strong ties to the sorors around her, as they treated her like a pariah. It really came down to fear. Neither of us believed in monogamy. This formed the basis why we never dated anyone exclusively during our undergrad years. As I got to know and be with her daily, I understood why she didn't. Being inside someone long enough to know their fears, you reached a point where fear endured as this space, a compartment inside a person. The most bewildering kind leapt forward when a person feared those who loved her in the past would stop.

I failed to deduce how Diane viewed this as holding onto me. Perhaps she knew the danger awaiting me at Semline and thereafter to be greater than losing her to infidelity. The next option meant she chose the most vile method to push me away, to see if I would hold on. But I cannot, for my fear sat too close to my anger and my anger won out each time.

Constructed as an open campus, Semline had no gate nor security guard for visitors. Off I-90, one took a local road that bypassed the campus. The driver needed to know the turn onto what less than two decades ago remained a gravelly road. A quarter of a mile down the path, a large clearing, slate gray buildings, smooth limestone walkways greeted visitors. All campus buildings stood on this side of campus. Two large parking lots on opposite sides of the buildings. The buildings seemed to be stacked in rows, then followed by a clearing, a large grassy field used for concerts, picnics and outdoor classes. Beyond the open field were the dormitories, the only buildings not on this side. To get to them by car, one had to go back out and continue down the road. There, each entry needed a five-digit code to pass the thirty foot high security gate.

We walked in and faked as if we brought more joy to a crowded ballroom, where gents in tuxedos or their best dark suits spun dance moves and sultry lyrics to women in gowns, most showing bare shoulders, smooth necks and expensive jewelry. No one could have guessed any differently since MAX boys never needed to front to show love to each other and people not affiliated with us. We believed in love and all its many covers. Some of us wore macho poses. Others kept so kool one had to touch their skin to see if they were alive. I normally preferred the latter, but tonight I bore a jovial mask to greet people I had not seen in a long time; to smile at people I knew had thrown darts behind my back.

SBD, nicknamed Stay Black'n Die, assumed the role of our biggest rival. Firmly written in both our histories, the rift started shortly after the Women Suffrage movement and heightened during the Civil Rights Movement. Each year the separation got wider, specifically after MAX boys stopped acknowledging a sorority as our sister organization, while SBD had the ladies of SUM as their queens, practically their reason for being.

Many tried to make it more complex but the constant infighting sprouted from our refusal to have an equal, female branch to our organization. At the same time, SUM and many other women turned to MAX boys to settle their disputes with SBD, or when SBD failed to act on their behalf. We were the queen's army because they knew MAX boys shot first and dared anyone to question us.

Two people caught my eye simultaneously: Devon and Ken. Devon looked extremely depressed. My eyes darted around the room. Lucille, his woman was not here. Unlike Diane who became a recent constant in my life, Lucille stuck by Devon for four years and through the lowest of points. If anything had gone wrong, blame Devon. *Damn, D, what did you do?*

The shorter distance to Ken made me head in his direction. Ken was the type of brother who could easily have been a MAX boy. He had done athletics as a youth – a boxer – gained some notoriety but late in his high school years he started focusing on academics. As a former boxer and all-around tough guy, he fitted in nicely with SBD. Yet at six-two, a solid two-fifteen with brushed back wavy hair and dimples, the MAX history book gave hint that his family probably started on this side of the Society. He and Attitude bonded early in their freshman year. Second semester both pledged and wanted the other to pledge the other's frat. For Ken, the physical nature of SBD lured him. Whereas Attitude never really got into the *I wanna be a tough guy* thing.

To be honest, in a straight up fight, SBD would mop us MAX boys. Though we do have fighters, our frat attracted artists and intellectuals, and definitely lovers. Fly MAX Beta were the brothers whose style stole the show.

As a ballplayer, roughneck type, I looked more SBD than Max, but looks deceived and betrayed how my brain worked and the sharpness of my mind.

From the first day I met Ken, he breathed an air I wanted to test and cut short.

Barbara stood to his left. Though she tried hard to perfect the unruffled look, I sensed a discomfort in how her right foot pointed slightly toward the room's main exit. I met her years ago and introduced as Attitude's sister-friend, she took to Girard; and I to Hope. But nothing happened. For me, Hope simply teased my juvenile games, placing the two year edge she had over me as a barrier I would have to work too hard to eclipse.

In Girard's case, Barbara still held the throne as the only woman he ever flaked on. He claimed it was respect for Ken but they had yet to start dating. I still teased him that he couldn't handle that. Not only did Barbara possess a voluptuous solid frame, her beauty stood in stark contrast to the powdery fluff favored by men looking for a quick roll. A few years back I happened onto her on TGI's campus and flirtatiously asked, "How come I never see you all dolled up with make up, slinky hair, etc...?"

She answered with no hint of repulsion that I would ask this, "No more perming for me ever, and no make-up, unless I'm going to be on TV or for some special event, where the lighting might obstruct my beauty. Plus, as a natural Black woman I take the test when it is given, so there's really nothing to make up."

Though I sensed this as pledge program lessons she never shook off, it confirmed what I knew before I became part of the Society that SUM women were definitely a different breed. Not all SUM women lived and styled that way. In fact, far from it; the key was they were always willing and ready to take the test. I stepped toward Barbara and Ken instinctively held her hand in case I had forgotten.

I studied the look in Ken's face, how it dared me to walk the twenty feet. I nodded to the beat; hugged a couple of our little sisters, the women who helped during my pledge process; and then made my way to them.

"Ken, what's up baby?" I stood directly in front him, less than two feet away and kept bopping my head to the music.

"All's good! What's the deal?"

"Jokers, really! That's all. Just wanted to come by and greet this lovely SUM lady." I pivoted so that we now stood in this awkward triangle shape. The distance between them was less than theirs to me, but I could change it with two more sentences. "It's good to see you and your sisters and that the boycott has been called off."

Barbara appeared confused, possibly not in the know since she had graduated before our pledge class began. Her overly-perfect and formal tone and diction confirmed she was out of the loop. "Good to see you to Ernest! I am glad everything is back to peace."

Had Attitude not walked over with Bliss, my next sentence would have sealed the deal. In fact, I think Ken and Barbara ignored the warning on purpose. "Is peace better than love?"

Attitude's eyes told me he knew everything bu I could not tell if he wanted in or out. He hugged both Ken and Barbara then introduced Bliss as his wife. Unsure what bullshit he and Bliss were on, I stepped away to go check on Devon.

The room had gotten more crowded but I found him in a circle of frat and co-eds. "What's up! Where've you been?"

"Participating!" Devon sported an eager look like that of an animal about to be fed.

"Nah, D! Stay out of this one. Something is obviously wrong since Lucille is not here."

The shift of octaves from his voice hinted at his denial. "I ain't fazed by her. In fact this may be the last go around for us. She refuses to understand my platform."

Lucille by his side solidified Devon's image as a guy who took all risks no matter the outcome. If unattached, women would move more cautiously when he pitched promiscuity as standard fare. "D, she's not affiliated! Forget your platform! She stayed with you for years through everything. Lucille is a wonderful woman…"

He interrupted me. "Do you want her? I'm serious. You see this…" He waved his hand around the room, at the people, the ambience, the rivalries, the accolades. "I want this. You don't!"

His words caused me to take a defensive tone. "What makes you think I don't want it?"

"If you wanted it, Diane would have been heading up here with you. What could they have done if she broke her legacy right here and we made her our queen?"

"She wanted to but couldn't risk a war that goes back four generations for her family and I've only been down for less than a year." I stepped slightly to the left. "Look over there at Barbara and Ken. That's how uncomfortable Diane would have been."

"No, that's how you would have looked with her next to you. Diane is a rugged hardcore chick. She ain't scared of these motherfuckers. But I think, I guess someone else sensed your fear, that's why they attacked. If you wanted this, you would be begging me to participate. Who makes love better than me?"

Damn, Devon called it wrong in assuming fear held me back, but I respected him for having the gall to say something like that, especially to my face. "No, I want you to stay out on this one!"

"Is that an order?"

Devon's coldness did not surprise me nor that he made no attempt to make amends. Certain things about Fly MAX Beta one learned to appreciate even though they would always irritate.

Rank was one of them. Within each individual pledge line, there were ranks. Of the people listed so far from our line, the ranking went: Devon, Ernest, then Girard. And, that irked Girard the most because he was a fourth generation MAX boy, and this was only our first year in the Society.

Within the chapter, the founding line was one person: Attitude. So, he had top ranking. If we had no honor, Attitude would be dead by now.

The second line consisted of five brothers. When they heard of this particular war, they gave their standard answer to anything they didn't agree with: *that's some bitch shit.* Tonight G sided with them. Though he followed my order to declare war, he decided not to challenge SBD in this manner. Girard believed confrontation should be upfront and settled quickly, and that behind the scene maneuverings led to long-lasting feuds.

Of the remaining four brothers on our line, three joined the war, and most visiting brothers did the same.

>=<

The college's Vice-President for Student Life made a speech to welcome Fly MAX Beta as Semline's newest chartered organization. The Regional President for the fraternity then rose to present us our membership pin and rings. Each new member received two rings, one for himself and the other for the woman he had chosen for life. This tradition started back in the early 1900's and presented a challenge for us modern day MAX boys. Of the new pledge line, none of us had a woman present we could truly call our own, our personal queen. Hence our creed – *a woman for life; a man you can trust with your wife* – was something we could not uphold.

Girard did not push the issue that his woman make the flight from the Midwest. Mine kept wavering. Devon gave no reason for Lucille's absence.

Instead the seven of us, each walked to the podium with one of the women who helped us during the pledge process. We called them our sisters because for all they did for us but no official recognition came with that, especially since we each pocketed the ring meant for the woman in our life. To them, it did not matter, but the half-smile on the faces of the SUM women and other sorority women present spoke volumes. If we could change our ways, then MAX boys would not be alone. And, alone we were.

After the presentation, the bright lights dimmed and the sadness suppressed with smiles and drinks returned. I found myself sitting on a folded chair at a table thinking how it went so wrong so quickly, and whether it had ever been right. If so, then perhaps it could still be right.

The party was jumping; the women, simply beautiful; and everybody who was anybody was going to fuck tonight. What could be better? That was why the MAX family threw parties – to share the love. Before we pledged Max, we went to everybody's parties. Then last year, for the party celebrating us having made it into the frat, no affiliated person came. The few GDI's – got damn independents – who did come felt left out, but it was not our doing. We never asked them to simply observe. We always shared the love.

Last Call for Alcohol.

I needed more than another drink. To last the night, I dangled a shy smile at one of the pretty Barrington students who traveled an hour to work at Semline College. The affluence and smallness of the Semline campus made it unattractive to me when I came during college tour. I held the dreams and skills to make it pro and they had no MAX charter. The girl working as a barmaid caught my eye two years ago at Barrington, in her freshman year. I never really got to know her because of her bouncy personality and she hung out with a couple of upperclassmen chicks I had run through. Occasionally I would give her a nod, and during the Charter ceremony, those slight past acknowledgments gave me enough currency to approach her and say, "Do me a solid and bag a fresh bottle of Jack for me and leave it under my tuxedo jacket over there."

"Okay, Ernest."

I gave her a discreet pat on the butt with my left hand, like I would do to a teammate who'd made a good play. "Get my number from Devon and ring me next time you feel like coming to the city. I got you. OK?"

Big smile because I probably made her year. Even if she didn't call me, the ability to tell her friends what I offered would be enough status for her.

That's how MAX boys rolled - how we loved. So, to be alone and showing sadness meant the attack hit me hard.

I walked over to Girard. He held court with three women. I recognized them as TGI students but did not know them. He posed with both hands in his pants pockets and the tuxedo jacket folded over his right wrist. The stance meant he had no preference and whichever one made the offer, he would bed for the night. When I came over he continued his conversation with them, but went into *MAX speaking code.*

At its basic level, MAX speaking code mirrored normal conversation mixed with numbers serving as the cipher, the code. The numbers meant different things. The language evolved from slavery days as a method to pass messages from the house to the field to beyond the plantation. For example, while talking to his friends, Girard said, "Check it! A man with 17 votes out of 300 cannot possibly win this election. Even if the race was between 7 candidates, he would need to form a union with at least 2 others and be willing to share."

They were talking school politics and he obviously knew the women from his days of being heavily involved in student government, both on the campus and state level. Girard casually slipped the MAX speaking code into the conversation. At its most complex level, use all numbers with an occasional word. But even when alone, we were never as bold as to simply say: 1 17 300 7 2 of them.

> *Check it – signified the code switch. But other words also did the trick. Bust it. Yo! Guess what, and so on.*
>
> *A man was the number 1 – meant 'one man', which for us represented Attitude because he pledged alone and revived Fly MAX Beta in the region.*
>
> *17 – widely used to mean a wife because it was a prime number showing the union of 1 and 7. At this moment, Bliss was a man's wife.*
>
> *300 – widely used to mean a public room such as a hotel or motel.*

7 – was the number of people on our pledge line, and also meant me because I was the seventh person, the tallest.

2 – was Girard's number on our line.

Put it all together: Attitude with Bliss at the motel with me and Girard.

I didn't respond right away because we reserved code for absolute emergencies. I also didn't believe it, mainly because the share part meant Bliss concocted the plan. G continued the conversation with the two women to see if they could top Bliss's offer. I simply said, "I don't mean to be shady but I'm leaving in 15 minutes. If you don't catch me, I will ring you around 4."

I walked away but not before letting G know:

Shady Side motel would be a good place.

Fame (15) is something a man with his aspirations cannot get caught up in.

I am not with this episode, and I will be with #4 - Devon.

It took him another twenty minutes, and practically an empty ballroom to come by the table where I sat. I hid the bottle of Jack in my tuxedo jacket's left sleeve and bundled up the jacket because security would not let me leave the building with liquor. I couldn't locate Devon and most people had left. Girard's giggled as if the thoughts of killing someone had completely left his mind. "Them two chicks still on some courtship ritual bull, talking about let's go to the diner. When I passed, they gave me their numbers so we can do dinner in the city some time. Yeah right!" My lack of interest refocused him. "What is with you, Ern? Seriously!"

"Bliss ain't into that type of shit! You know how we roll – the 3 B's. I got the booze and the blow. You got the Buddah. Attitude probably got more blow. Let's just chill. We need to do some serious talking."

"A came up to me and told me she wanted to hang with us 'cause of the stories she heard about our high school days."

"You fools! Y'all be telling people the type of shit we were into. That's the past, son! I thought you wanted to run for elected office, and even have aspirations to, one day, be president."

G laughed and patted me on the shoulder. He sat and looked around the empty ballroom. "By the time I run for office, the stuff we used to be into is what will build the bridges to allow for my candidacy. That chick Bliss is thorough. Think about it! After all them other broads left us during the pledge period, she was the only one who stayed. The only one! Then she got like twenty other chicks who didn't even know us to stand by us. I know we don't have sisters and we, in fact, frown on that shit! But, Bliss, she's my queen! If she wants my loyalty, then she could have it."

"You make it sound like she's fighting a war."

"Attitude says she has Sight and Sound."

Sight and Sound. Sound was the formal name for what I described earlier as the MAX speak code. Sight was the other half, and as complex but we kept it basic. Since we rarely wore letters stating our fraternal affiliations, we used Sight to recognize each other and send signals, as in give direction. Like tonight when I walked in the room, all the MAX brothers in the room knew me so the fact that I gave sight meant to follow my lead.

Sight was simple: direct eye contact; subtly, look left then down.

To continue and give direction, I looked at the point of attack. Tonight I looked at the first SBD brother within my sight line - Ken. The MAX brother who I had given Sight repeated the process and targeted another SBD brother. Before doing so, he looked at me as the one giving direction. To have a successful plan of attack, no one moved too far from his original starting position until I moved away from my initial point of attack. At this point, everyone should have determined a target – a SBD's woman to sleep with.

Barbara had been my first choice.

LOVE TO THE MAX

I reflected on Bliss's claim to Barbra that she did not need *A Man*; he needed her. That bit of knowledge came too late. If I had deduced this as we left the ballroom, Bliss would still be alive. I never realized that her being out of control was not an act.

>=<

Girard and I left the Student Union Building and headed left to the larger of the two parking lots. Though a conservative campus, Semline allowing students to have liquor for certain top-shelf, on-campus events turned a pricey, catered ball into a spirited jam like atmosphere. To get the liquor license organizations had to use the catering services of a local brick-and-mortar establishment with a liquor license.

We trailed Attitude and Bliss by two steps. At that time my mind entertained the weirdest thoughts. Those two, Attitude and Girard were the only people I ever got into trouble with, and this had been going on for a decade. I really didn't know Bliss. She attended Semline so I never saw her on a daily basis or enough to determine her true nature. I followed Devon's take since he attended Semline and knew her since their freshmen year. At first, he thought the world of Bliss, but lately, slowly I began to see how he looked at her. That night, I began to understand that suspicious gaze, the same one I used in measuring Attitude and Girard. *I might have to kill these fools,* that thought danced around my head.

Classic example of why - Girard's antics as we walked to our cars. He used Sound to talk real bad about Bliss. He tested to see whether she would speak up and give way the fact that she knew our code, something as a woman she should not. Don't get me wrong! Some outsiders knew and used our code. Most times, they did not know we were Max boys.

How had they learn our sound?

Our sound started in the nineteenth century and it evolved over the years. Since we once had a sister organization, living members taught it to their children. Add to that the number of people who spent time studying us, spying us.

I figured Bliss got Sound from Attitude. Since he should not have taught her, she didn't count on Attitude telling us. I rarely used Sound so I knew I never said anything private around her.

So G sounded and talked of how we should get Bliss real drunk, give her lots of cocaine and after we fuck the shit out of her, drown her in the bathtub. Or we could simply make sure she overdosed and died. Where should we ditch the body? The last time he killed someone it was at Barrington and he knew those woods inside out. That the risk of getting caught with a dead girl in his trunk out here in Semline did not sit well with him.

I waited for Bliss to turn around and say something. I could tell by her stuttered gait some of what G said gave her second thoughts of coming with us.

The parking lot looked to be that of a large stadium. We arrived later than most so we parked further out from the building than Attitude. As he opened the passenger side for Bliss, G grabbed the back of her forearm and said, "Yo, let Bliss ride with us!"

She turned and punched him real hard in the chest. "You're a real asshole, you know?"

Girard laughed first then grabbed Bliss into his arms. "Why you fronting like you don't have Sight and Sound?"

"I don't know. I guess I knew you were just trying to be funny."

"S&S is some real dangerous shit! Don't ever use it! If you hear people using either, do not react! Got it?" She nodded as if not taking the warning too seriously and she hadn't, since a week later, she shouted "I don't need a man. A man needs me" in a room full of strangers.

G could tell she had no intention of heeding his warning so he shook her, "GOT IT?"

"Yes." I barely heard her though we all stood less than one foot of each other. Then G turned to Attitude, "Yo, I hope you haven't forgotten how dangerous love can be."

A brief pause while they stared at each other; the first to nod would basically state the other could have top ranking at this point. Again, I thought of my gun, in the rental's glove compartment. Girard broke the stalemate and nodded first.

Attitude kept rank. He pulled off by the time we got to our car. He hit the horn twice then once, meaning he was in room 21.

After such a festive night, at a little after two in the morning, I heard of not one after-party. Some people made the drive to either of the neighboring schools, my alma mater, Barrington, or to Attitude's alma mater, TGI. I had become familiar with Semline and its rhythm from various visits. Tonight the empty streets spoke of the town people's fear of the event Devon organized. Though not outwardly hostile, the town never got comfortable with too many Blacks congregating in one place. Unlike the actual town, with its focus on blending science with the spiritual world, Semline College never bought into the racial disharmony at any point during its existence. The campus hosted spiritual retreats while embracing science and engineering as its key subject areas. It once served as a sanctuary for fugitive slaves and many in the abolition movement.

My mood asked only for Jack neat and substances to heighten the sensation. If the Jack's burn proved to be too much, I would take my drinks on the rocks. Of course, I would puff some weed and snort a little blow. I wanted to fly, away from my troubles, thoughts of Diane, killing my best friends, and the war I declared.

As I parked the car far away from Room 21, on the other side of the motel, G made to speak but I just shook my head from side to side. I did not want to hear his input. He should know we did not want to be seen in a place Shady Side motel. There could be so many misinterpretations if someone drove by and saw us alone. So many more, if someone saw us with Attitude and Bliss. Nothing that happened at Shady Side motel lent itself to an easy explanation.

Perhaps in its early years, because the town had no trees in its three other sides, the name and location represented solitude, rest, and such imagery. Over the years, development went away from the motel so this side of town now looked like a ghost town; mostly old-timers lived there. Students found on this side were usually up to no good. Whatever the shenanigan, it had to be kept so low, not even death should bring it up. As pledges we came here, for pledging purposes, and other times to hide liaisons with women.

Bliss looked real good but I never really dug her like that, nor was I one of those guys who wanted to immediately befriend her and treat her like a sister. Since most folks gave her a passing grade, I must've missed something when it came to what kind of draw she had.

When we entered the room, Bliss had already reverted to her animated self, seemingly dismissing G's warning about Sight and Sound, and his standoff with Attitude. I pegged her as a hardheaded broad but that did not faze or affect me, as long as she kept me out whatever hair-brained scheme that made her think being here with the three of us was a necessity.

I sat in one of the desk chairs near the small table. A few feet away a lone standing lamp illuminated the room. The local Top 40 stations played *"Girls just wanna have fun!"* Yeah, how appropriate! Bliss alternated between singing and lip-syncing. In between she took off her clothes, not suggestively, but more like the way one undressed after a hard day of work. She got down to her bra and panties then headed to the bathroom and closed the door. As she ran a shower, we each prepared our drug of choice. A and I compared who had the better grade of cocaine. His caused less drip so we stood on those lines. By now we had taken off our formal shirts and we all sported white t-shirts or tank tops, and our tuxedo slacks. The way the scene played out, with no one sweet-talking her, meant Bliss controlled this scene.

I still was not with it. To me, she was really saying nothing.

She came out of the bathroom, wearing the motel's cheap bathrobe. I wondered if she still had panties on. She dried her wet hair with a towel. G offered a pull of the blunt, and she turned it down. "Don't tell me you don't smoke weed!" Then as if he had come to some sort of recollection, G added, "Word! When we were pledging, all the other girls were boozing and generally going hard on the drugs. You sought protection from Ted."

Ted was number six in our pledge class. A seventh generation MAX boy and the only other from our pledge class who stayed out of the war I declared, he stayed out, not because he didn't have my back but because he hated the method.

Bliss balked, "Protection? I didn't seek protection. We connected."

G laughed. "Then why you dumped him a few weeks after we went over?"

Her raised voice shrieked as if mortified that people thought that. "We were never dating."

G messed with her, needling her on two fronts. One, he asked questions to which we had all already jumped to our own conclusions as to what happened. Two, we made sure no one polluted Bliss during the pledge period. Devon went to Ted and told him to make sure Bliss did not get involve and stayed unaware of anything that happened during the pledge process. Devon did this at the very beginning of the underground process and he did it again once we surfaced. G knew this, but he wanted to know if Bliss could handle herself in a dangerous situation.

Up to that night, I voted no.

The room had two full-sized beds. A and G held similar poses on separate beds, back to the headboard, drug of choice in hand and staring at nothing in particular. The room's quietness felt like a stalemate, and truthfully, we could have left without doing anything and it would have been OK with everyone. Deep down, we loved Bliss like we would our queen! To hear us talk, the game of chess came to mind, with its allusions to warfare and capturing the king.

Bliss also saw it this way. She thought herself as a queen who had to make the power moves.

But MAX life and war differed from chess. We kept our queens protected, in the dark, away from our dark side. Most MAX boys married ultra-good girls because we knew how we could be. That lone point confounded me and many others, on why I dated Diane. Many claimed she would be impossible to reform so I settled on only wanting to hold her hand and steady her gaze, for her to fully realize what she had in me was not worth losing.

I could tell Bliss felt the same about Attitude. She wanted him to veer to a path where money coupled with fame superceded everything he wanted to accomplish in life. A's withdrawn eyes meant he'd rather be anywhere but here, and I wanted his voice to say it. "Yo, A where you at?"

Attitude answered in code. "Next Saturday is the closing of my show. After that I go to Switzerland and tour Europe for a while."

His speaking in code made no sense since we all knew Sound. "Yeah, I stopped by there one afternoon. Did the gallery tell you?"

"Yeah!"

"Good shit!"

"Thanks bro!" He nodded as he spoke, and I nodded back. The MAX nod served as both a salute and communication symbol. The simple sentences spoken in code told why Bliss chose us. Attitude had decided to step out of the MAX life and go neutral. This new mission meant he may never come back, or at least no time soon.

A woman for life. A man you can trust with your wife.

We talked in simple sentences that had two meanings. *A woman for life.* If your life is in trouble, you don't call your woman unless it's for her to call for backup. Life represented what she gave, as in your child, your legacy. *A man you can trust with your wife.* Sex was nothing to us. If you sexed a brother's wife, you tell him. But you should never sex a brother's wife unless he gave you permission.

With Attitude leaving for good and The Outsiders unable to hold top ranking, leadership in our chapter would be up for grabs. That night became more interesting, but I still remained on the sidelines.

G shifted the conversation, "Yo Bliss what you think of us MAX boys? Really think of us!"

"You guys are very dangerous. But most times the danger is to yourselves."

Only G laughed. Some people lived for danger. Include G in that group. Bliss had chosen tonight as her audition. I knew of no reason why she would want to get in deeper with us. With Attitude leaving, she could simply go back to a normal life the way the other little sisters had. Yes, Sight and Sound made that difficult; the knowing of one and possibly more hidden languages being spoken around you. Positioning herself as an adversary to MAX life showed her involvement to be more than she let on. She appeared to be the force behind Attitude going on a dangerous mission by pretending to be neutral, shortly after his name became billboard and print material. The brother always had name recognition, but to be out there in bright lights in the big city contradicted his style. She probably facilitated or challenged him. And, if I peeped that, so had G.

With G's ambition, a woman like Bliss who liked danger would serve him well. Kool, he could have her. But he really could not, at least not in the open. He had a main girl. True, she lived in a different state, but everyone knew she would be back. It's like G's girl maintained the distance so he could get this whole being a MAX neophyte out of his system.

So that left me. Not to necessarily be Bliss's man, but to provide the cover for G, the next king. OK, but she had to tell me something. Being near naked with three men in a motel room and playing with G's toes, slowly working her way to him, the soft kisses on his face, slowly working her way down, as he puffed the smoke into the air, I'd seen similar scenes and she was really saying nothing. I didn't know she floated on that high a skill level or whether G's excitement had gotten the better of him but his first nut cracked in damn near record time. He said, "Damn, girl, you go hard! High five baby!"

Chick actually gave Girard a high five! Then she headed to the bathroom and I could hear the water running and the sound of a mouth being rinsed. "Yo G, pass me the blunt! You want some of this?"

"Yeah, OK! Like I'm really gonna put that shit up my nose. But you could pour a brother some Jack!"

"Neat or Rocks?"

Girard took it straight. The music went from bad to worse, but as Bliss made her way back into the room, the DJ threw a little flavor. *I feel good...* She started talking about how she loved James Brown's music. G interrupted her, "You should let me hit it to this beat."

"You're not hitting anything." G only laughed, as if knowing he would soon enough. Not letting a silent moment sink in, she pulled Attitude's left foot. "But you can hit it anytime."

Attitude laughed and I tried to catch his eyes but Bliss taking off the robe blocked my sight lines. First she faced forward and straddled him. As the pace increased and he gripped her lower back, she slowed him down by doing a slow one-hundred-eighty degree spin. In this new position she faced me. I returned her stare, my eyes saying *nothing. You ain't really saying nothing.* Yeah, I meant to be real hard on chick. She put on a real good show. I had seen professionals who couldn't flow the way Bliss handled herself once we got into the room. Now her up and downs kept perfect measure of his length and girth. The only moans came from him. We were all friends but she communicated something devious; she eliminated all my preconceived notions that sex meant more for a good girl. Even after all this, I still saw Bliss as a good girl. Even after G asked Attitude to move her this way, so she could be on the bed on all fours, while each stood pole position on opposite sides.

Sex was sex, but did she see it as a commodity to buy our loyalty?

Were G and I loyal to her before this? Yes.

Would G be more loyal to her after this? Yes. Sex does transcend. They came in her simultaneously but on opposite ends. Sex transcended because of the mask that had been removed. To be naked and say I will do anything for you. I will even love you.

I admired the way she came to us, with no hurdles for us to jump. She came to us the way we approached women and asked them to join us in our struggle – straight no chaser, whether our struggle be the curves to multiply quickly and then disappear, or the straight shot of one night filled with simple brushstrokes.

But I still remained unfazed. As she returned from the bathroom, no longer pretending to need a robe, she seemed spent. Then I realized the dim bulb under the lamp's yellowing shade caused me to see Bliss in silhouette, now that she had turned off the background light from the bathroom. Her subtle curves including the arch in her lower back and the graceful manner she moved hinted, not at remorse, but a deep contemplation.

Attitude set himself to leave. After buttoning his shirt and putting on his jacket, he nodded to G and tossed her his car keys. Then he pronounced the words, "G has rank. Here are my car keys! Get home safe."

Not sure why he bypassed me since I technically should have rank, but I wondered on the transparency of my demeanor and look, whether I gave way to my thinking, that I might have to kill Bliss. But, A had made it known, no matter what this Bliss chick did, she had standing as his wife, drove his vehicle, and he personally guaranteed her safety. Had he left the broad's transport to our doing, not given Girard top ranking, who knew what could be? The hit I took from Diane earlier that night further confirmed my distrust of ambitious women. That type of episode, in a dump like Shady Sid motel you cannot trust to an ambitious woman, especially one as sharp as Bliss. Her ambition rivaled Girard's who summoned her, "Yo, come here for a second!" She went to him. "Have a drink!"

She sipped then came to me for a refill. I barely looked at her. She took the drink on the rocks and went back to the bed next to G. Lying on her side, I could not see but her motion clearly indicated the use of her right hand to work him back up. Minutes passed and then he stood up; t-shirt still on, dick unable to point to the ceiling but holding enough energy to be parallel to the ground. He discarded the pants from around his ankles, while reaching in his jacket pocket for a three-pack of condoms. At first, he banged away in the missionary like he was just trying to let one go, then her slow up and downs relaxed him.

These fools started making love. These motherfuckers!

Their sounds went from the slap happy, quick-rhythm bumps of unskilled or rushed lovers to slow circular gyrations mixed with the rise and fall of two people opening up wider in their effort to consume one another. This sequence went for a good twenty minutes. Next they kissed, long, deep passionate tongues, sucking each other, looking into each other's eyes. Every now and then, I could hear their whispers though the words remained inaudible. She moved her hands slowly from his wrists to his elbows, shoulders then back. Her hold on him grew stronger, and then I could hear her fighting it, as if this whole episode was not for her benefit. That she should not be affected by it, especially not through pleasure. She stifled her own breath, tried to throw his rhythm off, sped up the pace so she could throw his rhythm off, or him out of her. But she couldn't.

A little more time went by then the second part of the frat call and response, "MAX Beta!" Simultaneous orgasms.

Girard took about a minute before getting off her. Bliss's expression bawled it to be the longest minute of her life, not because of his physical weight but because she came, perhaps to the realization that sex could not move a MAX boy. As he got up, she rolled her body sideways to avoid his eyes. He turned her chin and looked at her. "I love you, Bliss."

Bliss had come to the realization that only love, real unflinching love moved a MAX boy.

A slight pause confirmed her confusion. He really didn't expect her or need her to say it. In the silence, they could hear me snort a line of coke. In the silence, I heard a faint sound: most likely the quick beat of her heart. "I love you too, Girard."

As he walked to the bathroom, he shouted, "It's all love, baby. It's all love."

The sound of the shower gave her enough of a window to confide in me, to explain this shift in behavior. As far as I knew she was not in trouble, and this was not her type of scene. She knew we would not tell anyone about this – what she did would stay here and die here. But, why did she want to do this, be this? She had to tell me something. My watch showed five in the morning. The sun would soon rise. Though the motel had a noon checkout time, I planned to be long gone. Bliss stayed under the covers. We ignored each other. The bathroom to her back, she stared blankly at the curtains of the window facing the parking lot. When G came out the bathroom, his eyes met mine but he did not look at Bliss. His subtle code of affirming Bliss to be kool with him and that she could sleep here. "Damn, Ern! You still hitting that bottle and standing on lines?"

His voice did not startle her but it sounded an alarm in her. She got out of the bed, showing that nude, nicely shaped body. Girard dressed in T-shirt and boxer briefs and made ready for bed. She rubbed his stomach, "You're good?"

"I'm well. Thank you for a great evening, sis."

She smiled and thanked him then walked to the bathroom. Seconds later, she started the shower. G got into the bed.

My words rushed out, "Yo, you're staying here?"

"Yeah this room is paid for. What's the point of going to look for a place to sleep? We'll get a room across town tomorrow."

We whispered, in case Bliss tried to play slick and listened at the door. "What about her?" I pointed to the bathroom. "Is she staying or leaving?"

"That's up to you. She's still here only because of you." My face must have told him I had no clue on how he figured that. "Talk to her, man! She was really pissed when she heard what Diane did."

"How does she know?"

"Not only did word get around the grapevine. She also has S&S." I frowned at the thought the grapevine had gotten word about the man in my bedroom. Diane cheating embarrassed others, especially SUM women, but the man in my bedroom hurt me and MAX only. "Yo, you said put the word out. I didn't put that part out, but people got their sources. And, that's the main reason I told you we should have killed…"

"Shut up with that nonsense!"

At that, G just rubbed his face with both palms, used them to brush his hair back and let his back fall to the bed. "Good night, man!"

Bliss came out five minutes later. She sat at the table and greeted me as if seeing me for the first time of a new day. "Hi Ernest."

OK, I'll play along, I thought. "Hi Bliss. How're you doing today?

"I'm sorry about what happened earlier. You know I did it for you."

"Really?" I bought time as I knew this chick planned on trying to run game on me.

"I heard about what happened and since you MAX boys flow the way you do, I wanted to know why you feel it's so bad for a woman to flow that same way. I mean if you were in a motel and had sex with three women, what would be wrong with that?"

"I'm not puzzled by the sex. Only why you are acting out of character."

"Have you forgotten the Free Love Society?"

"No, they're the girls who you got to help us after all the other females left."

"And, the things they did with the pledge line and some of the big brothers."

I tried to keep the conversation on one track. "They're not the first. Every line it's the same thing."

"Probably so! But they helped you guys because I was a member, not because of MAX. Don't get me wrong, they grew to love you guys and you've bonded. But as a society our love has always been free."

"Yeah, but the word on you was that..."

She broke in, "I know the word on me but love is not sex, nor is sex love. So, don't hold that against Diane. Something must be happening with her or to her."

"What? I'm supposed to go home and make everything nice?"

"No, I told her not to expect that..."

My anger rose on its own. "What! You called my girl?"

"Yes. And she's scared, Ernest, and not necessarily of you. She's scared, Ernest."

With three neighboring schools, people who you often thought were strangers did have their linkages. And this Bliss chick knew something. "What did she say?"

"I tried to pry it out of her, but she didn't say anything. That's why I know something is wrong. All she kept saying was that when you get back, she will talk to you and you will understand. Do you?" She grabbed my hand. I didn't say a word or offer a reaction. "I don't either, but together maybe, perhaps I can help you understand."

Bliss leaned over and gave me a soft peck on the lips. I backed away, letting go of her hand and avoiding the eye contact. She picked up the folded dollar bill and the straw and did a line of coke. Virgin nose. She shivered and held back the sneeze. "The cut is harsh, not like Attitude's."

"He's never given me cocaine."

"Then why are you doing it now?"

"There are things I have to become immune to."

"Not this! This shit will take you." I grabbed the blow out of her hand.

"Can you roll me a joint?" I shot her a funny look. "I have smoked before."

Thoughts of Diane tried to come to me, but there sat Bliss trying to plead Diane's case. The way Diane and I drank the hard stuff, smoked small joints, did a line here and there. Diane grew up a hard chick; I met her that way. She got harder after pledging SUM. Something about beautiful women who stood firm always bewitched me, and Bliss knew it. Danger always lurked around the MAX life and though she flirted with it, she never embraced danger. That night she wanted to sleep with danger. So I grabbed her hand to get her full attention. I communicated with her using only sight: Bliss, to sleep with danger, you have to dance with hate, pelvis to pelvis, a slow grind with your back against a scraggy wall. White panties stained because two fingers poked through the sides. After that point, no more needed be said. Only one who could save you was your God.

Bliss sat on my lap, facing me. I was partially limp so we moved slowly. Her kiss felt soft, yet very wet and hungry. She had no smell, except that of the motel's industrial soap. I began to feel this chick, the way she wound her hips to an island rhythm, one closer to how couples danced calypso near a party's end, no longer showing off fast unbridled movements, and more focused on grinding pubic regions so there'd be no need for foreplay once the clothes came off. I achieved the rock hard-on I sought and it took every bit of self-convincing I could muster not to go into her raw dog style. After I slid the condom down to the base, she reassumed the position of rump on lap, the flat of feet against the wall's dingy white paint, with me holding her elbows for motion. Slip. Slide. She took it all the way in. Through the wetness, I understood the wilderness, the underbelly of a man's subconscious, the reason governments formed. To have a species running with no order while knowing this side of bliss rested deep within every woman, humans would be extinct through sheer lack of progress due to over-copulation, overpopulation. Our sex metamorphosed from an exploration or even a destination; it inclined into an effort to distance ourselves from the banality of our existence. She now moved up and down, not the high bounce of quick hits and misses and high climaxes, but the passionate stir of a bowl allowing needy, prowling fingers to probe for mouths eagerly waiting to lick its mix. Though I had not looked at the clock when we started, I sensed time moving more rapidly than sixty ticks per minute. I felt like the walls around me had been built of my own designs and were now allowing me to transmute matter. To have my form merge into it, to either stay in or come out the other side. And this woman, this queen needed my loyalty. Not to always be there; perhaps to never again be with her, but to simply understand the danger around me. And, to face it head on.

I did not remember falling asleep and neither did Bliss. We probably would not have awaken save for G's voice. "Yo, y'all still at it?"

She woke, turned toward G's voice then back at me. The tranquility in her eyes embraced me and I knew it to be a reflection of mine. She nodded to me and I back at her. Then she got up. Though mostly limp, enough blood flowed so that the condom had enough support to still be on. I had fallen asleep in Bliss, and the nonchalant manner she moved while taking casual clothes from her small travel bag showed the coolness that had embraced me. She folded last night's clothes into the bag then went to the bathroom with her toothbrush and paste. G and I didn't speak because mere words could not describe the feeling. Bliss.

She came out of the bathroom and noticed the quiet. "What? What's wrong?"

"Oh, nothing." We both said at the same time.

"I'll see y'all at the family picnic later. Ok?"

We nodded and she left. Strangely enough We did not compare notes nor did we speak of our time in Bliss. Ever. We took turns showering and ironing our clothes, without uttering a word about how we felt. The secret rendezvous so foreboding, we even snuck out the room's window to get back to the car. We may have felt changed, but Shady Side Motel still implied sleazy escapades.

HOME ALONE

That weekend changed all of us, for the better. Freedom came to us. We knocked down a wall that had been closing in on us since we were teenagers. We grew up coaxing women into sex, especially group sex, *trains* to better visualize the colloquialism. That guilt fractured a large part of my thinking, created a paradox supported by what I later learned to be The Madonna-whore Complex. Bliss knocked down that wall by making us judge her not ourselves. Our eyes became her mirror: admiring the way she strutted in the nude; and how it barely differed at the family picnic, witness her still giving hugs and shining a wide smile to everyone who appeared near her.

Girard drove calmly, fast but calm. He listened to jazz. When one station went to commercials, he sought another. When he couldn't find another, he settled on classical music. In a nutshell, the boy was in Bliss. Normally no matter the mood, G strictly *vibed* on hip hop. The music captured the expanse of his moods. So, blasting jazz, during a four-hour drive back to Brooklyn, not mentioning anything about the war on SBD, Diane or Bliss meant a dreamscape captivated him. G dreamt big even though everyday it became clearer that indeed *it was a small world (after all)*.

I kept myself grounded because the world had no true directions to go; nowhere except for out. No up and down. For every positive, there existed a negative; and for every negative thing, finding a positive often proved too difficult. For me the jazz music and G's blissful state distracted but only for brief intervals. I had to go home and deal with some real shit. I had to be cold to a woman I committed myself to loving. No marital vows bound us but I thought, in time, she could protect me from that side of myself. Now a hole occupied that space. I always felt this urge to shoot at openings, believing ghosts hid in those shadows. The shots would force them out to kill me, to be killed or compromised.

Diane seemed to be fishing for a compromise. The clean apartment and the meal she cooked for my return meant unfinished business. I loved her cooking but tonight the food on my plate went in the trash. She grasped at the possibility of a phantom truce. "At least hear me out! It's not like you haven't cheated on me."

"Fine distinction, baby! But you put my life in danger."

"How? You're the one with the guns. He was not…"

"Exactly. What if I killed him on the spot? Then you, 'cause you're a witness."

She forced a laugh, one encircling a question accented as a declarative statement. "You wouldn't kill me!"

I sat on the sofa, not bothering to look at her. I stared at the television though I hadn't turned it on. "It's a real easy choice. One of us has to move out, tonight. Together one of us will die by morning."

"What are you talking about? Is this some of your MAX boy Code of Conduct bullshit? I am not scared of you Ernest."

"Oh, I know that! But, I am scared of you and for you. You have a death wish, and I don't want any part of it." I got up and went to the closet to pack some clothes for work.

She pleaded, "I can't afford this place on my own."

"Look, I will call a moving company to get the rest of my stuff tomorrow."

"What? You're really moving out? It's over between us?"

"YES! What is it you don't get?" I placed my jacket on the back of a chair. I grabbed my small gun, the .32 caliber Beretta from the inside pocket of my tux. I got this one because I could easily hide it, and if I faced a do or die situation where being captured alive being the worst possible outcome. Safety off. Trigger locked. I pointed it to my temple. "It's either me or you."

She fell to her knees and started crying. She failed in her act when she could barely bring a line of tears down her right cheek. In between sobs, she repeated "I'm sorry, Ernest." In between, she tried to reason the whole thing about how she never meant to hurt me, that she never brought him here before. This went on for about five minutes. I just sat at the dining room table and waited her out. I really liked the apartment and wanted to continue living there. She finally said the words, "I don't have any money to pay for movers."

"I will pay for it."

"Can I leave in the morning? I will sleep on the sofa."

"No. Tonight."

"I have no place to go."

"Call one of your sisters."

"That's real fucked up, Ernest. How you could do me like this? That's real fucked up." She got up fast and so did I.

I grew up with four sisters, two older than me. For a number of years, they outsized me. Diane's posture meant the thought of physically fighting me swirled in her head. I balled my fists because of what my mother told me whenever I ran crying to her that one of my sisters hit me. She told me to never hit a woman, but for damn sure, never let one hit me, except for her, of course. But my mother never hit me, she would scold then hug. If I had done something real bad, then she would tell my father. My father never hit me. He would hit my eldest brother and tell him why. But my eldest brother never hit. He would hit my other older brother, who would hit me. I would fight him. For years he would beat me, but eventually as I got bigger than him, and the fights got longer and harder for him, he stopped hitting me, though I never actually won a fight over him.

I grew up in a loving home where we rarely struck one another. We mostly yelled and gave each other hard looks. I preferred my mother's look.

Her cheeks would swell and her eyes would show confusion, as if asking "Really? You're that tough?" From there, she would clench her fists.

My fists were clenched and Diane knew I would not hit first, just like my father knew my mother would not hit first. He would pound a fist on the table, say his peace then storm out of the room. I always wondered what would happen if my father hit my mother. I once asked my brothers and without hesitation, they said, "We would kill him." Maybe not right then but that would be the plan. So I never got into the whole hitting someone scene, especially a woman. Diane knew this and obviously raised in a different place where people hit each other then made up, that frustrated her. I guess one day I would have to learn and understand such a place. But it would never be my house.

She finally decided on the best choice. "I gotta make a phone call?" Then she played on my guilty conscience. Diane made seven calls, saying the same thing, but never a name. "Hi. What's up, soror! This is Diane. I need to crash by you. Can you hit me back on my pager?" On the seventh, someone picked up as she left the message. She unhurriedly packed two bags and cried, murmuring under her breath, as if I should care to ask her destination.

Finally, two hours later, at ten o'clock, she left.

This was not a time for a sigh of relief. I pressed redial to check the phone Diane had dialed. Hope answered with a casual hello. I hung up without saying anything. SUM women honored their sisterhood until death, even when a sister was in the wrong. Six of them passed on Diane meaning she could die for all they cared, but Hope stood tall. I wondered whether it was for my protection or Diane's.

The next steps fixed whatever could be interpreted as my doing Diane wrong, by putting her out as the clock neared midnight. I made a series of phone calls. Diane had to disappear and I had to make it good. As MAX boys a good part of our training dealt with letting go of past lives. But true to MAX form, we never fully started over; we found a way to replicate the life we left behind. I called the 800 numbers for five realtors, five storage companies and one temporary housing agency. I used Hope's work number as the call back. Then I called a travel agency and paid for a one-way ticket to Switzerland to be delivered to Hope's job. We used the word, Switzerland, as code for any safe place and a way not to divulge exact destination.

I then called a twenty-four hour locksmith to have them come and add a lock to the apartment's door ASAP.

Two days passed and not one phone call but I knew it would soon come.

>=<

Lauren needed to see me because she too had her world shattered by Diane's actions.

Her call came to my office. She contacted Devon to get my number. Lauren pledged on the same line with Diane, and learned on Sunday, right before Diane's distress call the details of Diane and her boyfriend of over three years. He was a SBD brother who graduated one year before us. I always thought of him as a duck. Had it been him in the apartment this past Friday, I might have just pinned him down and took his manhood in all kinds of ways, and called the matter even.

She said the sloppy seconds had not bothered her because she knew of Diane's dalliance before she started dating him. Her anger came from how Diane swore it to be done, something to never be revisited. Lauren hated how she could never satisfy her boyfriend's needs. She called them kinky; perhaps one could label them such, particularly to her, a girl schooled on skirts past the knees; knees together, not crossed; smile, don't laugh, and if you must, a slight chuckle, the most; and don't bring it from you diaphragm.

She could not imagine herself doing the stuff he needed. So, to him, women like Diane filled that void. Diane was a bona fide lover. If you dreamt it, she would make it a reality.

But ultimately Diane's fantasies and needs got her in trouble, and the reason why I made her my woman. We could talk during and after sex. With most chicks I sexed I found I couldn't really talk to them. They didn't understand complex sentences. If you threw any punctuations besides a period, they would be completely lost; throw in conditional phrase or a conjunction, they would take the part of the sentence that most affected them and deal only with that. With Diane, I could have the following conversation.

"I like fucking you up the ass, but I am more into getting my dick sucked, so even though I wear a condom when we take the back country road, I still feel that it's somewhat dirty."

She looked up at the ceiling as if considering my needs and reconciling them with her own. "I clearly understand. Perhaps we will not do both acts during the same session. I really cannot go without getting it up the ass. At first, I enjoyed it because of the pain and pleasure and the taboo surrounding anal sex, but now I just love how you stick it up there while biting me as I bite your fingers, while you use your free hand to stick fingers or a dildo up my twat. I can't give that up. Can you?"

So, this chick Lauren came to my crib seeking revenge on her man, and though I am not impressed by her innocent, schoolgirl lyrics, I am noticing how she blossomed over the years. I did not want her to think of me as the shoulder to cry on but I had to admit it to her, something to let her know that she had a little leeway, to tease; that she didn't have to put out tonight. Yet, in the back of my mind, I envisioned what I could accomplish with a woman like that – a loyal bookwork known to have a vindictive, strike back quickly demeanor if rubbed the wrong way. I could put a crown on her head and a smile on her face. I made a quick play to test her reflexes. "Damn, you're beautiful! Give me a kiss."

I hesitated on letting her coming over when she called earlier because I had slept with too many women to be doing community service and training some young chick in the ways of love-making. I needed her to adjust to my new level, a realm with some old rough shit - biting and punching, in places where the public eye could not see. The last time Diane and I made love, she begged me, "Hit me!"

Situated on my left elbow, doing a slow up and down stroke, I admired the beauty of her jaw line when the words finally registered. She repeated herself. My right fist nailed her so hard, below the last rib where she had nothing but skin and a little bit of baby fat. She must have been waiting for me to question this new need of hers, for she had not braced herself. I really did not focus on how my fist nailed her, flattening her back to the bed, or how spittle slipped out the side of her lips, as she let out a cough so that she wouldn't choke. I saw her wide open eyes. I felt how her inside, from throat and crotch compressed. I had no room to move and my cum readied to jet out and spray inside of her. But I needed to see the feeling she had given me, to share it with her. She rubbed it on her stomach and chest, all the while trying to catch her breath.

Wednesday night with Lauren turned out to be anti-climatic. Inside of me a feeling sprung that she deserved more. It's one thing if a person refused to explore, but to have never been given the chance caused the hurt and feeling of betrayal. Her well-crafted image had betrayed her. She had gone out of her way to not be seen as a vixen, forgoing the forgone conclusion that most vixens are what most men consider to be dime-pieces. An hierarchy built on a foundation where only a super-naturally pretty, shapely woman could be considered a dime-piece. At five-four, slim upper body with wide hips and long, thick butt cheeks, Lauren beamed in that beautiful wife baking cookies model. She with the symmetrical face and the almond shaped eyes. Eyes that held your first glimpse and bequeathed you to eye contact during conversations. Their clarity showed purity, a regular night sleep and confidence, and no drugs or alcohol. Her smile bore a slyness but it really said nothing mischievous, and that was where I could have my most impact. Whenever she smiled, people would comment on the difference in her new smile. They would debate whether they could trust because of its complexity.

Regardless, they would be drawn to her smile. I could think of it as *Ernest's Statement*.

The next day my coworkers had this urge of wanting to talk to me. Normally no one talked to me. I even got invited to join a group of co-workers for lunch. It took me hours to realize I had a new smile, not that I really wanted one. I became curious about *Lauren's Statement*. Throughout the day, I expected to hear from her about last night. When I didn't, I went to the gym after work. I got home to find not one message on the answering machine. That worked fine because all I wanted to do was to shower, eat and read myself to sleep. By night's end, I planned on finishing Alice Walker's, *"The Temple of My Familiar"*. Attitude recommended it a few weeks back, saying it really helped him deal with structure in his art, particularly his most recent collection, *Voices from the Margin*.

As I fell asleep, my thoughts drifted to several women and the one thing they had in common - SUM women. Would Diane take my advice and move out of town? Hope, who should have called by now. Was Lauren sitting by the phone? Did Barbara realize I was prepared to kill Ken right there in the ballroom had Attitude and Bliss not walked up? The last one shocked me because, at that time, I barely knew Barbara but the pattern remained the same – all paths led to killing Ken.

Friday afternoon and the phone still had not rung. The coworkers kept getting friendlier, wanting to be on my good side, not realizing I had none. My kindness only extended to those who managed to get inside my small world. But as easily as you entered, one false step I spat you out.

I survived this way because life was the game, not people.

I got home and Lauren's phone call came as the kitchen clock chimed seven o'clock on a Friday. I had had a tiring week, not just from the increasing workload, but dealing with the changing office politics, suppressing thoughts of Diane. And her! The nerve to be calling on some old little girl shit, not speaking what she wanted to really say. Go ahead curse me for not calling you. She could not do that because I had an answer. In fact I had many answers. The first one, I asked it out of nowhere, to nullify her game. "Do you want to move in with me?"

She danced around it. "I can't move in with you…"

I stopped her midstream. "I know you're a girl and you just want to have fun, but I'm a grown man…"

"I think I'm older than you by a few months."

"Age ain't nothing but a number!" I zeroed in on the problem at hand. "Life has aged me and the things left for me to see cannot be shared with…"

She tried to get me out of my zone. "What are you doing tonight?"

"I'm chilling at the crib, watching porn. You wanna come through?"

Another pause. Then I heard the phone click followed by a dial tone. My hope shifted into one where our paths only crossed in public or group setting. By then, we could share a knowing hug, that although a brother cared for you, he could not play that game, for he competed in the major leagues of a deadly game in which he was the target.

Lauren did not want to play this game or she would have called the next day. She knew I could not call her, not after experiencing a bit of the stuff her sister, Diane and I explored. I had no intention of deceiving Lauren into leaving her nice, safe boyfriend for a guy who just evicted her sorority sister. A guy who believed marriage to be a conspiracy against manhood, slightly one step above celibacy and possibly more tortuous.

ABSURDISM IN THE TIME OF WANT

Ten o'clock. Smoking a joint, head-nodding to some konpa I borrowed from my oldest sister. When the bell rung, I could not believe it. At first, the sound, a two-second double buzz hit me wrong. I could not believe Lauren's audacity to show up without warning, especially after she hung up on me. Another part of me remembered the true her, the one I never saw as prey, and who never saw me that way. Everything about me lit up because I needed a woman. I needed her. The place smelled like weed. I quickly reasoned she knew I got high. She never saw me blazing, but word traveled. I ran to the bathroom to wash my face and rinse with some mouthwash so I could give her the biggest kiss, caress her and talk to her.

The buzzer again.

I didn't even bother to use the intercom, to ask who. I just buzzed her into the building. I stood by the door and waited. I could hear the clatter of heels coming up the steps and making the turn to my door. The bell chimed. I waited a second and opened it. The thoughts popped to the front of my head, but in situations where one's caught off-guard, I learned to remain quiet.

She spoke in that melodic voice that alternated between being pleasant and annoying. At that moment, I was not in the mood. "You look surprised but you are not saying anything. It's like you expected to see someone but not me. Coming up the stairs I swore your first question would be 'Bliss, what are you doing here'?" She said this as she walked into the apartment, taking off her coat and sizing up a comfortable place to put it.

"I try not to do what is expected of me."

With her coat off, I looked at her outfit and placed two mental images in my head: her launching point, and her destination. Bliss wore a sheer, actually see-through silk dress that, when hit by the light at certain angles, revealed everything since she wore no undergarments. "Where are you coming from?"

"Manhattan." My pause let her know I needed more information. I waited. "Attitude gave me your address."

That last sentence cleared her to stay because no one except other MAX boys or my nuclear family knew where I lived. "Did he also give you my phone number?"

"If you are expecting someone, I can leave."

"What about if I don't feel like having company?"

"In those situations, would you kick any of the brothers out?"

"Touché." I walked back to my place on the sofa and offered her a drink. Bliss came and sat right near me. I never heard word of her to be a nymphomaniac. Her body did not send out any vibes, except smelling good, wearing see-through clothing and sitting close to me. Bliss ignited a struggle between my manhood and my humanity. "What's up? You look sad."

"Aren't you?"

OK! That was why I never got close to Bliss. Her need to dig deep asked for no emotional connection. She kept at a distance and fired questions and ideas, as if puncturing holes into a person's argument, the shield he used to cover his weakness. "Why should I be sad?"

"Attitude is leaving tonight."

"That is why you here?"

"No. I am here because you need a woman."

The feeling of thoughts being read. Or not wearing my armor. "Why because Diane got the boot?"

"No, because you are not famous!"

"What the f..." I caught myself, realizing I could do without cussing. "Oh! I got it. This is what this is about. I heard you were or had become Attitude's muse. You have come to the wrong place. Over at Girard's might be better."

"He called me on Monday." She paused to show slight annoyance. "Wednesday. Thursday."

"What? You didn't call him back?" I held back the next thought to see how Bliss planned to play this since Girard was her protection, the one Attitude gave rank to – *a man you can trust with your wife.*

"There was no need to call back. We spoke each time he called, and he always told me when he would call."

"Then why are you not over there?"

"He has a woman. And the word on her, she's real mean."

"Nicole's back?"

"I don't think so, but he gave me the impression she might move here to be with him. He tiptoed around the rim but only one aspect seemed to stick with me though. It would be up to me to knock her out of his life."

"And?"

"Please. I am not getting killed over some man, especially one as ambitious as Girard."

A MAX boy's indoctrination forced him to constantly strive and the woman in his life must either stay out of his way or be as ruthless. "You just dissed the whole frat!"

"How?"

"You wouldn't marry a MAX boy?"

"One can never say never, but it couldn't be Girard or Attitude. They live for this."

"What, a brother gotta give up the fight to be with you?"

"Yes, in essence, to do so would be to choose peace and freedom. But, you only see it as being a coward."

"You don't know how I see it. In the same vein, Monk, a brother you've always shunned gave up the fight." I needed to know why Monk dropped line, meaning why he left the pledge program, being that his legacy goes back to the very beginning of the Society.

"I don't know Monk like that." The pace of her sentence meant she lied.

I kept at her. "He's always with Attitude, and you're A's wife." They married only in a personal vow since a public wedding never took place, but the MAX vow meant she agreed to carry a child for him, if he needed her as a last resort, to extend his legacy.

"Yeah but Monk and I have significant, fundamental differences. That's why I can say I don't know him. He gave up his legacy in the fraternity. On the one hand, some might say it's a peace offering. Or it can be seen as the start of a much bigger, deadlier war."

I got the information I needed. Now I either wanted her to leave or let me get off a good one. I grabbed a few hair strands and made eye contact with her. Bliss rolled her eyes the other way, but I pushed. "What's the matter? I can make love to you only when you want to?"

"Make love! Ah! Ernest, you're a comedian now? Is that what you considered what we did last week in Shady Side motel?" She got up and went far from me, to the dining table near the apartment's entrance. Being this far, she had to talk loud. I would eventually need to tell her to lower voice because I have neighbors. I entertained her zaniness, the way she used proper diction even when using slang. "You don't know what love is."

"You are right."

"Really? I am surprised you admitted that. Come here." I picked my drink off the coffee table and walked to her. "Tell me about your art."

"Why?"

"If we can change your art, then we can change your heart."

"I don't tell people about my art. I let them see it and make up their own minds." She simply shrugged her shoulders. "Oh that's it! Attitude told you about his art and you fell in love."

"In love? You are a real comedian. We were not in love. There was a challenge."

She stopped and said no more. I did not let her off that easy. "Who won?"

"Monk officiated. He said I won."

"If so, why do you look so sad?"

"I don't like the prize. I realized they did a flipside maneuver on me. His ambition. Having spent time with him. To sleep next to him. Internalize him. I feel dark." She paused and looked in my eyes. "Do I scare you?"

"No." I lied.

"Really?" She turned her head to the side, to get a different angle on my eyes. "I think I scare a lot of people, even some of the MAX boys."

I tested her honesty the way one administered a polygraph. Everything stated before led up to this question. "Do you think Girard is scared of you?"

"Yes. Why else would he have called me the next day after some cheap, scandalous motel sex? MAX boys don't call the next day. Isn't that your M.O.? You didn't call me the next day." She paused, giving me room to interject. I didn't. Bliss picked up my freehand, my left and kissed my palm. "I like that about you."

She passed my test.

When a man got a feeling, it was sometimes a slow process. Even when it came suddenly and he felt the rush of blood, he anticipated the feeling. I do not lose a feeling. Time passed and the feeling faded, but one did not lose the feeling. That moment I sensed myself losing the feeling. Immediately.

It was okay though. It felt different to be sitting on a Friday night with a woman I had no biological link and not feeling like she had to let me get one off, or go home. I wanted Bliss to stay so I offered her a smoke, a drink, some food, but she turned it all down. She asked for something I try not to share with women.

Diane became the first woman who validated my art. It happened before either of us started our respective pledge process. I needed someone to fully understand my search, in case I died or did not finish the process since not becoming a MAX boy would have been akin to death. To forever walk around after having bared your soul and leave it behind, how then could I consider myself an artist?

A tough chick, around the way girl, total dime piece; the one you imagined with your eyes open then acted a fool the moment you did set eyes on her, Diane became my confidant because all other chicks I met up to that point in my life, they came looking for what's missing, basically their father or their last boyfriend or baby's daddy. Diane quickly understood my art represented my gain, not someone's loss. And, no one, no man, no woman understood this; not the professors, fellow students nor friends.

I needed Bliss to understand but it was too soon. Though she carried herself as multi-faceted and could express her shortcomings, I wondered whether she appreciated the same from others. "How come you didn't come to Attitude's closing tonight?"

"He didn't invite me."

"Come better!"

"I know I could have come without an official invite, but I stopped by two weeks ago during the day and saw the exhibit. I already gave him my kudos."

"You say it like you didn't think it was all that."

I gave another test, this one to rankle her sensibilities. "His art is pop, as in soda, the taste is decent but it's really all sugar, fluff. It's the sort of stuff white folks support because it reinforces their beliefs about Blacks. The superfluous bull where Blacks are shown as being stuck in their environment, interacting only with each other; and when they do come face to face with what is deemed as the powers-that-be, race is treated as a crime that has victims but no culprit."

She put her hand up for a high-five. As I shot my hand out to connect with hers, she moved her hand and said, "Syke!!!" In a way I had to give her credit for not agreeing with me because I only criticized the surface level of Attitude's art. Beneath the surface, in his case, this current exhibit *Voices from the Margin,* the top layer was the setup. True, he had to explain it to Girard and me, early in its development, and I doubted he would tell Bliss. Strangely enough after he developed and made it more transparent, some people saw it, but many did not. Bliss knew there exited something else, and to probably appease her nagging, he obviously did use her as his muse, but only for the surface. No way, he would have told her the messages encoded, on how and where the money got moved. "Actually you are correct about the surface. What got me was how he drew the lines."

I nodded. Bliss had a good eye, and probably a good ear, one waiting for me to add more. I did not.

We talked until four in the morning, about nothing in particular. As I played CDs in random, I lit joints and downed a few more drinks. Eventually she took a few puffs and fixed a drink or two. She proved to be more than kool company, so I offered to sleep on the couch. "I can't put you out of your bed."

"It's OK. I wouldn't feel right leaving you out here on the sofa."

"I'm not sleeping on the sofa. I am sleeping in the bed with you."

"Don't push it!" She simply laughed and followed me into the bathroom. As I brushed, she squeezed the toothpaste onto her right index finger. She brushed using the index and the middle. "You are way too much."

We finished and headed into the bedroom. As I looked for a pair of my smallest shorts and T-shirt, I turned and got a good look at her. Last week the motel had been poorly lit, and all I could really see were her curves. Bliss sported the lithe body of a dancer, complete with revolutionary titties that stood on edge as if pointing forward to a brighter day ahead. She threw me a fake smile, to say stop staring. I handed her the clothes. "I don't need those. I am comfortable sleeping in the nude."

"I don't sleep in the nude. And, we're playing by house rules." She put them on and went to the mirror, making a face to show her displeasure in having to wear the oversized gym clothes. I turned off the light and she ran and jumped to my side of the bed. I rolled her over and she responded by giggling. "That's my side."

I lied with my back to her. I normally faced the other way, away from the light in the backyard where four-feet high fences separated connected lots. Some of them had gardens made by hobbyists beautifying what they came to accept as their dream homes. Though not the property's owner, they staked claim to their rented apartments though the neighborhood, block and yards separating the two blocks, stray dogs howling, cats in heat had long been run over by double parked cars, blaring horns and the drug trade. Bliss, who should have been back to back with me and as sleepy, now pressed against me. She still wore the gym clothes, but her forehead bounced softly, rhythmically against my shoulder. Her right arm slid across my right rib and her palm rubbed my stomach. First my stomach then it wandered down a bit, and I knew where this would head. She slipped her had through the side of my shorts, slowly working me up. "I am surprised you're soft. Have you been soft all night?" I rolled over to my back, as if to say I give up, do what you want. She took her hand out of my shorts and tapped me on the chest. "OK. You can sleep but tomorrow, technically later today, you're giving me some dick."

"You're crazy."

"No I'm not."

She placed a soft peck on my lips.

That night of sleep emerged as the best one of the week. All week I battled this feeling of being alone.

>=<

That Saturday morning I did not feel alone, but I was. The lack of noise coming from the outer rooms reverberated to somewhere in the back of my mind where the thought of Bliss in the kitchen making breakfast became a quick and fading one since Bliss did not look or act like the cooking type. I reasoned her departure to be a good thing. As we fell asleep, it sounded so natural when she talked of later today. Normally I would not let some chick make that sort of decision, to plan my day like she bought a stake in my affairs. Bliss progressed from being just some random chick grouped with some others to help us during the pledge process. For a few hours, she stood solo when the others quit. Then she became the recruiter and leader of twenty women who proved to be the kind anyone would want by her or his side when things got tough. Yet somehow MAX boys rarely dated or married one of the little sisters. It basically came down to how well they knew us; and for us, what we had put them through in order for us to get by.

But Bliss was here.

She knocked on the door even though the bell worked. She carried various bags and wore the clothes she had slept in under her coat. "Did you get locked out? Where you coming from?"

"Let's see. I went to my car to get my bag then decided to keep walking and go get breakfast. This is a real interesting neighborhood…"

"OK, Bliss. It's eleven in the morning. Let's work our way up to full conversation."

"Well you have to catch up. I have been up since seven. First, I lay there quietly even though you were snoring up a storm. Then, around nine, I decided to go get my clothes. I have been walking around since then, hoping you would be up when I got back. But just in case, I didn't ring the bell."

I went into the kitchen to get plates for the breakfast she bought from one of the local luncheonettes. "How'd you get into the building?"

"Mrs. Leland from 1F let me in."

"You rang her bell?" Though a small building, neighbors stayed as strangers to me. I didn't even know her name.

"Yes, I saw her as I left and introduced myself. She told me to ring her bell when I got back. She even gave me an errand to run."

"You what? You introduced yourself. I don't even know that woman."

"She knows you by name. Let's see how it started. As I was leaving she said hello. So I said, Hi I'm Bliss. She asked, Who are you visiting, Ernest? He's the only guy in the building I can see you with. She just kept talking and even said, I'm glad he got rid of the other girl. You're much better for him."

"She didn't say that."

"Yes, she did." We went and sat at the dining table. "I think she got a little crush on you."

"Oh please, Bliss. You need to stop. That woman's like 60 years old."

"She's 67 and has lived in this building for 43 years. Her husband died a few years ago. She doesn't seem lonely in the needy sense, but I think she could use some manly attention."

"What? Please stop! I am trying to eat."

"What's the matter, old ladies can't get any?" I ignored her, but Bliss being Bliss she continued. Chick never stopped talking. "I mean when you are married and that age, you're not going to have sex?"

"I am not getting married. My sex life is too important to entrust to just one woman."

"I didn't know you didn't want kids. For some reason, I saw you as the family type."

"Oh, I'm having kids, lots of them."

"Out of wedlock? I guess we're different in that aspect." She took a bite. "I want the marriage and the love that turns into friendship. But no kids for me. The way I see it if there were no kids, we would never get old."

It was too early in the morning to have that debate. "Food's good, right?"

"So! How're you going to do it?" My face drew a blank so she added, "Hook Mrs. Leland up!"

"You are really crazy." I said it with no malice intended.

"No, I am not and stop saying that!"

"That woman has grandkids older than me. I've seen them come visit."

"How do you think she was able to have grandkids? By having kids. By having sex."

"Which you do not want."

"Let's see. She had me buy sugar, fruits and cereal. So all you have to do is stop by one night and tell her you ran out of sugar."

"Are you for real? You want me to go ask that little old lady for sex?"

Bliss looked mortified. "No! Of course not! You know better than that. Never rush a grown woman. After you ring the bell, it's up to her to ask you to come in, and let her take charge."

"You are crazy."

Her mood changed to a rage that would scare most people. She flipped not totally, the way one makes pancakes, more like an omelet turned to its side. "You call me crazy again, I will smash you upside the head with this glass."

It took less than a second for what she said to register. I gave Bliss my mother's look and shook my head. "You're crazy but not that crazy."

She held the glass for a moment then slowly placed it down. "I'm sorry."

I got up from the table to bring the plates into the kitchen. I planted a soft kiss on the forehead. "Sorry, baby. I was just playing with you. Promise I won't say it ever again. Okay?"

"Okay." She puckered and I bent over to meet her lips.

Though I offered her a subway ride into Manhattan, the early morning walk peaked Bliss's interest of my neighborhood. She asked questions about things I took for granted from having lived there most of my life. After a short bus ride to get us to the heart of it all, we walked nearly a third of Flatbush Avenue. One of Brooklyn's main thoroughfares, Flatbush Avenue ran from the Manhattan Bridge up to the Belt Parkway, a good 12 miles. We focused on the stretch from Prospect Park to Flabush-Nostrand Junction. The Caribbean folks controlled the food trade while other nationalities balanced out the other shops. The avenue's congestion stemmed from shoppers looking for clothes, household supplies, and residents simply milling about.

Bliss showed me a different side of her personality. She no longer had an opinion and explanation for everything. She took on the role of student, letting my voice be her guide as to what I deemed important, and asking questions only to get a deeper sense of what she saw and not rhetorical ones. She wondered about the life of the people as they moved, their accents pronounced as if they had never left their islands, simply moved the culture to a safer or more prosperous place. I could feel her adjusting to the various accents she heard and glances the people gave her. She wanted to know about roti, grios, ackie. She blended yet still stood out, not because of appearance; the way her head turned and fingers pointed obviously screamed tourist. The casual steps gave hint she wanted to camouflage herself to allow people to carry on without her stare. The walk took three hours because of our constant stops. Somewhere during our conversation she got me to agree on us going to three vacations - a Caribbean cruise, a trip to Haiti, and a month-long tour of Africa. All things already on my agenda, so I didn't mind letting her join me. She asked why I quit the team and whether I still thought I could make the NBA. I didn't really go into either but I did say that I could make the league if I focused for a year, did grad school at a top university to use my last year of eligibility.

"Do you plan to?"

"Nah, it's really about my art."

"Is it that good?"

"I have never not been good at anything in life. But, with art being so subjective, it's really up to me how I define success." We rode the bus back toward home, even though Bliss was game to walk back, possibly explore a different avenue. Her boundless energy and fitness surprised me. She attributed stamina and mental strength to not tire to years of playing sports, taking music lessons and dance classes. As the youngest child, she lived the burden of fulfilling both parents' vision of what their child would be when the older sister bailed early on all of thier lofty expectations. We admitted, at least for this juncture of our lives, to forego other people's expectations and be ourselves.

"Most of all I want to be free," Bliss said.

"I am not sure I'm willing to pay that price."

"Isn't that why you chose the arts over sports?"

I simply laughed and rang the bell for the bus driver to stop. Darkness came slowly. The food-related stores were still open. The night maintained the same coolness as the day but without the sun one could feel winter trying to barge its way into autumn's domain. I put some left-over rice in a large pot and reheated it, stove-top. Bliss ran cold water over two plates and dried them with a kitchen towel. Slowly I began gazing a different her. Perhaps the house rules influenced her to meet my expectations. Either way it felt good having her there. She didn't enjoy the jerk chicken as much as I anticipated. The peppery spice took some getting used to, but only if one already enjoyed spicy food. As she cleared the table to wash the dishes, I went to my bedroom's closet for my personal portfolio. The antithesis of the portfolio I developed in Barrington's classrooms, some of the pieces lined the apartment's walls; no one, including Diane, knew I had done them. Those sketches were traditional sketches with the abstract message buried so deep, unless a person knew I created them, they would not know where to look. With the signature different from those I did for school and work, and even my personal portfolio; with the signature being EARL in cursive script, how could they know unless, they thought deeply and knew my full name: Ernest Andre Roland LeGagneur.

My personal portfolio veered far from traditional, industrial and not just because I developed the pieces without the school's technical limits in mind. I got great grades doing what they thought I would not be able to do, but I never took it too far, by delving into a deep study of century old masters. I studied enough and followed the guidelines to say I could do this. In turn, at times, the professors inflated my grade, as if buying into their myth of the limitations they placed on me. Though I never politicked with my classmates, I hung on their scene enough to see how their original styles showed the clash between their aesthetics and their political correctness. That told me they were either cheating themselves or each had a hidden, personal portfolio.

Mine was crowded. A black soft cover binder, yet very sturdy, I started compiling the pieces two years ago. Some pieces I created as far back as my last semester in high school, back in February 1987 when I knew I could have more impact with my art than my jump shot.

The portfolio did not impress Bliss. She breezed through the pieces as if searching for something specific. Her confusion would not allow her to be in awe. Then she went back and discussed each piece. Her dead-on critique of each, starting with the first to the very last; each piece seemed to counter everything her upbringing led her to believe and everything she hoped to achieve. "You've fallen into the trap society sets for smart Blacks. Your art says it all. Whereas a soothing touch here and there could transform Attitude to Davenport, yours is a lost cause. You believe winner takes all. You will never be famous and make enough money to live on. That is unless you are willing to start completely over."

I laughed because she talked of death, not physical, but stopping midstream in the middle of the passage. "Now you see why I didn't want to show you my work?"

"Seriously Ernest, as artists, you both believe in solid straight lines. Whereas Davenport's extends to the edge of the canvas or the preset margins, yours end short and form a maze." She pointed to a piece I created while pledging. "I see how you did this one. Afterward you placed the color and images on top of the lines yet within the confines of the boxes. That alone could be accepted and buyers would say OK and part with their money. But the kicker is how you show that the maze has many exits. That is really messed up, to say the people want to be trapped or boxed in."

Though she referred to him as Davenport, like other citizens of the art world had recently started, she really understood Attitude's *Voices from the Margin* series. OK she had spent enough time with him! But to look at my stuff and bang: clearly decipher it! I didn't care she did not like it for whatever reason. But no way she could have scoped the methodology so quickly.

Bliss was not who she claimed, in that the stuff she knew, she did not acquire them naturally. The information came either via theft or some other source or person. I camouflaged my suspicions, the fences I normally put up. "You just don't get it."

She continued, "Even if it were the truth, no one would admit to it. Everyone believes in their own sanctity, in that he or she is walking a straight line with only one ending."

"Do you?"

"Yes, being here with you, at this point in time is my destiny. And, even when we physically no longer see each other, the line that connects us continues and extends to the margins, even past them, even if we are walking in opposite directions."

"What about when we turn? We form a box."

"We do not turn. We never turn our backs on each other."

"Then how are boxes made?" I thought of Bliss's friendship with Diane but I never explained the ideology to Diane. How could Bliss know? That eventually we turn our backs on each other. "Then I guess I will have to die for you to show you that we eventually do turn our backs on each other."

"No, Ernest. I need you to live. I need to live. I need to be free. Don't box me in!"

I always felt that art should be like a punch in the mouth. It was meant to wake sleepers. Those who were not asleep would have to fight back. Swing punches! Call me names! Do whatever but fight back, but Bliss no longer wanted to fight. I went for the jugular. "White people are too free."

She responded. "Everybody's death is a suicide."

"Never judge Black at face value."

I might have saved Bliss's life right there by telling her my suspicions. But, I realized we were in different places, some sort of theater of the absurd. Our lines had intersected and we now traveled in different directions.

"Art is a mask. Making love is the only reality."

I gave her my standard line, the one I use when I was about to sleep with a woman I felt could trap me in a long-term relationship. "I want nothing past intimacy."

"Do you think I am lonely or lovely?"

Seeing Bliss like this brought forth an image of writing in your journal, and seeing your favorite pen bleeding all over the page, the words forming with smears and the ink on your hand. Heaven forbids the ink was blood red. "Today's man needs yesterday's woman. Today's women need each other."

"I need you like today was January 27th, and you were the first day of spring." And I tried to desperately make it there, to reach Bliss. But she got up. Her rise seemed rapid, because she had not been moving - still like a statue in front of a museum, the ones with legs and feet but no arms. Using the remote, she simply pressed play on the stereo. Still on random, the CD changer played something from my classical mix. Bliss started twirling. To me, the untrained eye, her form seemed perfect, like the ballerina I saw during an eighth grade school excursion. In this case, my living room served as the stage and the side windows overlooking the walkway to the courtyard provided the spotlight for the soloist. She seemed to be recalling a happy moment in her life, perhaps when she felt the most free. True to herself, the clothes had to be peeled off, to the rhythm and pattern of the ballet. Though she undressed, she emitted no sensuality. As she undressed she came closer to me, but this was not a sexual exposition. Something had come over her and she had to free herself of it. I think it was, free herself of me.

The song ended and I carried Bliss to my bed. I undressed her and then myself. We lied nude, on our backs in a brightly lit room and looking up at the ceiling. Her voice, soft, but not apologetic, confessed, "I did it for you. I am the reason Lucille broke up with Devon. Something I call the 'breakup to hook up'. It's where I breakup a couple then place one of them with a person he or she is best suited for. I did it because the way Devon got her right before you. It had to have been a setup. You know Lucille still talks about you. Her tone always shows the remorse."

Various emotions ran through me but I had to deal with what rested near me: Bliss in a vulnerable state. My art exposed her to the reality that I was not the man she thought. I had a real dark side, filled with naked ambition and could get dirty with the best of them. But tonight could not be the time for her to learn that perhaps my dark side was my norm, my only side.

Lucille continually dreamt of me? I wanted to tell Bliss that I had come to view Lucille as one of those women who liked a man who put his foot down, even if it landed on her neck. But Bliss did not want that, and I loved her for that. I would never treat her like that, unless she became one of those women who could not understand that it was ok for their husbands to dream of becoming an old man on the corner, or playing cards or dominos inside or in front of the barber shop that his friend owned. Not every man wanted to be a baller, a big shot. I agree that a young man playing the corner soon became a mural emblazed with the letters R.I.P. At the same time, a young man gotta blaze new trails even if it looked like he was only chasing tails, his and others.

It hurt me for her to think of my life as an exercise in futility. Mine and all the other MAX boys. Bliss may have Sight and Sound, but she didn't have a dick, therefore I could lie next to her and lie to her face that I would accept her plea and take on her stupid mission and date my brother's ex who would ultimately go back into his bed. Yet, he would never wife her, would only sex her until she just turned into a rag doll with holes a man tells tales of when boredom replaced want. Years later, in sorrow admitted only in dark rooms over a brew and a smoke, when two people were alone, he and I would sing the hymn – *Lucille was a good girl.*

UNTITLED

The next morning I woke to an empty feeling in the room but not in my heart, for I loved Bliss. I really did. But, just as she came, Bliss vanished. She called that afternoon to let me know she made it back to Connecticut safely. For the next few weeks, we called but made no plans to see each other. She left messages but I did not. Though she lived with her parents, she had her own phone in what she often referred to as this big old house. Those frequent pronunciations extended unspoken invitations. We played this mind game, and I knew what I had to do to make it stop.

A Thursday night in November, a week before Thanksgiving, I passed on my favorite gym night. Normally I didn't get home until after 10 p.m. After not seeing Bliss for four weeks, I skipped the gym and instead bought flowers for a lovely woman. Mrs. Leland flashed a beautiful smile that even dentures couldn't erode because she had a cute little mouth. She grabbed the flowers with her left, simultaneously thanking me and guiding me inside her apartment, by grabbing my left hand with her right. The apartment smelled of wood cleaner on antique furniture and barbecue chicken. I planned to only bring the flowers, make small talk and head upstairs for a quick workout of light weights, pushups and sit-ups. She had a different idea. First, she showed me her albums, from childbirth to grandchildren, all the while holding the same baseline of her heyday. She played piano, classical and jazz, and had recorded on several albums. Knowing the music to be more a labor of love and not something she would jump hurdles to make a living, she got a civil service job with the city. She retired a few years back. She could tell I enjoyed her company and the trip down memory lane so she invited me to stay for dinner. Before I had a chance to say yes, she added "Do you have any smoke? I could use a nice buzz before dinner."

I didn't even try to suppress my laughter. "I have some upstairs."

"OK, go get it. I will fix our plates." We smoked over Coltrane and ate over Afro-Cuban drums. "That was some real good weed. Who's your pusher? I need to tell my grandson because the stuff he brings me is garbage. He was supposed to come by but I think some young girl got him open, or it might be the other way around." She laughed, openly, bringing it from deep enough to let joy-filled tears bubble in her eyes. The laugh seemed to fade away the creases near her eyes as if time raced backwards, bringing her appearance closer to the picture atop the piano. The weed and good food talked and moved my thoughts pleasantly to where I could accept the life a woman such as Mrs. Leland could bring. I told her where to get the good smoke and she said she tried that place and they told her that they didn't sell.

We both agreed to my words. "That's what it's like being a senior citizen. They probably think you're with the neighborhood patrol."

It neared eleven o'clock and I realized I didn't need to make up some lame excuse to leave. I had stayed long and truly enjoyed myself. She resisted to my wanting to leave her the rest of the twenty sack, so we compromised that I roll her a couple of joints. She gave me a grandmotherly hug and we thanked each other for a wonderful night. I didn't even bother to call Bliss. Mrs. Leland would do that.

The next day work was work even though the coworkers and I had long moved past just quick greetings. We now traversed office politics over occasional drinks after work. I rarely went to the gym on Fridays as I viewed it as something losers with no prospects or social life did. I entered to a crowded main lobby. Every room filled with people sweating out a week of work, from weights, aerobics, racquetball up to the basketball courts. Unlike Thursdays, the competition was only average so I used the time to work on my passing and practicing defensive strategies.

I got home and had no messages on my phone. Good.

I thought of knocking on Mrs. LeLand's door, just to chat and have someone to share my assistance but it was after ten o'clock. Since sex with Bliss weeks back, my only hookups had been with the two chicks who served as my bench these past few months. They both had boyfriends so I left it up to them to let me know of their free time.

It felt weird being alone. I knew of the fellas' plans and I contemplated catching up with them. Instead I settled back into the zone I inhabited since Diane moved out. I enjoyed being home in the middle of a restless city; being still while others emphatically searched for a diversion. I knew I could get to like that unattached status. I sparked a joint, kept the stereo to a medium level and reviewed my newly-created art work.

At eleven the next morning, I heard a knock on the door. It could be no other than Bliss. We kissed like lost lovers, trying to swallow each other whole. I missed everything about her, particularly her. Breath. Her voice. It radiated with the exuberance of a soul discovering a new musical chord. "I brought a six pack instead of food 'cause I'm sure you have food in the fridge."

I motioned for her to lower her voice. "I'm not up yet."

"Man, you need to wake up earlier. I have been downstairs for nearly two hours with Mrs. Leland. She thinks you are wonderful." After going to the fridge to put away the beers, she followed me to the bedroom. Undressed. In bed. On me.

In between, we ate and I drank beer. She said that her body didn't feel right these past few weeks and she wouldn't be joining in smoking or drinking. "Is that OK?"

"Of course. I prefer it that way."

"When are you going to stop?"

I nearly choked on the beer that went down the wrong pipe.

Bliss had a plan, a platform she stood on, and the next day, Sunday around seven o'clock as she prepared to leave, I leaned against the closet door, near the room's entrance. The closet is where I kept my secrets. Art.

Guns. Nude pictures of some of the women I had been with; all flicks taken voluntarily, of course. Some of the images were quite graphic. I just kept staring at Bliss, trying to figure out how long she would be gone this time, wondering why she felt she had to leave. "When is lunch with Lucille?"

I evaded Bliss's question because I did not know if she was bluffing. Though she probably got the information through the grapevine, Bliss knew our personal history. By our, I mean Lucille and me.

>=<

I made lunch plans with Lucille and we shared a near moment of passion but it did not feel right to either of us so we stopped. Instead of letting myself go through absolute withdrawal, I fed my binges with the other two women. Since their mental makeup varied from Bliss, conversations with Mrs. Leland brought me to the amplitude where Bliss resided. She spoke glowingly of Bliss, yet she never hinted that Bliss and I would end up together.

I adjusted to only receiving an occasional phone call from Bliss because I grasped the emotional toll our union took on us. My art developed along the lines it had veered before Diane moved out. Bliss sought to change this but her meddling and hints forced me to dig deeper and enhance the transparency of my message; that, she feared.

Days passed and life became blissful. Though she stayed away, I felt her presence in every step I took, each breath, each thought. I wondered if she lived the same. Of all the women who could have helped me rebound, Bliss helped me move forward and not look to the past in a way that had me walking New York City and not looking to bump my shoulders hard into someone. Not looking to shoot down a coworker's idea, no matter how poor. She reconstructed me into a man with deep convictions about love and peace. One where deep inside I no longer feared the hurt of not wanting anything past intimacy, and no longer yearned for the need to be alone. As if sensing, perhaps mistaking her symbolic gesture, her act of self-sacrifice, the essence of MAX becoming a reality, no more than two sentences into my phone call to her, Bliss began rambling about her first and only true love, Frank DeLoose.

She still dreamed, believed, better yet knew they could be together. I took no offense, experienced no hurt to know she had moved on, nor doubted she'd ever been here with me. She really meant everything she had said and done. I was just sorry to have never bowed to the queen. To that she just laughed and replied, "You will have your chance." To confirm that our love lived on various planes, she rambled an idle thought to start a fight, not a war, to test how far she had moved me. "There's nothing about a man's makeup that says he cannot be monogamous."

I chuckled. "When is the last time you took a biology course?"

"As humans, we have surpassed our biological limitations. That is our advantage over most animals." We paused at the same time. My quietness because she had dug a hole, totally countering the MAX code of life. Now we waited to see which one of us would jump in. She continued, "We don't have sex to simply reproduce. For humans, sex has become an emotional link. And, a woman's emotional makeup with its complexities dictates that she can love many men within a confined period or over a lifetime, and still keep them feeling loved. The average man cannot do that for women. When he tries to, for lack of a better word, to juggle women, he invariably drops the ball. He then leaves behind a lot of emotionally damaged women - women who then go on to hurt others, men and women. That is why you have to stop being a ho."

OK, she shifted from talking at empty spaces, transmitting other people's words, to challenging me. Bliss had a calling, but no matter its mission, she needed to be pushed back. "I never said I was a ho. I am a lover." I paused long enough to give her a chance to correct herself. Again, I knew this could not be how Bliss felt about me. But, if someone did and that person had declared war on me, Bliss needed to take a side, my side. "So, that's what you walked into my life thinking? That I was some kind of cheap trick?"

Bliss remained silent. And, the feeling I once harbored for her disappeared.

Feeling more exposed and vulnerable than ever, my job and art helped to bury the emptiness threatening to consume me. It would have been easy for me to give up what I always fought for: Choice. And, Paulette was choice. To an unobserving eye, she could be seen as a safe girl to have, not affiliated with any side, anything. Yet she epitomized the most dangerous avenue I could take. Whereas other women in my life knew so much about me, they in essence served as guards protecting my kingdom. When Paulette looked at my album and listened to the short stories that made up my life, she drew no quick conclusions, nor tried to push me in any particular direction. I had never been one of those men who wanted a sister only because she stayed out of a brother's path. Paulette was not that nor did she function as an obstacle. On our first date she spread her truth like an open road I could take and wherever I ended up would be my destination. Her presence in my life became a secret. Same as my art, most friends knew of her but had never met her. They could bump into her at the local store and not make the connection. And, in the future, after our bond had fully developed and when being introduced, each party would smile, search their memory but never recall the place and time, where they had seen each other.

>=<

With her in my life time flew by, regaling us to the role of stationary objects, mere light poles on a highway, helping cars speed by. The greater scheme no longer mattered to us. On a Thursday night when in the past I would be with the boys, we were at home, playing dominos, and the bell rang. Her intuition and eyes said she knew a woman had come knocking, a challenger who felt comfortable enough to do so without calling first.. Early on Paulette asked whether she would be occupying another woman's space because my apartment felt like a woman lived or used to live there. I understood the question and told her about Diane without stating the exact reason she left. Paulette was the only one I entertained at my place. All the others I used one of the apartments MAX boys paid dues for, in order to have sexual escapades without complicating our personal lives; no one actually lived in those places. They were just places for parties, poker and poking.

Paulette's calls always came at hours she obviously slated for herself, what could be deemed safe hours. Something about me obviously gave out the vibe that I got around. Eventually I planned to confront her but then Bliss rang the bell, as if it was the most normal thing, to show up at eleven o'clock at night unannounced.

Fully expecting me to be alone, Bliss stepped into the apartment without hugging me. Something had excited her but then she stopped like she got hit by cold water. There existed a contrast between the two, and it only took them five seconds to get over it. Though no sense of fear or distrust came, I got a glimpse of the sisterly bond that women shared, and why it often betrayed them. Wrapped in a crème bed sheet and fighting to keep her embarrassment from communicating the wrong idea, Bliss turned to me and said, "I'm sorry I did not know you had company."

"Family is never company." I put my arm around her shoulder and we walked to where Paulette sat. After the initial greeting and conversation, I asked, "Where are you coming from and where are your clothes?"

Then, for the next hour, Bliss recounted her date with her first true love. Her sheer joy of them making plans to marry carried her into the streets, and I was the first person she could think to tell. The notion of marriage brought a euphoric state over them. Paulette ushered her into the bedroom to find her a t-shirt, boxers, long crewneck shirt and sweat pants to wear. When they came back, Bliss recounted how we had attended neighboring colleges, and how we became family. Paulette explained how we met a few months back at a food court near my job. The question still hung between them and I felt perhaps my presence in the room did not leave enough room for them to maneuver and ask it. "While you two talk, I think I will head to bed."

"Oh! Again I'm sorry. I have to be heading home," Bliss excused herself.

Paulette said, "Bliss, you don't have to leave. Stay, we can hangout all night."

"OK, but I have to call and leave a message so the school can have a substitute ready for my third graders."

Then it dawned on me. "Bliss, does Frank know you're here?"

"No. I left when he went to the store. I will call him after the weekend."

One could never separate Bliss's silliness from her cunningness. Neither could she. Tonight was not the time to start but I knew soon I would have to sit her down and explain how her zaniness sabotaged relationships.

Hours later, I heard giggling coming from the front room. The clock showed three-thirty in the morning. As I stepped out of the room, I smelled the weed. Those two rolled a skinny, poorly shaped joint and each had a glass of booze near her left knee. The joint hung loosely between Paulette's lips. They were playing one of those patty-cake hand-slapping games and continued moving fast even after noticing my presence. "Do you know what time it is? Aren't you going to work tomorrow?"

Paulette replied, "No. I am taking your advice and finally taking a day off. I'm calling in sick." Coupled, the two of them were doing things that alone they would not do. They stopped so Bliss could take the joint, and each sipped her drink. "You should take the day off also."

"No, I have a project to finish." At that I headed back to the bedroom, thinking how each infused a part of her carefree attitude into the other, I added, "Keep it down so I can sleep."

I barely made it under the covers when without turning on the lights, I heard their giggles near me. "Slide over to the middle. I am sleeping on your side of the bed tonight."

"P, stop. I have to get some sleep. You sleep in the middle."

Then Bliss interjected, making it clear Paulette had asked the question and felt comfortable with my history with Bliss. "I thought your manly ways could hold us together."

Paulette concurred, "Yeah, Ernest, get in the middle." I slid to the middle and turned my back to Bliss, thinking Paulette would have her back to me, but she faced me, sandwiching me. Her hands were cold but not enough for me to push them off. She rubbed my stomach then her left hand went below. Her mouth stole quick breaths from mine and alternately blew into my mouth. As I reached the edge, she asked "How is that?"

Hearing my sound, Bliss said, "Damn, girl you've got skills!"

At that Paulette giggled and rubbed the sperm in her right palm onto my stomach, pushing me on my back, slowly rolling me until I faced Bliss. That turned into the breaking point and I realized the best thing to do was fake a snore.

They laughed.

When the alarm sounded neither budged. I had slept on my back and awoke seeing each of them with an arm across my body. I felt their hands on me throughout the night, caressing just to soothe, massage a little; with the interesting points being when their hands grazed against the other's that they quickly pulled away.

Work that day breezed by. I made my in-house presentation for the design part of what would be the largest account the firm ever won. The faces smiled and some sat with their mouths open. It had been over a year since my hire, and since that time, the company hired three other Black employees. Though none of us worked on the same floor or department, we knew of each other's presence. The dude was kool. I invited him as a guest at my gym a few times and eventually we discovered that one person, the one degree of separation.

The older woman played the role of serious sister. We shared a taxi after a company gathering one night. She never smiled until away from the office and other workers. From that point, her biting sense of humor chewed everything, making it fodder for inspection: her coworkers, her marriage of nearly thirty years, her two children and most of all her husband.

The last person remained a mystery, and I understood why. As a young Black woman, she did not want to give the wrong impression. I didn't pick up on it right away, not until I asked her to lunch and she quickly said no, even though she had to sense I only wanted to provide myself as a workplace ally.

As fate would have it, on that Friday, when my mind wondered of the mischief Bliss and Paulette conceived and if it in any way would shatter the simple peace I had found, that Bliss had found, they called my office to let me know their plans of heading out to lunch. Bliss added, "Mrs. Leland would love for you to be there."

That last giggle from Paulette confirmed that Bliss had jokes! It made me wonder why everyone, male and female, could not simply use her ways to build peaceful unions. To get to the lunch spot they selected, I had to cross Canal and Avenue of the Americas. When one driver decided he could squeeze his mid-sized sedan across the intersection, so did another. The traffic jam forced me to cross the side street and walk up Canal. I then heard a voice using my nickname from the distant past. I totally shed that name as soon as I arrived on the Barrington campus. The first article written put it in a context I thought of but never had reason to question. In those days, as far as I knew, no student got paid for playing high school ball. Of course, we got free stuff given by friends of the school. Once in a while, a rumor spread of a game being fixed.

Though a losing poorly-regarded program, Barrington still resided in the larger college sports world and to be considered a money player with the nickname, "Ern-Money!" did not sit right with me. So I approached the student reporter who wrote the profile. He fully understood and told the editor of my wish to simply be Ernest. The word got around, and by the next series of articles, both the local and national press complied.

"Yo, Ern-Money!"

"Oh snap! My man, Slick! What's up, baby!" The first to pick me for his squad in a game versus older players, Slick signaled my quick transition from boy to man. We hugged. Then I noticed the young woman accompanying him. As we let go, I said hi to her.

"You two know each other?" He smiled at the coincidence.

"Yeah, we work for the same company."

"You didn't tell me you knew Ern-Money!"

"We don't exactly know each other. I asked her to lunch but she turned me down." I threw it out there because I thought it would eventually come up later when they were alone. I could tell by her quizzical look she would have never mentioned it. I could tell by the casual comfort in which Slick leaned into her they were friends and lovers. He looked shocked. "It's nothing like that. I guess she was just representing your name properly."

Slick laughed and put his arm around her shoulders, turning her a little so she could face me. "You see this man. We go way back; that's my man forever! *We were beginners together…*" He gave me a pound. Though he kept talking, the surface telling of how we met and grew up, those words stayed with me. Slick pulled them from a song that would come years after our youth, yet recount and connect it with today's youth. AZ rapped on Nas's album, *Illmatic*:

> *Cause yeah, we were beginners in the hood as Five-Percenters*
> *But something must have got in us 'cause all of us turned to sinners.*

For most of us, being a Five-Percenter did not apply, though a few Gods and Earths lived in the neighborhood. Our crew of friends was like a United Nations summit; every country and culture had its representatives. Slick maintained a true, positive presence then and though I heard of his hard times, I could tell that he rebounded and made it through. After we talked basketball and other sports, he spoke the only remaining question, "How's the love life?"

"Great! I am with this real gem."

"I know the feeling brother." Slick placed a kiss on top of her head. "When she first told me she got a job with that company, I was definitely curious as to who kicked the door open."

"Nah, it was nothing like that. The lady in HR, Jen, is real kool!" Slick laughed and gave me a pound. I laughed too then we exchanged business cards. "Next week after work, let's do something!"

"Definitely!" We hugged our farewell. "Ern-Money be good 'cause it will always be love."

"You're right, Slick. It will always be love."

Seeing the past and how life turned out for a childhood friend made the day and work more enjoyable. After we finished reminiscing, I could not join the women for lunch and returned for the afternoon meetings. As the speakers expounded on our campaign and solidified our standing with the client, I drifted in and out, looking forward to hearing what adventures the women got into.

The apartment had the aroma of a pot luck dinner, an international concoction of the different dishes and cultures; from Mrs. Leland's southern touch, Bliss's New England seafood specialty, and Paulette's traditional Haitian flavor. Each of them gave me a big hug and kiss, with only Paulette's meeting my lips. To let me know what was known and shared, Mrs. Leland started right in, "I was telling Paulette how when I first saw her entering the building I would duck. And, each time I spoke with Bliss on the phone, I knew not to say anything, even if she brought up your name."

"It's OK Mrs. Leland I know you have my best interest at heart. I would have never put you in such an awkward position."

I rolled a bunch of joints, close to ten. We used the first set to whet our appetites. After dinner, we played cards while the stereo soothed, first with recordings on which Mrs. Leland had played piano, then with random selections from my collection of Jazz standards and konpa that Paulette brought over in previous visits. She often surprised me with music from my youth. Recordings I either had never heard or long forgotten. The hours passed and Mrs. Leland excused herself and hugged everyone good night. The thought crossed my mind instantly, and being Max, Bliss took the opportunity to make her exit, "Oh wait for me! I am walking down too."

"Oh don't leave, Bliss! We were having so much fun."

"Don't worry sis, I will see you soon. I have to get back home, tell my parents the good news and call Frank first thing Monday morning. Bliss winked at me, knowing that thought was on my mind. She hugged me and whispered, "Take care Ernest! I love this sister. Don't screw it up!"

Paulette hugged her next. "Don't worry! I will not let him."

The four of us laughed and then Mrs. Leland and Bliss were gone.

Who knew I would never see Bliss again? As family, periods pass when we did not see each other and we grew accustomed to that. The telephone calls did not come as frequently, from either side. I took this to mean her life mirrored mine, nothing but Bliss. As Paulette and I began to make plans of a life together, I first convinced her to get her own place to live. I needed to see how she lived without her parents hovering over her. My life became total peace. Until one night. A Sunday night when the doorbell rang at ten o'clock, and A Man returned to say his wife was dead.

THE WAR AT HOME

Time continued to blur but I knew it was a Sunday, one of the few Paulette chose not to come over. Shortly before ten o'clock, I turned off all the apartment's lights and lied on my bed in a pitch black state. News of Bliss's death came as a message on my answering machine. Devon's voice gave way to his anger and also his guilt. That same guilt ate at me the moment I confirmed the news with him and then Girard.

The bell in the lobby sounded, a rapid version of the two-second double buzz. I turned on a few lights and without asking for his identity, I pushed the button to let him enter the building. I had not seen him for two years, since that night in Shady Side motel. I didn't need to see him to know he had once again morphed into someone, something else. I saw Manny Davenport evolve from boy to man. Always moving to bigger and better things, he tracked his own progress by constantly changing what people called him. This served as an unofficial marker as to when a person made his acquaintance. I knew of five options: Manny, The Man, Attitude, or Davenport. In private and in MAX code, we called him A Man, or simply 'A'. He now encouraged us to call him Davenport when in public.

I heard him running up the stairs, two steps at a time and making his way to the door. I opened before he had to ring the doorbell. As soon as I closed the door, he bore into me, "What happened? I left Bliss with you."

"Where were you?" I turned my back and headed to a seat at the dining table. "And you left her with G and me!"

"I was in Switzerland, taking care of the mission she sent me."

"Bliss sent you on a mission? We don't have sisters! We don't take orders from women." I screamed to emphasize the last word, knowing full well I had gone on two missions for Bliss. Mine had been minor ones; his had taken him away for years, with no word on whether he was alive or dead. He remained silent so I could recant what I had said. I held my silence to show A Man the error of his ways, of whatever he had done by getting Bliss this involved in our MAX way of life.

We both said it at the same time. "What have I done?"

He kicked the inanimate object nearest to him. The standing lamp fell over. A metal lamp with a shade, it made a small thud and the bulb blew. Attitude went over and grabbed the smaller his two traveling bags and went into the bathroom. He closed the door but from the living room, I heard the clippers then the shower. I sat on the living room sofa, blankly staring ahead. My pulse raced. The guilt slowly left me even though I held myself responsible for Bliss's death. I connected it to Diane and my revenge at the Semline Charter ceremony; the war I declared.

As I thought of the beauty she yearned to bring into every life that came across hers, Attitude's emergence from the bathroom proved Bliss had an ugly side. We ignored this but to honor her we had to avenge her death. No longer could we hold onto the theory that we could make love not war to defeat out opponents. Attitude traveled here to cut his dread locks, shave his head bald. He shaved the beard and mustache. I had never seen him with less hair than a Caesar, a closely cropped haircut popular during the late seventies and early eighties, to resemble the helmet of Roman soldiers during Julius' reign. In recent years, he let his hair grow and lock naturally; it eventually grew past his shoulders. He also wore a thick goatee with trimmed sideburns; at the very least, he kept a thin mustache. The man before me had morphed, evolved into someone new within a thirty minute span. All because I had no answer for him. He trusted me to look after his wife. She chose Girard and me, then simply me, as Attitude knew she would. And, I failed him. I failed to protect her from herself.

"I need two soldiers to help me find Bliss's killer. Are you with me?"

"A, Bliss committed suicide. In her bedroom. That's the word!"

He stepped closer to me. "Are you with me?"

The fact he asked the question again without acknowledging mine meant he wanted to know the why of her death and not the how or at whose hands. "Yes, I'm with you."

"Do you have a number for Monk?"

"Yes, in the phone book by the phone."

He dialed a number, and hung up as if he got blocked by the answering machine. "OK! I will see you at the funeral."

"A, the funeral is not until next week."

"I know. But I can't stay here. I've got to keep on moving. They're coming after me."

"Who's the other soldier?"

His eyes asked the question whether I had forgotten or thought he had. "Who do you think?"

For him to agree to that particular MAX boy meant this would be a dangerous mission. He wanted to make people overreact to our presence. I answered, "Devon?"

At that, he grabbed his bags and left.

When a man left home and didn't return for years, we easily assume he had forgotten. But, home was not something you forget, especially since you carry it with you no matter where you went. Some carried more of it than others, but everyone carried a piece of their home throughout their life. In times of war, returning home was the only thing a soldier really had to hold him together. For A Man to come back from the war, even go A.W.O.L. when he heard his wife, the holder of his life, his legacy had died, was a feeling I could not begin to match. Bliss was not my wife nor did I make her my muse, still I felt as if I had lost my home, my life, my legacy.

The doorbell rang and since it did not have the urgent, panicky sequence, I knew Attitude had not returned. "Ernest, sorry to be ringing your bell this late. But as you know my window faces the front and I saw this angry man come and go..."

I stopped her by grabbing her hand, leading her to the dining table for a seat. A shame passed over me in having to tell her. I choked back the words as tears spilled out my eyes, followed by heavy sobbing. "Bliss is dead."

"What? Why? What happened..." Mrs. Leland gave me a blank stare to indicate she needed details. She had a right to know what I could tell, that was not considered a secret. For she loved Bliss and Bliss loved her, so she had a right to know. She already knew that love kills, and *life's a bitch and then you die...*

But she did not know that *we were beginners...turned into sinners.*

Part Three

RETURN OF THE ANGRY BLACK MAN

SOCIETY GIRL

That Sunday I did not rest, nor make it to church. Something felt wrong the night before when I stopped reading and headed to bed. Her call came at the hour when chickens crowed, and before the three little birds woke me. I showered, brushed but did not eat before rushing out my apartment. The rain never came though the grayness enveloping the Manhattan skyline made me weary, on the verge of a mild fear that if we lived in biblical times an ark would be needed for two of each creature. The suspense hinged along the lines of the clouds seemingly perched on the tip of the skyscrapers. The fall colors dissipated into a charcoal blend, nearing black, bruised like purple. The world as we knew it had ended – Ken had left Barbara.

"Hope, he left over some nonsense." Her sobs overlapped her words, sloppily conveying a misstep, one she took six years ago when she allowed herself to fall in love because of a courtship fashioned out of sentimentality, comfort and trust during a time of personal crisis. Theirs made sense on the surface because she on appearance with the half-smile at formal events, and booming laughter amongst friends; she was the girl Ken longed for when he first came to me. He and I understood behind the façade, a society girl's longevity relied on more than just a razor-sharp wit. He needed the calmness, the slow tempo behind closed doors and between the sheets. The first emergence of a raised voice, she claimed, he ran.

I listened with half an ear but with two wide open eyes on the dissolution of love when it manifested itself into an ultimatum. She needed the two rings - a diamond, a band: platinum, not a catchy song and dance; and a child or two. He needed space, a place for when he had something to ponder; much more than the studio apartment he kept even after he moved in with her. Ken kept everything, from his looks – wavy hair, café-au-lait texture, dimples, natural bright smile, chiseled body – up to his focus on career and removing any obstacle to his traveling ways. A top salesman for a budding technology company after years at a Big Six accounting firm as a consultant, Ken boxed life in terms of priorities and conquest.

By the time I arrived at her apartment, her tears no longer flowed, only trickled from eyes whose dark circumference made me ask, "When did this happen?"

Four days and the cough, sobs and dry heaves that bulldozed a woman whom I witnessed take punishment and barely wince even when her body gave, her back smashing to the floor. I never once saw her knees touch the ground. She remained flat-footed as her forehead touched her knees. To see her disheveled, going days without a shower and apologetic brought me a small, hidden joy. Still not the time to celebrate for I needed to dust her up for another battle; for the war was far from over.

Nothing Barbara said connected as to why Ken would leave her. The risk to himself was too great. I convinced her to shower as I cleaned up the apartment, all the while thinking her display had an angle. Shifty and words along that line best described her, and that's why we endured as the best of friends. Yet when dealing with her, I learned to n*ever forgo adages, old wise sayings,* just because we live in a new era: *your best friend could be your worst enemy; keep your friends close and your enemies closer.* I took a step back from her dilemma to assess the trap, if any, being lain for me. Pressing play on the stereo gave me Miles Davis' "Kind of Blue". I knew this off-hand because of my father. She knew Jazz because of Ken; his music embodied her thoughts. I checked the television and it too channeled Ken - still tuned to ESPN. The refrigerator, somewhat empty, with remnants of food, takeout and half gallon of milk on the verge of spoiling. Four days and nothing? No movement, no change, then a call to me – to say what; that she had given her live-in an ultimatum. And, after he spent the night on the sofa, she woke to find a note, and his traveling bag gone, along with some clothes and basic necessities. She called to find the phone at his studio had been disconnected. She called me because I did not do pity-parties. I did lunch, after work drinks and dinner at trendy restaurants. Crying over a man was so passé, in fact never in my repertoire – something Barbara and I always shared. So, this felt like a trap of the highest order.

She came out of the shower with the towel draped across her right shoulder. Her body still amazed me but never as much as she loved to think. I had my own body. It was just as luscious though not as voluptuous. I held my words to see if her seductive stare conveyed dominance or sorrow. Forever a hard read, I did not accept her reach and her plea for me to follow her into the bedroom. She made a move to kiss me but I turned my head to negotiate the terms. "I told you I'm seeing someone."

"Come on Hope, you've been saying this for a year. Who is he? The Invisible Man? You still have not introduced him."

"No one needs to know him but me."

Barbara brushed it off. "Fine but why does that mean you can't comfort me in my time of need? Remember that time you came to me…" She made to kiss me again. "Come on."

I moved my head. "I said, no. What is it with you? One minute you're crying over Ken. Next you want me to put myself in your bed, in the middle of your mess…"

"Oh, forget you then!"

At that moment, thinking she would turn to walk away, I balled my fist, prepared to bust her eardrum. I was seriously tired of this chick. No matter how many times I came to her rescue, she never acknowledged it with any kind of appreciation. But then she fooled me by dropping to her knees. A soft kiss to my navel. Even over the fabric, I felt the wetness of her tongue. Her forehead on my abdomen, she waited for my push-off. Frozen in the moment. Her warm hands moved under my skirt, from my knees to my thighs to my waist. The elastic on my panties, taut against my stomach, gave me another two seconds to push her away. I muttered God's name in vain then let out a faint murmur for her to stop. She looked up as both her thumbs stroked gently across my lips. Minor orgasms always made me feel like running to the bathroom. I would then realize my surroundings and give way to the moment. Spreading my legs as she simultaneously kissed and pushed up my skirt. I kept my hands to myself, holding my head, and whatever sane thoughts I still had left. We leveled ourselves onto the area rug – she on top, below my navel with her palms caressing the heaves pulsating under my silk blouse. Though I rushed to be by her side, I thought we would simply talk and be done in enough time for me to catch the late service. The glass coffee table reflected the stereo's amplifier lights, the green fluctuating as the yellow and red stayed steady. She felt no need to hide her hunger, devouring me in the open space of her living room, readying herself for the moment I would curl into a ball, the satisfaction and confusion reverting me into a childlike, feeble state. Our words merged the way Indian ink begged to form calligraphy under the fingers of adolescents, instead the pen drew blotches. We coalesced in raw form, a passion between two beauties; I a svelte five-foot-six quote-end-quote cutie pie with an hacksaw for a mind; she a towering five-nine brick-house who calculated moves in the manner of a chess master. We took slow yet careless steps into her bedroom. It smelled of musk with a tinge of lavender fighting to emerge under the unmade king size bed with four posts, clean linen. The beige light cotton fabric felt cool on my skin. The sheet confirmed Barbara spent the past few days on the sofa or living room floor. The palatable loneliness crushed any misgivings holding a flight pattern in my mind. My first ever taste of her body, down there, as I never trusted what she wanted, never yearned to have this conversation with the sound she made. Her moans, raw and heavy, let me know just how long she had waited for this moment, eight years, when we first met on TGI's campus. Her hands tried to be gentle but she wanted my face closer. In no time she shivered, then a thunderous groan led to a cool sweat on the rustic glow emanating from her skin. I made to head for the bathroom but she chuckled and kissed, no; she licked my mouth, face, neck, then bit my lip, not hard but a soft nuzzle as she looked into my eyes. The dark of her irises spoke of a love she could not utter, a passion she had held in check. I felt faint, small, worried that I could not return the sentiments she held. I needed a drink to numb the fear swirling in my head; more along the lines of a drink to feel a burn on my chest, sort of the sting rubbing alcohol ignites on an open wound.

The hours moved to the melancholic rhythm of the jazz CDs being played in sequence in the outer room. Each CD had played its full compliment, from Miles, to Budd Powell, to Cannonball Adderley, then to now where John Coltrane's greatest hits bellowed a sultriness reminiscent of a dark room, a joint, of tables for two, booths for four and high chairs at the bar where dames tilted a bit so a gent's charge could speed along. We ordered delivery, Italian dishes: linguine with clam sauce topped with calamari; and vegetable lasagna. She wanted richness but without the extra weight. I loved variety, spice and the unfamiliar. I loved the Society, while she inched out of it, thinking I had not picked up on her slow steps. Tonight a different side of her emerged. She had skipped a beat. I ordered wine to further mellow me as the lovemaking though slow, melodic and having reached a crescendo above eighty beats per minute had steadied the way top marathon runners glided across urban landscapes. The rain fell in drizzles, un-momentous, not disturbing the groove. Slight raps against the windows then it would straighten out whenever it got heavier, falling to the pavement, creating a bass line, with car tires sliding across to heighten the acoustics. The traffic lessened when the night came, and the cars turning off the main avenue would slow, throwing caution to the wind and slickness off the road. Over countless meals and girls night-out she had seen me let down my guards as red wine overtook my blood and my laughter masked my apprehensions. My mind calculated how, years ago, she explained how we could be everything to each other while pretending to uphold monogamy if either married a man. To her, my saying no meant I loved her in that emotional 'if I can't have you, I don't want nobody else' way. Truth was, I loved the freedom she enjoyed to take my body and me in her mouth; use her hands like a tool; use a sex object as if it were attached to her body.

Until that rainy Sunday I never tasted her that way. All I knew: her tongue was long, and her breasts more than a mouthful. Still she kept the pretension of we could be and would be there for each other. Years ago, it felt good because of the curiosity to experience what I read in books and came to know in art, of how women satisfied each other while men fought wars to conquer more women.

Twelve hours had gone by and I needed her to tell me something to interrupt my thoughts of whether I should make a call to my boyfriend to explain I cannot come by for dinner. I needed her to exclaim this to be better than she ever imagined but she was dry, out of words and the way her body shifted told me the same deal she wanted years ago, still on the table, constituted her best offer. "I need to shower."

"You're in a rush?" Her response meant I beat her to the punch. Chin in palm, elbow on the pillow, she searched for a way to keep me there. "Why don't you call your 'invisible man' and tell him to come join us? I'm sure he'd like that."

I cut her a joking look. "Is this your new offer – that I share my man with you?"

"Whatever it takes for us not to go another four years without feeling this good?"

"Extra towels still in the same place?" She nodded and I walked to the hallway then the bathroom. Not even five minutes, before I lathered, she came in and joined me. She tried her playfulness, her norm at least with me, to distract my thoughts. She caressed me from behind, building suds with a washcloth, nuzzling my neck as her right hand probed. I turned to face her. "What do you want?"

Unflappable to the core, my stern tone had no effect on her, "For you to spend the night."

"I can't. I have work in the morning. And, you also have to go to work. No more calling in sick."

"OK on both. But I wake early so you'll have enough time to get home to get ready for work. Plus, you can take my car."

"Nowhere to park in Manhattan. That's why I don't own a car." I left the shower to dry off as she lathered and rinsed.

She entered the bedroom as I finished dressing, and sprung the surprise. "Well don't rush out. Wait to at least say hi to Attitude."

"WHAT?"

"He called when you went into the shower."

"And now you're telling me this?"

"If you were staying, I would have waited to see your surprised look."

"Is this why you called me this morning?"

"Oh no, here we go again! Hope, I haven't heard from him in two years just like you. You're always thinking I'm part of some huge conspiracy to undermine you." She went into a tirade. "Who helped you find and buy that condo in that exclusive building? Who helped you get your job by writing over twenty letters?"

"So, you got connections. So what?" The desperate way she threw those two items out there meant she really wanted me to stay. She never mentioned either over the years. "Why is Attitude coming here? Why is he calling you and not me?" She did not answer. "You're up to something! Does he know I'm here? I don't want to be here when he gets here."

"No, I wanted to surprise him too." She did not challenge why I put myself to be more important in his life. "I don't get you. After all we've been through. After today…You think…What is it you think?"

Thoughts were the first things to betray a person. One's mind contained a barrel of ideas as well as facts. I had miscalculated the start of the final battle. I never thought this could be it when I entered the apartment this morning, as Ken leaving made no sense. I had to stand my ground. "Barbara, you know what I think. I think you underestimate me. You always have."

She laughed. "You are my partner in this madness. We are SUM women. Strength. Unity. Morality. Please don't tell me you're dropping all three and deserting me."

I walked to the mirror atop the dresser, fluffed my hair. I took a good look at myself in the mirror at the youthfulness, the worry-free round face that still passed for a teenager. "Your biggest mistake is that you keep thinking you got something to lose. You have nothing. NOTHING! My family has seventy-plus years in this Society, in SUM. And, you're questioning me? You don't fucking last this long in this Society if you cannot sift through bullshit. Before Attitude gets here, tell me why did Ken break up with you!"

"I don't know. I told you he gave me a bunch of nonsense about not being sure if he wants a lifelong commitment, kids, and so on."

Ken and Barbara. Attitude and Hope. That was how people saw it; how I often imagined it but the reality was that Ken and Barbara were a couple, and Attitude and I had divided loyalties, though fighting for the same cause. "OK, whatever it is you did, the price you're going to pay is major. So, let me help you. I can get you out of this, whatever it is. I will sacrifice my king for you. But if he dies, you owe me eighty years – 4 full generations of your family. The rest of your life. Your children. Their Children. Their Children's children."

"What? What type of help is that?"

"You called me, right? You know something is not right. Ken cannot simply leave you. You know this. I know this. So you decide!"

"I pass. Girl, you're sick. You ain't no friend of mine."

Before I had a chance to answer, the door bell rang. Not the downstairs bell – the one in the hallway, near the apartment's entrance.

TORN

I slid to the side and leaned against the wall behind the door. The open door shielded me but allowed enough air for eavesdropping. I kept count of the seconds and spied her movements through the crack of light between the hinge and panel. My eyes sought how she would signal they were not alone. Attitude walked into the apartment as if he lived there. He placed the large duffel bag he shouldered in front of the coat closet, right of the entrance. Their strong hug and her jubilation brought memories of two disparate souls who somehow locked each other into a familial ring. The first thing he noticed further substantiated the care, the constant worry for her. The picture of Ken and Barbara on their most recent vacation, a small frame holding a five by seven snapshot, depicted a comfort level, of a woman's bare shoulder under the lightness of a hand that would always be there. They streaked no smile, baring teeth to show an overflow of joy. Their pose did not match, Attitude's question, "You still with that duck?"

An odd thing to hear him say as he and Ken never bickered over her, even in the most trying moments. Two years passed and the most visible changes made him look younger: a bare upper lip, jaw line and scalp. The cut of his dread locks and unkempt beard meant a change in identity, a confirmation to what I suspected and feared the last time I saw him.

That day and night propelled me to a new dimension. I needed to see Ken to put the puzzle together. The four of us became a square, a chess board with four remaining black pieces battling insurmountable odds. They worshipped Barbara in a way that the naked, untrained eye would mistaken her for a queen, the way Bliss had, the last time I saw her and Attitude. Ken was the king. Attitude played the role of bishop, a monk who took a vow of celibacy just as he vowed, only to, himself to become my knight. Unfortunately, he never fathomed the impossible truth: I abdicated my throne to give him safe passage. Now they, all three could potentially use me to save Barbara, a mere pawn.

I was not in the mood for Attitude or any of his games, until he asked, "Is Monk here yet?"

"If he was, where do you think he would be?" My voice turned him toward the bedroom door but he did not see me, not yet. I stepped out into the hallway. His short smile and steady gaze at my lips, and the slight tilt of his head led his pretense, a detached cool play that he expected to see me here. The irony, the counter of such an act cleared his name in my book, meaning whatever Barbara's scheme for calling me this morning did not involve him. Yet she welcomed his return, as he pretended my being here to be the most natural thing. We exchanged a soft hug, a feeling, and then I sized up his anxiety, the blink of his eyes, the muffled way he asked for Monk, the street-slang he had used to disapprovingly describe Ken while questioning their union.

Attitude knew something, and needed her to push Ken out of her mind.

Attitude left over two years ago and never followed up, never reached out, at all - not even a postcard. True, the rumor; I came to accept that he was dead. But this return meant he needed to clear his slate, start over, the way one overwrote a memory file. Yet, why start here, her apartment at midnight. Perhaps her place personified a place prodigal sons, distant relatives and the like came. And, he showed upon his return, with no worry or thought to ask whether Ken would be here. Even though I put my arms around him, I truly was not happy to see him. When he let go, I did not give him a chance to get his bearings. "What? You don't know anybody? You leave and nothing? Nothing!"

"Relax, sister! Yours was my first call and the number I had for you is disconnected."

Not exactly my primary concern, but it did feel good to know he tried to come to me first. "No! Not just tonight! Where have you been?"

He simply stared into my eyes then chuckled. His eyes coupled with the slight upturn in the right corner of his lips gave me the information, the hint I needed. He was dead but he could not admit this, not in front of her. All he said, "When I left I told you I was going on tour and will probably end up staying in Switzerland. I come back and the last number I had for you no longer works."

The brother had disappointed me in so many ways that I could not hide the hurt. "How did you find Barb's number? She moved also."

"I called Monk and he gave me her number. How come Monk doesn't have your number?" Barbara walked to the kitchen and started boiling water. She knew the routine. To show love Attitude and I sparred, hard. We battled over everything, even though we shared very similar views. We sat on the sofa, facing the entertainment unit. I read his movements while he held his silence. The jittery fingers drummed against the arm of the brown leather sofa. The right knee moved in rhythm but not that of the music, Wes Montgomery's *Bumpin'*.

As Barb brought the three cups of tea to the living room, the downstairs doorbell rang. Attitude said, "Make that four cups!"

She chimed in, "Nah, Monk doesn't drink tea."

My mind rotated right, to reconnect dots from the past, of actual events and gaps for events I might have missed.

"How much do you wanna bet?" They made a simple wager of one dollar. "I'll get the tea. You get the door."

I joined in, "No, I will get the door." The playful tone overtook me, the way toddlers spread germs to each other. Plus, I wanted to get Monk's reaction when I opened the door to Barb's apartment. I used my most flirtatious tone, the one that led to seduction, fast and hard, no teasing. "Hi stranger, where have you been all my life?"

I could tell no matter who opened the door, he would be this angry. "Hiding!" He stepped over the threshold and gave me one of those quick hugs for people who could barely stand each other, complete with the non-rhythmic two taps to the shoulder and well above the lower back. He came to a complete stop as he stepped into the living room and scanned his surroundings. His eyes moved a bit then stilled as if giving his ears a chance to seek out faint sounds. "Is that Wes Montgomery?" An inconspicuous body, Monk moved through life unfettered from rules because he lived *by the book*. Yet, he entered this room, where all signs pointed to a final battle to come. He then exchanged a hug and handshake with Attitude. I looked for a clue but could not detect whether they exchanged the frat grip. I needed to know whether Monk was a MAX boy, whether he had taken the oath. He asked Attitude, "What brings you here?"

Monk sported a black trench, not the classical Columbo detective style but a heavy denim blend with small metal buttons. He took it off and tossed it onto the love seat near the window. It gave me slight pause – enough to break out of character and sequence, to think specifically of two years ago when those two, Monk and Barb, first met.

"Oh, I almost forgot." Attitude's excitement broke my concentration. I watched him run to the closet and take a knapsack out of the duffle bag. Then, he took out a square gift box from in there. Barbara returned to the living room and chiming with her best melodic voice, poised to win the wager, until she caught Monk's serious look. I told her about that look but she had only laughed. His flat lips seemed to extend past his cheek bones, betraying the slenderness of his face. His charcoal gray sweater, a crew neck revealing a white tee under it, blended, more like disappeared, under his Adam's Apple; its firmness when he stayed silent and froze into that icy glare; that look froze me the first time I met Monk. Attitude handed her the gift box. "Open it in private!"

The secretive tone in Attitude's voice released her from Monk's hold, only to put her into a different quandary. I loved it. She handed Monk the cup of tea. "We're drinking tea, and I made you a cup."

In the space to say he didn't drink tea, Monk stared at her real hard until she broke eye contact. With his right hand, he motioned her to him. She approached. As he took the cup and saucer from her hands, she greeted him with a soft peck on the lips.

"When did y'all get that friendly?" I failed to focus on it, when Attitude told how he got Barbara's number. I tried to soften my inquiry. "Did I miss something?" I lied to keep and reestablish my cover.

Monk placed his tea on the coffee table and stepped to me. "What's the matter, baby, you want a kiss too?"

I did not answer. He took two steps to me and leaned down a little. A soft kiss. His tongue explored only a bit, up to the little space behind my teeth, as I had not fully opened my mouth. My body swayed.

The kiss pushed me back two years to 1991, to Attitude's opening reception at Bienvenue Gallery. A night that was more of a closing, a chapter in my life that being here with the three of them threatened to reopen. I had not seen them two since but here I stood in the room with these two men who complicated my life, my love of it, my amorous intentions more than any other.

I remembered when Monk entered the gallery. The space blared an emptiness, a duplex, loft with a balcony, white walls, bright lights, refinished hardwood flooring, nearly three hundred people looked in his direction even though he wore an unassuming look complete with an even gait. They all turned away for he stood by someone who had no bearing on the scene being played out. As the crowd lost focus on them, I stared and read Monk and Barbara's lips. He simply leaned next to her, against the smoked glass plane near the entrance and asked her, "Do you know me?"

"You look familiar. TGI, right?"

"No, I'm Monk from Semline. Theodore Perkins."

The smile came naturally and showed that she was impressed. She never believed me when I raved about this young boy from Semline, who carried tradition so lightly. Though not handsome in the classical sense, his contrast to the definition of soft male beauty melted my heart the minute I first landed eyes on him. Barbara joked, "What's up, you want some pussy?"

Not stated as a joke, but more of an audacious quip she once told me to use on him, so I could rid my nerves the next time I found myself near him. He smiled and seemingly bonded with her. Her offer had nothing to do with why he made the next offer. "I'll take a rain check. Check it! I'm not sure what you're doing here, or how you got so deep into these people's story. There is no easy way out but I will promise you this. If anyone ever asks you for a name, any name…you give them mine. Theodore Perkins."

She repeated his name, "Theodore Perkins. Monk from Semline."

He nodded. "If they don't already have it, they will ask for my phone number. It is…" She made to reach for a pen and paper from inside her bag. He told her, "No. Memorize it. Brooklyn's current area code. 555-1917."

She said, "Got it!"

"Now if you are ever in trouble and need immediate protection, call that same number and simply ask, 'May I speak to Monk'. Not my real name. Just Monk. Whoever answers will take care of you until I can come."

She repeated with a silliness yet she still held the seriousness of what he had conveyed, "Are you sure you don't want some pussy?"

He chuckled. "No, but next time you see me, give me a soft kiss on the lips."

As he made to walk away and deeper into the gallery, he caught my eye dead center and looked left.

Though I knew it to be no more than ten seconds of thought, it allowed me to connect the past two years, so I knew precisely where to pick up as if I had earmarked them. Barbara flipped through television channels as my mind moved like a CD changer on random.

For Monk to have her number, she would have had to call him recently. Seeing Monk's smile made me want to go back deeper into the past, to ask the question I held inside ever since we first met. The very first night I met him and learned that if he took the oath, he would be the seventh generation for his family in the Society. So, I interrupted by asking it point blank. "So, Monk, why do you fill the hatred you feel with a lot of superficial stuff?"

"That's really deep." He paused to find the right way to code it so that only I would understand the scope of his reply. "I have read some of your published pieces. Your analysis never really attacks the artist, but the line you cut through the work does make it seem like it is personal."

His retort, a loaded statement gave light to the fact that he read the magazine where I worked. He cared that much but never showed it. I played along. "What does that have to do with my question?"

Attitude answered, his face holding the same seriousness as when he first walked in. "It's simple, Sis. Race is a game of Truth, Dare and Consequence. Whether you speak the truth or live a lie; dare to change or live "race," the consequence is death."

"I live to uphold this legacy." Monk then said it as if it were common knowledge, "And, that's why Bliss is dead."

Barbara jumped out of her seat. "Bliss is dead?"

She overreacted so it meant she knew. I studied her for years and had her pegged. Now the real question was how far back did she know? Did she call Monk because Ken left or because she heard of Bliss's death? "How you're gonna come in here all casual then after all of this small talk drop this news like it's nothing?"

Monk spoke while staring at Attitude. "I thought y'all knew because when I walked in, he was already here. Why do you think I drank the tea? I thought it was some sort of communal thing to soothe our nerves."

"How come y'all don't know Bliss is dead? It happened this morning. The news has been spreading like wild fire."

"I haven't been home all day." I threw in my disclaimer to stand as far away from Barbara as possible but did not include I've been here, with her all day.

She jumped in as if I would become her alibi. "I had my ringer off until a couple of hours ago, and I have my answering machine off as not to accept any calls from Ken."

I stood up and called her bluff. "You know who killed her, right?"

"What?"

"Come on! You're always in the know about stuff."

She leaned away from me like my breath stunk or something. "Chick, get a grip!"

Attitude stepped between us. "You two are scaring me. Her death has been labeled a suicide. She took a butcher knife to her gut."

Monk stepped closer to me. "Yeah, but you two are talking as if something was in the works."

I deflected his suspicion. "Why are you looking at me and not her?"

"Because you slept with Devon and Bliss saw you coming out of the motel room with him the night after Semline's Charter ceremony." He said it so fast the accusation entwined with any disclaimer I could use.

Attitude and Barbara asked at the same time. "Is that why you abdicated your throne?"

Thoughts bunched up from the corners then raced to line up to the front of my mind. Those two men had a clear misunderstanding of how SUM women operated. My next thought begged me to deny Monk's claim but he countered before I could utter the words. "Call me a liar! I dare you! And, no, Devon didn't tell me and neither did Bliss."

I pondered whether Monk planned to help me by putting my cards on the table. "Then how do you know?"

"It doesn't matter how he knows. Does Miranda know about this?"

Barbara knew better than trying to get me to tell the ending of a story that goes back to 1860, as if my small piece were the first chapter, especially when my having sex with Devon really did not matter to her. MAX boys knew this, and as a SUM woman, she knew sex with a MAX boy did not matter unless you planned on marrying him. But did Monk know this? If yes, then he must have taken the oath to officially be a MAX boy and should know I only slept with Devon to protect his legacy, the one minutes ago he claimed to live to uphold.

"Bliss is dead?" My sobs coughed out the words and tears flooded my face enough for them to think it was a performance. I wanted them to doubt my sincerity. I looked at each of them, shook my head from side to side and ran to the bathroom to compose myself. In the five or so minutes it took me to gather myself, I listened at the door to pick up on anything being said that would help me decipher this day. Their silence flowed over the keys of Horace Silver and remained so as I came out and headed to the closet to get my jacket and purse.

She ran toward me and made to grab my arm. "What's wrong? Where you going at this hour?"

Unsure of what Barbara knew and when she came to that knowledge, I made it clear I wanted no part of it. "As far away from you as I can."

Those words gave Attitude and Monk enough pause, and warning to look at Barbara in a different light.

THE CONSCIOUS DAUGTHERS

Mission accomplished; the plan started to play itself out. I ran down the steps, not slowing when I reached the vestibule with the cathedral ceiling, polished tiles and two wings. If I went outside, I would not know whether they left because the building had two side exits. My mind raced with infinite possibilities of the conversation they held upstairs, and what she would be willing to do to get them to believe her. The street, dark and slippery, coiled around the bend leading to the parkway's underpass. Chasing a stray cat into the street would do the trick but the wetness might cause too big a crash and force them to stay upstairs until the commotion died down. A car alarm and a small but not too tiny of a rock. The large tree adjacent the bus stop gave me a good cover. If anything went wrong, I would hop the short brick barrier and dip into the park. I crossed the street and positioned myself sideways behind the tree. As I cocked back my arm to hurl the rock through the driver side window of the car nearing Barbara's parked car, I spied the two of them exit the building. They walked evenly, a uniformed gait of hands downward into their coat pockets, hoods over their heads, and that slight b-boy bop made famous by dudes who had grown up at the end of the pimp era and the start of wild style, graffiti-smeared bravado. I knew Manny's walk more than Monk's because I had only seen him five maybe six times my entire life but I replayed his moves, inflections and gaze the way one does a favorite music album. Unlike Monk's interactions that could fill only a few pages of an album of still shots, photographs one returns to when in doubt of a person's existence, Attitude's imprint haunted me, constantly replaying and adding sequels like a horror movie that captured the nation's imagination. Them two crossing a side street and entering a car to drive off pushed me to think of what I missed.

The last time I saw either of them, Bliss was there – the opening night at the gallery – what had I missed? Nothing. Perhaps it happened the week before the gallery, at the Semline Chartering ceremony. It had to be that day. Monk had given me the clue, the timeline. The night I slept with Devon. Should I start or end there?

Monk knew about Devon. WOW. What did I miss that night?

OK, Barbara and Ken. Attitude and Bliss. No, Attitude and Bliss came up to us only after Ernest approached. He came up to us and fired the first shot. He declared war with me standing there, with no cover. He did not acknowledge me even if only to protect my allegiance to him, a simple hello and we could have avoided all this.

I found myself frozen behind the tree. A slight drizzle. A choice to make. Bliss was dead. Attitude was technically dead.

I had no choice but to protect my king.

I stared up at the lone window of her apartment that faced this street. The others faced the side street overlooking the pay phone I needed to use. I saw her curtains and the lights illuminating the living room, bathroom and bedroom. Cars passed in intervals. With the traffic light showing green, I didn't need to worry about someone detecting my movements. Before any other move, I had to get my boyfriend out of town because he had nothing to do with this war.

He picked up on the second ring as if he had been awaiting my call. I spoke in a measured tone but with enough control so he would not interrupt and simply follow. "Hey baby. No I'm fine. I need you to get out of town and disappear for a few months. I don't know. Anywhere from two to six months. No, quit your job. Simply leave a message. No need to go into details. No, no, I'm fine. I'm worried about you. You know how you always say I don't share enough of my life with you. Well, I killed someone and need to kill someone else, and I don't want any of it to come back to you. No. No, seriously I'm fine. I only have one way out of this. But I would die if something happened to you. No, seriously. I will call you when it's time to come back. NO. OF COURSE NOT. I'm not going to get caught. I'm not even going to be there when the person dies. Oh, don't go too far because I might need you to come back at a moment's notice; travel a day away at most. Oh come on, not that again. No I'm not going to say it. I have no time for love. Of course you'll see me again. OK OK! I love you too. Ok, I will. Bye."

I headed for the subway station thinking of the things I had to sell and do. Bliss would most likely be buried in a week so I had enough time to sell my furniture, call my realtor to sell my apartment, and find me something smaller, less expensive with good security. The rain trickled, the intervals a quarter of my hurried steps toward the Union Turnpike subway station. The distance, a nice walk under the sun on warm day but at night, with temperatures in the low fifties, the seven blocks counted enough so that the doubts circled my brain at least three times. Only two people on the platform and I stood far from them so I could cry in peace. I cried for Bliss even though a part of me hated her. I tried hard not to like her because she reminded me of the girls in my high school, the ones desperately trying to blend in; the ditty-boppers with pom-poms and tight sweaters. Take away the sing-song voice, the bouncy steps, she reminded me of Barbara, because that Bliss chick also moved two steps forward in every situation. They had dissimilar dispositions, but that was not the reason she too brushed Bliss back.

They first met at the Semline Charter ceremony, nothing more than an introduction from Attitude of Bliss to Ken and Barbara. The next week at the gallery, Barbara iced her because of a jealous streak she possessed that I never witnessed. Bliss had come to admire Barbara, from afar, because she had mistaken rumors and gossip as truth. A rumor and gossip Bliss should never have been privy to, had she been who she claimed.

For her part, Barbara misread Bliss's appearance and eagerness to please as weakness. Barbara did not understand how sex could lead to love, something I failed to pick up on until tonight, though it existed when I first met Barbara.

September 1985, my freshman year at TGI. We met the first weekend on a Friday afternoon on the campus's open quad. The Welcome Back party started as an outdoor event that would eventually end up inside the Student Building. The twelve-hour party, the flyers announced. Billed as the lone must-attend party of the semester, it bridged the gap between graduate students, upper and lower classmen. I stood alone, not too far from a few students I met earlier in the week in my various classes. Barbara stood in a group of those new acquaintances. She stared at me and smiled. I looked away and saw another girl looking at me. They approached from different angles and with the same proposition.

"I'm Barbara Wilson. MC Barbwire."

"I'm Miranda Lopez. I go by Miranda Writes."

They smiled at each other and waited for my name. When I didn't offer it, they talked across me as I sized them up. The Spanish chick had on doorknocker earrings and a set of knockers on her. She wore a LeTigre polo top – light grey with multi-colored horizontal stripes, with brown the dominant color. A bit shorter than me, the tightness of her Calvin Klein designer jeans showed Miranda had hips for days, to go with full lips, a mess of mascara and make up, and bright red lip stick. Her hair so dark, shoulder-length, she turned heads in all manners. Necks craned, bent at odd angles. Some clearly checked out the other girl, the one in the acid wash denims and sporting a white Izod Lacoste polo top. Her gold necklace, a small rope with a name pendant looped around it. "We should form a rap group." They talked over each other like they rehearsed their lines for days. "The Conscious Daughters. See them two dudes deejaying, what do you think?"

They stopped talking and looked at me.

I threw them for a loop by using a hardened street slang betraying my preppy attire. "Y'all serious? Straight up! It's not gonna work. There's two of them and three of us. I'm here in this school for two reasons. Become a SUM woman, and find the love of my life."

"You're hard up like that?"

Miranda proved to be the one in the know. "I've been here one week and you're the third person I've heard mention SUM woman. What's that?"

"Do your research and choose between the first two people who offered it to you." I sized Barbara up. "So, which one of them two dudes you got?"

She sucked her teeth and walked a few steps away from us. The people near us formed a semi-circle. Her moves were fluid, a mix of the day's popular party and break dances. They ogled not just her steps but her body. She had a polished body, the way a great sculptor envisioned a stocked female body. Her painted on two-tone jeans, with no pockets, pressed every curve from her ankle to waist; along with her gyrations, her seams magnetized the bass, the treble and the eyes of the crowd. Not only did the two guys deejaying acknowledge her with scratches of the turntable, they started a mic chant. Barbara did a pop-lock move to motion Miranda forward. Miranda top-locked, then pirouetted so perfectly it hinted of light formal dance training. As she rocked to the beat, she stared at me. I started off with four simple bars:

Barbwire, Miranda Writes and a girl named Hope
When Conscious Daughters in the house all the brothers scope
Fly girlies rockin' a break beat at the Student U.
Bogarting Mesmerizing Tantalizing just for you.

Each of us dropped four bars and others took over the cipher and the break dance from where Barbara and Miranda left off. The DJs made it official by crooning, "This freshman class featuring The Conscious Daughters is live."

We partied all night. That proved to be the best party for the entire semester and my entire six years on the campus.

>=<

I would see Attitude around campus, had heard his name and recognized him as one of the two DJs at the semester's first party. When I first actually saw him, I thought he was a SBD brother because he mainly hung around with them. The first month, I would see the flyers with his artwork and tag. He did everyone's flyers and deejayed a few parties. Our paths never really crossed because he was hard to figure. He walked a fine line, as if the dividing line between the black mainstream and the liberal students of various ethnicities. No matter the rally or sponsoring organization, he would be in the western quad supporting it. His style varied from preppy argyle sweater, khakis and loafers; hard core bboy with gold, frames that were not prescription and new sneakers monthly; up to military jacket, boots and worn-looking sweat hoods.

He had a slight tilt to his walk, a drawl to his speech though no discernible southern accent. Strictly Brooklyn, the tell was the slang; deep in the heart of it, where people crossed lines to live and make friends, or else stayed in the house. I spied him hard that first month trying to figure if he had a woman. Then I heard about his reputation. Barbara first brought it to my attention. After our impromptu freestyle, she and I kept up with each other though we had no classes together and no interest in the same things. She lived for rumors and gossip. I learned from her that Attitude belonged to the wrong family – *Fly MAX Beta*. They were nearly extinct as an organization. I never met a MAX boy, but throughout my family, no matter who you spoke to, you would hear the stories. Though no definite consensus as to whether they were good or bad, one thing remained clear – when dealing with MAX boys, you better stay alert for the potential double-cross.

We sat in the open lounge area, at a table facing the entrance. When alone I sat in the back on the large fluffy cushions in the corner. With Barbara she preferred front and center. We debated the name for our rap group while waiting for Miranda. I felt *The Conscious Daughters* would limit what we could talk about. Barbara felt that rap would turn and stay black nationalist. To kill time she dared me to go and introduce myself to the group of upperclassmen seating in the right corner behind the entrance. "It's not a big deal for me to go over there since SBD and SUM is my family's family."

"Then how come it's one month into the semester and you have yet to introduce yourself?"

"No need for them to know me until they announce when the pledge class will start."

"Yes, but they need to at least know me beforehand 'cause unlike you I'm not a legacy."

"You can't become a SUM woman unless someone sponsors you."

"I figured you would." Before I could say anything, she added, "Miranda already got a sponsor – Louise Grimsley. That one over there."

"Don't point!" The girl stared in our direction. "See now I have to go over there. But I cannot sponsor you unless my great-grandmother gives the OK."

We left our food on our table because I figured it would be a quick visit, but as soon as we arrived, Attitude said, "Hi. I wondered when you would make your presence known."

"Excuse me." Everyone was confused except Barbara, and then it hit me. "Oh I get it!"

I laughed as he continued, "You know I asked Barbara about you the day after that freestyle session on the quad." Then he did the introductions, "Hope Kendall…"

Everyone at the table stood up – male and female. I didn't say anything because I didn't want to come off like I expected them to bow to me or something. I simply shook hands with everyone. I did not introduce Barbara and they understood why. Attitude gave me a confused look. She introduced herself, "Barbara. Barbara Wilson."

Ken was the only one to shake her hand, then he asked me, "How come you didn't introduce yourself from day one like most legacies do?"

I smiled to hint that he broke protocol for asking me this in front of two non-family members. But I was not looking for conflict even though some would see it that way. "I am taking the Legacy Exemption."

THE LEGACY ACCEPTANCE

Under The Legacy Acceptance, one simply signed her name into the membership blotter once the pledge class was sworn in. Doing so makes one ineligible for leadership in the organization.

.

Many organizations started at TGI because it was a combustible campus. Its past as a military fort, then later a military institute became a stronghold for students with many ideas and earned the school a strong reputation for student activism. Though not the founding place for SUM or SBD, it became the most instrumental place for its growth. The formal nature of the organization started when three white female cadets felt they could take a more active role in the burgeoning abolitionist movement of the nineteenth century. The three cadets convened other classmates, males and females, in a late night secret meeting in what was at the time the lone dormitory. They learned others had similar ideas and espoused the same ideals as an organization started by free Northern Blacks for recently freed slaves. The existing organization had no name but it had two secret passages to identify one's self…

Call a spade a spade.

Do you believe in the kindness of strangers?

The first was to simply identity yourself as a supporter of the African's right to be free. The second was to offer a person help if her life is in immediate danger.

The TGI campus remained a place for rabid student activism. On a normal day the quad looked like a battleground for ideas; placard protesting against anything and everything, from abortion, apartheid, funding for organizations, shorter class periods down to the cafeteria food. Barbara and I gravitated toward Attitude because he treated us like his sisters. She hardly attended the activities. I did to get a better sense of him and the issues the students impacted the most. Unlike the other guys he didn't come at us hard just because we were Freshmen, fresh meat.

Though I carried a SUM legacy, even the SBD brothers tested my resolve to see if I would become one of those girls who lost all common sense as soon as they arrived on a college campus and faced personal freedom once away from their parents' guarding and prying eyes. With few trees in the center of campus and its pathways, the fall winds swirled and batted away any warmth the sun offered. The shade lied on the edge of the campus and eastern quad, where students lounged on the grass edging the paths to dormitories or running against the walls adjacent entrances and windows. The five dorms sprawled obliquely away from the circular path leading to the main quad. At night, the lone light near each entrance illuminated barely enough to give presence to the sign stating a building's name. Past the glow, near the shadows, around the side, on the grass leading to the woods filled with century old trees, cloaked with hoods, wandering eyes and lust, students talked rendezvous. On days I had a late class or attended a meeting, a walking partner would start with subtle hints then make a bold push to dabble.

Within the family, three of the four SBD brothers on the campus tried hard. Their maneuvers came as a shock. Stating I would not go under my family's legacy, gave me a sense how they bartered a young woman's yearnings with their personal vow and quest for secrecy. True discretion helped both parties but the forwardness of having to win over a man's hand seemed too heavy a burden.

Not taking The Legacy Acceptance puts one's legacy at risk, for if I failed to make it my family would lose what amounts to four generations of SUM and SBD membership and entitlements. Part of the SBD reason for trying to court me was in case I made it, the sheer power of our union.

>=<

Attitude did not roll like that. He sensed the chemistry between us, the reason we argued like third graders, debated everything and waited by each other's classes to grab lunch or sit in the open lounge and chat. Ken joined us often but his quietness made me wonder if he showed up for Barbara or me. He never said much nor walked with us across the quad to Poe Hall when we tagged along with Barbara just to see what the extreme whites were into. Attitude never struck a conversation with these white students. Poe Hall was the first dormitory built. It stood on the eastern-most point of the quad, directly across the faculty building, some 275 yards. The other four dorms sprung up clockwise, with King Hall the closest to the main entrance to the campus, roughly 100 yards from the main parking lot. The library, the lone structure constantly undergoing improvements stood across the quad from King Hall, a bit to the side since it was on the edge of the other quad.

In the distant past, Poe Hall housed the male cadets on the top two floors and female cadets in the basement. Always a battleground, TGI endeared itself to progressive values from the onset. The first academy to admit women in the military before it was even legal. The women did not fight or carry arms onto the battlefield but they received the same training as the men. The women served as covert operatives, utilizing any means to bring down the enemy. Three of them in 1861 decided to extend the training they were receiving to a group of Blacks congregating in New York City.

Over the years, the building faded into a dirty graying brown both inside and outside, its industrial carpet stained with fallen drinks and dried vomit. It became a place where indifferent students worshipped nothing but an Animal House frat boy mentality. I hated coming to Poe Hall and tried repeatedly to get Barbara to move into King Hall and be my roommate. She said she enjoyed living there because its distance kept people out of her business. I held my laugh thinking what business - the girl was a virgin who did not smoke or drink, a total contrast to her white female roommate. I had nothing against Lena even though she had the worst reputation I ever heard. Moving from The Bronx to Westchester County I experienced a culture shock at age twelve. I went from living with my mother and older sister with a major self-induced, self-esteem problem, to being under the watchful eye of a father, step-mother and two older half-brothers. In my previous school I was the norm, a young brown girl with a smart mouth and a quick temper. In the new school, I became a minority, with Blacks making up less than three percent of the student body. There were few Hispanics and Asians. I did junior high school there and by high school, everyone including the Black girls knew the deal, we smiled, we took pictures, we saw each other in hallways and the cafeteria but it would all be over soon, so no need to get too friendly or emotional.

I held the same posture with Lena and she took it to mean I did not like her, at least that's what Barbara thought, especially when I kept pressuring her into moving to King Hall. I really could not tell her the real reason she had to move out. It was almost November and she let it out she wanted to become a SUM woman. She needed to be up close, next to the other women who would make up the pledge class. She did not get that and asked me the weirdest question.

We sat in her room listening to a radio station experiencing major static interference. We put up with it because their broadcast kept us current on the latest songs. I had smoked a joint after dinner and stopped by to make one final push for her to become my roommate. The brightness of the room's regular light messed with my high so I asked her to put in a color bulb. It never dawned on me that she would take it that way. I had spent the night at slumber parties with other girls, daughters of SUM women, legacies like me. She had spent night, she said, at pajamas parties with other girls and the common questions were about kissing. Yes, so were mine; we talked about boys, SBD legacies who we would one day marry. She asked if I had ever done it with a boy. I told her the same thing I told her when she first asked me, "Yes, this guy, a couple of years older than me. He's SBD from my eldest brother's school. He was my prom date."

She giggled like it was her first time hearing this then she asked, "Have you ever done it with a girl?" I didn't answer because it was the dumbest thing I had ever heard. She continued, "I did it with a girl before, a few girls, a few times…" She started laughing. I thought she would say that she was lying but then she asked, "Do you like me?"

Her voice carried a pleading sadness into the room. I turned to see her eyes as best as I could. The pathetic stare moved me one way, toward the door. She caught me by grabbing my left palm. Her grip did not hold because a nervous sweat had seeped from underneath her top layer. "You take one step forward, I will punch you dead in the face."

"And, what do you think happens after that?"

I squared up to let her know that I had been in many fights. Her shoulders squared and her fists balled. She chuckled and bent her neck so that her lips were but inches from mine. I held my ground daring her to take that next step, that next misstep. She sat back on her bed. I thought of simply walking out but my curiosity took the first step. "What was that all about?"

"I don't know." Her voice, whiny and confused, begged for my understanding. "There is so much going on up here on this campus. Every day someone is offering me sex. Men, women, professors but I'm scared and thought if I started with someone I could trust then…" Trust that she actually said the following, "I like living in this dorm because I don't have to worry about the Black men on this campus."

"What do you mean?"

She crossed her arms as if to hold warmth in her body. You see how they do the sisters? One for every other day of the week."

"What do you think goes on in this dorm?"

"I don't have to worry about these guys. If you know what I mean."

"No." I paused to be clear to her that my answer mattered only within the context of our current conversation. "I would date a white guy."

I had only known chick for about two months, and was ready to be out and be done with her. My college plans rested on clear goals: get good grades and pledge SUM. I couldn't afford to be associated with scandals and Barbara had the makings of a scandalous chick. Not necessarily her curiosity about sex but her need to be involved in things of no particular importance or meaning to her. At first, I dismissed what I kept hearing about her roommate, reported to be one of the campus's biggest sluts. I excused it because dorm pairings for the most part were random occurrences.

I sat back down and took on the role of older sister though we were only one month apart in age. "You should get with Attitude."

Before I got into my next sentence, she said, "Not him. That boy is in love with you…" She kept talking but my ears reverberated with the word love; an echo chamber of thoughts. "But he says that you are destined to be with Ken. Why is that?"

I knew but could not tell her. "I'm not sure. But you can get with Attitude. That's not a problem with me. I mean we're only talking about some college sex, and who knows…"

"Nah, he's like a brother to me. The big brother I lost out on when my brother went away for twenty-five to life." She started crying. She told me the story a few weeks ago, of how her brother, Lincoln, in taking up a fight she had gotten into at her middle school, ended up killing this white kid at his high school. His plan was to rough the kid up a bit but the kid's resistance proved much stronger than he expected so Lincoln threw the boy around a bit more, banged him against some lockers then stomped his jaw when he finally got him down. "I'm sorry Hope."

I reached to console her. I put my left arm around her neck. As I pulled her closer to rest her face on my shoulders, there was a misunderstanding. She slipped her tongue into my mouth. Not only was it wet from her lust but mixed with her tears, the taste overpowered me. I made no effort to stop her because something inside me went BAH! like that first firecracker, an M-80 on Independence Day. The Roman Candles followed it; they lit up the sky in a succession of small exploding balls. Then the sparkles flared in my eyes. She got on her knees without breaking the contact between our mouths. Her lips suctioned mine; the fullness, slippery, soft. Though my face moved to keep the right angles with hers, my palms stayed on the bed. Hers squeezed my breasts the way the little horny boys did when they convinced us girls to play Run, Catch and Kiss. Her touch was rough, hungry, desperate. She unbuttoned my blouse and unhooked my bra. I parted my legs so she could get closer and just as I started to lean back, Lena came in. She stumbled into the room and the hallway light barged in, the fluorescent bars in the ceiling felt like a spotlight. I ordered her to close the door but she came inside. I meant for her to get out but she said no. The shock on her face reddened her; her eyes and hair seemed to glow in the dark room. There in one instant I saw and understood why she slept with all those men. Her beauty covered everything about her. It forced her into hiding herself in meaningless exploits, under-priced booze and a quick tongue.

I covered up and bundled myself in my jacket, and left Poe Hall in fear that I had thrown my family's legacy down the drain. If I simply took The Legacy Acceptance even if such a rumor were to make the rounds, nothing could happen. It would take me a bit longer to find a man who understood, or would it really? Were men concerned with, fearful of female sexuality on this level? That would not matter because though my being a Kendall guaranteed me a spot on the pledge class, the path I would walk just got tougher. Even if Barbara swore her roommate to secrecy and she kept this as the ultimate life and death secret, my paranoia would overtake me. I had no choice but to carry her into the Society, drag her through the darkest places in a Black woman's history.

THE LEGACY EXCEPTION

*Under The Legacy Exception, a person with
no previous link, or a lost legacy is vouched
for by a member in good standing. Once
sworn as a pledge, all activity is independent
of the person providing the legacy, though
the Voucher no longer has a legacy to pass if
the pledge fails to complete the process.*

Days went by and I avoided all direct contact with Barbara. We shared no classes and no other links, only our common friendship with Attitude caused us to cross paths, which eventually led to us making the peace. Even then I only made the peace because I hadn't heard a peep of that night in her room.

Black nation on the rise.
We gotta educate, agitate, organize.
Black nation on the rise.

Black Solidarity Day on the TGI campus illustrated how less than ten percent of the student body dictated campus life. Not sure if it was by default or a conscious decision but white students except for classes and social protests ventured into the connecting town for their activities. This left the campus desolate after 6 p.m. in colder months. The campus though modernized came across as an enclave of dingy mossy brown buildings, a clearing in the middle of a forest. It felt and smelled like a swamp. For Black Solidarity Day, the Monday before Election Tuesday, the Black Student Alliance held a dinner in King Hall. After dinner and heated debate regarding campus, local, state and national politics, the BSA marched across campus chanting freedom songs, with the most popular being *Black nation on the rise*. Preparing dinner was a collective effort between various organizations. In reality, through a cluster of independent student organizations, BSA served as no more than a front for SBD and SUM to recruit new members. Since the change to a liberal arts college, the campus did not give charters to paramilitary organizations and Greek-lettered organizations. Though many students wore letters of their respective organizations, the campus did not recognize the organizations, so they could not throw parties, organize meetings, rent campus space and so forth. The change took place after the 1960's because the liability hazing brought to the institution. If not for the State school, Barrington, coming into existence, this sort of campus life would have died out completely. With Barrington's liberal policies, the SBD and SUM family did as the Greek-lettered; they moved their charter there, instead of Semline College where though open to charters had restrictive guidelines for all student organizations.

So the Black Solidarity Day dinner at King Hall became a tradition, a standing room only, daylong gathering of all the organizations from the tri-city schools united under one banner, that of the Black Student Alliance. To be clear, none of those organizations knew they were under our family's banner, for none of our members could join a fraternity or sorority, and no person who ever joined one could become SUM or SBD. We shared only one tradition: standing on line in size order. We only did this behind closed doors to a select public on the first night, appropriately called Surface Night. From there outsiders would never know who continued or when the process to become SBD or SUM ended. Years ago rumors spread that pledging into our family was a lifelong process.

Barbara entered the common area in the basement through one of the side doors. Some had gathered since three o'clock to help set up to get themselves a seat. Others came just as mealtime started. She came toward the start of the first caucus and looked around for an empty seat. Various tables in the room had one; rarely did a table have two. A person from practically all of them waved for her to come sit with them. The sororities wanted her to become a sister. The fraternities wanted her to become a little sister. Even the SBD family wanted her to become a little sister. Doing so would give her some insight to SUM life, and probably earn her a Legacy Exception. But she just smiled and waved to them. She looked around the room. I looked straight ahead. I stood alone but in between some folks chattering about classes and campus life. My paper plate was nearly empty. She saw I avoided her eyes and she kept searching for a familiar face. Miranda saw her and avoided her eyes, hinting not to take the empty seat next to her. Barbara knew better than to go over there. At least she should. No one from the SUM table invited her to sit – they were the lone table not to wave her over. Though people could sit anywhere they wanted to, enough people knew who sat at that table. When I came in, they looked at me, expecting me to come over. A few other standing people looked at me. This gave me a clear indication of who would be pledging SBD and SUM when they announced the next class.

As Miranda got up to go get Barbara the plate of food one of the SUM women asked her to get, she cut me a real evil look. Though we had not kept up with each other, Miranda was not my adversary and I did not plan on treating her like one so I just averted my eyes.

The room broke into various segments to discuss and vote on the primary issues affecting Black America. I headed to the economics caucus being held on the second floor. Attitude caught up to me by matching my stride then slowing down a bit so we could talk out of earshot. "You know you're going to get that girl killed if you take The Legacy Exemption and put her on the same pledge class with you, right?"

"I don't want her to become a SUM woman."

"You told her this?"

"Yes."

My answer surprised him. "Then what is it with her?"

I turned to face him but kept my eyes off him to shroud the importance of our words. "I have no idea. I told her to pledge one of the sororities or something but she's not listening."

"Well, then put her under your family's legacy for protection while you take The Legacy Acceptance."

"Why should I do that?"

"Come on, Hope! She's had a hard life with no real family. That's all she's looking for."

"I thought about that but she likes me in the wrong way."

"Like how?"

"Like how I like you." I got closer to him.

"Now you know I can't touch you like that."

Murals covered the hallways of King Hall. Their various colors under the bright light symbolized a coming together of various countries, cultures and aesthetics. The school erected this newest dormitory in 1972 with no complaints from any of the groups that protested everything. Each of the four floors had meeting rooms, TV lounges but only the basement had a kitchen in each wing and open space to convene large meetings. The school, though, never fashioned King Hall as a residence only for Black and Hispanic students.

"Why not? I see you touching a whole lot…"

He chuckled, "No. You're taking The Legacy Exemption. It's one thing for Barbara to get on with no history and put herself at risk but nothing her family did can be held against her. How well do you know your family's history? Not the cute, Sunday dress up stuff they told you when they thought you would just take The Legacy Acceptance."

"What are you trying to say about my family?"

"Nothing. I'm standing here, right? Our two families got in around the same time. We never had any quarrels. I'm here for you."

I smiled then took another step closer to him. Wearing my pumps, my nose reached his mouth. I tilted my head up a bit so that our mouths could touch if he just leaned forward. "So, let's go then. My room. You know where it is though you never come by. Let's go. Right now. Let's make it happen. Put it in writing that you will stand there with me."

Attitude moved his head back a bit. "You know I'm a MAX boy, right?"

"Yes, and…"

All he said was "WOW" two times, and then he walked ahead, down the hall toward one of the caucuses.

The caucuses ended at ten o'clock then we headed out. About five hundred of us participated in the candlelight march around the campus. We stopped at each building and sang a song. At this late hour only the academic buildings did not have people in them. With each building, as part of tradition, people, mainly non-Blacks, would come out and join the march, since they were excluded from the earlier activities. Each building someone came out, except Barbara's dorm. Students looked out of windows but none came out. The light in Barbara's room was on and she stared up there for a brief moment. Then we marched on, to finish at King Hall. Ken said a prayer and poured libations for the ancestors who paved the way that we could march in these parts, march anywhere in peace. At the end, I waited for her in the direction she would use to trek Poe Hall. She offered a smile. I smirked and we did not mention what happened. We walked across the quad. The night quieted except for faint noises in the distance, in the trees leading to, and in the woods themselves. Nature moved a bit faster up here as autumn lasted eight weeks at the most. The forty degrees, on the campus elevated on a mountainous bank, even without wind, with the constellation of stars visible; the chill stood at a standstill the way a pond prepared its water to freeze as a variation for its form of hibernation. Barbara dug her hands deep into her pockets and I noticed the exaggerated sway of her hips, when she stepped down with her left foot, had faded to no more than simple allure, the charm of a street girl reclaiming her sweetness.

"So, you really want to be a SUM woman?"

"Yes, you are right. I should have moved out." The unnecessary defiance she had used, who knew for how long, no longer snickered when she used short sentences.

"No. No. You can live wherever you want. We need brave sisters like you who are willing to buck tradition."

"Like what you are doing?" The soft syllables did not drag to embrace colloquialism; they simply struck their lyrical chime and waited for a response.

"Yes, and you need to stop messing around with the SUM women. They have very short tempers and long memories."

Yet, a defiance woven with the naïve confidence still pulsed from her chest. "Well, I figure the more I stay in their faces the easier it will be to get their vote, even if they do it just to try to get rid of me."

"The best thing to do is become a SBD little sister when they start tomorrow."

"Tomorrow?" I disclosed a secret to her and wondered if it would stay that way. "When does SUM start?"

"When I say so! It can start tomorrow if I want."

"Why is that?"

"I'm the reigning legacy on campus."

Her eyes cleared the way for her excitement. Those eyes espoused the old adage of early to bed. "So, let's start tomorrow."

"I had planned to but I don't like how things are done on this campus."

"Now look who's bucking tradition." She laughed.

"Plus, Attitude made me realize that I should put you under my Great-Granny's legacy."

"Cool. Let's go call her."

"No it doesn't work that way. We need to get you ready to meet her. First things first. Call Ken and tell him you want to be a little sister."

"But I don't."

"Why not?"

"Whenever I'm around them, it's Hope this, Hope that…"

"What? I didn't know that."

"Yeah, I know I sound petty but I get a little jealous."

"Why 'cause the brothers like me?"

"No not of you but because I don't have a brother looking out for me."

"Yeah, you do. Attitude!"

"But, he's a MAX boy."

The way she said it hurt me. The disgust showed not only in the tone of her voice but the way words, subject-verb-article, rushed to form one word, then the exaggeration of the accusing word. No matter what rumors she heard, she knew nothing of him and MAX boys. "What's that supposed to mean?"

"After hearing so many people say that, last week I asked him to come by after class. I finally got up the nerve to ask him in a way that would not cause any rift between him and the other brothers." She paused to gather her thoughts. "He simply smiled, looked into my eyes and told me to take off my top. And then my bra."

She stopped and looked in the distance as if wanting to choke back the words. "Then?"

Her head tilted downward to shield the sad turn her eyes had taken. "He took off all his clothes, stared at me for a bit then got dressed and left."

"You two didn't do anything?"

"I wanted to. I spent hours playing it in my mind. I ran it past Lena as a hypothetical, something that happened to another girl with some other guy." A half smile formed on her lips and she inhaled. "She said the girl was supposed to give him a blow job to start it off."

The word, what, got stuck between my throat and nose, and made an odd sound.

She continued, "So the next day I go to visit him to see what that was all about. I take a cab to town and go all the way to his house. I ring the bell and a woman's voice says to come in. I open the door and she's a few feet from the door, topless and wearing only these little yellow panties. He's on the sofa, naked and smoking reefer with some other topless girl next to him. There's this other girl in the kitchen wearing a long t-shirt and probably nothing else. I hear all these voices, male and female upstairs and in the adjacent rooms. I smiled and just said that I would come see him some other time."

I started laughing. She joined in. Then we said, "Those fucking MAX boys."

THE LEGACY EXEMPTION

Under The Legacy Exemption, a person eligible for a Legacy Acceptance opts to complete the full pledge process. If successful, the person starts a new legacy tree while maintaining all previous entitlements. Failure to complete the process, breaks the existing legacy unless the holder of the legacy disowns the person prior to the signing of the pledge.

Hope never told Barbara about Attitude turning her down on Black Solidarity Day. She found Barbara hard to figure out. She joined SBD as a little sister. Their role was to simply learn the organization's history. Nothing more as they would get only two things from their affiliation: a closer friendship with the current brothers and the pledges who made it through the process. This would in turn help have them lobby a SUM woman to offer her a Legacy Exception. Members rarely gave out exceptions, though the Society created it as a way to bring new life into the S.P.A.D.E.S.

In 1860, months before the start of The American Civil War, a plantation burned down in Virginia. Among the survivors were field negroes who did the heavy lifting, and the house negroes who served as a communication pipeline between them and the slave masters. The fire took the life of seven slave-owning masters and their wives and children who had come to the plantation to discuss secession plans from the Union in light of Abraham Lincoln's election. The cause of the fire was never discovered and neither the whereabouts of some forty-odd slaves, while the bodies of nearly two hundred other slaves were found burned beyond recognition. No one could say for certain who escaped. With help from various abolitionists groups the survivors integrated into northern cities and other places where slavery did not exist. Unlike many other slaves the abolitionists aided to freedom, these slaves planned their own escape, this onslaught on their own for years, from start to finish. The timing just happened to mix with the recent presidential election and political climate.

Since they existed long before without the aid of outsiders, the forty-odd slaves secretly divided themselves using the name of the seven abolitionist families gave them to serve as cover. They then formalized their own secret organization and named it SPADES, or Society to Protect Africans from Doers of Evil and Sin. The seven families only trusted each other and felt that in 80 years they could begin to trust outsiders. To protect each other they branched into two sides: Strength, and Pride.

Contrary to popular belief and mythology, skin color played no role on their division. They just knew it would serve them well in targeting enemies. Strength consisted of five families, and Pride of the remaining two - in this case the lightest and the darkest. Pride's tasks involved working with the abolitionists. Their stated mission was to infiltrate and integrate any and every organization – by any means necessary.

In those days though Strength did not necessarily agree with Pride's strategy, they backed it as they saw how it could help the Society. Pride's initial goal was to test miscegenation laws and theory in order to turn the United States into mixed race nation. Strength, since it had the most people, became the army to carry out this mission and keep the original foundation and tradition of the Society. To do so, Strength maintained a policy that their female legacy could only be passed down through the daughters born of male and female initiates, and the male legacy through the sons of any male initiates.

To hold the color line, the two Pride families could only marry those in the larger society with hues similar to how they started for, at least, the first four generations – 80 years. This mandate limited the growth of the Pride side.

At the end of World War II when SPADES convened and saw that the resulting Society had inadvertently excluded white women because they had no way to carry on their legacy even if they married on the light Pride side.

By the late 1950s, though turbulent years for America, the work done over the years carried into the judicial system and helped overturn the two cases that had formed the main focus of SPADES activism: *Plessy v. Ferguson*, and *Pace v. Alabama*.

SPADES decided it was time to fold the Pride side back into Strength. Pride refused, renamed and remade themselves while still retaining the SPADES legacy. SPADES to them became Society to Protect Africans Doing Evil and Sinning. Pride side felt the risks they placed on themselves and their families since the late nineteenth century was what allowed the Society to advance.

It was the Pride side who had to work behind the scenes yet directly with friends and foes alike. Strength countered that they were the ones on the front lines and first to die when something went wrong.

Still with much work to do, they decided to maintain their connection though the Society, though the organization had split. Their visibility heightened and the need to build up recruitment, led the Society to modeling the organization after the popular Greek-lettered organizations. They went by many names, with their official names showing their linkages.

SBD: Strength Brotherhood Delta
SUM: Strength Unity Mu
PMB: Pride Morality Beta
PLT: Pride Loyalty Tau

A quick study of the names of the organizations showed that the females on the Pride side had no link with the Strength side. In less than a generation – twenty years – SPADES as it had existed ceased when Pride Morality Beta and Pride Loyalty Tau disavowed one another, and the latter disbanded. The former became Fly MAX Beta, a renegade male organization setting its own agenda while keeping minimal ties with the Strength side.

>=<

Though written in the rules from the first generation in 1860, no female had ever taken The Legacy Exemption. Then in 1985, a young woman showed up on the campus of Trafalgar Garrison Institute to say she wanted to unbury the old bones, that of her Great-Grandmother, Celeste Leonora Kendall.

People were nervous and the word spread across the nation to the entire membership. That first semester went by without any flare-ups. Unlike most Black students who received a full scholarship - academic, athletic or needs-based - to attend, Hope applied and got into TGI because of the financial means to pay without mentioning that her great-granny Celeste was the first Black female to enroll at TGI in 1921.

The military institute had changed to a liberal arts college but not before accepting its first two Black males. Unbeknownst to the TGI administration they'd had a Black enrollee as far back as 1887 – a Black man able to pass as a white. He was a TGI legacy, the son of Carol Eleanor Duval, one of the three female Cadets who connected with the Society in 1861. That son carried his mother's last name because his father, being a Pride Side legacy, a MAX boy, never avowed to a monogamous life.

By the time the first two official Black enrollees registered for training at TGI in 1917, Paul E. Duval had become a Trainer in the Espionage and Encryption division. He was particularly hard on the two Blacks students selected from the first set of soldiers to integrate the armed forces. They never responded to his harsh treatment. He kept pushing, to the point even students rumored to be part of the local and state white supremacist groups objected to how he treated the two Blacks. Paul answered he was just *calling a spade a spade*.

To be certain of Paul's claim, the one of the two who had taken the oath of Strength, to *SBD – stay black and die* if ever caught executing a dangerous mission met him in the woods one night. He accepted the microscopic brand onto his left rib, and the mission that came with it. The wound was like having a broken rib and would prevent him from leaving for Europe in two days with the rest of the unit. Paul covered the rest of the lie and got him medical rest, then additional training and a job at TGI.

Edwin J. Kendall remained on U.S. soil during World War I, at TGI to further his studies. Kendall also worked in the Recruitment Office and searched for a woman he thought could withstand the required training, while Paul worked at developing a counterintelligence mission for which they needed a colored woman.

Great-granny Celeste laughed as she recounted the mission to them. Barbara listened intently, never uttering a word. The front porch reminded her of those she saw in black-and-white movies, featuring the Antebellum South. Hope heard the story throughout her life, whenever she visited.

"I lost my husband in that town and still don't understand what he was doing with that white woman out in those woods. Nowhere in the mission did Ed say anything about him being out in those woods. They lynched him, cut his nuts off and stuffed his dick in his mouth. He hung there for days before I got word where he was."

"How do you know he was really out there with her?"

Celeste did not stop to turn and look at Barbara. "He was on that campus for over four years and I was there for almost a year before I got pregnant. Nothing ever happened except for someone hurling ignorance at us." She squinted and shriveled her nose. "I am sure a MAX boy was behind the whole thing."

"A MAX boy, why would they kill a SBD brother?"

"No, he didn't do the killing. But, those MAX boys are sloppy even when they are effective." She leaned back into the chaise. "That part of New York opened up after that. So many racists were either jailed, suffered unfortunate accidents or simply got murdered in the next few years."

"Did they ever catch who killed Ed or all those people?"

"Oh, you don't catch a MAX boy! They die and take their knowledge with them. If a MAX boy were to get caught alive, it could destroy this entire Society."

Barbara loved learning about this part of the Society. "They never thought to question you?"

"To them, I was a little country Black woman, a nervous wreck those next years, thinking that any moment they would come get me and my baby. I never left the campus or town because I felt safe there but I never ventured into those woods again. In the end it was worth it. My Ed died a hero. TGI opened up to more Black admissions and my legacy is strong not only through my only son and all the children he had, but from all the students who joined SUM and SBD those years I studied and worked there."

"That's a great story Mrs. Kendall."

"Story? Why you little bitch!" Great-granny Celeste had a short fuse especially for those who stood, even if by accident, to trivialize her life's work. "It's not a story. It is the SUM of what we live for, to put ourselves in harm's way so that our sister and brother can go free, so that our children can live to fight another day."

Born in 1903 and though she received a TGI education after it was converted from a military institute, part of Celeste Kendall's training dealt with survival and intimidation via interrogation. She became a trusted voice not only to whichever Black students enrolled, but also the people who governed the institution. Everyone loved her quiet demeanor, the public persona, but behind closed doors she could tell with two pointed questions which student would hold up in war as well as those who could make it into the Society. She initiated both first classes of male and females on the Strength side on TGI's campus. She accomplished this during the Society's fourth generation, the one that lifted the burden each side felt they carried, the period leading to The Great Depression and eventually World War II. While doing all this, she reared a young son.

The "burden" as the Society called it invigorated the Strength side but they were fine, returning home from war and living in a separate, segregated society, as long as no one bothered them and it was their choice. They saw how the Pride side lived, not just off art, patronage, politics and any other industry or mission that enabled them to hobnob with Whites. Strength never understood the utter chaos and degradation required to live a covert existence as those on the Pride side.

By the 1950's the roles reversed, Strength side wanted integration while maintaining nationalistic values. Pride wanted separation not only from the larger nation and Society, but from each other – along color lines, gender, economic status, and so on. Not able to reach common ground, the Pride women disbanded their association in 1957, with most taking the Legacy Exception and joining the Strength side. The remaining women just left the Society.

Few as they were, the Sixth generation on the Pride side became the lynchpin of the Society as the men of Strength who had passed "the burden" to join the Pride side could not succeed.

With only two original families remaining and most other members having no real legacy going past one generation, the MAX boys as they came to be known needed SUM women, the women from the Strength side to preserve their legacy. SUM women were a special type of women because their strength lied on the fact that as their letters stated they could Stand Under Morality, their own. In times of perpetual war, with only a few you can trust, a man needed a SUM woman.

The Society started with 7 families – 5 of them on the Strength side. In 1980, the seventh generation, there were only 15 families on the Strength side, and 5 on the Pride side. There was just too much risk to a family's legacy in trying to bring in a new member, to offer the Legacy Exception.

So what Hope had in mind, Celeste could not even fathom.

>=<

It was the summer of 1986, the previous semester had been rough academically for both girls but they got the B average both needed to even be considered for initiation. Barbara had also gotten a peek but only a slight one of life behind the Society's closed doors, for during the Fall 1985 semester all three men aspiring to SBD life had quit. The legacies had taken the Acceptance, which was really frowned upon by other males but knowing what one had to go through in order to become SBD, it happened regularly. The Acceptance meant no vote in family affairs, and taking the hand of an arranged union to a SUM woman even if you were already legally married.

Keeping the family vote was the most important thing to the original standing legacy especially for SUM. A legacy's holder expected a young woman to take the Acceptance, and to never dare bring a friend, especially one she's only known for a short time, home to the legacy's holder.

So Celeste could not fathom what Hope had in mind when she said, "GG, can I bring a friend with me for this year's visit?"

"Sure, darling. Anyone I know?" That part of the phone conversation ended there.

The aerial view of Celeste's street showed a house central to the cluster around her. From the street level view, off the main road, two right turns, a left and then a quick right took you to the house. Trees lined the short block on both sides. No picket fences to gate the homes. Wide porch, her banister painted yellow, a bench swing, four lounge chairs, a glass card table holding a pitcher of lemonade, a bucket of ice, a bottle of Jack, a bottle of Southern Comfort. An octogenarian wearing a sun dress, orange with white daisies smiling as her great-granddaughter who not yet out of her teens makes the introduction. Celeste held her smile, hiding the confusion that creased her mouth when the taxi pulled up and she saw a young woman next to Hope. She had learned in tougher times to smile in the face of danger, to keep her mouth shut when the voices around her speculated, and to cuss a motherfucker out when trying to intimidate.

This girl with her Hope reminded her of those girls who thought they could take the Society's oath, but the mere recitation of the pledge brought them to tears, and their actions, their cowardice to their knees, asking to serve any master who could help them escape Celeste's wrath. This was before the SUM training got easy and across the nation each school wanted to hold its own charter so that only it could be held accountable for its membership. They accomplished that by modeling themselves after the sororities, but SUM was no sorority even though the women nowadays called themselves sorors. This young woman with her great-granddaughter had hips for days, bust out to here and full juicy lips.

Celeste could not even contain her curiosity for two more minutes after retelling how she formed her legacy on TGI's campus. They had been there less than an hour and even before letting them into the house to show them where to put their suitcases, she felt compelled to ask, "Who's Elizabeth, and who's Leslie?"

That sassy one laughed. "Neither of us. We're just friends."

Celeste looked at Hope. "You know how I feel about liars, darling. What's going on?" She motioned them to get up from the table and sit on the swinging bench.

Hope's feet did not touch the ground because she knew the drill. Celeste pushed the swing as hard as her weakening frame allowed, for not only had the gray overtaken her hair leaving it mostly salt with very little pepper, her bones cracked when she bent too quickly and she had come to occasionally rely on a cane. The swing did not rock because Barbara had kept her feet on the ground. The force in GG Celeste's voice, its gust alone could have moved the bench. "Get your feet off the ground!"

Hope's fear came to the forefront. "Nothing's going on, GG Celeste. I brought Barbara here…."

Celeste cut her off and stared at Barbara who held her eyes. "I will look at her to see the fault lines. With each response you give, I bet she cracks." She inched her face closer to Barbara's so that on the down swing, their noses were but one inch apart. "And you, you keep your mouth shut and your eyes on me! Hope, you look east, away from us!"

"Yes, GG."

"Have you two ever been intimate?" Barbara's nose twitched.

"Yes, but only a kiss and a little…"

"Oh stop! Oh stop! Oh stop…" Celeste did not want to hear the details. "You brought her here so I can help arrange a marriage for you after you enter SUM, one who is comfortable with your little situation?"

Barbara's eyebrows raised.

Hope answered, "No, it's nothing like that."

"Her eyes says she's open to it."

No movement from Barbara.

"I brought her here so that you can write a letter for her."

"What? What type of letter? Please tell me she got kicked out of school or something minor like that!"

"No, she needs a Legacy Exception."

Celeste Kendall was trained in all manners of interrogation, first as the receiver then as the administer. She pushed the swing again, with both hands, one on the armrest Barbara rested on, the other hand on that space where her knees should have been touching had she been sitting like a proper young lady. "For this little trashy girl? I would rather have been correct that you two were together, together. But no, you want me to risk my life, my life for this girl. I bet this girl has never even been with a man. Is she a virgin?"

Barbara held her stare.

Hope answered, "Yes."

"No she's not. She's had sex with 4 boys and 7 girls." Hope turned to look at Barbara. "Did I tell you to look my way?"

As she moved her head back, Hope mumbled, "That's what she told me."

"Let's see what else she's told you." Celeste stopped the swing, and then sat at the table and poured herself a drink, Jack on the rocks. "What do you want darling?"

"I will take Southern on the rocks."

"What about you?"

Barbara meekly said, "I don't drink."

"Yeah, I know…" Celeste fixed her a tall glass of lemonade. Barbara looked at the drink then at Hope. Celeste sipped on her Jack. "Why are you looking at her? You came to be my great-grand-niece. So look at me! Tell me about your father who ran out and left you! Tell me about your jailbird brother! And your little brother who you want to save and the reason you come to us."

Hope looked at Barbara. Barbara remained quiet as her stare into Celeste's eyes intensified. Neither knew whether Celeste was doing a quick profile or had done research and knew of their friendship. Hope hinted at it, "So who have you been speaking to at TGI?"

"Don't insult me, darling! Do you think I need to check up on you? I know you, love you, trust you…until today. I guess I will always love you but the other two, I don't know. How dare you be so gullible and bring our enemy to my house? Look around you." Barbara continued staring at Celeste. Hope looked up and down the block. The sun, soon to set, held low on the western sky; that far away, it gave relief to what had been a day with temperatures in the mid-nineties. Hope had never taken in the maze this block formed. She just realized it only had one exit. Celeste's house sat dead center on the walled-off side of the street. Across hers, closer to the corner from where the taxi had come, a man pretended to be watering his lawn. The side street across two women chatted and glanced in their direction every now and then. "So, tell me, what's the plan? You can talk now. Why do you want to be a woman of SUM?"

Barbara remained quiet. Hope nudged her to speak. "I don't have to answer because she's not going to write the letter."

"You damn right I am not going to write no f'n letter for you. I've seen your kind before. I give you three days before you start talking about there's a death in the family. Five days before you reach a compromise with some boy or boys and bend over for them so that they can cover your back. Seven days before you disappear for weeks then when found lounging somewhere comfy, claim you could not find your way out of the woods. I know your kind, you are weak, unstable, pathetic, ugly, smelly…" Right there, Barbara fell into tears. She made to go wipe her tears with her left but lost her balance when Celeste kicked the bench. The pushback caused her to fall forward. "Who the fuck told you to get off the bench, you little tramp?" She jumped back on the bench as her sobs deepened. "Oh, you disgust me, you little weak fucker!"

Celeste grabbed her drink and walked into the house. When she was out of earshot, Barbara stopped crying and chuckled, "Your great-granny is hilarious."

Taken back by Barbara's performance, Hope showed her surprise by saying, "I thought…"

"Only way to stop her is to give in before it gets worse. And, trust me, it can get worse. So cry when she comes at you or this can get ugly." She heard Celeste retuning so she restarted her sobbing. "I'm sorry Mrs. Kendall. I did not mean to come here and try to fool you into thinking I was something I'm not."

Celeste ignored her and fixed another drink. "So, do you want a drink or not?"

"No, Ma'am."

"So what happens when you go in the field and the mission requires that you get drunk, smoke some marijuana….Oh I almost forgot. You little heifers hit me so hard with your girl-on-girl action that I completely forgot." She shouted, "You got my shit?"

Hope went to her traveling bag and pulled out a large Ziploc bag filled to the brim with buds. "No I did not forget."

"Come on! Roll a fat one! We got hours and days to go at this!" She sipped her drink. "Where was I...yes, so when you're in the field and you're on a business trip and your boss gets the drinking started and the client you're pitching has that hungry look in his face. Oh no, let's not skip to that yet! You look like you got some strength to you. What happens when things go out of control, and even though we are and have always been against sisters striking each other, especially pledges. What happens when shit just gets hectic and the sister loses her cool and just smacks..." SMACK "...and just smacks the shit out of you?"

Barbara did not cry or move, only stared into Celeste's eyes, to show the anger rising in her after Celeste's smack. "Nothing. Ma'am! I do nothing. For if these were real combat situations, I would be surrounded just as I now am, and any move on my part would surely mean my death."

"Oh fuck that! Anybody put their hands on you, you strike back! You hear me!"

"No you don't!" Hope said.

"Who the fuck asked you?" Celeste snatched the joint from Hope's fingers and flicked her lighter at it. Hope poured herself another drink. "So now you decide to intervene, after sitting here and letting me completely trash your friend?"

"I just felt that meeting you would give her an indication as to what she will be up against."

"Oh, shut up!" Hope did. "Listen, you don't smoke, you don't drink, you probably don't suck dick...so I'm really not sure how you plan to survive in the field."

"I am hoping to qualify as an Analyst."

Celeste almost gagged on the smoke. Her coughs forced her to bend over as if it were a reflex, a training to regain her footing. She took one deep breath, coughed then spat out a gang of phlegm. "Oh man, you two· little bitches are really trying to kill me. Not only are you bringing me this little skeezer from a dysfunctional family and environment, she wants to bypass at the minimum twenty years of duty, to compress it into what…"

"I think I can do it in 5 years."

Celeste sat back, crossed right leg over left and for the first time really looked at Barbara. The clearness in her eyes, the conservatively-styled hair and the square shoulders spoke of a purity that contrasted the overpowering physicality of her body. Celeste took a long pull on the joint and repeatedly nodded her head. "You do know the basic training is no more than ten weeks, right? And if you are willing to serve under someone, you can get your three letters in about two or three years? You do know that, right?" Barbara nodded. Celeste nodded and motioned the joint to her. Barbara took it but was slow to put it in her mouth. Then Celeste handed her the rum glass after spilling in two fingers of Jack. Barbara took a swig right after she blew the remaining smoke out, through her nostrils. "You know you failed, right?"

"No I didn't."

"I'm not giving you my Legacy Exception."

"Oh, I knew that."

"Then why did you drink? And smoke?"

"I knew it the moment I came onto the porch and you didn't shake my hand. It's the same reception the SUM women on the campus gave me."

Celeste nodded her head several times. "Then why did you answer my questions?"

"Because I have the utmost respect for what you went through and your ability to live this long under constant pressure and surveillance." Celeste motioned for her to return the joint. "No, I will finish."

"That's what I'm afraid of. Pass the weed, girl!" Barbara laughed. Celeste only smiled then continued. "You're very crafty. So, let's say you are able to take the pledge, do you trust her?" She didn't look at Hope, who nearly choked on the weed smoke. "Do you trust her with your life?"

"Yes."

"How do you know she didn't walk you into an ambush on purpose?"

"She told me since November that you wouldn't give me the exception."

Celeste turned to Hope. Her words had to sneak out the corner of her mouth because of her sneer. "Then why'd you bring her here?"

"I figured after you met her that you might change your mind." Hope passed her the joint as she sipped on her Jack

"Let me see if I understand this. She trusts you but you don't trust her?" Celeste was staring at Hope and motioned for Barbara to look away. "Barbie, you do the answering."

"She doesn't trust me."

Hope did not blink.

"You love her but she doesn't love you?"

"She loves me."

Hope did not blink.

"Hope, does Barbara know you're a cousin-fucker?" Barbara turned her head and Celeste motioned for her to look away. "Yes, her first lay was her cousin." Hope did not blink. "You thought I didn't know. I mean you were so pathetic that your older brother had to get you a prom date by coercing the guy he gave his SBD Legacy Exception into being your date. And, what do you do? You fuck him on prom night. And from what I hear – you got BUSY!"

The way the smoke gushed out of Celeste's mouth and blew into her face unnerved Hope so she talked out of turn. "Richard's not my cousin. He's a first generation SBD."

"What? You're telling me I don't know my own family? His family was one of the original five. They lost their standing around the same time I gained mine. He's your fourth cousin on your mother's side." Celeste started laughing. "I mean all you had to do was tell your mother who your prom date was and she could have filled you in. But no, you don't talk to your mother 'cause you hate your mother." Celeste turned to Barbara. "Did she tell you she hates her mother?"

"I don't hate my mother."

"Who is talking to you, you little cousin-fucker? I'm talking to Barbie. What's the matter you don't trust her to speak for you, yet you bring her here?"

"This is not about her. It's about me."

"It's not about you. It's about me. It's my legacy on the line, not yours. Maybe when you're my age…"

Hope interrupted her. "I'm taking the Legacy Exemption."

"You're what?

"I'm taking…"

"I heard what you said. Oh, oh, you two did come here to kill me. I'm trying to live to one-hundred something. I don't have time for these little games of yours. You are not taking the Exemption, and you are not getting the Exception. That's that. Now drink up. Smoke up! And please shut the fuck up! Both of you!"

Barbara sipped her drink and glanced at Hope who was not going to let it die. "I am taking the Legacy Exemption. There are many things that do not sit well with me, especially the Exclusion of 1950."

"That has nothing to do with my legacy. I stood tall. Fuck what you might have heard." Celeste stood up and shouted so that everyone who was still milling outside could hear. "I stood tall."

"I know GG Celeste but we can go so much further if we remove the Exclusion. By the twenty-first century, wouldn't you like to have it stated that under your continuing legacy, white women were allowed into the Society."

Celeste and Barbara said it simultaneously. "Fuck a white girl!" Then Celeste reached out her right hand so that Barbara could slap her five. "Word!"

"Your roommate is white and you live in a white dorm."

Celeste answered for Barbara. "So? You do what you have to do to survive."

"What, now she's all of a sudden not your friend?"

"Of course she's my friend. I love that girl but let's be real, I ain't trying to worry about her and my SBD brothers."

Celeste looked at her and corrected. "Those ain't your brothers! Those are your future husbands, fathers of your children, or misters, if you get put on the back burner like her mother was."

The way Celeste moved her head when she said "her mother" enraged Hope. "There you go again starting some shit about my mother."

"Little girl, watch your mouth! Do you know who you're talking to? Forget that GG Celeste bullshit. I can bury you alive right here in this fucking lawn and no one would even come looking for you." Hope didn't say a word. "Have you met her mother?"

Barbara nodded. "Third Generation SUM which means her grandmother got in the same period I did. But if you look down their history, not one daughter made SUM. Not one had the moral fortitude, the academic standard, and this little bitch has the nerve to walk in here, as my only great-granddaughter born of a SBD and SUM union who has the qualifications. She has the nerve to walk in here, and bring you along, three hundred-somewhat miles from home to talk this nonsense."

"You don't seem to understand how the Exclusion hurts our standing as women. People think we cannot compete on a level playing field."

"Well let them, darling! Let them know we tote the hoe, and asked for more. Let them know when the crops in the field drowned in blood that it was not our period. For it was an era, wherein we stood tall, next to our men and they by us. From whips to spit, we are SUM women and we ain't scared of shit!"

Barbara chimed in. "Yeah! Fuck a level playing field when we're already winning with the odds stacked against us!"

Celeste smiled. "Sweetie, you make me want to take out my dentures and tongue kiss you."

Hope swung one more time. "We are doing our men and ourselves a disservice. Look at the other side of the line…"

Celeste interrupted. "Oh, that's it! That's it! Oh my! Oh my! I gotta sit down. You are in love with a MAX boy. A MAX boy – wow! Who?"

Hope cut Barbara a look that pretty much said, I will kill you right here. "No I meant, look at the other side. The women who walked away from the Society. They are free GG, they are free."

"Let them! Let them be free, my darling! You too are free. You can do anything you want. You can marry anyone you want, including a MAX boy. Just do yourself a favor. Always be able to Stand Under Morality…and uphold this legacy."

"I'm still taking the Exemption."

"Then you gotta leave."

"We're here for the week."

"No, you both get out. I will call you a taxi and give you enough money for a week's stay at a posh hotel. Once you leave here tonight, I don't know either of you unless you both become SUM women. Not just one of you, but you both. And, you…" She pointed at Hope. "If you do take the Exemption, don't think I will not try my best to kill you. I can always get a young woman to take the Exception to continue my legacy. But the stuff you are trying to accomplish, I seriously wish you'd reconsider. The field is what it is, what it is meant to be. Before you can change the playing field, you have to show proof that it exists. And guess what, we're the biggest secret in the world. We do not exist. WE WOMEN DO NOT EXIST!"

RUMORS & GOSSIP

The taxi took ten minutes to arrive but GG Celeste never came out of the house. Barbara and I remained quiet. I could feel and smell her fear the moment she rushed off the bench to sit at the table. The scant turn she took to look over her shoulders and past the house's open front door spoke volumes. She would rather leave as night fell than sleep under my great-grandmother's roof. Though I had seen her angry, GG Celeste's scolds never scared me, not even when she ridiculed, using a tone similar to the one she used tonight. The foul language hinted her spiel to be, at least, part act, for I had never heard her use such off-color words. Plus, her enunciation was off. She often chided me when I dropped the letter 'g' when using the progressive form.

I came to spend a week with her every summer ever since I could remember. As I got older and entering high school, she always handed me an envelope as a taxi pulled up. The envelope would have cash and a note of things on which to focus the next academic year. These ranged from class lessons and life lessons, particularly what rumors were spreading, and to avoid gossip at all cost.

That night my envelope had one-thousand dollars in crisp one-hundred bills but no note. Barbara's contained five one-hundred dollar bills. No words or hugs for either of us, just a slight frown she could not conceal. My shame stemmed from her charge that I purposely brought Barbara into an ambush. Though not the case, I did want Barbara to get a sense of the graveness of the choice she wanted to make. My miscalculation shamed me the most, as I never realized that great-granny Celeste lived trapped for a choice she made at age nineteen. It consumed her through an intense military-style training and bounded her to a creed she cherished more than her life. She retired the year I was conceived yet she still carried the burden, the mantle, the torch to this day. My great-granny was beautiful in the way old Black ladies born at the turn of the twentieth century were. Never one to wear hair to her shoulder, her hair coalesced into tight curls, a starched look to them as they caressed the back of her neck. That look took her from age twenty to eighty, up to when her hair thinned to the point where she let the natural texture return, its coils overlapping two colors, black and gray, shaped into two circular braids that met at the base of her skull. Her crown, she called it; a crown it resembled. My entry into SUM could simply be added after-the-fact as her legacy, while my failure even if not linked directly to her legacy would be an asterisk to an otherwise stellar career.

The direct links listed three direct SPADES families started under her watch, and one hundred and seventeen human deaths from her work. For what she created multiplied into children and children of children over a sixty-year period; while those who died and their ancestors never knew why, because women like my great-grandmother did not exist. Now she held me in contempt for making her existence known to Barbara, who still had not said a word.

The same taxi driver who picked us up at the airport showed up. I distinctively recalled flagging him down, but it could have been him awaiting us, letting other taxis go ahead so he would be next on line at the taxi stand. When he pulled up in front of the house, we descended the steps and turned for a simple wave good-bye. GG Celeste returned the gesture, but offered no more. I thought when we opened the envelope there would be an Exception letter for Barbara, but nothing besides the cash. I contemplated about a taxi with no destination, turning onto the main road. The right play would be to tell him a fake destination and switch to another cab, but I sensed he already knew our hotel.

The trust required when the word got put out on you became the same as being the food taster for a marked despot. I needed to know Barbara's thoughts but the taxi driver had not turned on the radio.

Three or more streets in this town resembled many other small towns, a tony suburb feeding off a cosmopolitan city. From the main road heading onto the highway, the sights of Arlington Cemetery, the Pentagon and other monuments in the distance clarified the magnitude of my next undertaking. Crossing the Woodrow Wilson Bridge moved us past my yearly visit, the best part of my summers, where I vegetated on the living room sofa and read, smoked and drank with great-granny. I was twelve years old the first time she gave me a drink, my first ever. She asked if I had ever done it; I said no. She laughed and labeled me a good girl. Then she explained to me what made a woman a woman, at least to her. GG Celeste defined herself not by her conquest, by men, by anything tangible. She said her spirit, that feeling she had knowing that if anyone stood close enough to her, she would not need to utter one single word for the person to know exactly how she felt about him or her. "It's a sense, not so common but anyone can learn it – female or male. Yes, when you stand next to a man and he can sense you, and you can sense him. That's when you know. Other than that, it's ok to do it with them, do it to them, but don't feel it, at least not like that, not in that place that makes you a woman."

The Hilton Hotel in the Capitol, off K Street coming into sight loosened the tension from my shoulders. The driver shook off the tip and smiled. We got to the registration desk and our names were already in their log, for a deluxe suite with two queen-size beds, and a rental car - paid up for the week. Barbara gushed about the room's posh furniture, polished cherry wood all-around, a sofa, love seat, two table chairs at a desk, a small dining table with two chairs, brass portrait mirror in the living room, a full-length one in the bedroom across the closet door near the window, with the two beds separated by a standing lamp, and flanked on the outside by two reading lamps atop night tables. The feel and smell of real money after the royal treatment the service workers bestowed upon us wowed her. Though familiar with it, it was not something I took for granted. My initial thought would have been a motel for two nights and use the rest for clothes and weed. I reasoned this selection to be something GG Celeste used to show Barbara the rewards of making it into the Society.

I had a grand to play with in DC but first I needed to clear the air. My great-grandmother said so many things in less than two hours, things that countered what I took as truths and some I never imagined nor understood. Before this went further, I asked Barbara, "I thought you were a virgin?"

"I am." She said it as she opened drawers as if hoping the previous guests had forgotten valuables.

"Four boys and seven girls?"

She laughed to prompt me to think it the silliest thing in the world. "She threw that out there and it shook you. You have to do a much better job than that when questioned."

"Why those numbers?"

"Rumors and gossip."

"What do you know about Rumors & Gossip?"

"I've been a victim of it ever since late middle school. And, by my count that would be the number of people I've had sex with. So, it tells me your great-grandmother is much more than she's ever even told you."

"How so?"

"Once people started throwing out words like SUM and SBD, I asked questions. For every half answer I got, I did research in the library, pulled old newspaper clippings. By the time I got around to your GG, I was floored. The pictures. The houses you, your family, the people you've associated with for close to eighty years. I knew I wanted in but I also knew she wasn't going to sign off on me...unless...unless you were convincing."

"So you're blaming me?"

"No, I'm saying what you don't know how to say, what you can't rightly say, what your GG came out and said."

"She was wrong for that…"

"No, she wasn't. It is what it is. What I have to overcome. This is my big chance – to marry one man and stay that way until death. To raise one family. To pass that knowledge to my little brother." Barbara slowed her pace, to adjust the words, as if wanting to make sure she did not offend me, "You take that for granted."

"No, I don't."

Accusatory notes seeped from underneath her pleading tone. "Yes, you do. If you didn't, you would have never brought me to meet your great-grandmother." I tried to interrupt but she put her hands up so she could continue. "If you did, you would have come to visit her and tell her that you're taking the Acceptance. Then next year, after you were in, you could then convince her to write the Exception for me."

"What, you hear some rumors and gossip and you think you know my family? What I'm about? Before moving to my father's in Westchester, I grew up in The Bronx, the heart of it. By no means poor but you've been to my mom's house you know the deal. You out here acting like you grew up in St. Mary's just 'cause your parents grew up there."

"That's not what I'm saying. I'm saying that you underestimate how dangerous this is. You can bypass the pledge process. You can start above an analyst level, above managerial and go right up to be a director…and you came here to tell your great-grandmother to fuck it, fuck all the work she did, her life's work."

We stood face to face but not in a confrontational way. We were baring, lowering the barriers erected between us ever since that night. But before this went on any longer I had to correct her faulty thinking. "No, I am honoring her legacy by letting her know that her walk was worth it, letting her understand that I internalized all the lessons she taught me. This whole idea of accepting a legacy is totally ruining the Society. This is supposed to be a meritocracy but all everyone cares about is themselves and kickbacks, as long as the money flows up."

"Money? What money?"

My laughter drew her in. "Well, you're the one who did the research. You think the pictures, the cotillions, the big homes, the people who are named such and such the third or the fourth. What you think all of that is for? Show? This is the SUM of what we live for, what we fight for: Money, Power, Respect. You get what I'm saying?"

"Wouldn't you make or get as much as a director?"

"Yes, in due time. But I'm talking about 1920s, 1940s, 1960s and now 1980s. Four generations. All those names you came across in your research, anyone after my great-granny pays up to her, and bows to her. She pays and bows to the people before her. Now I'm walking in and inverting it, and not just up to the 1920's either. I'm talking back to the 1860's."

"Is that why she threatened to kill you?"

"Yes, if I don't make it, her legacy in SUM is broken and in a generation or two, we might be dirt poor and straight-up outcast until the end of time, or someone offers a family member an Exception."

"What's the point?"

"What the fuck you mean what's the point? How do you feel when people say four boys and seven girls?"

"I feel no ways about it because I know the truth."

"There is no fucking Truth. There is only Rumors & Gossip. And, the sooner you get that through your skull, the better it is for you."

"Correction, for you and me. Remember your great-grandmother said we both have to make it or she never wants to see you again."

"So? I don't care if I ever see her again. There is no you and me. When this process starts, keep in mind that you have to trust me. I don't have to trust you."

"One day you will."

I only smiled to agree and say, "You're right. But by then you will be so deep in this Society, you will know enough to keep your mouth shut."

Barbara smiled back and made to grab my hand like syrupy words yearned to pour out of her mouth. I pushed her hands away and told her to hit the shower so we can go clubbing. I went to the suitcase and took out a large Ziploc of weed and a bottle of Southern Comfort. "Wasn't that for your…"

"Her loss, right?" With that I rolled a joint as she headed to the bathroom.

>=<

We stayed in the District until Friday night. We did some tourist stuff and learned about the district's layout and design. We thought of partying that last night but after a week of recruiting during the day and partying at night, we were dead tired. In this instance, recruiting meant visiting all the local campuses even those with no formal SUM chapter. For the ones with charters, I employed the normal way to find a SUM woman or any member of the Society. Simply sit on the front steps, the left side, of the school's main library. We did two or three schools a day. We hit Howard University first. The main campus blended with the neighborhood, but once you passed the entrance off Georgia Avenue, you felt as if you entered a different world. The Quad. The Founders Library. Even in the end of summer with few or no classes in session, the campus felt alive, like home. We waited, hoping someone would eventually show, even on campuses with no known charter. The membership was nowhere near where it needed to be, not when compared to fraternities and sororities founded after our Society. But, that was fine because we did not need that many members but we did need to have close to twenty-five hundred members for what I had planned. The power of the Society also lied in the people who were not a part of it but enjoyed the benefits of our work. Those people knew enough to talk about us, our existence but nothing relevant, only the untruths we leaked. Eventually the word got around that there were two SUM women on the campus. Even though I had yet to take the oath, my legacy gave me close to all the privileges of a sworn member. I told Barbara how to sit to look like a member and to not say a word.

Someone in the family, the Society would eventually show up as word spread about the two women sitting on the library's steps. Their chit chat would be different than that of the outsiders. It would go from either a recognition symbol or they would sit close enough to listen to the conversation I pretended to be having with Barbara.

The week's mission was simple. I needed someone in the Society to take Barbara's virginity, even if she really wasn't one. I needed someone to bed her and give her a Legacy Exception.

No takers.

Everyone understood our indirect conversation, the offer being made, including Barbara. By Thursday though no one had extended her a hand, enough members knew I planned to take the Legacy Exemption. So they had a choice to side with me now or pay dearly later. I got less than a tenth of the support I expected. Finally on the last day, a Friday afternoon on the Morgan State campus, I came direct, hard at a young boy of no more than sixteen. He moved with the swagger of a boy whose older brothers had taken the Legacy Exemption and, in a few years, he who would do the same. He introduced himself as Sterling Mansfield, the youngest of the Mansfield boys. "How come? You're trying to tell me you don't want this full-bodied grown woman?"

He circled his bicycle around a small dirt patch off the grass. The crisp baseball cap with the brim tilted up to show bushy eyebrows towering over sneaky eyes, broad nose and a bold smile. "I do but I ain't trying to die over no chick."

"Then what do you plan to die over?"

"My own woman."

I called his bluff. "You ain't got no woman."

"I know but I will in three years."

I maintained the jovial back and forth because he exuded a good energy. I also sensed, this near to my GG's zone, he knew my legacy and the offer I made too good to pass up. I knew the family name as third generation SBD with no SUM women out of a birth, only previous marriages. "What's wrong with now? I doubt you will do any better. Look at her. Full-bodied and sexy as hell."

He thought about it for awhile. "Nah, like I said, it ain't worth dying over. And, I'm not talking about you, beautiful." Sterling gave her quick smile. "You're definitely worth dying over but it's just that there's a name on you."

"A what?" Barbara spoke even though I told her to never open her mouth in a closed conversation. Her words did do something. It confirmed that she was indeed a virgin. The way she balked, thinking someone had claimed to having penetrated her walls. "Who the hell?"

Sterling looked confusedly at me, because she had no idea whose legacy she was representing, which honestly put three lives in danger if the boy chose to run away and tell someone just that. That she didn't know the name of her protector. "It's OK. Your secret stays with me."

"What's the name?"

"A Manny Davenport."

Some odd reason, in my mind, I already jumped to assume Ken would be the name. "Manny, he's a MAX boy."

"By choice."

"What? I looked up his name…"

Sterling interrupted and I could sense his discomfort in aligning with us. He rushed his words. "By choice. My father got pull and pulled his file. It has to do with his father. Something about the Freedom of Information Act."

"He's one of us?"

"Not anymore. But I tell you one thing. The dude got good taste." He spun his bike around and talked to us over his left shoulder. "Do you know how many SBD brothers congregated after your visit to Howard on Monday?"

I stood up. "And not one stepped up?"

"Ain't nobody trying to mess with that dude. It would take at least five years to get to him. It's easier to just kill her and be done with it, and then let him come after the culprit."

"What's the word on me?"

He turned back to face us and sized me up. Right there, I thought of the three years and knew I could wait. This little boy had an appeal to him. He said, "You tell me."

I thought about it. "Four generations and better? That leaves only like twenty men and what, only five or six available?"

"I like your math."

"Thanks but tell them they're wrong. A brother doesn't have to be my equal or higher to step to me. Just love me for who I am."

He dropped his bike and startled me. He rushed toward me. "I'm in."

Flattered, I said, "If your father gives you permission, come to my hotel tonight. I'm staying at The Hilton in DC, on 16th and K Streets. I'm there until ten unless you show up."

"If he doesn't, can you at least give me something to remember you by?"

Taken aback by his forwardness, I asked, "Like what?"

"Can I feel your titties?" He chuckled.

I smiled to show I had not taken offense. Having two brothers and hearing of their priorities, and remembering the joy of grade school boys, I said, "Sure but be very discreet." He made to give me a hug and took a good squeeze with a hand on each breast as he made his way to caress my back. Inside his bear hug, I slid my right hand to the front of his pants and gave it a gentle squeeze. He was rock hard. His moan revealed his innocence and I gave him a soft peck on the cheek. As he backed away, I said, "If you can't come by tonight, don't forget to put your money on me."

"How much?"

"I think the slots are one hundred. If you can put one-thousand dollars, in ten years, you stand to make a million."

"Are you sure?"

"Yeah, especially now that we got Davenport on our side."

He boarded his bike and gestured his head toward her. "But she got the look of someone who's bound to get a brother killed."

I sat down and put my arm around Barbara's neck and though I felt her slight jitteriness, I said. "As long as you worship pussy, you got nothing to worry about."

He looked at us, smiled and nodded. As he pedaled away, he said, "True. That's true!"

WHO INVITED THAT WHITE GIRL?

At best, a legacy without a daughter would want in on the SUM side or a SBD brother who knew the benefit of claiming a wife early would extend his son to Barbara. But, somehow we surpassed all expectations, an abandoned legacy came through and she was free to use it and have the value of a fourth generation SUM woman if she completed the process.

Attitude never spoke much of his family. Last year the winter break we all hung out but we mostly met in the city for clubs, Greek jams or sight-seeing. In the summer he stayed up at school to catch up on classes and would occasionally come down. I asked him to pick me up at home but he passed, and drove right past. His excuses never added up - that he didn't feel like getting off the highway and getting lost on some back road. I only laughed, thinking he knew better than to think I lived in the country or woods of a podunk town. Most nights it would be just the three of us, but in the oft-chance it was just me and him, I got a chance to sense how he felt. On the surface it felt like hanging with a homie but his persona kept every male at bay.

Night fell quickly as I had waited Sterling, the young Mansfield boy. By the time we finished eating at some around the way eatery off I-95, sleep started calling me. Barbara did not have a license, not even a learner's permit. Even without those papers, I would have let her do the driving but she did not even know how to drive. The opposite of the Nassau and Suffolk County girls I knew, I realized she was actually country. Most of the L.I. girls I met were legacies like me who grew up with access to cars and expectations to grow up fast while remaining above the fray. The highway fascinated her. I picked up on this during the bus ride down to the airport. Her face practically glued to the window, reading signs, gazing the landscape and checking out passing vehicles. Her shelter did not come from the cocoon of being homebound but by a radius of six miles, and hurdles of access and navigation. The road from Baltimore through Delaware shrunk when we got to the New Jersey turnpike. I cruised the right lane not so much out of no hurry to reach home but pacing myself to understand the fear that appeared on her face when she learned Manny got her onto the pledge class via a Legacy Acceptance.

But now it made clear sense. He understood the norms of this side. They did not apply to him as long as he lived the choice to fight for the Pride side. On this side, I would be his wife at first touch. Whereas being rejected by a guy should cause a woman to feel unloved, Attitude's brotherly love had layered me with more confidence. He allowed me the choice to decide whether I wanted to deal with that insecure feeling that sex without love often caused. For Barbara, she would forever be his sister or his wife – his choice. With the family history sealed, she wouldn't have to fight any old battles, but she knew this acceptance gave him some control over her.

On the rare occasions I convinced Miranda to come out to hang with us, she never wanted to be near Attitude, simply because he was a MAX boy.

Two semesters had gone by and the three of us went from being The Conscious Daughters to three women contending for one prize. It really did not have to be like that. In fact it was not like that, especially if everyone stayed in their place, played their role. I came in as a fourth generation legacy. Miranda got an Exception from a living legacy who never bore a daughter so they set her protection to the Nth degree. She would have to do something dastardly, offhand, unbecoming not to make SUM. Barbara also walked in with major protection, also under a fourth generation legacy, yet very vulnerable since Attitude had become a MAX boy by choice. Who did that in this day and age? Who did that with their numbers down to less than one hundred members nationally. True, many more were alive but they did not participate in the Society.

She accepted the legacy but under fear and panic. I had never seen her so jittery and so quiet, not even when GG Celeste gave her a sense of the resolve she would need for initiation. She knew something about his family or him but could not say, and I did not want to know because my feelings for Attitude could not affect any decision during or after the process.

Scheduled to start on the first week of September with a large party at the house used by the Society for all social and initiation activities, the pledge process had two levels. The first level consisted of various socials to get to know the family. People would travel from near and far, to any town and speak their approval or disapproval. Every available bachelor down to four years a man's or woman's junior could come and make a case for a hand in marriage within the Society.

This went on until the campus's annual SUM Surfacing Party. On that night all pledges took an oath to give up what they had come to accept as their identity and enter the body as one whole. To do so, the pledges wore black everyday until the remainder of the process. All black everything to symbolize mourning as well as depth and that which should not be touched. At any point a pledge could wear a different color, preferably white, to end the process. That night she would be questioned using the standard format. If her answers were satisfactory, she would be welcomed into the Society on the day that all others completed the process. The wrong answers, she lost her chance to ever being admitted. So, the best thing to do was wear black until you were told not to.

For the Surfacing Party, all pledges were asked to forego vanity from that point forward, until the end of the process. This consisted of no makeup, no fashionable clothes and the removal of all body hair, specifically the head. Up to that point for the socials, the ones convened for a mate to be chosen, the women had been told to doll up and look their very best. By the Surfacing Party, each woman had a clear idea who their suitors would be, the SBD brother who would stand there, within the Society, and be their mate. This union kept legacies intact. It did not mean you had to marry this person in real life, but in most ways it was the easiest way to go about it. Our problem boiled down to having only three SBD brothers and nine of us women. For me, that did not pose a problem. For tradition's sake, Ken would come to me and I would accept because the Society expected legacies to align or the man's to be higher than the woman's. I knew he would end up with Barbara because as she noted, he extended his hand to her from day one. Within the Society, we could couple; in the real world, she could have him if she wanted.

No matter how simple that sounded, during the second social, he whispered, "You feel like having company later?"

He understood protocol too well to ask this and I knew a power play too well to say no. The night featured an October sky filled with stars, a clear, dark sky and temperatures in the low sixties. Thirty members lounged around the house. I noticed that of the males none really spoke to me while Miranda, Barbara and the others got the most attention from them. Though they feigned to be distracted with their own conversations, the SUM women observed and listened. They picked up on all sort of loose words, those they could use later to break down a pledge.

As Ken drove that night, he played the radio, a tape since the local stations did not play R&B ballads at night and he obviously did not want to waste time trying to fight through the static of the nearest station catering to a Black audience. A comfortable silence encircled us, reminding me we had never held a conversation without other people around. We had never been alone. OK, I decided, "I will bite."

"Where?"

The humor threw me a bit as he was the serious, silent type. His smile under a thick black mustache showed a man wise beyond his years. The sideward glance and shake of the head told me he had more on his mind so I pushed further. "What do you have in mind?'

"Do you like me?"

The words though a bit more to the point than I expected let me know he wanted to play for keeps. "Yes, I do. But the real question is do you love me?"

"Yes but only as much as you will let me." I held my words so that he could continue. "You do know that you cannot end up with Manny, right? Not in the Society and not even in real life."

Both were true if we played by the book but the second was easy to accomplish, if only Ken would just shut up. Even as a MAX boy, Manny could have attended the many socials but he never came. "Do you love Barbara?"

"Yes, but she's not going to make it."

"Is this why you're here tonight?"

"No, there's always been this thing about you. From when you came over and introduced yourself. Early on I misread it but now that it's clear to me, I believe in you. And, these last two months of seeing you everyday, how you can be alone in a crowded room and not care, I like that. A whole lot."

I smiled then laughed. "That's it? That's what you like about me, that leads you into loving me?"

"There needs to be more?" I nodded. "Well you're beautiful, in that deadly way. The way you hold back your smile, try not to blink. Should I go on?"

"What's in it for me? For you?"

"I've been in this thing two years. Forget the legacy, the four generations we both have and stuff, and just think of the two years. It's much more than you think it is. More dangerous. It turns you into…not to be…I will avoid the clichés, but you get what I'm saying."

"You want me to take the Acceptance! I get that but what's in it for me? You didn't. Why should I?"

"If I did, I wouldn't have ended up on this side."

"You're a MAX legacy?"

"We've been on both sides throughout, but yeah, mother was a SUM and father not affiliated."

That revelation threw me for a major loop. "So no MAX can touch you and SBD got your back?"

"I wouldn't say no MAX can touch me but it's pretty much so. You and me, whichever way you go in, we can become King and Queen of this Society in a generation or so. No one could touch us."

"Oh! For a moment I thought you were making a power play against me."

He pulled the car into the large parking lot across from my dorm. The lot behind the dorm meant the car planned to stay for a brief period. The large lot across, at this time of night, meant the car parked for the night. "Why would I make a play against you?"

"My mind works that way. So, let me ask you: as King and Queen even if don't take the Acceptance, what is the difference?"

"I am asking you to save a life, maybe many."

"That's not in my hands." He tried to say something but I stopped him. "It's not, so it's up to you. Look at me and tell me whether you love me enough to spend more than one night."

At thirteen my great-grandmother taught me a powerful lesson. She said to always make eye contact with a person. You don't always have to do it in an intimidating, confrontation style. Just look and see how long the person hold your stare. When you are convinced that you can always look in the person's eyes and know when the truth is being told as opposed to a lie, then you can look away. Yet, she added, there are those times where it is best to be the one to look away, rather quickly at that; times when a person's pain is such that he is looking to lash out at anyone volunteering to understand his story.

A person who looks away first from your stare is not necessary lying, she might just be fearful of your story. My story was that scary but Ken stayed that night. We could have circled to his off-campus apartment since he had no roommate. When I tapped my roommate on the shoulder and whispered I needed privacy she wanted the details. I shushed her and she left the room. I heard her gasp, her soft voice as she undoubtedly stared in amazement that my first campus conquest was the guy the women called "the prize". I listened as her slippers swished in the halls of King Hall.

My sheets were cold not only because we kept the windows open until bed time. My sheets were cold because my eyes used them as a cover to protect me as I slept. The nightmares did not come this night or the many nights during the next two weeks that Ken opened me slowly and moved patiently to where he needed to get to, to where he needed to bring me. I had been there, real fast the couple of times Richard, my cousin, had rushed in me as we banged against each other like bumper cars stuck in a bad corner. Ken entered and stayed in that place where the pulse throbs and the slow pump pushed sounds out of our voice box. He was soft in a place I never expected. I felt it the first time I grabbed his wavy hair in both hands as a small cannon discharged inside me. He whispered his love to me in a way that I could not answer even though I echoed his words. He kissed my cheek, nuzzled my collarbone, teased my nipples, encircled my navel with the wetness of his tongue. As he parted my lips and slid in his tongue, I let myself go and rolled onto my stomach. Anything he wanted, anything but his patience and kindness.

Ken's love mired in its respectfulness, partly because SUM women commanded that. Since the outside world treated us as women where chivalry was barely only an option, the brothers went out their way to protect and cherish. SUM Surfacing Party had come to be our holiday, the ceremonial night when we took the pledge to enter and to endure. Ken had not mentioned the Acceptance since the first night but it crossed my mind every night we attended a social. The women, SUM and pledges, had come to accept me and the men spoke cordially. The Exemption no longer presented the fear it had when they thought me a renegade. With Ken the current campus king, the prize by my side, they figured I would have a balance to my voice so that any platform I chose would be implemented gradually. With Ken by my side I felt good and drifted off to the days after Thanksgiving weekend when the process would be over and we would hold hands in public. With the family, the surprise was the word had not spread to those outside the Society who would marvel at the real life wonder of it all.

Friday October 3, 1986. At the time it really did not matter that the other two SBD brothers selected pledges other than Miranda and Barbara. I remember the night of the last social clearer than any other day of my life. The days leading to it, we each received one invitation, a formal one, to give as an invitation to a woman we trusted with our lives. That person might get a call one night and decide whether we lived or died. Then we took the oath.

>=<

Once a SUM woman took the oath, very little is known about what happened afterward. We do know that Hope chose a freshman girl she had seen around the campus a few times. See, though a great-granddaughter and daughter of a SUM woman, Hope never learned what happened once one said, "I do". She did know that a stranger might care more for your life, much more than a former friend. Under the pressure of just having had your head shaved, all your clothes taken and told to return home in nothing more than that hooded black shroud handed to you, most are quick to think on the short-term, imagining the call would come in a few weeks. The call might never come, or come many, many years down the line. Many women have stopped wearing black because the person they invited to the SUM Surfacing party got spooked the night they saw the pledge standing next to a group of baldheaded Black women and being dictated by other Black women and men.

This was all for show. Yes, all for show! SUM women did not line up, walk military style around campus singing songs. What SUM women did was ask questions, hard pointed questions. They along with the SBD men, who are allowed to participate in certain aspects of the SUM pledge process, asked repeatedly, in the soundproof basement after they requested that Lena leave. They asked over and over and Barbara kept repeating, "No."

So, they kept asking, "Did you invite that white girl? Did Attitude tell you to invite that white girl? Who invited that white girl?"

Hope never answered. The process allowed one to never say a word for the duration. Each pledge got that same instruction so Hope kept wondering why Barbara kept talking, not incessantly but intermittently. Hope knew she would eventually give a convincing answer, one that could jeopardize the entire process. She could tell by the slight sounds, the breaths of the women to the right and left of her that most would not make it. She did not pick this up during the first two months when the pledge period and process consisted of mainly attending various socials.

She still sensed Barbara could make it even after making that error, the move Hope felt might have been a calculation to help Hope's platform of leveling the playing field, by overturning the Exclusion of 1950. Barbara had either mistaken Hope's goals or invited Lena for some sort of insurance.

Barbara's demeanor changed ever since the drive back from the District. During the study sessions, she obsessed over every word of the Society's history yet missed the key points, the very ones that led her to inviting Lena. During the socials she stayed to herself unless approached which she often was but her small talk felt stifled, forced. Before Ken came to Hope, he tried to smile at her, to remind her their initial connection but Barbara was not thinking real life, only the Society.

That night she answered with one word, "No" but that's all the SUM women needed to continue with the questions. On the third hour, she lied and said, "Attitude told me Lena was the best person to invite."

The room fell silent and Hope searched the eyes of the SUM women. No one believed her. Barbara then spun an elaborate tale how it happened. It left them with only one conclusion, to reveal why they kicked Lena out. "The taxi that brought her here has probably already been talked about. Let it go for tonight but get rid of her by Wednesday."

The words sounded so final so Hope had no choice but to break her silence. "I have a say and need to understand precisely what the plan is."

The second level of SUM pledging deals with learning what exactly was being said and to not get caught up in the Rumors & Gossip. After the oath most things said are usually fabricated with the truth hidden in the middle. They called it "talking around the margins". Their voices aimed to confuse the pledges into thinking a rumor actually happened as stated, or they attributed an event to a person other than the real culprit. "Why would you have a say?"

"The Exemption does not preclude a legacy's right to truth."

"And, what happens if these others do not make it to full understanding?"

"They should know enough to keep their mouth shut."

Another SUM woman said, "That white girl saw too much and she has no reason to keep our secrets. So she dies."

"Thank you." Hope did not care for truth at this point because she knew the risk of this even becoming a rumor, forget a reality. This would be in her file. This pledge class was in her name unless she also died.

The SUM women ordered them to fasten their blindfold and undress. Everyone left the room. The minute they were alone a few pledges made to relax and not stand on line next to each other. Hope stood still and did not say anything until she felt the opening of the first mouth. "Shut up!" She ordered. "You are not alone even when you are alone."

>=<

Sunday, Monday, Tuesday. All three nights the same thing. Stand naked in a room for hours without speaking. They showed up at 10:30 p.m. and pulled an all-nighter. They knelt against the wall to nod off. Then a foreign voice would either laugh or ask, "Is she sleeping?" The nudity bothered some. The silence played tricks on their minds. The sleep deprivation edged to break them. Hope knew that during the day they all snuck a nap and she did too. But for the past two days when she got to the campus, she searched for Lena. She didn't dare go to Poe Hall for they were forbidden to go to any dorm but King Hall, the cafeteria building and administrative buildings. Those, like her, who lived in King Hall got to nap on their own beds and since the process was not meant to bond them as sisters, no one extended themselves to help another, for fear of divulging a secret or slice of her life that could be used against them during the process or afterward.

On Wednesday morning, Hope took a risk and snuck by Barbara's class and told her she had to tell Lena to withdraw from school. She needed to get her off the campus. Yet as Hope left the cafeteria at 5 p.m., when dusk started to give the campus that spooky haunted Hitchcockian look with dark birds perched on semi-bare tree branches, she spotted Lena. Though she wore a depressed look, she walked as if she had not a care in the world. They were about fifty feet apart but she needed to get Lena's attention. Hope stopped and stared dead at Lena. Her eyes expressing "I can't believe it's you". Though she doubted Lena knew Morse Code, she blinked SOS and mouthed, "Get lost!"

The quad was filled with people. She put herself at risk knowing someone could go back and say she warned Lena. That would make her an accomplice but not telling her was a far greater risk. Hope wanted a curious person to intercept the message – a person with no ties to either of them, but with military training or versed in coded languages. Hope prayed that someone even if they did nothing about it, as far as warning Lena; just as long as that person knew and could testify she had warned the girl to get lost because her life was in danger.

Friday night. The first rumors hit. The white girl was nowhere to be found. People think she's in the moat. No, she went home last night after import night with some guy from the next town. No, she withdrew from school because she heard that someone was trying to kill her.

Whereas those rumors brought relief and peace of mind to Hope, the others turned into chatterboxes. All except Miranda and Barbara. Hope wondered with a week under their belt why were they talking especially while wearing a blindfold. She did not know where and how they were being observed but that did not matter. The room was padded with industrial foam, no visible holes, a square room centered within the dank basement. The first voice came from behind them, inside the wall. "Who told you about the white girl's disappearance?"

The second voice, "Don't act like you don't know what we're talking about."

Three of them started blabbing. Hope thought, if any of these chicks mention my name, I will take off my blindfold and beat the shit out of her. She listened carefully to their words to see if they had picked up the craft of talking around the margins. Hints here and there but not skilled enough to truly mask their fear.

The first voice replied, "So what are you scared off? What did you think this Society was about?"

On Saturday night, only The Conscious Daughters showed up. At first Hope did not believe the six others quit that easily but she saw them on Monday, Tuesday, Wednesday. She saw them wearing no hint of Black, and not a speck of white.

SISTERS OF HABIT

Only the three of us remained and we loved each other, at least I loved them. We kept quiet as children who learned to not speak even when spoken to. The walls around us no longer felt intrusive to our naked self. We had been rid of vanity. Our minds became quiet, still. The words, the rumors about so and so did not penetrate the meditative trance, the transformation we underwent. Even when a male voice spoke none of us made to cover our breasts, our pelvic area or hunch our shoulders in discomfort. The basement no longer felt damp, with hints of mold. It became a shelter we ran to immediately after class, after our meals. Often when in study hall, we rushed through our assignments and absorbed the material with an acuity we had never possessed. Our grades stayed the same for the subjects we cared little about or those whose professors could not teach. For our majors, anything less than a B+ grade on an exam we regarded as failure. That semester, those weeks in the basement strengthened us with a multi-dimensional view of how women lived through the Society's various eras. As the 1980s ended we would be tasked with pushing forward the Society's agenda. The sisters spoke of us, of themselves, as individuals. They passed on wisdom on how we were to carry ourselves. The sisters told of the sanctity we held, of that clear mental space to revisit when in duress. By calculation, Tuesday before Thanksgiving, November 25, 1986, we would become SUM women. That would make three weeks underground and ten above. No rumor told in that room shook us, for we learned truth did not exist unless we gave it life. Our words would be the only actions capable of moving us from here to there. So why speak of what was done, especially when there existed a real possibility it never truly occurred. We as women of SUM had a responsibility.

Those lessons of history and perception occurred nightly; their intensity heightened the moment the other six women deserted. The three of us stood there and never uttered a word, except when asked, ordered to talk about stuff we stated during the interview and the socials. We talked academics and career. We made sure not to get too chatty, to remain focus. Still somehow the sisters felt what we knew and with which we were quite comfortable. Yet, a divide dwelled amongst us, a deep mutual respect but a divide. Since the start, Miranda shifted from musical aspirations to fashion design, to plans of traveling the world, and eventually teaching on the university level. Barbara, who undoubtedly possessed the talent and look to make it in music, even if only with her writing skills, she had done a complete one-eighty into a focus on elementary education and social work. I stayed with my original major of English, specifically a strong interest in examining Art and Literature.

Once I spoke the last words the room got quiet but I could hear a slight murmur, something returned after a hiatus and I knew if I could hear it so could everyone else. The heart rate, the anticipation on both sides. Miranda on my right. Barbara on my left. I thought of breaking my thoughts by telling them to calm down but that would only lead to hours of interrogation. I knew I would not break but one, and possibly both, of them began showing weakness. I could not sense why, for it was very clear that this Saturday night, with less than three full days remaining; that this Saturday night would be the last we'd have to endure the darkness, the voices in the dark, on the margins of our existence. I pleaded, sent shock waves to their brains to stop fucking thinking.

The sisters told us we could leave for the night as they themselves wanted to attend the last big party before Thanksgiving break. We could leave the basement, the house. The SUM women left and headed to Barrington. They instructed us to gather our thoughts, go find a place to sleep and use tomorrow as a day of worship, and they would see us Monday night. We had not been sent to sleep on our own beds overnight for over six weeks. It was not a trick. We had basically completed the process. We had reached a freedom that only death could take away. We were for all intents and purposes, though not yet recognized or able to recognize them; we were women of SUM, as well as SUM women,. I wanted to release my tears as I heard the house empty but my eyes were covered, their eyes were covered, their hearts were beating, their thoughts were wavering.

"I am so horny."

"Girl, who you telling! This had to be the worse part of the process," added Barbara. That to me sounded like an act but how could I be certain? Perhaps being denied while not explicitly told not to do something awoke something in her.

I kept expecting to hear the voices interrupt us but we took off the blindfolds and the silence returned as we dressed. The house sat on the western hill flanking TGI. To get to it from the campus, one left out the main gate and drove or walked two miles on the first road. When the road ended, a flashing yellow light signaled the dead end street; one made two quick rights and the house lolled on a small hill. Cars could not climb it so passengers disembarked down below. The odd thing, there existed a shorter way to the house, just as there were shorter ways to get from leaving or entering TGI without going past the main gate. Through the woods, listen for the sound of the creek into which the campus's sewer system spilled. On the other side that creek sent water into a filtration system that funneled back to the school. Some of the paths led to nowhere and only caused one to end up back on the campus. The paths were not paved, no real trail to use as a guide unless one knew or created the markers needed to get from point A to B. Many endings since there were many points of entry from the campus. The administration never closed off the ditches on the edge of the perimeter wall because the original students, when TGI was a military training center; those students created them to sneak off and to bring people on campus; those students never told the administration they existed. I knew of them because my great-grandmother spoke of going into the woods and knowing that people often went there. She only went one time; from the campus and how did she get there from the house with the body and with no one seeing her, I could never figure.

I spent all of last year mapping the woods once I learned the location of the family's house. We called it the family's house because that's what it truly was. Ed Kendall bought it when he graduated, and he and GG Celeste lived there while she took courses. She being his wife made her admission much simpler. She talked of the love they shared, the duty he had to a mission he never spoke of. On the night she left the campus to go confirm the rumor that her husband, missing for three days, had indeed been lynched, she walked the path from the campus. So, I knew there had to be ways to get from point A to point B that had to do with the paths less traveled.

I showed the path to Barbara and Miranda, not out of some sisterly affection but because I needed them to know where to come and look for me in case I ever needed to get lost. The normal walk back to campus would reveal what time we left the house. Something told me some new rumor had reached, or this could be a final test. We would fail the test, that is the way of the process but it would be something we could make up in due time as SUM women. The key was to make certain the test would not divide us, The Conscious Daughters.

The woods were not completely dark since even the slightest moonlight penetrated through the forest of trees, especial this time of year. In the fall when the leaves' bare branches and stems crash to the ground, an off-step traveled for a mile. When a car on the main road went over thirty miles per hour, the head lights looked like a spaceship flying above. They were scared even though I held their hands and guided them. Each noise caused them to stop and look around. To reassure them I would motion to keep silent, or sign for them the object - human or animal - that could have possibly made the noise. That seemed to spook them more since they did not understand sign language. I meant deer, owls, furry harmless little ones, not bears, wolves and the like. Fraternities and sororities often took pledges into these woods since they could not hold charters and pledge people on the campus. Like all other organizations, they used their houses and occasionally sent the pledges into the woods for scavenger hunts. In fifteen minutes, we hit the point where the path curved a bit and landed behind the perimeter wall where a drop into a ditch and ten steps forward placed us on a slope muddied by the recent rains. The campus perimeter made the woods less threatening. To rid the mud, we dipped our feet up to our calves into the pond. "Now go get some sleep and talk to no one," I ordered.

"What? I'm gonna shower and go get me some."

"It's almost two in the morning, just go to sleep."

Miranda took a step toward me and said, "You wanna smell me?"

"What? That just sounds so nasty."

"Exactly," she said. "If I asked any guy that, right this moment, it would be on until six in the morning."

Barbara chimed in, "Yeah, I gotta make a few phone calls myself to see who's worthy."

We stood by the side door of King Hall. We lowered our voices as a few students walked by. "What the hell have you two been up to?"

"One thing this process did is make the right guys take notice. The dietary restrictions, the exercise, the stress. I have lost so much weight but mostly baby fat, and I'm the finest and fittest I've ever been. I'm ready. Are you ready Barbwire?"

"Oh yeah, even if it's by accident, if a guy looks in my direction, I'm grabbing his dick."

Miranda laughed.

"Ok you two need to stop. I'm begging you. Just three more days the most. Keep yourselves hidden. Keep your hoods on when in public. Talk to no one. And wear black."

"Who said we were going to stop?"

"Then what the hell are you two blabbing out? Talking about how horny you are when standing naked in a crowed room?" I walked away in disgust and with certainty that I had driven my point home.

I did not see either of them for the next two days. We worshipped differently. I went to the Methodist church in town, Barbara the Baptist service in town and Miranda the Catholic church over in Barrington.

Both nights had been quiet except for my roommate's excitement in seeing me. She did not know what I was doing but claimed it had to do with pledging. She talked of all the sororities and never mentioned SUM. She was a Freshman and had I not been focused on accomplishing SUM, I would have chased her out like I had done last year with my previous roommate, an upperclassmen at that. But this girl had a kind heart, kept lots of food in the room and disappeared the moment I indicated I needed space. Both nights she talked and caught me up on the latest happenings for the three schools. As she talked I imagined her having to stay quiet for an extended period of time. She was a plain pretty girl, in that skinny long limb body typified by young girls who ran high school track. Less than two years younger than me but I felt aged. Not one to ever having felt young since I first sat at my great-grandmother's feet, I wondered how this young girl looked naked, not in a sexual way, but the way we SUM women learned to harden ourselves under the discomfort peering eyes brought.

I never left the dorm room except for church but I rushed back in right after the service. I did the same for classes on Monday, anticipating our last study hall session. It should be our last since our night time sessions started after ten o'clock, and we'd have to rush on Tuesday to finish by midnight. I thought about this day, this night for so long in my life that at 6:23 p.m., I just cried as the young girl rambled about how good the party had been over at Barrington. She saw my sobs, apologized and made to leave the room. I stopped her and hugged to say, "Don't leave, sister. I love you."

She told me she loved me too, and I fully understood why we SUM women, though out of habit we call ourselves such, do not really consider each other sisters. We would not feel right to exclude others in this bond. We stay in the Society and keep it secret to preserve a tradition, to fight in the shadows to benefit the young girls who have a right to be free, in whatever they do. I donned the black robe and hood and went to the library. I waited on the left front step until 10 p.m., thinking perhaps Miranda and Barbara were together, thinking I missed something, as far as a scheduled meeting. Just as I left for the family's house, I spotted Barbara coming out of Poe Hall. She turned toward the front gate instead of coming toward the library. Across the quad, I saw Miranda exiting King Hall. We joined by the turn off the visitors parking lot. I pretended to take our silence as our customary stance, but I felt the deep divide between us.

Some nights we walked, particularly when we left the library early enough. Though we had no set time to assemble, we always tried to reach the house by 10:30 p.m. and always together once the other women stopped their process. The one time we arrived after that time, there was a discussion in full swing and we never got the substance of the conversation and that kept us off-balance for days.

The basement was empty and voices, from behind the wall, male and female, debated the day's best musical group. We undressed, piled our clothes in corners, respective wall spaces we had chosen as our own then we placed the blindfolds on each other. We stood as we normally did except the SUM women ordered us to remove our blindfolds. We teetered on the verge of the process being over – minimum one and half hours, or one more full day. With the blindfolds off and seeing the various women who had participated in our process enter the room; face to face, there was no way we walked out of there without becoming SUM women or quitting the process.

I felt my heart beat a second or two raster before the sister who had extended Miranda a legacy spoke. She was in her late thirties, a third generation SUM woman who carried her accomplishments on the surface like a badge, her quiet demeanor and wit matching her beauty. She tilted her head to side and looked at Barbara, then me, then Miranda. Then she let out a laugh. The other sisters, at least about thirty of them, in the room joined in until one said, "Wow! Y'all went out and got busy in your time off!"

These are the things SUM women could read so well in each other and other women. Not just sex but fear, doubt, arrogance, complacency, weakness, disunity, immorality. I gave Miranda and Barbara an order to stand together for just two days. "Another one said, you know what, I ain't mad at you. I lasted only twelve days and paid dearly for it throughout the process. We were worried about y'all three for a second. You women got everything it takes to make it but if you can't trust a brother, a man, you don't make it in this Society. Don't let no woman or man tell you differently!"

In SUM you never let your guard down, Miranda had been schooled from her first month on the campus up to this day. It's like her process started last September. Barbara got only a taste of it when she helped the SBD pledge class that quit early last year and those couple of hours with my great-grandmother. I grew up around SUM women. When I met them, they were all already in the Society and they never spoke of their process.

These women kept their words to a minimum so all this talking meant a bit of vicious gossip had hit us, all types of rumors were spreading, and these sisters were not going to let it stand amongst us.

Two weeks. Four weeks into this part of the process, I might have let the chips fall where they may. On the eve of completion, with the clock twenty minutes away from a midnight, a group of elderly women, sixty to eighty year-olds walked into the room and they too got naked. In that room everyone shed their clothes upon entry and a man who entered did so naked, for all to see and married the woman he came in to save. So, no man has ever entered when the women were naked. There was a price to pay if a man entered that room. I didn't know the exact fee and certain no one in the room did. But, there was a price to pay.

The elderly group remained silent but their eyes spoke of an unknown danger. The sister in charge took the lead back after everyone greeted each other. "The look in our eyes, very gentle but can also be very harsh. To make yourself known as one of us, after a slight stare inhale once to create a slight flare of your nose, a soft inhale that should give off a slight noise especially if you take care of your body as you had done these past months. Look at us beautiful, strong women who stand united under a banner of morality. We are a legacy of women who have faced our fear and can detect it by a simple stare and a soft inhale."

Everyone in the room looked into our eyes and inhaled softly. We were told to counter the recognition symbol. We were SUM women.

The sister continued. "Your work begins now but only you dictate what you follow but nothing that changes our current agenda moves unless authorized by the Queen. It is from her I send word to welcome you and to build your legacy. The Society's paperwork is grounded on the birth certificates that tell who was born to whom; as such for women, a legacy is upheld only in matters of matrimony, in monogamy, in motherhood within the Society."

Both their hearts were beating rapidly and mine wasn't so an elder woman spoke. "Is there something you would like to tell us?"

The sister in charge, "Excuse me!"

"I got a call to come in and I want to know if it's true."

"We do not entertain such outlandish rumors."

"My nephew is a man of his word."

"Does he wish to state a name?"

"No, I am fine to holding it for all three women."

The sister in charge agreed. "Noted."

"No," I disagreed. "We have not come this far to be subjected to that which will tarnish our legacy."

Before the sister in charge had a chance to speak, the elder woman rushed in with, "A woman voluntarily in a motel room with three men. Her doing, her way to determine the mate who would stand by her side no matter what." I made to speak but she stopped me by raising her hand. "I know it wasn't you since I can't smell you from here."

I was standing between the two of them and did not think either would do such a thing. I really did not care whether either of them had done such a foolish thing. "Why raise it after the fact? We are now SUM women."

The sister in charge, Miranda's sponsor said, "We cannot take physical action against a pledge but we can break a sister's legacy."

"Why would you want to break your own legacy?" As soon as the words left my mouth, I wanted to swallow them back and choke on them. Miranda's sponsor took a hard step toward me. I did not move an inch because I knew I could kick her ass in any form she presented. But, Miranda, my dear Miranda, I accidentally placed this as her burden.

"No, it was me." Technically a closed conversation but with the process over, Barbara could chime in. Even with the misstep I took, I could have protected Miranda by choosing my next set of words carefully.

This was just a nasty rumor. Nothing you hear in or about in this Society was the absolute truth. Barbara should have known this by now. Even the damn truth was a lie. So they knew she had lied but still she would pay for it. They accused her of sabotaging us by sleeping with three of the men we could be linked to in the Society. To clear this, one or all three men had to walk into the room and cop to this lie. I definitely did not expect any of them to do that.

I begged in my heart of hearts for the men, any man to stay out of the room.

With so many women and so many years in the room the rumor took a life of its own and as the minutes turned into hours, they decided on the only viable solution, to break Barbara right there. She already confessed, so all she could leave the Society. No tarnished legacy would be linked to her name, making it as if she never went through this, never existed. But Attitude's legacy on this side would be forfeited, forever broken. Truthfully that might have been the best solution except that she did not break. She held my advice:

to never raise her hand on a sister. I figured the first couple of people would hit her and it would be done with and eventually they would cop to it being a rumor.

By the fourth hour and her having hit the ground several times, I knew she had to fight back. They wanted her to fight back but then, who knew what next. No one had yet to hit her on the face but I saw that the next punch would strike high, possibly the temple.

So I grabbed the sister's arm and said, "A woman's morality should not be tied to her sexuality."

"Get off my fucking arm!"

"A woman's morality should not be tied to her sexuality." I repeated my words because she did not scare me. "You call whoever you need to call but I didn't take the Exemption to have someone's death on my hands."

The sister in charge said, "You already have someone's death on your hands. That white girl she brought in here. Don't you see this woman is trying to sabotage you?"

"Get off my fucking arm!"

I needed time to think and the only way to buy the time was to smack the sister whose arm I held. In SUM we protect and cherish each other. Even when we pass on the streets, in the walks of life and bother not to glance in each other's direction, we value and treasure each other. The biggest affront within the Society is to strike another sister.

She made to hit me back so I let her even though I could have dodged her swing. I knew there would be heavy consequence to this but I needed time to think. Barbara as my enemy did not make sense. Miranda stood still like this had nothing to do with her, the right approach. I tried another track. "We're fighting a race war, and you're killing people over sex?"

The sister in charge asked, "Where do you think the race comes from?"

I still needed time to think so I twisted the other sister's arm. I then punched her in the nose and heard a crack. Blood rushed out and I pushed her to the floor. Another sister, this one also in her early thirties, came rushing at me. She looked a bit stronger so I sidestepped her charge then countered with a left to her jaw. My hand felt the pain as much as she did. She wobbled a bit as a rush of sisters came at me.

Ken barged into the room. Even in times of ugliness, the beauty of him radiated; his limp cock dangled mid-thigh and I could sense that behind the walls he had used mental gymnastics to prevent getting aroused at seeing so many naked women. The horror of the fight had slowed the blood rush and reversed it to a flaccid state. His light brown eyes stared ahead, to the brow of the sister in charge. His voice apologetic yet carrying a charge said, "Stop! Stop!"

The women gasped in, not shame, but shock that he entered the room.

A male voice from behind the wall said, "Did this fool just see my wife naked?"

"I will stand by this woman."

"Which one?" Before I could signal for him to save Barbara, he pointed at Miranda. Barbara held onto her left rib and coiled up on the floor. Though I later realized Ken made the right play, I often wondered which of us he indeed wanted to carry his legacy in the Society. "Were you one of the men in the room?"

"Yes."

A piece of me died right there. This would remain as part of Barbara's legacy, lodged on the historical record as to how she earned her membership in the Society. A total lie conjured out of disgusting gossip, she would forever have to stand tall and learn to ignore it, for it is a war she could never win, unless she destroyed the Society.

As the sisters came toward me, I dropped my head to accept the blindfold. They put the robe on me, leaving my clothes crumpled on the floor. Though the degrees would say otherwise, this had to have been the coldness night since I enrolled at TGI. A group of the sisters walked me down the dip that led into the woods. They walked me off the path, in circles and as the sun started to rise. They said, "A woman's morality should not be tied to her sexuality? We believe in your cause. Now let's see how you plan to achieve that when you're a nun for life."

"How do I escape this fate my sisters?"

"The day we forgive you for striking the Queen. She came tonight to see you, for herself, to see this brave woman, the first to ever take the Exemption. And this is how you repaid her? By bloodying her nose?

"I didn't know she was the Queen."

"Every sister should be afforded the same respect you extend the Queen."

They ordered me to count to one thousand before removing the blindfold. I heard their steps drift further away from me but I counted to two-thousand to see whether they would return, and to confirm I was truly alone. The woods did not scare me. A former girl scout, camper and lover of nature, the woods did not scare me 'cause all I had to do was listen for the water

I sat on a tree stump and enjoyed the silence a day in the woods brought, the clarity. How the national Queen, the leader of the Society felt so threatened by me, who would only become a queen on the campus level; that she came out of hiding to stop me on my last night.

No matter what I thought of Barbara before, she cemented herself as the chick I would bring into any battle, no matter the odds. She was willing to die for me. She technically took a bullet for me. We might never be the mushy girlfriends oft-portrayed and seen. We might never be sisters in the sorority sense but this was a chick I would kill for. This chick took a beat down for me, simply by linking her name to a nasty rumor.

Now the only question remained, would I need to kill the Queen or would she simply hand over the crown, ring and scepter and let me run shit my way?

That was the only real question.

LEVELING THE PLAYING FIELD

The woods brought me a sense of serenity, of peace, the opposite of their aim. Putting me out here as daylight neared meant they wanted me to be there a few hours, but to return by nightfall. To go under any of the possible passageways under the wall, into the woods bordering the campus would get me nowhere because I risked being seen. Though many campus activities were held in the woods, including classes, some wilderness exploration, natural earth as the soil and rock formation, the administration disciplined any unsanctioned activity.

True I had struck the Queen but why make their play now, and not wait until I become the campus queen for SUM when my visibility made me an easier target. The more I sat to ponder and listen for the water, the more obvious it became that the leadership long desired my platform but never knew how to implement. Still I had no interest whatsoever in whatever sexual power games that clouded their agenda. We had much more important items to combat. First I needed access to students' transcripts and exams. This would allow me to expose the grading curve that kept minority enrollment in check, and impacted future employment, graduate school, etc...

In the distance I heard the first voices and footsteps. I had to start moving. I set the first marker so I would know my starting point. Then I had to think counter, as in counterintelligence, they needed me to question myself, get me to go in another direction. They would do the very opposite of their objectives. To implement such a plan, they would need a man, someone familiar with the woods. I set a second marker about thirty yards from the first. With the sun behind me, I wondered why they would place me on the campus' eastern side, behind Poe Hall. If I chose to circle east I would end up on the road to Semline, about seven miles away from campus. To go back west, I risked getting lost as making a semi-circle might push me south, only to return back here. I definitely could not go north - too far a distance, one back road that circles back to Semline, and the only veer-off led to the more affluent side of town, where Attitude lived. With no choice but to head straight south, I turned in the direction that I heard sounds of water.

The hours moved rapidly and the sun now stood directly above me. Any sound I heard turned out to be a small animal or deer looking for the highway. I followed one a bit but then lost it when I heard and it felt a human presence. "Hey!" my voice echoed back to me from the west which hinted the Adirondack mountains and the campus wall was in that direction. I increased my pace, knowing in less than five hours the woods would be pitch black, and that in less than twelve hours my legacy would be broken. My great-grandmother's intact since I finished the process, but mine would vanish, with a notation labeling me the first and probably last SUM legacy to take the Exemption. I would become a warning, as in "remember when..."

I came back to the first marker but knew I had not walked a circle.

"You didn't walk a circle. You passed one of your later markers without even realizing it. I did the same thing when I went through it."

I was surprised but not shocked to see him there, about ten yards behind the first marker. "Attitude, what are you doing here?"

"I was trying to lead you out without you seeing me but you kept listening for the water."

When I got near enough, he wrapped his arms around me. That surprised me because it felt passionate. I could not get distracted because he should not have been there. "I don't have time for small talk. How did you know I was here?"

"Why does it matter?"

"What, you think I'm stupid?" He handed me the canister of water and a sandwich. I walked back to the tree stump to enjoy both. I turned my back to him. "Who sent you?"

"They left you out here to die. Don't you get it?"

"No. Did you die when they left you?"

"Yes, but that was always my aim. I wanted to walk away from the Strength side for what they did to my father. You belong with me, on the Pride side."

"Who sent you?" I asked a last time.

"Ken got word to me but no one can know this."

"I will die with the secret but please go. You cannot be seen here."

He turned and went in what I previously considered east but was actually north. I laughed to myself thinking how I failed to realize the first opposite. They put me in the woods behind the house. I counted sixty-seven when they led me out here, which meant about an hour and seven minutes into the woods from the house. Subtract a measure of time for the turns we took so I could not count paces. What would they do? Since they went out back, they would not disguise distance which meant I was no more than fifteen minutes from the family house.

They would not disguise distance unless they were really trying to kill me. I could starve out there. They had to know this. I could be found by strangers and be held for days, years under adverse conditions. They had to know this.

Night fell and the sounds of the wind and the forest animals mixed with my hunger kept me alert while rattling my nerves. The sun set, by my count, two hours ago. I had roughly four hours to make it back to the house. Though I no longer circled back to my original markers, I did not make the progress I anticipated. I needed help but it could only come from two people. I had to think like them as they would be the ones sent to find me, something Ken did not fully grasp. It showed when he entered the room, and when he sent

Attitude. This! This was a woman's world! Women who needed men for only one thing.

I spotted the faint moon and dashed in its direction. No more than two minutes passed when I heard, "What the fuck? Where did you run off to?"

"How did you know where to find me?"

Miranda's beauty especially under a soft light predated the European's arrival. The first time I visited her room, she took out her albums and scrapbook. Her family ranged the spectrum of hues and shapes, and she embodied a bit of each branch of her ancestry. Her soft face, peach-colored, flat with puffy cheeks; normally cradled by hair that went a good four inches pass her shoulders. Getting her hair chopped had not fazed her; having to stay silent for weeks brought no response. A tough read from her forehead to waistline, Miranda radiated a tender sexuality that curved wide near her thighs and caused men to rush by her side the way ants sought out crumbs on dirt patches near picnics. She smiled her words, showing the relief she felt. "What? No hello? How're you doing? Thank you?"

"No, no. Thank you. I was beginning to think I would die out here."

"All you had to do was stay put and someone would come for you. We're The Conscious Daughters. We're girls from day one."

I almost told her that Attitude had come out for me. "It didn't dawn on me until a moment ago but did Ken send you?"

"No. Why?" I just shrugged. "Anyway what you showed us last night worked in these woods too. I figured you would find your way out and show up at King Hall around 4 p.m. or so. When I didn't see you and night fell, I got scared so I came looking for you?"

"King Hall? No! Why are you not with the sisters, at the house?"

"I left during the party and went to get some sleep. Plus, I ain't trying to be with them like that. I am glad I'm a SUM woman but this Society shit, it's fucked up and it's not for me."

We walked and she led the way. "You can't just walk away. It's not that simple."

"Oh I know the mantra: 'Enough to keep your mouth shut!' It's not like I'm going to say anything to anyone."

"No, I mean you're going to want a piece of the action. Just stay quiet about how you feel about this. I will not tell anyone. Just go with the flow, and you will see. OK?"

Miranda's eyes widened because the money was the secret part no one ever spoke of or put in writing. "OK!"

"Now how did you know about these woods?"

"It's in the historical record. It's the one where they lynched your great-grandfather, and Celeste Kendall came to bring him back to the house. They talk about it all the time so the minute they left with you, Barbara figured they were taking you to the woods."

"Barbara! How is she? Where is she?"

"In the hospital…"

I interrupted her, "Oh no, damn…"

"Oh it's nothing! She's ok. She was just acting."

"No she wasn't. I was there. Remember!"

Miranda laughed then touched my shoulders. "No, they were hitting her hard but those blows couldn't hurt her. That girl is hard as a rock from all the jogging and weight training she does. I knew something was up when that lady, she looked like she was pushing eighty-five; when Barbara groaned on that punch, it told me, not to move. I mean I punched chick…"

"You punched Barbara?"

"Hell Yeah! One night early last year, I went to her room and chick pushed up on me, on some 'it's so lonely up here' rap. Then she tried to kiss me, and touched my tits. *BAWW!* Yo, and chick didn't even move. I mean square on the cheek. I was aiming for her nose like you did the Queen." Miranda laughed. "Then Barbwire goes, 'all you had to do was say no. It's not all that'. I apologized. She laughed. And everything went back to normal."

"What do you make of her?"

Miranda raised both hands. "Oh I love chick but man, she's stupid. I mean she walked into this Society without a SUM woman to guide her, and under a MAX boy's legacy. WOW! They made me do a full year to get in. I wonder how many years she will have to do."

"But she is a SUM woman."

"Yes but they already showed they'll kill her without giving it a second thought. Do you think she can walk that fine a line?"

I didn't and saw no reason to lie to Miranda. "No, but I don't think she's planning to."

"Then why did you jump out to save her when she's the one who could have been out here?"

"She copped a plea to something she did not do."

"Let's say she was in the room with the three brothers. Would you have still put your life on the line for her?"

"I don't know. Even if I did I don't think I could ever look her in the eyes again."

At that, Miranda rolled her eyes away and a smirk formed near her mouth.

>=<

When we entered the house only the matriculating SUM women were there; all except Barbara. The sister in charge said, "You took long enough. Go take a shower and get dressed. We have lots of work to do."

I made one thing clear. "Pledging is over. You don't order me. Fourth generation Kendall compared to third generation Gardner."

"I'm in charge until next fall semester. Keep in mind, we finish under this court. Plus, it's not even about that. This is work we all have to do. We just want to update the two of you…"

"There's three of us."

"If you say so, sure! But we've been doing this for years and no one ever ended up in the hospital. We know where to hit people, without leaving marks, break bones and draw blood, unlike some people."

They all laughed.

"So what's the plan?" I asked.

"Go take a shower and get dressed."

"Miranda come here." At first Miranda did not move then my thoughts transferred to hers: even though she now had her own legacy and she helped carry on the Gardner legacy into a fourth generation SUM legacy, she had to go along with the Society until such time she would start reaping the benefits. Miranda went to her. Cynthia Gardner took off a necklace she kept out of plain sight, hidden under buttoned blouses and sweaters. She fastened the necklace supporting a diamond-crusted pendant and put it around Miranda's neck. The other women gushed at the value. "My great-grandmother's sister, long deceased; she died in the struggle; she gave me this. Not from my mother to me, but from her directly. She was born right before The Great Depression, came into the Society right before Vietnam, during the Civil Rights Movement. So you know how much this means to me, but still I want you to know it's not how much money it's worth. It's about the love in her eyes when she gave it to me and said, 'Only to a woman you will die for'. I just want you to know that from the first day I saw you, I knew. I knew. Sorry it took this long. It really would not have, had Hope simply not being in love with that Barbara girl and pledged last year."

Miranda hugged her, shaking off a slight hesitancy right before the squeeze that brought their bodies closer. Miranda could not act as well as Barbara but at that moment I felt no one peeped she did not want the gift, because of the words that tried to divide The Conscious Daughters.

>=<

The three of us got acclimated into SUM life. The various activities informed us on the division between SUM and SBD. They had Brotherhood. We had Unity. Barely discernible on the surface, our loyalty was all-encompassing. For them, there existed points where they sided with PMB. The B, the brotherhood was strong though dwindling. The SBD process had become too physically challenging and in this first era where people were quicker to shoot you than stab or fight with their hands, SBD needed an influx of new families.

For us, after the winter break, we put word out that this charter would no longer take the Legacy Acceptance. That we would make more of an effort to recruit from both neighboring schools. The first drew criticism. The second received cheers. We explained our willingness to write letters of recommendation for any legacy who enrolled in the future and they could go in under another school charter's name and we would forgo the strength in numbers and the money it brought. In exchange we wanted any and all women, even those ineligible, since we would carry on this new rule for generations. This meant that women who had already entered other organizations could have any direct female relative enroll into any of the three local schools and get a fair chance at becoming a SUM. We lifted some of the requirements to receive an Exception with the caveat being that all legacies had to take the Exemption.

They put my name on the new rule though many had formulated it, dating back to the 1970's but no one could get it passed. With my family name, Kendall, on it, no one would challenge it. They would not even dare call GG Celeste and ask. We implemented the new rule at TGI, Semline and Barrington, one we hoped would gain national acceptance. I went along because the sisters showed me how it would help repeal The Exclusion of the 1950's.

First order of business, we reviewed files from when The 23rd Amendment was enacted and TGI unequivocally opened its doors to minority enrollment. Even on a campus like TGI where GG Celeste got them to admit more Black women, our final grades did not reflect the true scholarship we produced over the years. We now wanted to attack campus policy, the ripples of which would cause waves from grade school up to corporate board rooms.

We had the evidence but the brothers voted against taking action. The brothers said to consider the grade deflation the toll we pay to cross this bridge. We questioned their dedication and said a change had to come. The sisters promised to try again next year, even though they feared the result would be the same.

This was my platform, why I took the Exemption. I pleaded for us to try harder, that the entire female student body there and many other places were counting on us. We made ourselves visible, well not fully, but more visible. We had young women doing their own work and that of other students to get proof on grade deflation and discrimination.

We had to act.

>=<

May 1987. I had not seen Attitude since that night in the woods. He could go underground for days yet the attendance roll of his classes and common exams would never reflect his absence. A week before the start of Finals Week, he showed up on the steps of the library and sat behind me. He wore a green army jacket zipped up to the chin, under a full beard. His hair had grown since I first met him. Each strand close to three inches, knotted, in no specific pattern. I then realized since last summer I had not seen his head as he always wore a hat. In the woods, it was under his sweat-top's hood. "Oh, you're a Rasta now?"

"At first sight that's what people think and say."

"That's not what it is?"

"It's whatever you want it to be."

"You're still mad at me?"

"No, just confused why you have people looking for me when you know where I live."

"From what I hear your house is always crowded. Plus, the neighbors said they had not seen you since November. I looked everywhere for you."

"Come on, you know what's up!"

"Did you really expect me to walk away from my family…"

I stopped his initial words but he knew. "I don't know. I didn't see it like that. For months, over a year, I was telling motherfuckers that I would have the baddest chick in the Society carrying my name, my legacy and you played me. You played me."

I stood up, turned and made to grab his hands. He pulled them away. "Don't play that shit with me. We're now forever on opposite sides of the Society."

"But that doesn't make you my enemy."

"Maybe in reality. In reality, what are you to me?"

"What do you mean?"

"The vote is always the same as the vote has always been. If you are willing to publicly put your name on it for everyone to see, I can get you a sit-down with the Board of Trustees."

"What? All we want is the faculty committee to…"

He cut me off, "Fuck the faculty committee. Who do you think have been voting it down for almost twenty years? There are only three students on that committee. Compare that with twelve voting faculty, one for each degree-granting school. What is the most problematic?"

"The Art school. It is way too subjective. Even in music, we don't graduate with honors. Can you believe that?"

"What do you want me to do?"

I switched up on him to see if he really loved me. "I want you to love me like I love you."

He got up and went inside the library.

I didn't see or hear anything until the end of the week, Friday. All the administrative and student life buildings were empty. I knew this because a fire drill came right before. The people in those buildings evacuated. A bit more detailed than the normal fire drills, the firemen went into all the buildings on the western quad to make sure no one ducked into a hiding place. They issued an edict to not repopulate any of them except the cafeteria.

The fire trucks left.

Thirty minutes later, we heard gun shots. The family was together, the nine of us sharing a meal. We heard gun shots. Two followed by two more shots. Ken asked, "Who the fuck cleared the MAX line?"

Again. Then again. Two gun shots followed by two more shots.

"A MAX line?" Everyone turned to look at me. "Don't look at me. I didn't even know anyone was pledging."

"Five of them," said Ken, "But they don't have clearance. No legacy on the line and no PMB legacy on the campus to clear them."

We ran to the window and all our faces registered the same thought-which came first: the fire or the gunshots? A fire raged on the top two floors of the faculty administration building. A few tenured professors lived on those floors. All of us made to dash outside as Ken said, "Those stupid, fucking MAX boys!"

Miranda grabbed Barbara and me. "No, don't go out there. Let's go out the back! And back to our dorms."

"What? We stand together."

"If your name is really on this new rule then you don't want your face seen. You will have no way to deny it."

"I have all these witnesses that I was here and no one can say I was out there when the shooting and fire started."

"But they can say you ordered it. Sister! Hope, don't go out there!"

Barbara sucked her teeth and ran to join the family. I did the same but I turned to look and saw Miranda head out down the stairs in the back.

When we got to the quad, more students had arrived. The white students caused the most destruction. They threw bricks through windows since the guy on the bullhorn ordered them not to burn the library, only the faculty building. Campus police came but they stopped behind their cars when they saw the hundred or so students on the periphery holding rifles, shotguns and machine guns. Attitude stood off-center but more toward the middle rows of those gathered. He had five guys next to him. Each had a handgun and every once in a while they fired into the air and screamed, "Beta" with the response being, "Fly Max."

The show of force was too great to ignore. Except for our family, no other Black students came onto the quad. Then, I spotted them. Two young dudes. Young, maybe two or three years younger than me. The shorter one had the look. The look Attitude had when I first saw him and mistaken him for family, way before he grew his hair out. The SBD stance. Bboy from Brooklyn.

I nudged Barbara to follow me. We slipped away from the family and introduced ourselves. Barbara started talking up a storm, but not about the bonfire. I stayed quiet, studied Girard. She knew something and wanted to communicate it. I needed a diversion so she could use plain English to tell Girard what she needed.

I offered the other food. "Ernest, right? Are you hungry?"

"It depends on what you're offering."

"Cafeteria food. It's over there in the building to the right." As we walked away, he glanced at my butt. "Did you just check me out?"

"Yeah!"

"Do you know how disrespectful that is?"

He scrunched up his face as if my words had pushed him back. "Actually I stare at sisters to acknowledge them in a cold, empty world. To let them know they're beautiful to me."

OK. I blushed and gave him a big smile, bigger than I planned. His eyes were hard but hidden, so by tilting my head a bit I saw a softness in them. I slowed my gait, putting a little twitch to my stride. "How do you know Girard and Attitude?"

"Who's Attitude?"

"I mean Manny."

"How do you know we're looking for him?"

"My family has been in this for over sixty years. In total I will say I have had about fifty members of family in this. And you?"

"I'm not in it."

He knew of the Society but not about the Society. "That's why I am asking how you know Girard and Manny?"

"Friends from around the way." I nodded to let him know that I knew something and he needed to figure it out. TGI erected the cafeteria building in the past decade to move away from the previous one with the simple layout, once used to feed soldiers preparing for war. This new one housed three different cafeterias, the larger one on the mezzanine catered to the freshmen meal plan. The two smaller ones accommodated all other students including faculty and staff. It offered an array of cuisine and two scenic views of the campus. I steered Ernest to the more private one, with the windows facing the woods. I needed his attention away from the bonfire on the quad.

He ordered food and I paid with my meal card. We sat in a booth, against a wall not far from the cafeteria's entrance. He kept trying to move the conversation into a direction, straight to the bedroom. He asked me if I had a man. I said no. Then Ken and the other two SBD brothers approached. They had a protective pace to their step, like someone had stepped on their toes.

Ernest said, "Ken, right?" Ken lied. Ernest continued, "Summer before my freshman year in high school, you made the papers often, for boxing. You had a chance to go to the Olympics, but I never heard any more on you after that summer."

Ernest said it as a challenge, to basically call Ken's bluff. Ken ignored him and started talking to me, as if baiting Ernest to be on some gangster, tough-guy stuff. I could tell something was bothering Ken by the way he tried to pass himself off as some sort of college preppie, pretty boy. Ernest just kept eating his food. The other two brothers stared at him, trying to scare him. "Yo, let me bounce before I have to kill these fools."

I spoke to make like his words had never been stated. "He's visiting Attitude." He seemed insulted that I felt he needed someone to vouch for him. "This is Ken. He and Attitude are like frick and frack."

"I know who he is and he knows who I am."

Ken's voice drew a bass and street accent I never heard him use.. "Yeah, I saw you out in the quad. What's the deal? You think you're coming up here to run the games, I heard y'all be running on chicks?"

I ignored him.

The brother on my right spoke. "What? You think you're hard? I'll knock…"

I stepped in. "Hold up! All of you are out of line. Come on Ernest, let's get out of here."

Ernest did not back down but never even bothered to look up at them. "Nah, I ain't finished my food."

His words left me a bit perplexed. "Oh, so you are just like the rest of them? Always looking for trouble. I should have figured, being that you roll with Attitude."

I squeezed my way by Ken but he grabbed me and said, "Stay!"

Ernest looked up but still took them very lightly. "What's up! Y'all want to grab some food and sit?"

"What, you think this is a joke?"

I saw Ernest's eyes move the way a trained fighter's does. First, he would have to kick the dude closest to him. That way he kept his hands free to grab Ken and swing him into the booth. By time the third one reacted, he would sidestep him and punch him. If need be, as a last resort, he would start spraying bullets. Ernest made a last attempt. "Are we talking two different languages?"

"Exactly! You're smarter than you look." At that Ken moved over, as if telling me to go outside. I didn't move. "What else?"

"Who ordered the hit?" Ken didn't respond. "Who is the target?"

Ken asked, "Who do you think?"

Ernest grasped he would not get a clear answer and the action was outside on the quad. He should have known I pulled him away so he would not be implicated in whatever hair-brained scheme Barbara had in mind. Still, he ran through the building, his right hand fighting the urge to pull out his gun. Then he realized he could not go outside running in full stride. He stopped before pushing the door open. Took a deep breath. Then strolled.

I caught up to him. As I got next to him, I cut my eyes at him, "You still don't know who I am, eh?" He shook his head to indicate no. "You have to figure out things quicker, to follow my lead or the orders I give you."

Attitude stood next to Girard and Barbara. Ernest grabbed my arm. "I need to talk to you."

I pulled away from his hold to let him know if he ever grabbed me like that, especially in public, to be ready to shoot joints. "Get your hands off me! Don't you ever pull on me like I'm your kid or something!"

My anger was real and shocked him. He turned to Attitude to get a clearer reading. "Yo, what's up with your hookers?"

"Hookers?" Barbara spoke out of turn, again. Ernest needed to focus on me and Attitude to get a clearer reading but she once again hijacked a conversation that had nothing to do with her. "Attitude, what's up with these young boys? They're on some sex shit."

"What, a brother can't get no love?" Girard dropped the smooth boy repertoire and talked street to her, like he had classified her as a dumb girl. Not saying that Barbara was dumb! Just saying Girard practiced his B game.

I tried to get the conversation back on track. "I already gave you love! I fed you." I said it to Ernest as if I were reading a script and trying hard to prevent something. To let him know the whole cafeteria scene was just that – a scene.

Not sure who else caught on, until Girard said, "This one didn't give jack! When you gonna show love?"

"I'll visit you in jail." Barbara's sarcastic reply hit the wall.

Girard knew something but not the key point that though Barbara carried on like a fourth generation SUM woman, she just got into the Society, on an Exception at that. Ever the willing soldier, he asked, "You want me to kill your man? Sure, who's the duck?"

Girard said the magic words, but possibly only to let Ernest gain a clearer picture as to why Attitude asked them to come visit – a reconnaissance trip, to scout the target.

Ken and the two brothers came out of the building and walked toward the rest of the family. The timing was too perfect to have been staged. I looked around to see who else backed this operation. Attitude jumped in. "Yo! Yo! Stop that shit! What's wrong with you?"

Barbara smiled; her smile, an act, a major diversion. "I don't know what either of you are talking about."

"I was just joking!" Girard said it to recover.

Attitude stared at us, to make certain we knew to stand down and that this served as a test, a drill. He walked away to join the five new MAX boys.

As it was in the beginning when we first walked over, Ernest faced and stared at Barbara while using a sideward glance to eye me. He had the poise of a guy who could get far. He went by the letter, and in this case that tall, sculpted bodies would seemingly be drawn to each other. But his eyes and the way he nodded let me know that he got the message loud and clear - that if and whenever the time came he needed to follow my orders, mine only. Until then just play along.

I returned to stand next to the family. More people vacated the quad. If I guessed correctly, he now understood there was a hit out on Barbara's man. No one knew who put in the order. It could be that I would ask Ernest to protect him or kill him. He really could not tell because he did not know who was Barbara's man.

He was blind to this Society, and it really did not bother him. As a queen it would be an unconventional union to make Ernest my king, but I would rather marry a blind man than have a king who thought I wanted him only for his power.

THE FALL AFTER THE UPRISING

Monday morning while people walked around confused as to what would happen with Finals Week since there had been a general announcement that all students must stay on the eastern side of campus near or in the dormitories. The administration only allowed students across the quad to the west side to get into the cafeteria. The bonfire burned well into Sunday and died on its own minutes after dusk. Even though the protest ended early that morning, campus police made no effort to arrest anyone or stop the demonstration. Our family only stayed for one hour or so on Friday, shortly before practically TGI's entire student body made some sort of visit. No one said anything as to what our words would or should be if called in for questioning. No one said anything because we did not think we had to prepare for an interrogation.

Then at 7:55 a.m., I heard a series of knocks on my door. Authoritative banging followed by the words, "Ms. Kendall, open the door!"

My roommate made to stand. We sat on our respective sides of the room and on our beds, reading over notes for upcoming exams. I motioned for her to sit back down and keep quiet. I tip-toed to the dresser and quietly opened the drawer with my t-shirts, shorts and exercise outfits. The gun, small, a silver .25-caliber semi-automatic pistol. I double-checked the cartridge. I got it as a gift from my father for my thirteenth birthday. It came in a box with a short note: Don't let them take you alive! Never let them take what you are not willing to give.

The next set of authoritative knocks shook the door.

I approached the door. Shoulder perpendicular to it to sense how close they were to kicking it in. "Yes. Can I help you?"

"It's Campus Police. You need to come with us. Trustee Winston Trafalgar the Fourth wants to talk to you."

"OK." I stalled and recalled Attitude saying he would get me a meeting with the Board of Trustees. "I need to get dressed. I will be right out."

Their next response would let me know whether I needed to bring a gun. "OK. We'll wait."

I put the gun back in the drawer and motioned and lipped for my roommate to not touch or even recall seeing it. I made some more noise to indicate to fool them into thinking I searched for clothes. The time had come to put the SUM training to work: Your eyes can fool you, so shade them to make you blind. Focus only on your thoughts and think positively and only the truth. A skilled interrogator could read your eyes so what you did not want to state, you shield from your mind. That which you do think but never spoke, allowed you to never be on record as informing on another.

The weeks as a pledge and a lifetime in the Society trained me not to smile even as the students of King Hall walked behind me and chanted songs of solidarity. We walked out of the dorm and I could feel their presence but not once did I turn my head.

Black nation on the rise.
We gotta educate, agitate, organize.
Black nation on the rise.

An officer on each side of me, and two behind me. Outside four squad cars with four officers in three of the cars. Lights flashed from all of them. They led me into the second car, and the two officers behind me entered into the backseat with me as the other two got into the front. The students followed as the cars motored slowly down the path leading to the other side of the campus. The squad cars had to move slowly because along the path other students, mainly whites with a few Hispanics, Asians and the few Blacks who did not live in King Hall joined the chant. The drive to the other side took about five minutes. They followed us up to the building and the chants stopped as we entered the building.

I kept my mind clear because I had no answers since I did not know the question. The faculty building smelled of burnt paper and wood, and molten steel, a mix of bonfire and train wreck. The four officers led me to the elevator and into an office in the back of the third floor. We walked through a door marked as an exit and to my surprise I entered the most beautiful room I had ever graced, bar none. I walked each of these building's floors for nearly two years and never tested this door. Above each corner door on the floor, a clear EXIT sign illuminated by a bulb behind a red glass screen. I knew that each of the other exits had a staircase including this one but if one turned right there was a hidden door. A door none of the officers entered with me. This door led to another and then a large room, an executive's office with all the amenities representative of a top executive in the private sector. The furniture: mahogany, brass handle antiques, framed original oil paintings of people including General Trafalgar. This told me the guy standing in front of me was no impostor.

"Why would I be an impostor?"

My thoughts had seeped through but how could he tell? I shut down quickly and blanked my mind. He asked that I sit across him. The table, somewhat smaller than a large dining room table, sat six. The chairs dwarfed me with their cushioned leather backs, headrest a good three inches higher from the top of my head. Winston Trafalgar IV looked to be in his late thirties, with sandy brown hair that he parted on the left to camouflage thinning and a receding hairline. He wore a pinstriped shirt – blue with light gray lines; starched collar, cuff links. The charcoal gray suit jacket arched over the back of his chair. His head only one inch below the cushioned headrest. He seemed fit not muscular, the solid body of a tennis player, a golfer, a man comfortable when standing naked in front of woman.

His next words shocked me more than his first question. "You've grown into such a beautiful young woman. I remember the last time I saw pictures of you."

My confusion must have shown even though no words came to my mind. This seemed to confound even him. From this point on, for expediency's sake, know that his answers correlated to my thoughts.

He got up and went to the cabinet in the far right of the room, near the desk. A modest television sat in the middle portion. He used a small key on his key chain to unlock the upper portion. A photo album. The early pages, by page three, showed a young Celeste Kendall. Black and White photos. Her broche slightly above her heart; varying degrees of smiles, porcelain fine mahogany skin; the eyes, an easy read.

He flipped the pages, instead of turning the album over to me, which indicated the amount of pride he took from owning it. I saw a few pictures of my great-grandmother with the man he identified as his grandfather. "Oh no," he said, "It's nothing like that. My grandfather was crazy in love with Auntie Celeste."

I looked up.

"Well, we could have been kin. Had she agreed to marry him the many times he asked. But he understood why she couldn't. Her biggest fear was to appear that she had been co-opted. She said it would interfere with her work up here as it would look like she had picked sides. She needed to be friends with her enemies so they couldn't know she thought of them as such."

I frowned at the thought. Toward the back he pointed to a picture of him in shorts, sitting on GG Celeste's lap.

"You're beginning to scare me, Hope. Hope G. Kendall. My, if you weren't the one who authorized this attack on what we stand for, we would have killed every student who stepped foot on the quad these past two days. Anyway, my point is that we could have been cousins. If only you were a bit older, I would have definitely asked Auntie Celeste for a meeting one of those summers when I visited."

My face stiffened.

"Yes, I visited until my freshman year in college. My grandfather passed away and I went to tell her. She told me she would always love me like I was her own grandson but she could not risk getting the security clearance for me to come visit. I totally understood. Young people, we want to blaze our own paths, so I understand why she could not trust what I would pick up along the way. Is this what happened to you?"

"Nothing happened to me."

My voice surprised him. He waited for more but I shut down. "Auntie Celeste took down an entire militia piece by piece, and through her decades here no one knew about her relationship with my grandfather even though my grandmother suspected something happened before she came into the picture."

I sniffed.

"No need to be angry because you're the one making these assumptions. Once my grandfather married, their romance stopped but he always loved her. He only told me about it so he'd have someone to carry out his legacy. And, I am proud to do so. I just wish you would have come and introduced yourself when you got here. I wish I knew you had even applied for enrollment. But I'm not blaming you. I should have contacted Auntie Celeste over these years. How is she?"

"She's doing well."

Winston smiled. "So, how do we resolve this?" At that, he pushed a piece of paper in front of me. The words on the top indicated all the organizations had contributed to putting it together. Further down the page, a list of organizations. SUM, SBD and PMB were not listed. Good. He continued, "I see a lot of names here and everyone's demands. The checked items are the ones we can implement immediately. The ones crossed out, we will not even consider. The ones in highlight, we will form committees to discuss the best ways to implement them. You will provide the names of the people to staff the students' side of these committees. How you derive your list is up to you! There are five councils that oversee admission, grading and other policies. You join one and directly appoint four other students to the others. All this is written in there."

He got up from the table, back to the cabinet. This time he unlocked the lower portion and returned with a box. I knew the box's contents before he opened it. My heart pulsed faster.

"Do you own a gun?" He paused and opened. "Good. Then you know the words, the instructions that accompany this. I bought it last year for my daughter but then I realized she's only ten. As much as we'd like to think children are aging or maturing faster, she wasn't ready for it."

He assembled the gun, a Glock 17, and clipped in the cartridge. I blinked.

"It's unfortunate that you got mixed up with Aman but that is the path you have chosen. I will let you make your own decisions but if the time comes and it will, use this gun then toss it in a nearby bush or something, so it can be found. But don't make it too obvious you intended for the gun to be found. My prints are all over it so use a glove."

I stared dead at him, clearly letting him know that I was not afraid but I did not know Aman.

So he spelled it out because he clearly did not believe me. "A-M-A-N!" When I still registered a blank, he said, "My sources said he had not been seen in weeks then they saw you talking to him in front of the library last Monday. You offered him your love and your protection but he turned you down."

A thought rushed to surface to the forefront of my mind so I scrambled it by forcing my mind to spin.

"Oh, I'm sorry. You didn't know who he was and what he was going to do," said Winston. "That explains it. I should have known you would not get involved with these terrorists, who are really a bunch of criminals using the struggle as a front for their activities."

I pleaded for him to continue.

"They infiltrated the town's fire department. Got into the building. Stole precious records, artifacts, jewelry, you name it, they stole it from the faculty offices and residences. They looted the entire building. Have you ever been to the top floors, inside the residences? The paintings alone are worth tens of millions. To cover their tracks they burned the two floors and staged a student protest."

"And, you say this Aman is behind this?" I had to ask.

"They were the first ones with guns to appear and doing the shooting."

I couldn't say anything about MAX boys since there should not be any such organizations on the campus, or in existence anywhere. "That sounds circumstantial at best."

Winston looked into my eyes, and I into his. "Ok. Fair enough. Do this! You infiltrate their organization. If you are successful and I'm wrong, you put word out there under your name, then I will give into his demands."

"What are his demands?"

"He wants a voice."

"A what?"

"He's this disgruntled artist. He and all his cronies."

"That would be too obvious. Instead I will do a review or interview of one of the others. Do you have a list of them?" He stared at me and his mouth moved a little. "You can trust me. I have great respect for what you have shown and told me today. If it turns out that I am wrong, it would be an error in judgment, not omission or duplicity."

He handed me a list from the stacks he had on his desk. I folded it and put it in my knapsack. Then he stood and stuck out his hand, "Thank you for meeting with me. I sent the police to not blow your cover."

I didn't take his hand. Instead, I choked on the words as I asked, "What happened to my great-grandfather?"

I could tell by the slow manner in which he sat back down and the sadness spreading across his eyes he too felt the pain. "Edwin Louis Kendall got a raw deal. A simple misunderstanding that changed the course of history. From the records and what my grandfather stated, Mr. Kendall was of impeccable character. My grandfather was a bit younger when it happened and not fully entrenched in campus activities. He never knew the truth and could never put the puzzle together, not even after he and Auntie Celeste became friends. It was not until he went away in the summer of 1927 and came back married that Fall did everything become clearer. Before then, he was satisfied to believe that Mr. Kendall did as stated, even though Auntie Celeste never believed it. Well, my grandfather came back with his beautiful young bride who had been quite sheltered throughout her life. Everyone was in awe of her but she walked a straight line her first days here, not even a slight turn of the head. At the very first social, one with all the faculty discussing their summers - vacations, research, conquests and so on, my grandmother saw a man and almost broke her neck to turn and get a better look. Quite a few others saw that look, including my grandfather. The next morning, the man was found shot to death in such an ungodly fashion."

"I don't get it."

"That man whose name they struck from the campus' historical record had been living among them, passing as a white man, teaching courses, recruiting students and pretending to be vehemently against Blacks. He was so loved by the racists in these parts even though he refused to join any of their organizations. They don't even say his name for shame in how badly he had fooled them and led to so many deaths amongst their ranks."

"Why did he let them kill my grandfather?"

"He didn't. He didn't. A rumor spread. This white woman told another she was sleeping with a Black man who worked for the Institute. She told of the love affair as a secret told to a friend who swore to never even think of it, but a rumor spread. Since Mr. Kendall was the only known Black man on the campus, the lynch mob came for him instead of the man who was passing as white."

I nodded.

Winston said, "I think that scarred my grandmother for life. She never stepped foot on the campus again and basically stayed behind closed doors. Auntie Celeste did not know what to make of it. On the one hand she got some sort of closure but I still don't think she believes the man they shot was a Black man. She told my grandfather they were just looking for a scapegoat as to why and how they were getting picked off, one by one. She might have a point since they kept getting killed for every misdeed they did."

I got up but he remained seated.

"You do know that's why she voted to exclude white women from the Society, right?" I didn't even blink. "In those days many white women had very little contact with Black men, and when they'd walk into a room where a man was passing, they would undoubtedly do something out of character. This then led to suspicion and complicated or ruined any MAX boy activity."

"That was over thirty years ago. We're not fighting that war anymore."

He got up but he looked at me like he did not believe me. I picked up the box with the loaded gun and put it inside my knapsack. We walked on opposite sides of the table and before he reached to open the door for me, I put my arm around his torso for a hug. He felt good, strong and smelled nice, like the finest cologne. I raised up on my tip-toes. He looked into my eyes and we both opened our mouths a little. Just a soft kiss and a little tongue.

I let go first, opened the door and steeled my eyes.

The police officers were standing on the other side of the door. They returned to the formation used when we entered. When we got outside, they walked away from me, and I headed into the Student Building and straight to the copy center. I asked for a rush order – one copy for each of the student organizations listed on the manifesto. Behind me, the students who could get through shouted questions. I simply said, "Call an emergency meeting for your organization and members. I will place a copy in each mailbox."

As the students met, a general announcement came. Finals cancelled. The campus was no longer on lockdown. Students could leave at their discretion. Grades will be whatever one would have received before Finals. Those with grades less than "C" will get an Incomplete and the option to take the final exam during the summer sessions or the coming Fall semester.

Since I was not leading any organizations that semester, I went to my dorm and packed a traveling bag and headed to New York City. I had to find a man, A MAN: Manny Attitude Davenport. I had questions he needed to answer. I had a gun with a full clip.

EPILOGUE: SETTLING OLD SCORES

Hope titled the piece, "Are You an Artist or a Racist?"

Within months after graduating Trafalgar Garrison Institute, Manny Davenport has garnered critical praise for his work as a painter. This coming semester, he will become the first African-American TGI alumni ever invited to exhibit his work on the walls of Garrison ballroom. I caught up with Mr. Davenport to ask him some questions as to why some praise his work while others demonize it.

Hope Kendall: I have seen your exhibit, your graduating thesis, many times and I do not know what to make of it.

Manny Davenport: In what sense?

HK: First, the title of the collection.

MD: Return of the Angry Black Man? I chose that title because there clearly is an effort to show some Black people as nonexistent, simply because all of us do not busy ourselves with confronting the dire straits our race face.

HK: Well, upon this return, do angry Blacks rectify this? In your paintings you show them in the exact environments which others use to depict them, for lack of a better phrase, as less than human. You have boys on the corner shooting dice. Women prostituting in alleyways. Drug peddlers. Stickup kids, and so on.

MD: In essence, the series is to show that through their travels and travails, angry Blacks have found peace with their past, the whole of it, including the negative aspects. So, within that framework, we are willing to celebrate our faults.

HK: How does seemingly bringing down the race help further its growth?

MD: All of our battles have always been to quote-end-quote fight the good fight. But, how do you go about raising the people on the bottom? How do you get them involved?

HK: Your work shows them in a noble light but in a negative environment? Is it your goal to give their experience credibility?

MD: That's a different proposition. I am not trying to replace street credibility with street nobility. I am speaking specifically about people with nothing to lose. You cannot involve them in the good fight. You have to allow them to set their own agenda because they are able to get into places that, for lack of a better term, "society people" cannot.

HK: No. I did not get that from your work. My primary question deals with how you represent the race. If a white person or any person of a different nationality was to depict the images you show, he or she would be considered racist and ignorant of Black culture.

MD: If it was a true artistic representation then what is the problem?

HK: Well then, are you an artist or a racist?

MD: I am an artist who uses race as my primary mode of communication. If in an artist's work, he or she is categorizing the work as a study of race, then yes, the artist is free to explore the underbelly as well as the glory of our race, no matter the creator's nationality. But if you are an artist who has a limited viewpoint of what constitutes Black life, whether it is high society or street life, and uses that limited viewpoint while not specifically addressing the race issue and pointing out the victims as well as the culprits, then you are simply a racist hiding behind art to push your agenda.

HK: Does that include a Black artist?

MD: Especially a Black artist!

HK: Does that extend into other spheres of life.

MD: Most definitely!

HK: What is next for you, in regards to your art?

MD: I have already started putting together the theme.

HK: I would welcome the opportunity to view it before you exhibit.

MD: I doubt I will exhibit this one. Most of the pieces you saw in the 'Return of the Angry Black Man' series were painted as gifts for friends. At the end of the exhibit, I will give each painting to the person who inspired the particular piece.

HK: You don't sell your work?

MD: Yes, but this collection was not for sale. It was for my people.

HK: I'm impressed.

MD: Thank you sister. I appreciate your admiration and respect.

The city's main conservative paper published the interview Hope conducted. I never knew why she chose them but it opened doors that should never have been opened. Neither of them were aiming for fame; they did it to detract those who had a clear target on Attitude. The piece did accomplish that on a broad scale, but it did set a spotlight on both of them, one that started during the bonfire on the campus. As that light widened, I put together a plan to move away from the crosshairs. Hope helped me do this though she continually begrudged me for taking that path, even when she gave me a few minutes with Girard by directing Ernest away from our conversation and toward the cafeteria. She miscalculated my plan and co-signed it.

May 1987, the bonfire started when students grew frustrated of the orders that halted their quest to burn down the entire campus. Many took off their tops and lit them on fire. The main quad's grass had always been so beautiful but seeing that circle of flames rise, and more people rushing toward it, throwing whatever they could into it, I knew I had made the wrong choice.

"This is the fire Baldwin spoke of." His face had a stoic, deep intellectual profile. It sort of created an imbalance with his Ralph Lauren navy blue windbreaker. The zipper up to right under his wishbone so he could show off the baby blue polo top. The shirt hung past the jacket's length down to the back pocket of his crisp dark blue jeans. Bluish gray New Balance track sneakers anchored his rugged posture. Hope sniffed them out. For me, picking up the scent, whether fear, anger, sexual energy, remained a myth, but she was right. The two of them, introduced as Girard and Ernest, had that hard exterior of two Brooklyn boys who strapped a weapon inside their jackets; or toted a small gun in the front pocket of their oversized jeans. Girard bore the cooler pose, kept his eyes in narrow slits, moved neither head nor irises yet scoped everything as if he had written the play and knew from where each actor would enter. "What's your name again?"

"Barbara. Barbara Wilson." He did not offer his. "And yours?"

"Girard." He stopped there even though he knew I meant the last name since I remembered his first name. He then asked, "What is it you don't like about this?"

"The not knowing. The violence as a means to an end."

He continued staring straight ahead and motioned for me to do the same. I wanted to look into his eyes and he into mine, to establish some sort of trust. "You cannot leave now, so ride it out until after coronation next semester."

"Then I can leave?"

"No. No. Don't tell anyone you want to leave! It doesn't work like that. You are in it. If your child decides not to accept the legacy but her child does, then you're still in it. It takes four continuous generations of inactivity including yours to be out."

"Nobody told me this."

"That's because it is so common for first generation folks to want out of the Society, especially after they experience a fall after the uprising."

"What's that?"

"The fall can be anything of value to you, but it usually deals with innocence." He bumped me with his shoulder to nudge me out of that fearful state. "Why do you want to kill the king? You know he could tell that's why we're talking?"

"Then how come he walked away to follow her?"

"Because he trusts you and me, but not Ernest and definitely not Hope."

"What can you tell me about her from first sight?"

"Real sweet girl. Has a conscience but was trained to make the hard call."

"The hard call? You mean like this fire and riot?"

"I doubt this is her work?"

"So, Attitude and the MAX boys are really behind this?"

"He's part of it but if the MAX boys were behind this, there would be dead people all over the place."

"So who's behind this?"

"Not sure but it has the King's backing."

"He voted against…"

"I'm sure he did but nothing happens without his approval." Girard turned his head towards the cafeteria and spotted Ernest returning. Hope was not far behind; trailing them, a few more steps, Ken and his two lieutenants, as he likes to call them. "Switch the topic to some dumb shit to throw them off."

"OK, but first, if you need a place to stay tonight, you can come by me."

"You mean to stay, like slide up in it?"

I laughed. "Yes, sex is on the table."

"Would love to. You're like the most polished body I've ever seen on a woman so young but you're the King's woman and I ain't trying to start no shit."

"I'm not Ken's woman."

"You are or will soon be. Just chill. To not get too deep into the Society, attend mandatory meetings and always vote *The Old Guard*. But the real way to survive in this Society is to serve others by doing good work."

"What about Progress?"

"And, what? You're going to stay the eighty years it takes to fight for it to get implemented?" At that, he changed the conversation to make Ernest and Hope think we were talking about meaningless sex and that I was not willing to put out for him.

I did not pick up on it that day because I assumed that since Girard was a legacy, Ernest was one too. Those things slipped by you unless you stayed in tune of the Society's happenings.

Summer came and with it *the fall* Girard spoke of. The report stated my older brother Lincoln died in a fire when two rival prison gangs clashed and sparked a riot. They burned mattresses, stabbed other inmates and barricaded a cell block for four days. When the rioters ended, they recovered bodies burned to a crisp. My mother and I made the trip to view the body, to claim it; a skeleton with no true identifiers, way too painful.

Ken and Hope were my rock that summer. If not for them, I don't know if I would have made it back to school, back to anything close to normalcy. I acted out a bit the next semester. Grades suffered then I refocused. Lincoln's death made me think of what it must have been like for Lena when she lost her two friends in that car accident the previous summer. Though I supported her during her grieving period in the summer, as soon as we returned to school I drifted off. I kept thinking I would run into her again. Some deep denial to believe they would kill her for simply walking into the family house and knowing who we were. I understood the secrecy, why they might have killed her to protect identities, and why most associate secret with shame or deception.

The big deception turned out to be that she was alive walking Manhattan having drinks with, of all Black men, my current, a MAX boy.

Hope told me she looked all over for Lena. Though her school records showed she finished the entire school year, no one person had actually seen her. The girl was supposed to be dead. I went by her family's house during that winter break. They said they hadn't heard from her, then weeks later they called me to say they filed a missing person's report on her. I stopped looking because I figured she did not want to be found, for whatever reason. Then six years later, she stood there with nothing in her eyes that told me she was in our Society. Since one could not deny being a member, she really was not a SUM woman.

I called the only man I always felt I could trust for he had put his name on the line for me. He had seen me the first week of school and said, "Hey, young sister. If you ever need anything, just let me know." I could only smile at the sincerity. It stayed that way for as long as I've known him until I read that interview he did with Hope. I still loved him but I stayed away because he was into something. I learned the hard way that I needed to stay away because of the fall after the uprising.

I found it easy to duck the Society and simply vote *The Old Guard* but it hurt me to not take his call or give him repeated excuses as to why I could not come to his parties, come by for a visit, meet him for lunch. He understood my fear and he never held it against me even though I was pissing away his family's legacy.

I buried myself in my career, in Ken's life even though he spent more than half of his time on the road for his job. The years started passing and I kept hearing the same questions about when I planned to marry, have kids. I kept hearing rumors. But I had been trained to not listen to rumors even if you knew the truth behind them. Then she showed up. Lena, blonde, slim, sexy, made up, perky and excited to see me as if she never left.

I phoned him the first chance I got. Attitude did not sound surprised to hear she was alive but he sure wanted to know who would be. He said the quickest way was to throw a party. I knew what he meant. A Society party but that would mean I wanted to be – back – in. Nothing had turned me back in that direction. Not the night Bliss approached me in the gallery and thought I was the SUM pledge who had been in the motel room with three men. She told me something that almost made throw up right there. Bliss said she wanted to be like me so she had done the same thing. I stopped her short from giving me the sordid details of the who, what, when because the why had disgusted me. Was this to be my legacy in this Society?

Then the chick became a martyr and Attitude, who I also thought to be dead, the way Lena was supposed to be dead came back to town. He gave me a small gift box. Then Monk showed up, again out of nowhere. With both of them there, Hope placed Bliss's death at my feet. Attitude and Monk told me to not make a move because whatever the small lies, the big lie was unraveling and the truth would soon come to light. They said to do as I had always done, live my life, stay out of the Society.

When they left the apartment, I opened the gift box and saw the photo in the locket, a photo of my brother looking two years older than me, eight years older than the age on his death certificate.

I waited and waited and was not making a move when I courted Ernest. I just needed someone to erase my loneliness. I needed something but didn't realize how deep he was in the Society – deeper than any first generation member should be. That night I saw him with Lena, I came looking for a final talk to look into his eyes to know the truth of why he kept pushing me away. Then I realized he did not know. To make matters worse, I did not know.

They were all, technically dead: Ken. Lena. Manny. Yet they walked amongst us, still using their names, seeking answers as to who put a hit out on them.

>=<

The party started slowly with my older co-workers showing up first accompanied by their husbands, then the younger ones came for what they figured would be the type of parties they frequented. They brought the bottles of wine, liquor and six packs. One of my administrative assistants asked for the smoke room. I giggled and told her to access the roof. She laughed and headed for the roof.

Ken came early in relation to the other family members. Most of them were paired up and so happy to see Ken and I back together again. I did not deny it so he started playing host. Just like that he was ready to come back into my life, no questions asked, no answers given. I let it play itself out until Monk walked in.

I didn't invite him and he let it be known, "How you going to throw a party and not invite me?" His loud obnoxious manner let me know to follow his act. He grabbed me to him, kissed me on the lips and patted me on my butt. Every set of eyes fell on me, with most speaking something, some sort of disbelief, amazement, wondering if Monk's my man., then how did Ken fit in? Monk continued, "Put my jacket in the closet and bring me the two Henrys."

I turned toward the closet near the apartment's entrance. I expected Ken to be staring, at either me or Monk, but this stare with mouth agape, complete with wide open eyes showed no inclination to attack or assert any dominance. Then Monk asked, "What the fuck you looking at?"

I just kept walking while glancing at the various eyes. None of the SBD brothers moved. In fact they all looked away. Monk stood at five-nine, one-seventy-five at the most; ripped but still. I processed that not only did Monk outrank every Society member in the room, he was on the attack. Attitude kept DJ'ing without even breaking stride.

Heading away from the closet and to the makeshift table bar by the kitchen's entrance, one of my younger colleagues said, "Henessey neat and a Heineken." She handed me the drinks because she knew I didn't know. I wondered who else could see through Monk's charade of claiming me as his woman. And even if they could, would they stop pretending? He thanked me for the drinks and then shouted, a series of calls and responses.

"Where my white girls at?" They responded, "Woa!" while raising their hands. The older ones just laughed.

"Any mamis in the house? Yo!" They responded, "Yo!"

"From the windows to the walls…"

Attitude kept mixing the beat and people danced but nothing too rowdy just simple moves to enjoy themselves. Ernest walked in next. He looked like he didn't want to be there. He took off his jacket and hung it in the closet. Unlike the respect shown to Monk when he walked in by not looking directly in his direction, the SBD brothers stopped their dancing and stared Ernest down every step of the way. I read the family's eyes. They did not know about my relationship with Ernest.

Ernest walked past Ken without saying a word. I liked that because he was not going to live by this Society's rules and acknowledge the king just because he had that title and rank. He nodded to Attitude, skipped over Major, then made eye contact with Monk. Monk broke the contact. Ernest then shook hands with Major, finished the greeting with a snap of the fingers. Ernest sat on the chair in front of where Monk was standing.

Attitude lowered the music so we could feel the tension in the air. Ken did not know which way to look. Attitude. Monk. Or Ernest. He then looked at Major as if trying to place him, "Yo, I know you?"

"Nah, B! And you don't want to." Major nodded repeatedly.

Ken simply said, "OK." I searched for his eyes but he had either cleared his thoughts or I was not advanced enough to read them.

The MAX boys were still, except for Attitude.

Our family made small talk around the room, mostly amongst themselves and some with my co-workers. The single women – all nationalities – were seductively looking across the room at Monk, Major and Ernest, inviting them to come say something. The MAX boys and Major did not budge.

The hallway bell sounded, the first person to ring it since the party's start. I went to it and got a big surprise. Lena was married. I never looked for a ring when I saw her because SUM women judged a woman by what her eyes · revealed. Hers did not reveal marital bliss nor strife. She introduced her husband as she walked into the room but as soon as she finished his name, she slipped up and whispered, "Monk?"

I made out the question mark after the name and only I heard the word. I moved out of her way to see if she would go to him. He never looked her way.

I felt giddy as the puzzle started coming together right in front of me. The hugs and happy welcomes she got from the family surprised her. She could not decipher that they all thought she was dead, and used their joy to not state, simultaneously relieving their conscious of years of guilt. Only Ken knew the truth; his eyes and shoulders gave him away. I long pondered why he always agreed with me when it came to her death but he never offered any theories about her disappearance.

She stared at him as if recalling the SUM Surfacing Party. She simply offered a hello, but no introduction to her husband. She made her way to the other side of the room as if she felt more comfortable next to the MAX boys- not the other white people nor our family, but the MAX boys. I looked at Monk then glanced at her. His eyes remained blank as he chugged the beer. Then I heard the words that caused everyone in the Society to look in her direction. Lena's back was to us so she didn't see the eyes shift when her husband told Attitude, "The Manny Davenport? I heard you were dead."

Attitude's next words allowed Larry McIntosh to keep his guards down. By claiming his death to be common knowledge, he continued to let Larry McIntosh hang himself. If only Lena's husband understood that the death never got reported, never got talked about to anyone outside the Society. Only those in the Society and those responsible would know of Attitude's death.

Everyone nodded except Ernest. The party went back to normal but I couldn't understand why Ernest had not nodded. I thought of taking him to the back but then it would complicate things and possibly raise suspicion.

Ken played good host as a burden seemed to have lifted off his shoulders. Then it hit me, seeing Monk then Ernest, he thought I invited him to the party to have him killed.

I turned in his direction and smiled. He read my eyes and his replied, "Hey I didn't know what to think."

By the time Hope arrived the party atmosphere mellowed into a cocktail party vibe with good music playing in the background. She walked into the apartment and luckily Lena did not look in her direction, for Hope's eyes spun completely and I read the question in them, "I thought you were dead?"

She then focused her stare at me and I smiled because I was extremely relieved she didn't know Lena was alive. At least I could trust her this much. I walked to her as she took a gun out of her pocketbook and I noticed the engagement ring: princess cut, small but of the highest grade. She secretly slipped the gun into Ernest's jacket inside pocket then hung hers and her fiancé's jacket. She told him to introduce himself to people and that she'd be right back. I followed her to the bedroom as she said only a quick hello to anyone who tried to greet her.

I barely closed the door when she stormed, "What the hell are you thinking ambushing me and probably everyone else like this?"

"I thought it was just some ruse to hold over us to keep us in the Society."

"Oh my God!" She sat on the bed. Beads of perspiration rose on her brow. "What the fuck are you thinking inviting a dead white girl to your apartment? And, who are those two white men with her?"

"One is her husband. The other is Attitude's friend Major. He's not white, only looks it."

"Oh that's Major? Ok we'll deal with him later." She paused. "Where is Miranda?"

"I told her she couldn't bring Devon and she threw a fit."

"That explains why Monk's here. Listen, stop putting distance between you and Miranda or you will keep getting into situations like tonight."

"That wasn't my plan."

"Did anyone vouch for her husband?"

"No, and he already said the magic words."

"Oh shit!" She got up. "OK, I need you to put on the performance of your life. We need to break up this party. Whatever you do! Do not let Ernest go outside! Do whatever you can to stop him!"

"Oh, I thought you were willing to sacrifice your King?"

"Yes, to save you but not for some bullshit like this. Plus, you didn't take the offer so what are you doing with him?"

"Well, you saw me leave with him."

"Yes, I figured it was a one night stand."

"It was but one thing led to another!"

"Yeah, I get it. But it's too late. He is the only one who might be able to set the historical record straight about you and Bliss so he must live." She went to the mirror, steeled her eyes then turned toward the door. "Let's end this party!"

Hope went out first and I followed two steps behind her. Ken was talking to her fiancé with a group of other family members. Hope greeted everyone in the room with a hug and chatter. She knew the MAX boys would not lose sight of their target. She knew no one got away with trying to kill a MAX boy, but if anything she would stop the party from happening tonight.

The only way to do that she let them in on a secret that only Monk must know, the only way Lena could be alive. Lena was a woman of SUM. A small distinction from being a SUM woman in that she did not know the recognition symbols.

I needed Lena to clear her mind and look into my eyes and answer the question, "How do you know this guy, Larry?"

She shrugged a little then she realized the confusion, the danger. She knew to get her man out of the crosshairs. Hope started her performance and all parties joined in, except the MAX boys who had bloodlust in their eyes. The performance reached a crescendo, Larry stepped forward but Lena pulled him back. Attitude said to Ken, "Stop trying to act like you're the king of the castle..."

For those not in the Society, we continued the performance even after Lena left. Eventually I had to kick everyone out. I did my best to keep Ernest in the apartment, but just as he didn't know the truth about what this party had turned into, I learned why Ken left me.

Bliss thought I understood the full meaning of the words, "I don't need a man. A man needs me."

>=<

A fear and sadness rushed over me as tears flushed my face. Less than two minutes later, the time it would take for Ernest to get outside, I heard two gun shots, followed by two more. I kept expecting more bullets to sound, to leave a man found shot to death in an ungodly fashion.

But no other sounds came. Nothing so I ran to the window but I could not see anything. To go outside would make me a witness or a suspect. The police would question me and the historical record had the standard answers to use in such a situation. I would say a quarrel started between several people, most of them uninvited guests and they took it outside. Larry McIntosh probably got caught in the crossfire.

But there were no other sounds, except that of passing cars, until I heard his knock at the door.

I jumped into his arms and said, "I am so sorry. I am so sorry."

He gently shoved me to the side and walked to the sofa. "Did it matter which man came back upstairs? Me or Ernest?"

"Yes, but this is all your fault! You did not tell me you were dead." His jaw dropped. "I figured it out when Lena walked in. What did she have to do with your death?"

"Nothing. I tried to put together a counterintelligence training for her and people I trusted turned on me. They took her but I don't know what they told her about my disappearance."

"So, you thought she was dead?"

"I wasn't sure. But she obviously knows enough to keep her mouth shut." He shook his head and fixed a himself a drink. I did not say anything because he obviously needed one. Heck, even I thought of fixing myself one. "It's a dangerous game you played tonight."

"That was not my intention. I ran into Lena in Manhattan and didn't know what to do. So, I told Attitude…"

Ken scolded me. "You need to stay away from those MAX boys. I told you this before."

"Why? When you trust him more than anyone on our side." He didn't say anything. "So, you're telling me that someone was trying to kill you though you're already dead?"

"As MAX boys, the first time we die, it's a rumor. The second time, we make it convincing. The third, we are really dead."

"But you're not a MAX boy!"

"I grew up with the training. But it still doesn't explain Ernest and Monk."

"Monk was here because I told Miranda Devon couldn't come so I figure he came to cover Ernest."

"And, Ernest?"

"Hope sent him for my protection, but then the party changed into something."

"Why would you need Ernest's protection when the sisters have always covered your back?" That proclamation confused me so I listened some more. "You're the reason they come out to the meetings and parties."

"Why is that?"

"You have a target on your back because of that motel room incident."

"I was never in a room with three men."

"I know. They know. But you pleaded to it, that is what the historical record will show. That's all the public will know."

"I still hate Miranda for just standing there."

"Why? She wasn't in that room. It was just nasty gossip to rankle you three."

"I'm not so sure."

"I am. I was with her the night the motel incident reportedly happened."

"You what?"

"I was expecting Hope's call. Or your call. But she's the only one who called and she needed me."

"You were with Miranda?"

"Yes, and who were you with?"

I smirked. "Manny."

"OK then stop begrudging Miranda for her choices."

That quieted me and my mind drifted to something Hope said about Ernest being able to set the historical record straight. "Well, you still ran and left me when you heard someone was trying to kill you."

"No, I ran to protect your brother since he was using an identity linked to my former one. I thought I would never return and that we both would die." I stumbled backward. Ken continued, "What? How could you not know? You're wearing the chain."

"Attitude gave me this."

"Yes, I sent him back with it while I worked on relocating your brother. Didn't he tell you? Didn't you open the back?"

"We weren't alone and then got distracted that night. He didn't get to even look at it. I opened the box the next day by myself."

Ken got up and took the chain and locket from my neck and revealed a secret compartment. Opening the backside of the picture portion, the locket revealed another panel, which left the front as just a cover, the photo as a divider, and the back a compartment holding a diamond ring. The note on the back of the small photo: *Barb, thank you for sending Ken to save me. Love, Lincoln.*

The engagement ring looked to cost about ten thousand dollars. "How much is this?"

"Less expensive than the chain and locket." He smiled. "Those two are worth about 280 thousand."

"How can you afford this?"

"Just say family heirloom."

I rolled my eyes thinking, those MAX boys. I put on the ring and gave him a soft punch to the chest. "But…"

"Tomorrow, we sort all this out. Tonight. Tonight…well you know the rest."

Ken picked me up and carried me to the bedroom.

THE END

About The Author

G. Dan Buford grew up in New York City and has spent many years residing in other parts of the country. Though he hopes this new novel is well-received, he is still weighing the differences in writing in obscurity versus infamy.